DATE			

THE CHILDREN OF KINGS

MARION ZIMMER BRADLEY
From DAW Books:

SWORD AND SORCERESS I-XXI

THE NOVELS OF DARKOVER

EXILE'S SONG
THE SHADOW MATRIX
TRAITOR'S SUN

(With Deborah J. Ross)
THE ALTON GIFT
HASTUR LORD
THE CHILDREN OF KINGS

The Clingfire Trilogy
(With Deborah J. Ross)
THE FALL OF NESKAYA
ZANDRU'S FORGE
A FLAME IN HALI

Special omnibus editions:

HERITAGE AND EXILE
The Heritage of Hastur | Sharra's Exile

THE AGES OF CHAOS
Stormqueen! | Hawkmistress!

THE SAGA OF THE RENUNCIATES
The Shattered Chain | Thendara House
City of Sorcery

THE FORBIDDEN CIRCLE
The Spell Sword | The Forbidden Tower

A WORLD DIVIDED
The Bloody Sun | The Winds of Darkover
Star of Danger

DARKOVER: FIRST CONTACT
Darkover Landfall | The Forbidden Tower

THE CHILDREN OF KINGS

A DARKOVER® NOVEL

MARION ZIMMER BRADLEY

AND

DEBORAH J. ROSS

DAW BOOKS, INC.

DONALD A. WOLLHEIM, FOUNDER

375 Hudson Street, New York, NY 10014

ELIZABETH R. WOLLHEIM
SHEILA E. GILBERT
PUBLISHERS

http://www.dawbooks.com

Jacket art by Matthew Stawicki.

DAW Book Collectors No. 1615.

DAW Books are distributed by Penguin Group (USA) Inc.

First Printing, March 2013

1 2 3 4 5 6 7 8 9

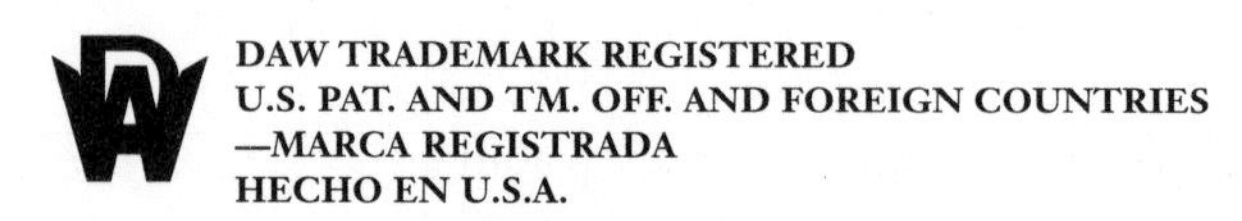

DAW TRADEMARK REGISTERED
U.S. PAT. AND TM. OFF. AND FOREIGN COUNTRIES
—MARCA REGISTRADA
HECHO EN U.S.A.

PRINTED IN THE U.S.A.

NOTES

Readers have asked me what it's like to continue the Darkover series, and after talking about working with Marion, I add that it's like writing historical fiction. I have to do my research, which means studying the previously published novels and as much other material—Marion's notes and letters. For this tale set mostly in the Dry Towns, I used not only *The Shattered Chain* but a very early (1961) "proto-Darkover" novel, *The Door Through Space. The Door Through Space* contained many elements familiar to Darkover readers, from *jaco* and the Ghost Wind to the names of people and places (Shainsa, Rakhal, Dry-towns). Marion was exploring a world in which Terrans are the visitors and adventure lurks in the shadows of ancient alien cities. She drew upon and further developed this material in *The Shattered Chain* (1976).

These books reflected the growth of Marion's vision, but each of them was also part of the times in which it was written. 1960s science fiction novels were often tightly-plotted, fast-paced, and short by today's standards. Most, although by no means all, protagonists were male, and female characters were often viewed from that perspective, what today we call "the male gaze." By the middle of the next decade, publishers were interested in longer, more complex works. Not only that, the women's movement and the issues it raised influenced genre as well as mainstream fiction, opening the way for strong female characters who defined themselves in their own terms. If Marion had written *The Shattered Chain* a decade and a half earlier, I doubt it would have found the receptive, enthusiastic audience it did. Her timing (as with *The Mists of Avalon* or *The Heritage of Hastur*) brilliantly reflected the emerging sensibilities of the times.

Now we live in a different world. This is not to say that the previous struggles have been resolved, but that much has changed in the social consciousness from 1976 to today. In writing *The Children of Kings*, I considered how Marion's ideas about the Dry Towns (and any patriarchal desert culture) might have changed over the last three decades. *The Shattered Chain*, with its examination of the roles of women and the choices (or lack of choices) facing them, focused on only a few aspects of the Dry Towns culture. What if we went deeper, seeing it as complex, with admirable aspects as well as those we find abhorrent? With customs that we cannot truly comprehend but must respect, as well as those that resonate with our own? With men of compassion and women of power?

As the Dry Towns developed in my mind, I turned also to the theme that had characterized the early Darkover novels—the conflict between a space-faring technological race and the marvelously rich and romantic Domains, with their tradition of the Compact and the *laran*-Gifted Comyn. And now, adding to the mix, the ancient *kihar*-based Dry Towns.

I hope you enjoy reading this adventure as much as I did writing it.

Deborah J. Ross

DEDICATION

In Memoriam
Cleopatricia Sanda (1962-2012)
Be at peace, dear friend

The disk of Darkover's Bloody Sun had barely risen beyond the walls and towers of Thendara, and icy chill still haunted the shadows. A brisk wind swept the sky clear of clouds. The branches of the trees in the gardens of the Old Town trembled. Lavender and white blossoms unfurled amid the new leaves. The air no longer smelled of old layered ice and sodden wool, but of fresh growing things.

The roads had been open for a tenday, even as far as the Kilghard Hills. Traders reached the city, bringing goods and gossip. The open-air markets offered spring onions and an array of early fruits, a welcome change from boiled roots and porridge.

The rising sun lit the ancient castle of the Comyn where it stood like a city unto itself, with its walls and spires, domes and courtyards, the barracks and training yards of the City Guard, and ballrooms and living quarters for the ruling families when they were in town. A crowd gathered outside the main gates. Their mood was festive, the dark hues of winter garb brightened by garlands of early-blooming ice lilies.

The gates swung open, and a contingent of City Guards came out, clearing an open path. Then came more armed men, mounted on sturdy horses. People waved and someone played a lilting air on a wooden flute. The leader of the Guards smiled and nodded, although his gaze never stopped moving across the assembly and one hand remained on the hilt of his sword.

Just inside the gates, a second, much smaller group gathered, household servants and a scattering of richly dressed Comyn lords and ladies. In the center of the courtyard, a party of riders mounted up. The horses stamped and snorted, their breath turning into plumes of white vapor. Servants and baggage handlers finished securing the coverings on a laden wagon.

From the shelter of an arched, deep-set Castle doorway, Gareth Marius-Danvan Elhalyn y Hastur watched the preparations for leave-taking. The slanting morning light touched his hair, which had darkened from childhood flaxen to red-gold, and the fine planes of his face, reflecting the compelling masculine beauty of his lineage. His cloak, although of soft lambswool, bore no badge or identifying mark, neither the blue-and-silver fir tree of his Hastur father nor the tree and crown of his royal Elhalyn mother. Neither of his parents was present, having passed the winter at Elhalyn Castle with his younger brother and sister. He was not alone, for he was rarely unattended, either by Castle Guards, personal servants, or the courtiers who lived in Thendara or had journeyed here as soon as the roads were open. Ordinarily, he was so well guarded that he had never yet had occasion to use the sword hanging at his belt except in daily practice. Today, however, no one attempted to draw him into conversation. Perhaps the early hour caused his presence to go unnoticed.

The foremost rider was a man of middle years, the gold of his hair laced lightly with frost. Like the woman beside him, he wore warm, brightly colored travel clothing. His fur-lined cloak draped over the rump of his horse, one of the fabled Armida blacks. He smiled and lifted one hand in greeting to the crowd beyond the gates. They shouted and clapped.

"*Dom* Mikhail! The Regent!"

The woman colored a little. Her horse, a gray of the same fine breeding as her husband's, pranced and pulled at the bit. She quieted the horse with a touch and, as she did so, the hood of her cloak slipped from her head, revealing a crown of feather-soft, coppery hair.

A sigh swept the crowd outside. The cheers diminished into whispers of awe.

"Lady Marguerida . . ."

Mikhail Lanart-Hastur gave his wife a crooked smile. "They cheer me, but *you* they offer greater honor. I don't know whether to be relieved or proud."

A trick of the acoustics in the courtyard carried their voices to where Gareth stood. He felt as if he were eavesdropping on a private family conversation and wished he hadn't come. He pressed his back against the stone doorway.

"I wish they wouldn't," Marguerida Alton replied in a low voice. "I'd much rather be respected for what I've achieved than for the color of my hair. We can't take a simple vacation without all this fuss."

"It's gratitude, *preciosa*."

"Mik, the Trailmen's Fever was two years ago!"

"Darkovans have long memories. Ah, Nico!" Mikhail smiled broadly as his eldest son and heir approached.

At twenty-two, Domenic Alton-Hastur was just a few years older than Gareth. By Comyn standards, he was simply dressed, a jacket crossed by the Alton tartan, and trousers tucked into swordsman's boots. He laid one hand on the black's glossy shoulder, looked up at his father, and said with a perfectly serious expression, "It's not too late to change your minds and turn back from this insanity."

"Nico!" Marguerida exclaimed, then laughed. "Not us leaving, but you staying to run this place—that's the real insanity!"

"The Castle is in good hands." One corner of Mikhail's mouth twitched. "I have no concerns on that score. We're in your debt for making it possible for your mother and me to get away at the same time. It's been far too long since all of us—most of us, anyway—were together at Armida."

A peculiar sensation, part ache, part something else, tightened Gareth's chest. He had never doubted the love his own parents had for him, but neither they nor anyone else in a position of power had ever trusted him as much as Mikhail trusted Domenic. It did no good to reiterate that Domenic was older, that he had been trained since childhood to assume the Regency, in addition to the discipline of his season in a Tower.

He has real work, work that matters. Nobody thinks of him as a useless ceremonial appendage.

Yet Gareth could not summon even a shred of resentment against his cousin. Neither of them could help their birth.

He will be Regent and I, the uncrownable King. As Grandfather Regis used to say, if we had wanted another destiny, we should have chosen different parents.

Meanwhile, Mikhail had nudged his horse forward and addressed the throng outside the gates. Pitching his voice to reach to the edges of the crowd, he thanked them and wished them a joyful spring and a bountiful early crop.

"I leave you in the care of my son and heir, Domenic Lanart-Hastur, and his equally capable advisors. I warn you, however, that he is a far sterner taskmaster than I." At this, everyone laughed. "I bid you farewell until the summer Festival season!"

Mikhail signaled to the Guard captain to proceed. The crowd pulled back as they approached, heading for the road to the Alton family estate at Armida. Marguerida glanced back toward the castle.

"He'll be fine," Mikhail said. "Danilo will send word at the least hint of trouble."

Lifting her chin, she nudged the gray forward until she was even with her husband. The party clattered over the paved street to renewed cheers, and the gates swung shut behind them. The onlookers began to disperse, servants hurrying back to their duties. The nobles milled around, exchanging comments and making sure they were seen as people of importance.

Gareth's stomach rumbled, reminding him that he had not taken more than a cup of water since arising. Perhaps Domenic, now talking with one of the Castle Guards, might be persuaded to breakfast with him.

One of the minor lords brushed against Gareth's cloak and drew back, clearly startled. "Your pardon, *vai dom*! How clumsy of me. I did not notice you standing there!"

Gareth schooled his features into a blandly pleasant smile. There was no point in telling the man to think nothing of it. Even though the Castle was echoingly empty, gossip spread like a Hellers wildfire.

"Gareth Elhalyn went to see the Regent and Domna *Marguerida off, can you believe it?"*

"Oh, yes, I bumped into him. He was looking very pale indeed."

"Well, what do you expect—he's an Elhalyn! He's probably terrified of his own shadow. They're all feebleminded when they aren't insane, the whole nest of them. Remember Prince Derik, a generation ago? As simpleminded as they come. And that business with Gareth after Regis died! You don't suppose he's losing what little sanity he ever possessed . . ."

No, his best hope was to avoid a conversation entirely. He inclined his head and murmured, "Excuse me."

Gareth reached Domenic just as the Guardsman bowed and took his leave.

"Good morning, cousin!" Domenic said with a friendly nod.

Gareth's grandfather, the legendary Regis Hastur, had been brother to Domenic's Grandmother Javanne. In his youth, Regis had formally adopted her son, Mikhail, as his heir, trained him for leadership, and kept his promise even when his own son, Gareth's father, was born. Dani Hastur had chosen a private life over one of public display, so the Regency now passed from Mikhail to Domenic.

"A good morning for everyone, I hope." Then, feeling he ought to explain his presence, Gareth added, "I came to wish your parents a safe and speedy journey." The words sounded pretentious, as if the difficulties of the road were subject to his amendment. *They had no need of my wishes. Half of Thendara came to cheer them. Why would they pay any attention to me, who did not even speak to them?*

Before Gareth could untangle his thoughts, they were joined by an older man who carried himself with the unconscious vigilance of a longtime paxman. Danilo Syrtis-Ardais was the namesake of Gareth's father and had been his grandfather's *bredu*, a term that meant "sworn brother," but in this case carried more intimate connotations as well, and to this day remained his grandmother's close friend. Danilo acted as Domenic's mentor and advisor when he was not traveling about the Domains in search of latent telepaths.

"*Tío* Danilo!" Gareth came, somewhat shyly, into Danilo's fatherly embrace. They hadn't seen each other since the last performance of Marguerida's opera. Danilo lived in his quarters in the Castle when he wasn't traveling, while Gareth occupied the townhouse that had belonged to Regis.

Danilo thumped Gareth on the shoulder. "You've been regular in your sword practice."

Gareth never knew how to respond to such comments. Did Danilo really think him such a sluggard? Even the most indolent prince must be seen to uphold the tradition of military training. He sparred, he rode, and he racked his brains trying to master both Darkovan and Federation languages. Danilo had encouraged him, as did Grandmother Linnea.

"Good lad." Danilo turned to Domenic, and Gareth caught the edge of a telepathic question.

Is there more, Nico . . . you sensed . . . ?

Domenic's eyes narrowed, the movement so subtle that if Gareth had not sensed Danilo's inquiry, he would not have noticed it.

. . . earth tremors . . .

Gareth's surprise almost betrayed him. Until recent times, each Domain had possessed a characteristic psychic Gift. Now the Gifts no longer bred true, and new ones arose unexpectedly. Domenic's was one such, the ability to sense geological conditions, although not even Domenic knew whether what he felt arose from the crustal layers or deep within the planet. Perhaps the Gift was genetically linked to his dark hair, unusual for the offspring of a blond and a redhead.

Earth tremors, Gareth repeated to himself. He had studied a little planetology but could not remember any references to seismic activity in the Domains.

As if in answer to Gareth's thought, Domenic pitched his voice low and bent toward Danilo. Gareth caught a few phrases: "Superficial . . . could be impact . . . if I didn't know otherwise . . ."

". . . not the Federation . . . no signals . . . Jeram's radio project . . ."

Gareth knew of the *Terranan* renegade, Jeremiah Reed, who had remained on Darkover when the Federation departed and had taken the name *Jeram.* Their paths had not crossed, except for public events like the Midsummer Festival ball. Jeram had set up a radio listening post, using the abandoned equipment at the old Federation Headquarters.

"Let me know . . . happens again." Danilo turned and nodded to Gareth in much the same way Gareth might dismiss a child. The two men headed for the city gate, heads inclined together, voices low.

Gareth schooled his features to reflect nothing of what he felt. He should be used to such treatment. If he ever expected to be taken seriously, to be treated with respect, then he himself must behave in a responsible manner.

"Your Highness? Is anything amiss?"

Gareth's attention snapped to his immediate surroundings. Two courtiers peered at him from a respectful distance. One of them, a Vistarin of Temora, was newly arrived in Thendara and had not yet built a reputation. The man had a little money from his family's salt trade and not a trace of *laran.* His companion, on the other hand, had been a minor fixture in Comyn society for as long as Gareth could remember. Stout and dressed unflatteringly in fur-trimmed yellow satin, Octavien MacEwain was always trying to insinuate himself into Gareth's confidence.

"I was merely contemplating the vastly reduced evening amusements without *Domna* Marguerida's musical compositions," Gareth said with deliberately affected blandness. "*Lady Bruna* was the jewel of the season."

"Her absence leaves us all poorer," the Vistarin lord said.

"And yet . . ." Octavien cut in smoothly, "within every disappointment lies opportunity."

Octavien's features betrayed nothing of his purpose, but Gareth had grown up in the treacherous and convoluted world of Comyn politics. What Octavien meant was that the absence of the Regent would be an excellent time for Gareth to assert his claim to the throne. Next, he would suggest that although no one had anything to say against young Domenic, the Council would surely support a legitimate king over a mere Regent's son. The Regency, begun two generations ago by Danvan Hastur, was never intended as a permanent transfer of power.

He thinks I'm sane enough to be crowned and weak enough to be controlled.

"Oh," Gareth said airily, "I'm sure we can all find something with which to amuse ourselves." With a suitably arrogant lift of his chin, he turned and headed for the nearest exit, which happened to be the gate leading to the city.

Not ten paces beyond the Castle walls, Gareth realized he was shaking. The back of his throat tasted of stomach acid, and his temples throbbed. The thought of food nauseated him, but he ought to eat something. Grandmother Linnea would know the moment he arrived for his lesson if he neglected the most basic self-care.

Gareth paused at a corner food stall where a red-cheeked woman stood over a small copper pot set on a portable brazier. The pot gave off the tantalizing aromas of sweet oil and fried dough. The clawing sensation at the back of Gareth's throat eased. His mouth watered, and his spirits lifted.

The woman used a long wooden skewer to fish out braided, palm-wide pastries, which she rolled in crystallized honey before placing them, steaming and fragrant, on a cooling rack.

"Apple buns, fine sir?"

Gareth bought two, wrapped in paper. Beneath the crisp shell, the buns were moist with bits of fruit and lightly seasoned with spicebark. The taste reminded him of Midwinter Festival treats. The apples had probably been stored since last fall, and the resourceful baker had carved out every useful bit.

From the dregs comes treasure.

"*Vai dom*," came a man's voice, heavy with long-suffering forbearance. "If you please, you should not be here alone."

Here meant out in the open, mingling with the populace. *Alone* meant without his bodyguard.

Nursemaid would be more like it.

Irritation flared, fueled by smoldering resentment. Gareth immediately regretted both. Narsin had served the Elhalyn family since before *Domna* Miralys, Gareth's mother, was born. The old man would have given his life for any one of them and did not deserve to be the target of Gareth's foul temper.

"I am sorry if my impulsiveness caused you distress," Gareth said. "As you see, I am in no danger. Truly, it was not necessary for you to leave the house at such an hour simply because I wished to stretch my legs on this fine morning."

Cragged brows tensed. The old man set his lips together, but Gareth understood his meaning.

It is neither safe nor seemly for the heir to the crown of the Seven Domains to be wandering around without an escort. Don't tell me you can defend yourself as well as the next man. Even a swordmaster can be taken unawares.

So Narsin had said a hundred times. Even as a boy, Gareth understood that an ordinary man had more freedom than a prince. And a prince who had once made a fool of himself in front of the Comyn Council must accept the consequences of his actions: suspicion and constant surveillance.

"Very well, then," Gareth said, "but don't hover at my elbow, glaring at every passer-by. There are no World Wreckers abroad this morning."

Without waiting for a response, Gareth headed back toward Comyn Castle, but slowly enough so that the old man could easily keep pace. It was early for his lesson with Grandmother Linnea, but he badly wanted to be off the streets. At the moment, he felt he'd had all he could tolerate of being watched over and whispered about.

There were no longer any World Wreckers, or any saboteurs, undercover agents, or Federation forces of any sort remaining on Darkover. Except, of course, the very few, like Jeram, who had stayed behind out of loyalty to Darkover when the Terrans withdrew their forces.

Gareth lifted his face to the sky, trying to imagine what it must be like out there, in the vast reaches of space. Darkover was an insignificant planet, considered irredeemably primitive by the Federation. Only its strategic location on the galactic arm, and then later its potential for exploitation, had granted it any status. Even that could not justify the *Terranan* presence once the Federation erupted into interstellar war.

What was going on up there? Who was winning, who losing? Darkover had had few enough allies in the Senate, even before the war. *And will they ever come back?*

When they do, we will be ready for them. So Gareth had sworn more times than he could count. Now the words sounded hollow. If the Federation returned, with its advanced technological weapons, determined to seize whatever it wanted, who could stop them? And how?

Since childhood, Gareth had been drilled in the importance of the Compact, the ancient code of honor that forbade the use of any weapon that did not bring the wielder within equal risk. In many ways, the Compact was the soul of Darkover, of the Domains, anyway. The Dry Towns had never sworn to it, but their inhabitants did not possess *laran.*

Laran. As the rambling complex of walls and towers of Comyn Castle came into view, Gareth tried to imagine a world without *laran.* Darkover was unique in the strength and prevalence of psychic powers, powers that, when amplified by the psychoactive matrices called starstones, were capable of everything from sensing the emotions of another, to healing mind and body, to charging batteries that could light a castle or power an airship . . . or bring one crashing down.

The *Terranan* had thought the Compact the superstition of a primitive race. They had not realized it was aimed not at their own technology but at the far more devastating weaponry of the mind.

Once, Gareth had been taught, *laran* warfare had raged unchecked across the face of Darkover. Many of the techniques had been lost, and most people thought it better that way.

But if the Federation comes back, our laran *may be the best defense we have.*

Was it arrogant to think that *he* could somehow make a difference? Under it all, he supposed, he was a hopeless romantic, a prince who wanted to save his kingdom. Or to prove himself worthy of it.

If Gareth had been alone, he would have used one of the side entrances near Comyn Tower. That would only distress Narsin further, though, for the old man envisioned ambushes in the rosalys arbor. It was better to use the main gate, where armed Guards stood at attention. Gareth paused for a few moments to speak to them.

Gareth and Narsin crossed the outer courtyard, a flagstone square lined with benches and trees, their leaves still bright green. Beds of yellowheart gave off a subtle, spicy perfume. Although the sky had brightened to full morning, it was still chilly in the shadows. Narsin furtively pulled his cloak around his bony shoulders.

"You need not remain with me, old friend," Gareth said. "Go home and get yourself a hot meal. I am safe within these walls."

"But, *Dom* Gareth—"

"No harm will come to me, I promise. Look, see how the Guards watch over me." *They are undoubtedly wondering what scandalous thing the mad Elhalyn princeling will do next.* "I have only to call out and they will be here to protect me. And I will be in my grandmother's care." *What could you defend me against, that a Keeper could not?*

Narsin's shoulders sagged minutely. They had been through similar arguments a hundred times before, and he knew how far he could push Gareth. He nodded, bowed, and departed the way they had come.

Gareth breathed a little more freely as he hurried along the maze of passages leading to the Tower. For a few moments, he need not barricade his thoughts behind a granite shield. His life was like a puzzle. Grandmother Linnea knew part of it; as his friend and Regent-heir, Domenic knew another; his parents saw him as the boy they loved so dearly; the courtiers and Comyn lords regarded him as either yet another of those unstable Elhalyns or else a pawn to their own ambitions. Gareth supposed it was like that for everyone, especially those cursed with noble birth. Perhaps his own father had taken the wiser choice in abdicating his claim to the Hastur Domain in favor of a private domestic life.

Gareth paused outside the door leading to Linnea's private chambers. Carved with an interlacing pattern of branches, the door always made him think of an enchanted forest and his grandmother as a *chieri* queen who lived there. She had been queen in all but name, for no one would have challenged Regis if he had wanted the throne.

Before Gareth's knuckles touched the fine-grained wood, Linnea called for him to enter. He lifted the latch and stepped inside.

Linnea Storn-Lanart sat before the hearth where a fire sent up flickers of brightness. She had set aside her red Keeper's robes for a gown of undyed wool. The room with its mantle of opalized river-stone was proportioned for a small, delicate person. It fit her perfectly.

She lifted one hand from her knitting to greet him. The light streamed in from the mullioned windows and touched her silver hair. For a moment, with her face softened by shadow, he envisioned her as she must have been, a young woman with a heart-shaped face and deeply expressive eyes. Then she tucked the needles and ball of wool into a basket at her feet, and he saw her as she was. Years had pleated her skin like the withering of a flower, revealing the strength of her character.

"How good it is to see you, *chiyu*. I was beginning to think you weren't coming this morning."

Gareth squirmed, although there was no censure in Linnea's words, only a gentle reminder that she had waited up for him after a night's work in the Tower circle. He decided not to mention the courtiers. She'd had enough of such machinations in her own life.

"Forgive me, Grandmother." Gareth drew up a chair. "Shall we begin?"

With an expression of pleasure, Linnea took out her starstone from its locket lined with insulating spidersilk. Gareth caught a flash of blue-white as the gem touched her skin. Quickly he averted his gaze. The shifting patterns of energy, manifested as twisting light, could be dangerous to any mind other than the one to which the stone was attuned.

Gareth carried his own matrix stone in the old style, in a silk pouch tucked under his shirt. Simple geometric embroidery decorated the outer layer, a gift from one of his Elhalyn aunts. With a practiced tug, he loosened the cord, and the starstone fell into the palm of his hand.

The stone, carried so close to his body, felt warm. Blue-white brilliance lit the facets, dancing through the patterns he knew so well. Sometimes, when he was first learning to use the stone, those patterns had haunted his dreams.

Gareth closed his eyes, focusing his mind on the stone. As he had been taught, he envisioned a single point of light. He imagined it moving through a prism, gaining in power and clarity. The starstone would amplify his own innate talent, but it could not grant him a Gift he did not already have.

What was his Gift? The Ridenow were celebrated for their empathy, particularly with nonhumans. Their skill with horses and hawks was common knowledge. And the Altons . . . forced rapport was not a thing to be taken lightly, and the unchecked anger of an Alton could kill. Other Gifts had been lost through dilution and the passage of time. No one living knew what Gifts the Aillards and Gareth's own family, the Elhalyns, had once possessed.

The Aillards, he reflected, were all but extinct, their Domain represented on the Comyn Council by a distant, collateral branch. As for the Elhalyns . . .

After so many near-psychotic generations, it is no wonder we have no Gift!

Immediately, Gareth regretted the pettiness of his thought. True, his maternal grandmother had been stricken with depression, delusions, and who knew what else. His own mother, Miralys Elhalyn, had never been anything but sweet natured, constant, and loving. It was unworthy to condemn her in the same breath as Old Stefan or Derik the Insane.

Or me, as I could have been.

As he might still be?

Concentrate on nothing else, only this point of light . . . came Linnea's silent command, cool as silver. With a start, Gareth reined his thoughts back under control.

The light . . . think of nothing but the light . . .

With a sigh, he lowered his barriers and allowed his mind to merge with hers. She took control with a Keeper's deft touch.

Gareth floated in a sea of misty blue-white. He poured his mental energies through his starstone and into hers, keeping the stream of *laran* power steady and even. Peace such as he had rarely known suffused him. Here, in this place out of time, there was no deception, no need for disguise, no schemes or plots, no consideration of rank, no past . . .

His next awareness was the touch of his grandmother's mind on his, a gentle warning before she broke their rapport. He felt himself falling, as he always felt when ending a telepathic session. They had not worked nearly as long as an ordinary circle would, but their goal was not assembling a higher-order matrix, mining rare minerals deep below Darkover's crust, producing fire-fighting chemicals or medicines, or any of the hundred things that could be accomplished with *laran*.

He wondered, not for the first time, if he should seek admittance to a Tower. Linnea believed he had the ability. Aldones knew the circles always needed more workers. That was why *Tío* Danilo spent the better part of each year searching out new talent.

To bury myself in such a world, a place of peace and fellowship . . . but one where nothing ever changed, where discipline and order were the rule.

No, he could not do that, either.

Linnea rose and stretched. "You did well, little one, once you settled down. I've rarely seen you so distracted."

"I—"

"No, don't tell me. It doesn't matter. We must leave all personal considerations behind when we work in a circle. That discipline is as necessary for you as for any Tower-trained *laranzu*."

Gareth hung his head, offering no excuse.

"Come now, you did not do badly. Did I not say so?" She brushed her fingertips against the back of his wrist in a telepath's feather-light touch. "We all have days when we are not our best, for are we not human? You are too hard on yourself. Sometimes I think you anticipate criticism by heaping it upon yourself first!"

"If I do not set high standards for myself, who will? Half the city can't wait for me to fail. The bet-makers are likely making odds that I'll do it in some spectacular and unseemly fashion."

Linnea shook her head. "You were very young when Javanne got her claws into you. She no more had your best interest at heart than do those toadies who dog your steps. It is they who are to blame, not you, unless you constantly remind me of it by this wincing."

"It is an old habit," he admitted, smiling.

"And one I should be happy to see you rid yourself of."

"For you, Grandmother, I will try." Gareth leaned forward to kiss her on the cheek. He bowed and stepped back, preparing to take his leave.

A thoughtful expression touched her face. "In some ways, you are very like Regis. He too had an adventurous spirit, although his rank forced him to set aside his own dreams. And he too expected more of himself than anyone else ever could."

"Grandfather Regis?" *The legendary Regis had stood against the World Wreckers and, if half the stories were true, became the living incarnation of Hastur Lord of Light when he destroyed the Sharra matrix.*

"Yes, he is best known for those things." Linnea responded to Gareth's unspoken thought, for they were still in light telepathic contact. "Before that, he led the Allison Expedition. Oh, yes, he was a mountaineer as a young man. Even as a cadet, he went alone into the Hellers at the time of the first Sharra disaster, when Caer Donn was destroyed."

"Are you saying . . ."

Linnea smiled. "I am saying that perhaps you need not hide your own dreams of adventure, at least not from me. It is natural for young people to strike out on their own. We all have private thoughts, and if you had been able to study at a Tower, you would have learned to keep yours close without drawing quite so much attention to them."

"I don't know what to say." His cheeks burned.

"Nothing is required. I only wish you to know that you are not the first young Comyn to want something more from his life than Council business, marrying for political advantage, and producing heirs. Go on, now. It is time for me to rest. If you will, we will speak more of this later."

There was no point in arguing. Besides, Linnea was right. With a Keeper's unerring instinct for the uncomfortable truth, she had put into words the focus of his discontent.

There had to be more to life than being polite to bootlickers like Octavien MacEwain or trying endlessly to live down his own past and escape everyone else's.

2

Gareth emerged from the Tower into sunshine. This part of the Castle was a jumble of architectural styles, an accretion of additions and remodeling that spanned centuries, perhaps millennia, and it bustled with activity. Servants chattered to one another as they hurried along the walkways, maids carried baskets of laundry, and scullions wheeled handcarts laden with barrels of apples, pottery jars of cooking oil, and braided strings of garlic. A nursemaid hurried along with a well-wrapped infant in her arms; from her expression, both of them had been up all night. Soon the place would be filled with children as the noble Comyn families began arriving for the Midsummer season.

Just as Gareth passed beneath the arched doorway leading to a garden courtyard, he spotted two men coming toward him from the opposite end. They were dressed alike in velvet hats and robes embellished with tartan ribbons. Copper links glinted around their necks. Gareth groaned silently as he recognized Rufus DiAsturien and Lorrill Vallonde. Only a few years ago, *Dom* Lorrill had schemed shamelessly to match Domenic with his daughter and, when that had failed, had shifted his ambitions to Gareth. Undoubtedly, one or the other of these two lords had influenced Octavien MacEwain. Gareth had heard rumors that some on the Council believed the time for a new Golden Age of Restoration had come. They would redouble their efforts to snare him with flattering talk and promises of power or a beautiful wife, because they believed he would be a puppet in their hands.

The two lords bent toward one another, speaking in hushed, urgent tones. Quickly, before either could recognize him, Gareth sidled back into the nearest doorway. His rising pulse sent a thrill through his chest. His vision sharpened. For a moment, he felt as if he were a boy again, pretending he was Special Agent Race Cargill of the Terran Secret Service, sent on a secret mission to save the Old Empire. He'd escaped his tutors on more than one occasion, prowling the back passages of Elhalyn Castle and pretending he was sneaking into Charin to root out The Lisse. Where Charin might have been and who or what The Lisse was, he had no idea, although his imagination had supplied many tantalizing possibilities. It often seemed as though he were living his life only through those adventures, and ordinary, real, daily events had nothing to do with him.

The two nobles passed through the courtyard and into the shadowed colonnade. Gareth made his way down one corridor through an older portion, once family quarters but now given over to offices, and then ascended a short flight of stairs. From here, he could stay hidden until he emerged near one of the outer gates.

At the top of the stairs, he glanced down the narrow corridor just in time to see Domenic and Danilo hurrying in the opposite direction. They both wore cloaks of the serviceable, ordinary type to be seen anywhere in the city. Gareth skidded to a halt, but with their faces hidden behind their hoods, neither noticed him. Clearly, they wished to avoid notice.

A tedious day had just gotten a whole lot more interesting. Gareth took a moment to make sure his *laran* barriers were secure, so that no telltale mental aura might slip through. He moved as smoothly and quietly as he imagined a catman might prowl. Following at a distance, he watched the pair slip through the same side gate he had intended to use. He marked the direction they took, then raised his own hood and hurried after them.

Domenic and Danilo kept to a moderate pace through the Old Town, passing corner food stalls and *jaco* sellers without pausing. If they sensed Gareth on their trail, they gave no sign.

As they entered the crowded Kazarin Market, Gareth almost lost them. By this hour, the market thronged with people eager to enjoy the fine weather, even if they found nothing to buy. He wove through a jumble of peddlers crying out their wares, shoppers and gawkers, street urchins and City Guards. For a time, he lost sight of them when a wagon loaded with furniture crossed in front of him, and by the time it had passed, he could no longer see them.

A moment later, he spotted them at the far end of the square. Danilo halted and glanced back, his eyes narrowed. For an instant, Gareth felt utterly exposed. What should he do? Race Cargill would not have been so easily detected.

Gareth's muscles unfroze. He whirled around, ducking his head to hide his face in the shadows of his hood. Behind him stood a table of leather goods. He fumbled to pick up the nearest piece of merchandise.

I'm not here, he thought, hardly seeing the finely tooled belt. *You don't notice me.*

So strongly did Gareth project invisibility that the owner of the stall, who had headed over the instant Gareth paused, drifted past him to greet another customer. Gareth counted under his breath, replaced the belt on the table, and turned around in as casual a manner as he could muster. He was just in time to see Domenic and Danilo leave the plaza.

Shortly, Gareth found himself in one of the city's seedier areas, the kind of place Narsin would have forbidden him to go, had he known. The streets were crooked, their paving stones cracked and discolored. A sour smell hung in the air. Many of the structures had originally been built well but had fallen into disrepair. He noticed the powdery mortar between weathered stones, the splintered beams, the sagging eaves and flaking paint. Men with weather-reddened faces huddled around garbage fires, warming their hands. They followed Gareth's progress with their eyes, perhaps calculating the value of his cloak and boots. He swaggered a bit, throwing out his chest and swinging his cloak back to reveal the sword at his belt. Rationally, the last thing he wanted was a fight, but he felt a twinge of disappointment at the speed with which the men hunched their shoulders and looked away.

Gareth returned his attention to the chase. What were they up to in this part of the city? This could be no morning stroll, no eccentric way of taking exercise. True, Domenic had acquired a reputation for unconventional behavior. His mother, *Domna* Marguerida, had been educated off-world and encouraged him to think for himself. This approach was not met with universal approval among the old Comyn families. One of the ladies attending Miralys Elhalyn, Gareth's mother, relished any breath of a scandal about Domenic.

"I heard," she had whispered to her friend when she thought Gareth was out of hearing, *"he consorts with common traders, Zandru only knows why!"*

"The Regent's son?" her companion had exclaimed. *"Shocking, positively shocking! But what do you expect from his lineage? I always say,* Blood will tell . . ."

Indeed, they undoubtedly said the very same thing—or worse—about Gareth. Maybe that was why Gareth held a particular sympathy for the young Regent-heir.

Gareth flattened himself against the rough stone wall of a wine shop just as the two stepped inside a similar establishment farther down the lane. The two-story building seemed in better repair than its neighbors and, by the presence of other patrons, was open for breakfast. The aromas of sausage, fried onions, and fresh-baked bread wafted from the door.

Odd to come all this way for a morning meal . . . But perhaps the relief from prying eyes was worth the walk.

The front door, although battered, opened smoothly at Gareth's touch. The interior was dark after the brightness of the street. He made out a bar running along the back wall. Three men in workers' clothing sat around the largest table, bent over bowls of meat-laced porridge and mugs of *jaco.* Several solitary patrons occupied smaller tables.

As Gareth was debating what to do, a harried-looking woman burst from the kitchen, balancing a basket of nut-studded loaves, a pitcher, and two platters of lumpy gray stew. Perspiration darkened the scarf that held back her gray-streaked hair. Gareth could not take his eyes off the wart on the side of her nose.

"Another one, is it?" She threw the bread down on the large table and bustled around to the others, hardly glancing at Gareth. She sounded as if she'd been engaged in a screaming contest with the crows. "Of all the mornings, with the girl out sick and my man not yet back from the miller! You'll be wanting breakfast as well, I suppose?"

It took Gareth a moment to realize she meant him. "No, nothing for me," he mumbled, imitating the common accent of the Castle servants.

"Then get yourself upstairs before I trip over you!"

By this time, Gareth's vision had adapted to the dimmer light well enough to make out a staircase at the far end of the common room. Places like this must have a chamber or two for private meals at a small additional fee. He went up. The stairs ended in a landing with two closed doors to either side.

Step by cautious step, Special Agent Cargill advances on the entrance to the secret chamber. Evil symbols glow on the ancient wood, but he must not shrink from his quest. The fate of worlds rests on him. He reaches out . . .

Which door? Both were perfectly ordinary, cheap coarse-grained wood. Gareth lowered his *laran* shields minutely, searching for the distinctive mental signatures of his friends. He tried to radiate as little as possible of his own presence.

An instant later, he sensed the familiar pattern of Domenic's mind . . . then Danilo's . . . and someone else's. This third man was no Comyn; his mind had no *laran* beyond ordinary intuition. Just about everyone in the Domains had some minor degree of sensitivity, or so Grandmother said. That was why telepaths cropped up now and again in non-Comyn families. The Comyn themselves inherited their psychic Gifts from the offspring of the earliest settlers and the ancient native race called *chieri*. The old families no longer held themselves apart, and over the millennia, *nedestro* children had spread the talent through the general population. Domenic's consort, Illona Rider, was one such, now working as under-Keeper at Comyn Tower.

Meanwhile, the third man presented questions. What was going on? A secret meeting? For what purpose? Danilo Syrtis had spent his life in serving the Domains, and Domenic was no less dedicated. Neither would have anything to do with criminal schemes or plots against the Comyn Council. Perhaps they met to prepare for the day when the Terran Federation returned to Darkover. Or to thwart some scheme of the Dry Towns lords? Whatever it was, it must be more exciting than the approaching summer social season.

And whatever it was, they would not be happy to find that he had followed them here. A man of honor, Comyn prince or commoner, did not spy on his friends. An image flashed across his mind of the door suddenly banging open and Domenic standing there, astonishment warring with disgust on his face, and beyond him, *Tío* Danilo reflecting disappointment.

I believed in you, Danilo said in Gareth's imagination. *I thought you were better than this.*

Cheeks flaming, Gareth scuttled backward so fast, he almost tripped on the edge of the stairs.

Idiot! Clumsy, stupid—

Hardly daring to breathe, Gareth hurried back down the stairs. Race Cargill would never have been so careless, not to mention so uncoordinated.

Gareth forced himself to slow down on the lowest stairs. It would do no good to escape notice only to attract it by suspicious haste. To his relief, none of the customers took any notice of him. The serving woman ignored him as she went about her work.

Taking a slow breath, Gareth ambled toward the door. At any moment, Danilo and the others might descend and find him here. He had not gone more than a short distance across the room when footsteps sounded on the stairs. Had he not been straining for any hint of pursuit, he might not have heard them. He dared not turn around or use his *laran.*

On a moment's impulse, he headed for the darkest corner, slid onto the bench, and pulled his hood over his face. Thus concealed, he hazarded a peek.

The man who emerged from the stairwell was of middle years, Gareth guessed, for his skin was darkly weathered. His hair glinted with the straw tints of Dry Towner ancestry, but he didn't look like one of the desert folk. His clothing was such as a trader or caravaneer might wear, a quilted jacket slightly ragged at the seams, knit cap, riding trousers, and laced boots. Without a glance, he crossed the room and pushed through the front door.

Heart pounding, Gareth sagged against the wall. He'd been lucky this time, but he dared not linger. Danilo and Domenic might appear at any moment.

Outside, the brightness of the day stung Gareth's eyes. The burst of adrenaline had faded, leaving a sense of exhilaration. Every nerve quivered with aliveness. The air tasted more intoxicating than wine. Even the rough walls, ramshackle buildings, and the drabness of the people passing him took on a new clarity and brilliance. He could not remember feeling like this, certainly not in all the interminable seasons at court. Was this why men climbed mountains or fought duels or ventured into the depths of space?

As he went on, the neighborhood changed, becoming even less familiar. The spasm of elation dimmed. He found himself headed in no particular direction . . . just like his life.

What a pathetic fool he'd been to derive such pleasure from a childish escapade. Only by luck had he managed to not be found out and his irresponsible behavior exposed.

His feet slowed to a halt. Around him, the brightness of the street faded and the sounds of the passers-by, the riders and carts, the children at play, a pair of itinerant musicians strumming an old ballad, seemed to mock him.

I can't face them, Tío *Danilo and Domenic. One look, one moment in my presence, and they'll know I've done something disgraceful, even if they don't know what it is. They're telepaths, both of them, and I don't have the strength to block my every thought.*

A man in sheep's-hide clothing, bent under a sack slung across his shoulders, bumped into Gareth and mumbled what might have been an apology but sounded more like a curse.

How could he go back? And how could he *not* go back?

The consequences of returning would be humiliating and degrading, but would they be any worse than what he'd already endured? He had no good name to destroy and no honor to preserve. And absolutely no reason to indulge in this disgusting spate of self-pity. Whatever he had created of his life, whatever he had done, was his responsibility. He would simply have to live with the results.

But if, oh, if only he could run away from it all! Join the Terran Secret

Service, if there really was such a thing outside the tri-vids. Hop on a freighter bound for the stars, if the Federation ever came back to Darkover. Join a caravan headed for the farthest reaches of the Hellers, venture beyond the Wall Around the World or the sands of Ardcarran or Daillon . . .

Gareth came to a halt. Instead of heading back the way he'd come, toward the Castle, he'd wandered to the outskirts of the Old Town. The place felt vaguely familiar, so he must have visited it before. He moved out of the flow of traffic, his back against a rough-sided building, and studied his surroundings. In one direction, he saw stables and fenced yards, in the other, blocks of warehouses. The mingled smells of animal dung and fodder hung in the air. He noticed many more horses and other beasts of burden than in the more populated city areas.

He must be somewhere near the Traders' Gate, then. From where he stood, he caught sight of a string of laden ponies, although surely it was too late in the day for any caravan to be setting out. A trio of women in the mannish garb of Renunciates stood outside a saddle shop, two speaking with a man in a leather apron and the third surveying the street, one hand on the hilt of her long knife. Her gaze paused on Gareth and her face tightened. He pushed himself away from the wall and, with as nonchalant an air as he could muster, strode off in the opposite direction.

There was always the chance he might be recognized, for he was a public figure. People saw what they expected to see, however, and who would expect Prince Gareth to frequent a livestock yard?

Gareth made his way past the pens and stables to an open square crowded with picket lines. Pack and riding animals of every description crowded together, everything from cart horses with thick shoulders and densely feathered feet to antlered *chervines*, young horses, and shaggy ponies. Everywhere men were talking, bargaining, examining the animals, and arguing with one another. Here and there, a man trotted out a horse on a leading rein to show off its paces.

Gareth wandered up one lane and down another, taking in the sights and sounds of the horse market. He'd never imagined such a place existed, although he supposed people must buy and keep their mounts somewhere. His horses had always been provided for him, most of them bred especially for his House and then cared for by servants. They'd all been superbly trained, of the finest bloodlines. No expense was spared in their grooming or feed.

Some of these animals appeared to be in decent condition, but most were far inferior to those he was used to. He saw many with old whitened sores on their withers, others with dull eyes and staring coats, bowed tendons, crooked hocks, and ribs like slats. A few appeared to be on the brink of collapse.

"Looking for a nice piece of horseflesh?" a voice drawled from behind Gareth's shoulder. Turning, he looked down on a hunched little man who might have been thirty or sixty. Layers of ragged, grime-darkened clothing obscured the contours of his body. Gray stubble covered an unshaven jaw, and the next words revealed several gaps in the man's teeth.

"Cut you a deal, nice young man like you, I will."

Gareth's gorge rose at the unsavory smell arising from the man, but he smoothed his features into the insipid blandness he affected at court. "I'm not sure," he said with a little careless laugh of the sort that usually resulted in nothing he said being taken seriously. "I might want something suitable for travel."

"Up or down?"

"I don't follow you."

The man sighed. "Mountains or Dry Towns? Do you want a beast that can climb like a goat or wade through the sand?"

Dry Towns . . . I could buy a horse fit for desert travel . . . I could disappear . . .

Images swept through Gareth's mind. He saw himself riding along a trail, leaving behind his life in Thendara. Out there, no one would know him. He could be whatever he made of himself.

He'd never been allowed to travel beyond the borders of the Domains, not even as far as Carthon. The very name hinted of perfume-laden night breezes, veiled women, men with strange accents and curved swords, exotic food and music—the stuff of tales of daring and courage.

He would need to be careful; like every other Comyn youth, he'd been brought up on stories of how treacherous the Dry Towns lords were. After the political machinations, the schemes and evasions and double-meanings of the Comyn courts, surely he knew how to handle himself.

It would be a brief visit, just long enough to clear his head and settle his nerves. Who knew what he might find, even in a day or two? He saw himself striding into Danilo's office, announcing, *"I overheard you speaking with the trader from Carthon, so I decided to investigate. I discovered—"* a dastardly plot by the Master of Shainsa or something equally spectacular, no doubt. In the next moment, he saw Danilo rising in astonishment and gratitude, and behind him, Mikhail and Domenic, Lady Marguerida and Gareth's own parents. *"Prince Gareth, your bravery and cunning have saved us all!"*

Getting a horse would be the easiest part. He'd need a disguise, a reason for his journey to Carthon. Maybe he could pose as a trader in small lenses or a buyer of whatever the Dry Towns had to sell—copper filigree jewelry? No, that would be too costly. Whatever he pretended to be interested in must not be worth the trouble of robbing him.

He'd also need a reason to be gone from home, should his absence be noted. *Narsin!* The old retainer fussed if Gareth was out of his sight for an hour, let alone a tenday!

The horse dealer was peering at him, perhaps calculating his next sales strategy. Gareth hardened his expression into disinterest. "I'll just look around a bit."

"You don't want to wait too long, young master," the dealer wheedled. "The best stock's already taken, 'cept for a few choice beasts I've set aside."

I'll bet.

"Then I'll come back another day." Without waiting for a response, Gareth turned and set off for another part of the horse market.

Gareth had not gone very far, no more than another row or two, when he recognized the man examining a dun mule. A youth held the lead lines of two sturdy horses the size of mountain ponies. He gestured in animated fashion with the older man, pointing to the mule's off rear hoof. It was the Dry Towns trader who had met with Danilo and Domenic.

Gareth froze in his tracks. A man leading a fractious, long-legged chestnut bumped into him, almost sending him spinning, and continued on with a curse at the idiocy of fools who got in the way. Gareth drew breath to demand an apology, but sense quenched his temper. Surely it was a good sign that he had been insulted and almost run down. No one here would dare to speak to him in that way if they'd realized who he was.

Feeling more confident, Gareth straightened his cloak and approached the Carthon trader. The boy noticed him first, stiffening. The trader straightened up from examining one of the mule's hooves.

"A fair day to you, friend." The trader's expression was mild but reserved, without any hint of the horse dealer's false affability.

"It is indeed," Gareth replied. "You look like a man who knows his way around horses."

"I have some skill with them, it's true."

Gareth was about to protest that anyone who earned his living by trading between Carthon and Thendara must have more than *some skill* with the animals upon which his livelihood depended. He stopped himself as he realized that the man's words amounted to reverse bragging.

"I'm in need of dependable travel advice," Gareth said. "It seems to be in short supply here."

The boy snorted and the trader looked amused. "What sort of advice?"

"I am to arrange transport to Carthon. The person—my employer's agent—who usually handles it is unavailable." Even as the words left his mouth, a story spun itself out in Gareth's imagination. The lens-seller pretext would work very well. Such articles were small, easily transported, and in demand. The Terrans had done much to improve the technology, especially for devices for detection of forest fires, but the scarcity of metal to construct proper furnaces still made the production of high-quality glass expensive. Growing up in a privileged family, Gareth had handled various kinds of lensed instruments. He owned a few such devices himself and could pretend to be showing them as samples.

"What would you be transporting to Carthon?" The trader's expression shifted to guarded interest.

"Myself and a small pack. I'm afraid I'm in a bit of a hurry, being already behind my master's schedule." Gareth tried to sound anxious.

"As it happens, I intend to depart the morning after next and can offer you the protection of my caravan. What's your name and business?"

Gareth stopped himself before he blurted out his real name. "Garrin. Garrin MacDanil." That was close enough to Gareth son of Danilo to make it easy to remember. "I'm to carry trade samples for my master."

"Trade samples?" One sand-pale brow lifted.

"Polished lenses."

"You speak with an unusually cultured accent for a merchant's apprentice."

Gareth tried to imagine having to earn his bread, what sort of work he might do. Even though he'd trained with a sword since boyhood, he wasn't qualified to be a bodyguard. He wasn't well enough educated to teach or fluent enough to translate. In truth, he wasn't much good for anything. Without his family's rank and wealth, he'd be extremely lucky to get a position as a merchant's apprentice.

The trader, seeing Gareth's confusion, dropped the matter and offered his own name with a bow. "Cyrillon Sensar, *z'par servu*."

After discussing the fee for joining the caravan and appointing a meeting place and time, Cyrillon agreed to help Gareth purchase a suitable mount. After sending the boy off with the horses and mule, he wandered through the picket lines of riding horses, pausing now and then to study one of the animals. Gareth knew enough about horses to understand that Cyrillon was evaluating their soundness. A keen eye could quickly discern the more serious faults, even without the precaution of picking up a hoof or estimating the age of the horse by the condition of its teeth.

After some looking, Cyrillon recommended a mare with a glossy, dark brown coat and one white sock. She was of middling years, "old enough to have sense," Cyrillon said, and was sturdy enough to carry Gareth easily. Her legs were strong and clean, and her hooves large and unusually hard. In addition, Cyrillon pointed out a second horse, a rusty black, to serve as a pack animal. Gareth thought it the ugliest horse he had ever seen, with its sway back, cow hocks, and ears so large it looked as if it were part rabbit-horn, but Cyrillon assured him that it was trailworthy. The dealer looked surprised that anyone was interested in buying it, so Gareth made a good bargain for the black as well as for its tack and a saddle for the mare.

Gareth paid for both horses and arranged for them to be stabled in the area. He didn't dare take them back to the little stable attached to the town house for fear of arousing too many questions from Narsin.

Whistling, Gareth strode back toward the town house. His scheme might have arisen in a moment's impulse and the soul-sick disgust for his life in Thendara, but it was coming together as if Aldones himself had commanded it. If Cyrillon Sensar had any doubts about Gareth's story, he'd kept them quiet. His apprentice wasn't exactly friendly, but what did that matter?

The sun had just passed midday, and the air was sweet and mild. He dropped his hood back over his shoulders and felt the warmth on his hair.

His hair . . . When he was younger, it had been as fair as a Dry Towner's. There might be some lady's product to lighten its color, but he wasn't sure if that would draw more or less attention to himself. As it was, he'd have enough to do—finding suitable clothing, packing the lenses, and laying a series of misdirections so his absence wouldn't be noticed. He doubted anyone in the Castle would miss him, at least until his parents arrived. The real problem would be Narsin. By the time Gareth strode up to the town house, he'd worked out a plan.

Narsin met him at the front entrance. The furrows between the old man's brows were even deeper than usual. His lips tensed, as if he were about to accuse Gareth of deliberately being late.

Gareth unclasped his cloak and shoved it at the old servant.

A grin came easily. "Narsin! I've got wonderful news!"

"Indeed, *vai dom*. And will you be wanting lunch?"

Gareth sat down on the bench just inside the door for Narsin to ease off his boots, then shoved his feet into felt house slippers. He gave orders for hot spiced wine along with his meal. Narsin arranged it all with his usual efficiency. The old servant might be a disapproving nuisance, but he never let his opinions interfere with the excellence of his work.

A fire warmed the smaller of the two parlors, where Gareth sank into the cushioned divan. The room seemed to enfold him with quiet and understated comfort. The furnishings, although beautifully constructed, had become slightly shabby with time and use. They probably dated back to the time of Danvan Hastur, who had been grandfather to Regis. Regis had refused to give up the town house, even when he had taken up quarters in the Castle. Gareth could understand why. Here there were no courtiers, no spying eyes. The house, especially this small parlor, felt lived in, a place where children might play before the fire, where parents might sit and talk after the children were abed. His own father had been born here . . .

Gareth shoved a cushion behind his shoulders and rested his head against it. When he closed his eyes, he could imagine his father as a toddler sitting on his grandmother's lap as she sang a ballad, perhaps one of the tales of Durraman's donkey or the Golden Forest of the *chieri*. The room might remember, but now there was no laughter, no child's delighted cries. No song. Just an empty, comfortable chamber. Gareth could not envision bringing any of the young Comynara to live here. Whoever he ended up with would insist on the Elhalyn quarters at the Castle and would doubtless spend the first years of the marriage in redecorating. The thought made him want to run away to Carthon and keep going.

Narsin returned to stand quietly beside the door. Gareth opened his eyes slowly, as if there were no urgency in anything he had to say. He hated the notion of lying to a man who had served him and his family so well and so long.

"I'm going away for a while, Narsin. I know it's sudden, but something unexpected just came up. I should be back in time for Midsummer festivities, but in case my parents arrive early, I want you to carry a note for them. You deserve a chance to go home—I believe you have family at Elhalyn Castle?" He was talking too fast, he knew, half-hoping that if he rushed over the particulars of his absence, he wouldn't have to explain further.

Narsin didn't question him directly. He was too good a servant for that. "When will you depart?"

"The day after tomorrow. If you leave in the morning, I'll be able to look after myself until then."

"My lord, is this wise?"

"Oh!" Gareth propelled himself from the divan. "I'll be in the best care, a man known to both *Tío* Danilo and *Dom* Domenic. That should be enough for even your demanding standards." He strode to the desk in the corner. "Here, I'll write the note right now. Well, get packing, man!"

"My lord—"

"Narsin, stop fretting. I'll be as safe as if I'd stayed in the Castle." He'd be safer than with the likes of *Dom* Octavien, that much was as certain as next winter's snows.

To Gareth's surprise and relief, Narsin withdrew without further argument.

Gareth scoured the library for every reference he could find on lenses. He learned the preparation of the different qualities of glass, the best types of sand for each purpose, and what minerals could be used to clarify or add color to the final product.

Confident in his pose as a rich man's son, Gareth went to interview the city's few glassmakers. To his delight, an elderly guildsman offered to show him glassblowing, and he spent the rest of the afternoon struggling with one failure after another. At last, he managed to produce a single misshapen flask.

"'Tis a fair first effort," the glassmaker said. "If you will pardon my saying so, young sir, but if you had begun your training as early as my apprentices do, you might now have attained at least a journeyman's skill. I intend no insult in saying so."

"No, why should any be taken?" Gareth said. "You are an honest man and a master at your craft. Here in your own workshop, surely you have the right to pass judgment."

The guildsman brought out various types of lenses, neatly arranged in padded carrying cases. With his advice, Gareth selected an assortment consistent with what a beginning trader might need. The outlay, modest though it was, would be expensive for anyone without the financial resources of a Comyn lord. Gareth did his best to convey the impression that he was putting his entire inheritance into the venture. He left with the agreement to pick up the merchandise upon payment. As he made his way back to his town house, the walls of Thendara did not press him as closely as they had before.

Shadows lengthened across the streets and towers of the Old Town as Gareth approached the town house. Light glimmered from the windows. Even in Narsin's absence, the household staff were efficient. He could expect a hot meal shortly.

Humming, he stepped through the door held open by another servant, one of the younger maids, and handed her his cloak.

"*Vai dom*, you are to go into the parlor," she said in a breathless voice, "if you please."

"Indeed." Not many people in Thendara had sufficient status to command the presence of an Elhalyn prince in his own home.

He went into the parlor, the larger one this time. The door had been left ajar, revealing the glow of a well-started fire. His grandmother sat in one of the armchairs drawn up near the hearth. She wore a formal visiting gown, and her hair was braided and coiled around her head like a crown, a subtle reminder of her status as dowager to the former Regent, as well Comynara and Keeper in her own right. She was not smiling, nor was Narsin, standing at a respectful distance behind her, arms crossed over his chest.

"Well, grandson, what kind of trouble have you gotten yourself into now?"

I haven't done anything yet.

Gareth was far from blameless, and he knew it. He had followed Danilo and Domenic, which was improper enough without also having eavesdropped on their private conversation. Once he'd made his plan, he'd deceived Narsin, who had served his family with devotion and loyalty. None of these actions was worthy of the man he wished he were. In a wild moment, he wondered if he would have behaved so badly had he not felt so useless and confined. He did not know what was worse, his life in Thendara or the loss of the hope, however fleeting, of escape. Even now, the road to Carthon, bright with adventure, vanished beyond reach.

"Narsin, leave us," Linnea's voice interrupted his misery. Watching the old servant bow and withdraw, Gareth realized that his emotional state must have leaked through his psychic barriers.

"Sit." Linnea indicated the unoccupied chair.

Gareth lowered himself into the seat and forced himself to meet his grandmother's gaze.

"I was concerned when you did not attend our scheduled session.

Then Narsin came to me with a tale of how you'd ordered him home on some pretext. He fears for you, you know." She clasped her hands on her lap, as if to hold them still. "As for myself, I had not realized how unhappy you were."

"It is not your fault."

"I did not say it was, only that as your teacher, if not your Keeper, I should have been aware."

Gareth looked away. How could she have helped, had she known? Could she have silenced the gossip, sorted the plots and schemes . . . given him something meaningful to do?

After a long moment, she said, "You attempted to send Narsin away. Your thoughts are of escape. Will you not trust me with the reason?"

Why not? He would never get away now. What little freedom he'd enjoyed would be snatched away. He'd be watched day and night, or else packed off to Elhalyn Castle like an unruly child.

"Gareth, I cannot help if you will not trust me. You know I will not enter your mind without your free consent. I have taken a oath never to do that."

She might not force a confidence, but once he'd confessed, his shame would be public. She and Danilo were still very close. Illona Rider, her under-Keeper, would surely pass along the report to Domenic. Before Midsummer, Mikhail and Marguerida, and his parents as well, would know.

One way or another, he must live with the humiliation. Perhaps it would be best to get it over with.

Then it came to him that he would not be the only one affected. Cyrillon Sensar had broken no faith, and yet his usefulness as Danilo's agent would end. What consequences that might have for the trader, Gareth did not know. It was one thing to risk his own tarnished reputation and quite another to sacrifice that of an innocent man.

Think what you will of me, but of me alone.

Gareth shook his head. To avoid even a hint of accidental betrayal, he kept his *laran* barriers as tight as he could.

Linnea, who had been leaning forward slightly, now sat back in her chair. "You feel very strongly about this. No, I have not read your thoughts. In all the years I have known you, since I held you in my arms when you were a babe, I have never seen you so determined."

"I have disgraced myself again and failed those who believed in me."

"Do you think anything you feel or did will shock me? By the time I was your age, my Tower training had shown me more of human folly than most people see in a lifetime. I may be sheltered, but I am not naïve. Besides, I suspect I know a great deal more about your character than you do. You are neither mean-spirited nor cowardly. Rash, certainly, and at times thoughtless, but what young man is not? I ask you again, will you not unburden yourself to me? I promise that whatever it is, I will love you none the less, and I will hold everything you say in strict confidence."

Gareth blinked. "You will tell no one?"

"Not without your leave." A smile hovered at the corners of her eyes. "Of course, if you tell me you are contemplating some felonious act—assassination, for example, or a violation of the Compact—then I will do my best to dissuade you. But if it is nothing worse than running away to seek your fortune in the Dry Towns, you have nothing to fear."

"Actually," he blurted out, "that's exactly what it is."

She sobered. "I think you had better tell me the whole story, then."

Linnea expressed no surprise as Gareth described what his days were like, the schemes to lure him into marriage or to turn him into a puppet king, and the days of idleness and surveillance. She listened, her head tilted slightly to one side, eyes thoughtful as he stumbled through his confession. She nodded, as if many things now became clear to her. At times, her focus blurred, as if she were hearing another voice and seeing another face before her.

Gareth felt a pang of remorse for having considered concealing the truth from her. As he stumbled through an apology, she smiled and said, "You forget that I have lived the better part of my life married to a public person whose every gesture was scrutinized for hidden meanings. We all need a place within our own minds where our thoughts and feelings, and dreams, too, are entirely our own."

Gareth had not expected such understanding. He had grown up

pelted by admonitions regarding duty and honor. "What else is there for me? I cannot find refuge in a Tower."

"When I was very young, I never dreamed of anything else." Linnea shook her head. "You are right. You belong too much to the world, and yet . . . Well, we will fly that hawk when his feathers are grown."

"That's—that's not the reason I tried to send Narsin away."

She sat very straight in her chair, her hands still. The tendons of her neck stood out, the only hint of her agitation. "Running away to the Dry Towns—you were not exaggerating, then? Have you any idea what those savages would do if they discovered you in their midst?"

"I have thought of that," Gareth said. "As the heir to Elhalyn, I run a particular risk. I am fully aware that I am no ordinary Darkovan. I will not be careless; I know this is no Midsummer Festival romp. Can you not understand? If I might someday be king, I must become worthy."

"Your sentiments are admirable. Do not, however, let unrealistic if noble motives get you killed while trying to prove yourself."

Passion hurled him to his feet. Raking his hair back from his forehead with one hand, he began to pace. "I've got to do *something*! If I don't find a way out of this cage, I'll truly become what they all think I am—just another useless Elhalyn. I want to be more than that!" He paused, chest heaving, and dropped back into his chair.

She regarded him, her eyes so filled with light that they seemed to glow from within.

He wanted to throw himself down before her and plead, *Let me go! Let me find my life!* but he could not, for reasons he did not entirely understand. Pride was not among them.

He sensed, in a moment of rapport, that she had *let go* before, that she saw not only this present moment but another, long past and infinitely more painful.

"I see that you have your heart set on this quest," she said, "and there is a great hunger in you. Although it frightens me to say so aloud, I think that if you stay here, some part of that heart will die."

Gareth could not believe what he had just heard. He had expected a certain degree of sympathy, but not such acceptance. He could not bear the intensity of the moment.

"I am not entirely helpless," he reminded her, trying to sound hopeful. "I've trained in swordplay and unarmed fighting since I was ten. I speak the dialect of the Dry Towns well enough to please my tutor. My hair's almost the right color to avoid attracting notice. I have my starstone and, thanks to you, some skill in using it."

The moment of overwhelming emotional intensity lifted. Linnea shifted in her seat, her expression once more practical.

"Use it for what? You are not a powerful enough telepath to send your thoughts over so great a distance. Sometimes, under conditions of great desperation, trained *leroni* have been able to reach one another's minds. I believe that Marguerida and Mikhail can do so, but their bond is extraordinary even among Comyn. As a piece of practical advice, if you find yourself in a position where you must try, it would be best to focus on me. I do not say this out of grandmotherly feeling but rather because I have been your Keeper. I am no longer as strong as I once was, but I am familiar with your mental signature. If anyone could recognize an attempted telepathic contact from you, I could. Moreover, here in the Tower, I have access to matrix screens capable of focusing and amplifying even very weak *laran*."

Gareth swallowed. "I hope it will not come to that."

"So do I. Gareth, the Dry Towners are a proud and cruel people. I fear that too many of them would consider it an ornament to their honor to unmask an intruder from the Domains. Should they discover who you really are—"

"I would die rather than give them a royal hostage!"

"You are so sure, then, that you can withstand the devices of men who have made an art out of torture?"

Gareth held his ground. "As well as any man, with the help of the gods. Clearly, the best solution is to not get caught."

"Your speech may not give you away," Linnea's gaze went to the silken pouch at his neck, "but that certainly will. Do you know what will happen if anyone but a Keeper handles your starstone?"

Dry-mouthed, Gareth nodded. It was one of the first lessons when he was given an unkeyed stone for his own. He had been ten, his *laran* only an occasional stirring, as distant as the storms of puberty, and yet he could still recall the words of warning spoken by Istvana of Neskaya, the Keeper who had given him his starstone.

"Once the matrix crystal has been attuned to your mind," Istvana had said, *"you cannot be separated without the gravest risk to your sanity. Even a casual touch by anyone except a trained Keeper can result in shock or even death. You must treat your starstone as if it were alive, an extension of your* laran."

Gareth could not leave the starstone behind in Thendara, not even in his grandmother's care. Once, as an experiment, he had tried locking it in a strongbox in his bedroom while he went to some official function. He had hoped that without it, he would be less sensitive to the psychic undercurrents of the assembly. That was when he still occupied the Elhalyn family quarters in the Castle. Before he had passed beyond the first courtyard, he began to feel dizzy. Each step intensified his unease until, retching and trembling, he'd been forced to turn back. The instant he took the matrix in his hands, his illness lifted. Fortunately, he was not expected to make any speeches, and no one paid him any heed beyond the usual insincere courtesies. He did not think he could have framed two coherent sentences in a row. For the next two days, he did little more than sleep.

He pulled the neckline of his shirt tighter. Perhaps he could carry the stone folded in his belt, where it would be less likely to be discovered.

"Belts and boots of leather make poor hiding places in the Dry Towns," Linnea pointed out. "The people there produce so little of their own, such goods are highly prized. I have a better idea."

She left the room and returned a short time later with a box about the length of his forearm and half as tall. Cobwebs dangled from one corner and clung to her sleeves. She sat with the box on her lap and brushed away the gossamer strands.

Gareth had no idea such a thing was in the house, but he had never explored the storage lofts. Broken furniture, discarded keepsakes, and chests of outdated clothing had never interested him.

Linnea caught his expression and smiled. "Yes, there's quite a collection of detritus up there. I never got around to cleaning out what had been left before us, and I'm afraid we were guilty of contributing our share. Regis always had so many more important things on his mind, and your father never cared."

After wiping her fingers on her skirt, she grasped the lid of the box.

It resisted her for a moment, then opened with a creaking of old, warped wood.

"I don't know why I kept this, except that it was too ugly to inflict on anyone else." She drew out an amulet on a chain and handed them to Gareth.

Both were of sturdy construction, although the metal was silver of the poorest quality. The amulet looked as if it had withstood hard usage. It bore a stylized representation of Nebran, the toad deity of the Dry Towns. Gareth agreed with Linnea's opinion of its ugliness.

"Thank you . . . I think," he said dubiously.

Linnea's eyes glinted. "Open it."

Gareth looked closely and saw that the amulet was in fact a locket. The clasp was well hidden. After several tries, Gareth found the release with his fingertips. The locket fell open. Each half was lined with a layer of something that looked like matted cobwebs.

"Place your starstone inside and close it."

As Gareth did so, the colors in the room went dull, as if all the light in the world had suddenly dimmed. His tongue felt too large for his mouth and his saliva tasted bitter. He recognized the same sickness that had seized him during that disastrous experiment when he attempted to leave his starstone behind, although much less severe. Unpleasant as these current symptoms were, he could tolerate them. He could even function with a degree of normality and perhaps use his *laran* to some small degree, unamplified by the starstone.

Linnea opened the door and invited Narsin inside. The old servant had been waiting a short distance away.

"Give the amulet to Narsin," Linnea said.

Puzzled, Gareth did as she bade him, although in the instant before the locket left his grasp, his nerve almost failed him. Narsin was an honorable man, and there was no question of his love for Gareth, yet he was no *laranzu*. Gareth held his breath and let the locket drop.

He had expected searing pain, but none came. In fact, he felt nothing at all as Narsin's fingers closed around the silver. Gareth glanced at Linnea for an explanation. She gestured him to wait, took the amulet back, thanked Narsin, and waited until he left the room.

"I don't understand," Gareth said. With trembling fingers, he pried the locket open and restored his starstone to its proper place. A wave of relief passed through him. His thoughts sharpened as the room grew brighter and warmer. His stomach no longer threatened rebellion. The muscles of his belly unclenched so that his next breath was deep and full.

"Is it—" he indicated the Nebran amulet, "—a telepathic damper like the ones in the Crystal Chamber? I did not know the Dry Towners made such devices." He could not imagine any metalsmith of the Domains creating such a piece.

Linnea shook her head. "I think the effect results from some contaminant in the silver. It's been here for a long while, from the days of Danvan Hastur, if not before. I discovered it on one of my vain attempts to organize the storage areas. I had thought to ask the *Terranan* scientists to analyze the metal, but one thing led to another, and I never found the occasion."

Her expression turned pensive. Then she gathered herself and continued, "Whatever the mechanism, the locket is psychically insulated and should protect you from the worst if it is taken from you. You will still face the problem of separation from your starstone, but at least you will not go into convulsions."

Gareth slipped the chain around his neck. The amulet pressed against his chest, so unlike the barely noticeable silk of the pouch. He assumed he would grow accustomed to the weight, and the more he wore it, the sooner that would happen.

"For now, we must part. I will speak with Narsin on my way out." Linnea brushed her fingertips over the back of Gareth's wrist. For a fleeting moment, he felt her mind touching his, her abiding love for him, her past griefs and present concern.

"I'll be all right," he assured her.

"There is nothing certain in this world but next winter's snows," she murmured. "Gareth, I would share what you have told me," *this burden, this worry,* "with another who loves you."

"My father, you mean?"

She shook her head. "Not unless . . . No, I meant Danilo Syrtis."

"*Tío* Danilo?" *He'd stop me from going if he knew.*

"Your fears wrong him."

He saw then the impossible position in which he'd placed her, to either go against his desires by forbidding him to go, or to bear in silence the anxiety of keeping such a secret.

"Tell whoever you must," he said, unable to keep a trace of resentment out of his tone, "but only after I'm gone."

"I have given my permission as your Keeper for you to go. Who in the Domains has the right to challenge my decision?"

Shame brought a flare of heat to his cheeks. He bowed his head.

"*Adelandeyo, chiyu mio,*" she murmured, brushing his forehead with a butterfly kiss. "Walk with the gods."

Gareth awoke before the first intimation of rose-pale light seeped across the eastern sky. After a hasty breakfast, he set about checking his clothing, his baggage, even the undistinguished but serviceable sword that replaced his jewel-hilted blade. After Grandmother Linnea had left him last night, he'd raced up to the storage lofts and found trunk after trunk of old clothing, some of it so worn he could not imagine why it had been kept. Besides the clothing, he had discovered a trail kit and the sword. In the end, he decided against attempting to alter the tint of his hair, for fear that the result might be so unnatural-looking as to draw even more attention to himself. He was rapidly becoming accustomed to the insulating effect of the Nebran amulet.

Mounted on the brown mare and leading the rusty black, Gareth passed the Traders Gate. The sky had been growing lighter by gradual degrees since he had left the town house. Night's chill clung to the earth like a lingering mist. He drew his cloak more tightly around his shoulders and pulled the hood over his head. To his relief, none of the people streaming in or out of the city took any special notice of him.

He was on his own now. He could go anywhere, do anything, be anyone!

A short distance down the broad road from Thendara, he spotted Cyrillon's caravan, off to one side. There must have been a dozen wagons and half again as many riders, some of them leading strings of laden pack animals. Cyrillon's apprentice moved among them, speaking with the drovers and checking harnesses.

Cyrillon waved a greeting to Gareth. "Garrin, you already know Rakhal, my apprentice. There is Korllen, our cook, and Tomas—" he indicated two men, one with a blond beard, who nodded silently in Gareth's direction "—and Alric there, with the waterskins." Alric, a shaggy, sun-browned boy, grinned shyly.

The apprentice made a thorough inspection of both the brown mare and the packhorse, paying particular attention to their feet and making sure the saddle pads had no folds or wrinkles and were thick enough to cushion their withers.

"Your gear is well balanced, but your stirrups are too short," Rakhal said, after adjusting the pack animal's breast strap. As he looked up, the sun fell full on his face. His cheeks were soft, innocent of any beard, and his eyes were the clear blue of an unkeyed starstone, except for a ring of gold.

"I think I know the length of my own legs." Gareth had been riding since he could remember and had been trained by the best instructors at Elhalyn Castle.

"For city riding, they are all right, but on the trail your knees will suffer." Rakhal turned to shout at Tomas, "No, not that way! The poor beast's spine will be too sore for him to carry a feather cushion after the first day!"

Gareth watched as the older man hurried to obey with the same alacrity as if the orders came from Cyrillon himself. Staring at the stirrup leathers, he admitted to himself that his resistance to changing the length came from his own inexperience in such stableman's tasks. His saddles had always been adjusted by someone else, not to mention cleaned and mended. Still, he would bring attention to himself by acting like a spoiled aristocrat. He swung down and fumbled with the leathers as Rakhal had suggested.

"On the road, everyone!" Cyrillon called when Gareth had remounted. "Let's waste no more daylight!"

Grabbing a handful of coarse, close-clipped mane, Rakhal swung up on a speckled roan. "Garrin, come with me. You're to ride in front."

The caravan got underway. Cyrillon drove the lead wagon, with the boy Alric sitting beside him. It did not take Gareth long to realize that the best position in the caravan was as far forward as possible. The animals churned up a surprising amount of dust. The drovers covered their mouths and noses with long scarves. One offered Gareth a length of worn, blue-printed cotton and indicated with hand gestures how to wrap it. Gareth did not trust the brown mare's temper enough to drop the reins, so he tried to do it one-handed. Unfamiliar with handling long strips of cloth, he flopped the scarf this way and that. When he thought he'd finally gotten it arranged correctly, it slipped down over his forehead. Not only could he not see, he could not breathe, for the folded cloth ended up snugged over his nostrils. He jerked it loose. By this time, he was the object of attention not only of the drover who'd gifted him with the scarf, but of everyone not driving a wagon, Rakhal among them.

Gareth flushed, waiting for the inevitable ridicule. The laughter, when it came, was good-humored, inviting him to share in the joke. He grinned sheepishly at his own clumsiness.

Rakhal nudged the speckled roan close enough to grab the mare's reins. "Try it with both hands."

Gareth complied, this time achieving a measure of success. The final result might have been comical and not nearly as evenly tucked as the others, but at least it filtered out the worst of the dust. To his surprise, the onlookers called out their approval. Rakhal grinned and booted the roan back along the line, where one of the pack animals—the stripe-legged mule—was threatening to kick another.

Past the outskirts of the city, the road wound through the small farms that supplied the markets of the city. A few farmers were loading their carts with the day's harvest—leeks, cabbages, and spring greens. Gareth grinned and lifted his hand in greeting.

By the time they stopped to water the animals at midday, Gareth was beginning to feel the effects of prolonged time in the saddle. In Thendara, he had occasion to ride for only short periods of time. He shifted in the saddle to ease a twinge in his lower back.

Rakhal must have noticed, for the young apprentice brought his horse beside Gareth's. "It will not slow us, should you walk for a time."

He thinks me weak, a soft-handed city lout.

"I can ride."

The apprentice shrugged. "Any fool can stay on a horse the first day." Then he turned the roan, kicked it into a trot, and went about his business.

The road narrowed at each crossroad until it was little better than a trail. They passed fields of early barley, rippling in the morning breeze. The barley smelled sweet, like new-cut grass. Fields of grain gave way to orchards and then to rocky pasture. The undergrowth rustled with living things. Rabbit-horns flashed white-spotted rumps as they darted for shelter. Overhead, a hunting falcon hovered on the air currents.

Now well into the hills, they encountered few other travelers beyond a caravan of pannier-laden mules and a metal trader with well-armed bodyguards. Near dusk, Cyrillon chose a spot well off the beaten track, where the grass was still lush. His men set about ordering the camp, digging latrine pits, placing the wagons, and setting picket lines for the horses.

Gareth watched them, trying to prolong the time before he would have to dismount. The twinge in his back had slowly burgeoned into a creaking stiffness that sent spasms down his legs. The mare shifted, pulling at the bit. She wanted the grass and it was not kind to hold her here without good cause.

Gritting his teeth, he kicked free of the stirrups, leaned over the pommel, slid his right leg over her back, and dropped to the ground. He caught his balance, leaning against the mare, and congratulated himself. A little stretching and his back would be fine. He slipped the reins over the mare's head and almost let out a yelp. Some imp from Zandru's coldest hell poked a dozen sharp needles into his knee joints. The next moment, he became aware of Rakhal smothering a grin. Gareth set his jaw, lifted his chest, and led the mare to the picket line. It was all he could do to take one step after another without wincing, but he managed it. If he had not taken Rakhal's advice about the length of his stirrups, he might not have been able to walk at all. He did not want to think what tomorrow's ride would be like. Still, moving about helped loosen his muscles. He managed to strip the mare's tack, pick out her feet, and hobble her to graze with the others.

The rest of the caravan was making ready for the night. Fires had been lit, and the smell of cooking food filled the encampment. Cyrillon waved from one of the fires, where his apprentice and his crew had gathered.

Korllen, the bearded blond man, had prepared a stew of dried meat and fruit over boiled grain, pan bread, and honeyed nuts. Gareth's belly melted at the sight. He lowered himself to an empty place in the circle. The boy, Alric, smiled shyly.

Besides the usual *jaco,* the cook had also brewed a pot of something hot and astringent smelling. He held out a pottery mug and indicated that Gareth was to drink it. The infusion was hot enough to scald, but Gareth managed a sip. It tasted much worse than it smelled. Korllen gave an encouraging nod. Another sip, and a fiery tingle spread across Gareth's mouth. The taste reminded him of vinegar and ashes. He grimaced and set the mug down.

"That's not a wise idea." Rakhal spoke up from the other side of Alric. "If you think it tastes bad now, it's ten times worse if you let it cool."

Korllen grunted and turned his attention back to the cook pot, as if to say he'd done what he could, and if Gareth was fool enough to refuse the drink, he was not responsible for the consequences.

You wanted adventure, Gareth told himself. *Well, here's yet another thing you've never done before.*

He blew across the steaming surface, as much to gather his nerve as to cool it, and then took as big a mouthful as he could. Warmth shot down his gullet, at first bordering on pain but quickly fading. Heartened, he downed another mouthful. Either his taste buds had gone numb or the stuff wasn't so bad. A sense of well-being seeped through him. His muscles no longer ached. He hadn't tasted any alcohol in the drink, but he felt the same sort of relaxation and cordiality as from several goblets of wine. When Korllen served up the stew, he accepted his portion with an emotion that bordered on delight. How delicious it was, how fascinating the texture of each component. He could not recall any meal at the Castle, even at the Regent's table at the Midwinter Festival banquet, tasting so good. Across the fire, Cyrillon nodded to him and then turned back to his conversation with one of his men, something about the horses that pulled the wagon.

After the meal, Tomas and Korllen went off by themselves. To gamble, Gareth suspected. Cyrillon called for songs, accompanied by Rakhal's reed flute. Gareth had never heard some of them before. He suspected they were either very old or came from deep in the deserts beyond Shainsa.

Midway through the singing, Gareth came back to his normal senses. He still felt relaxed but clearheaded. The warmth had settled in his tendons and joints. He suspected he would sleep well and awaken with far less stiffness than he'd otherwise suffer. The potion, whatever it was, had been kindly bestowed.

It was now full night. As the earth exhaled the last of the day's warmth, a chill sifted down from the sky. Of the four moons, only blue-green Kyrrdis shimmered from the swath of milky stars. The fires were dying. An occasional lick of flame rose from the glowing coals, each one smaller and briefer.

Gareth glanced around the encampment, what he could see of it in the encroaching darkness. Rakhal, Alric, and the others had gone off to bed. Only Gareth and Cyrillon and one of the drovers remained. A feeling rose up in Gareth, one he had never experienced in his life within the walls of Thendara.

The world was vaster and more vivid than he had ever dreamed. Somewhere out there in the dark, wolves howled in the wild lands beyond the Kadarin River. Banshees haunted the passes of the Hellers. Catmen prowled. Perhaps, in the farthest hidden forests, *chieri* danced beneath the single moon. Across the arid sands, *oudrakhi* moved like silent, lumbering behemoths. Men with strangely cut blades fought duels of honor. Veiled women watched from behind screens carved from rare and fragrant woods. He wanted to see it all, taste it all, dance beneath the moon and hear the secrets whispered in the perfumed night.

Linnea Storn shut the door to her sitting room, leaned her back against the smooth wood, and closed her eyes. Her muscles ached from the hours of forced inactivity during the night's work, and her spine felt as if it had turned to glass. She rarely felt her age so keenly. The past winter had seemed longer and its dampness more penetrating than she could remember. A thought hovered at the back of her mind, a truth she was not yet ready to face, the first intimations of her limits as a Keeper. Her mind might be as clear and her *laran* as powerful as ever, but her body would eventually force her to retire or risk the lives and sanity of the *leroni* of her circle. To gather the focused psychic energies of the men and women, to weave them into a unity and then direct it as she chose required not only skill and concentration but physical stamina as well.

At least, she would leave a capable, experienced Keeper in her place. If the gods were kind, she might have time to begin training another.

One of the novices had lit a fire, still brightly flickering, and left a tray with a pitcher of *jaco* and a plate of honeyed nuts and the dry cheese she favored. Linnea had already eaten enough to take the edge off her *laran*-

fueled hunger, and the smell of the food turned her stomach. Even the comforts of the room, the elegant hearth, the mantel with a carved box of her favorite biscuits and one of beeswax candles, the pair of cushioned chairs sized for a woman's small frame, the footstool and basket of knitting within easy reach, failed to soothe her.

In truth, she could not blame the weather or the years for her current fatigue. These last two nights, she had overworked deliberately, using the discipline of the matrix circle to keep from thinking about Gareth.

Had she been foolishly indulgent to let him go? The world held a litany of dangers—bandits and mudslides, falls and scorpion-ants. Carthon lay at the edge of the Dry Towns, and those fierce people had never been on amicable terms with the Domains. The men were said to be fanatic in defense of their *kihar*, their prestige, and as quick to engage in a duel as to blink an eye. Anything could happen there, especially to a young man accustomed to privilege—

Don't think it.

She pushed herself away from the door and went to the window. Half the sky had turned to light, or so it seemed.

And half remains in darkness.

What a maudlin mood! And at my age! She rubbed her arms through the layers of her knitted shawl.

Gareth was not much different from any other young nobleman of his time. He was a product of the ancient traditions of the Comyn—*and the Elhalyn, at that!*—and the society that had been changed forever by the starfaring *Terranan*. He'd said he would travel with a man trusted by Danilo. Was that the way someone truly feckless behaved? Was Gareth any less prepared to venture forth than Domenic had been, running away with the Travelers? Or Regis—

Ah, beloved! You dreamed of the stars but never left this one planet. Such was the price of your honor.

She and Danilo had laid to rest the frictions and jealousies born of loving the same person. Once she had resented him because he was the focus of her husband's heart. Their shared grief had done much to soften the distance between them.

Linnea roused. She could not admit a man, even her dead husband's lover, to her quarters while wearing her Keeper's robes. Rubbing the back of her neck, she dropped the shawl over the arm of a chair and went into her bedchamber. Here she changed into an ordinary gown, the old green wool she'd brought from High Windward so many years ago. Within a few moments, she felt less chilled. She wrapped herself in the shawl again and stood in front of the hearth, soaking up the warmth of the fire.

Gareth said Danilo knew this man, this guide . . . Then Danilo would be able to set her fears to rest. Some of them, at any rate.

She straightened at a tap on the door. "Come."

The door swung open, but it was not Danilo who entered. It was Illona Rider, Linnea's under-Keeper. Linnea had not seen her for some days as the younger woman had taken a brief rest from circle work. Illona wore a knee-length tunic over a long-sleeved gown, the sort of warm, comfortable clothing favored by mountain women, for she had originally trained at Nevarsin Tower in the Hellers. A butterfly clasp of copper filigree bound her hair in a coil on the back of her neck. A few silky tendrils framed her face.

"Oh!" she exclaimed, mentally catching Linnea's quickly masked surprise. A delicate flush suffused her cheeks. She looked younger than her years. "Am I intruding? Were you expecting someone else?"

"I was, but that does not mean you are unwelcome. Please sit down."

Illona glanced at the indicated chair and shook her head. She clasped her hands, then unclasped them. Linnea had never seen her so uncertain. Illona was one of the most self-confident young women she knew.

Concerned now, Linnea reached out with her mind. Despite Illona's evident anxiety, nothing of her inner state leaked through her *laran* barriers. Whatever she had to say, she intended to speak it aloud.

"Very well." Linnea drew herself up and composed her features. "Do you come before me now as one woman to another or as a *leronis* to her Keeper?"

"Both." Illona's voice did not carry the artificial brittleness of an effort to mask inner agitation. "I have just come from Michala," she went on, referring to the senior of the two monitors, on loan from Dalereuth Tower until Raynelle was experienced enough to work on her own, "and she confirms what I myself suspected."

Illona drew in a breath. "I am pregnant."

"Oh, my dear!" The words burst from Linnea before she could sort the rush and tangle of her own feelings. Any child was to be treasured—a son or daughter from two powerful telepaths to strengthen the ranks of the Gifted—*the risk to the unborn babe from matrix-circle work!*—what Illona must now give up, her work, her independence—a flood of memories. . . .

. . . Regis saying, when they first met and she had, in a moment of compassion, offered to give him children after two of his own had been lost to assassins—"*There are so few of you now, who can work the matrix relays. How can I put out more of the lights of our world?*" So she had chosen, first the demanding work that only she could perform, then to set it aside to bear and raise his children, and now a second life, one that was hers alone. But Illona still faced those choices.

Does Domenic know?

"Not yet. I came to you first."

"Oh, my dear!" There seemed to be nothing else she could say. The two women fell into an embrace, laughing and sobbing at once.

Linnea sighed. "I will miss you greatly."

Illona drew back, facing Linnea with her usual practical expression. "I have not yet decided on all the details—I must speak with Domenic first—but I have no intention of going anywhere."

Surely Illona understood why she could not continue to do matrix work. Every student learned the principles of monitoring the pathways of psychic energy in the body. The same channels that carried *laran* also carried sexual energy, flowing through nodes along the spine, the heart, and the reproductive organs. For this reason, puberty was often a dangerous time for a young telepath, as sexual feelings and psychic Gifts awoke, threatening to overload the energon channels. Linnea herself had suffered only a few transient bouts of disorientation and nausea, but Regis had almost died of threshold sickness.

A pregnant woman risked not only her own health but the life of her child . . .

"As your Keeper," Linnea declared, "I cannot allow you to work in the circle."

"Of course." Illona glanced down at her belly, still flat beneath her loose tunic and gown. "But I will not be an invalid. I can still work. We always have more applicants to the Tower than we can accommodate. I thought to use my skills in teaching until the babe is born."

"Sit." Linnea indicated the nearest chair with a flicker of her gaze. Illona responded to the Keeper's authority in the gesture, seating herself immediately and folding her hands into the posture of a student.

"I understand your desire to keep working," Linnea said, schooling a note of kindness into her voice. "Truly I do. I have stood at this same crossroads myself. I was very young when I met Regis, but already I was performing a Keeper's duties. I was doing what almost no one else could, and the fate of our world depended on that work. It was dangerous, for the World Wreckers had targeted telepaths. Such a risk I was glad—eager, almost—to face. So I recognize, more keenly than you can imagine, the choices that come to all of us in the Towers."

Illona, who had been listening attentively, now stirred. "I've grown up with stories of that terrible time, of poisonings and killings arranged to look like accidents, women dying in childbirth and the midwives murdered before they could speak. And—" here her voice faltered "—infants slaughtered in their cradles. However, those times are past. The Federation is gone. Who knows if they'll ever return? If they do, we'll be ready for them. That's why training as many Gifted young people as possible is so important."

"Yes, it is," Linnea agreed. "I was not referring then to any external threat. You are quite right, these are peaceful days. Evanda has blessed us with time to recover our numbers and deepen our knowledge. No, I meant that we as women have always faced difficult choices. The departure of the Federation may have resolved some problems . . . but not all."

Illona lifted her chin.

"A pregnant *leronis* is responsible not only for her own health but the welfare of her unborn child," Linnea said.

"I know that! I'm neither ignorant nor stupid. That's why I want to teach!"

She's off-balance, or she would see the truth for herself, Linnea thought with a rush of compassion. "Teaching carries its own responsibilities. You could teach for an hour, a day, even years without incident. But nothing is certain in this world except birth and next year's snows. Even the most talented student can lose control, and you as her teacher must be prepared to protect her and everyone else in the Tower. Do you understand me? In a Tower, a teacher does more than lecture. Our strength makes it possible for those in our care to stretch, to fly . . . and, occasionally, to fall, knowing that *we are there to catch them.* If such a thing were to happen . . ."

Illona had gone pale. She was, as she had said, neither ignorant nor unintelligent. She was an immensely Gifted *leronis* who would one day become one of the finest Keepers of modern times. Linnea felt ashamed at having lectured her.

"If I can't—" Illona stammered, "if it's unwise for me to teach, then what am I to do? I can't—I won't be carted off to Armida! I refuse to be cosseted like some hothouse blossom!"

"No, of course not!" Linnea's temper flared at the idea. Illona and Domenic might never be able to marry, due not only to her commitments to the Tower but to her illegitimate status and the hidebound conservatism of the Council, but she must not be parted from the father of her child. Among telepaths, such a thing would be unspeakably cruel.

"Then what am I do to?" Illona's eyes went wide and bright. "*Vai leronis*, what did *you* do?"

Linnea hesitated. She could not imagine how to explain all the things that had changed over the last two generations. During her own grandmother's time, a Keeper was expected to be not only celibate but virgin, kept forever apart. Men had been executed for daring a single lustful glance at a Keeper. Marriage meant a permanent end to matrix work, and noble families arranged alliances for power, prestige, and breeding for *laran* Gifts, regardless of the wishes or talents of the woman. By the time Linnea had trained as a Keeper, however, attitudes had changed. Cleindori Aillard had demonstrated that it was possible for a matrix worker to be sexually active if proper precautions were taken. Linnea herself had not been inexperienced when she and Regis became lovers.

Even then, she had not been spared.

"I had already ceased my work as a Keeper when I became pregnant with Dani," she said carefully. "And then Regis became Regent. As Lord Hastur, he needed a chatelaine for Comyn Castle and a partner and ally in dealing with the Council on one hand and the Federation on the other. Added to child raising, those duties were more than enough to keep me busy."

"But if you had not been forced into such responsibility, if you could have chosen your own life—"

"My life was with Regis." Linnea recoiled at the bleakness in her own voice. "If the price was taking on the position of Lady Hastur, then I paid it gladly."

Illona responded with fire. "So you gave up?"

"I did not *give up!* I performed the honorable and necessary work that was given to me! Just as you will, just as we women have always done. Child, you have both the yearning and the talent to act as a Keeper, so you have never had to face the hard reality when desire leads and ability refuses to follow. You have never had to grapple with the fact that we do not always get what we want, we cannot always *be* what we want, and sometimes the things we treasure most are taken from us. It is not fair, it is not easy, but it is the way it is."

Illona gulped, clearly taken aback at the force of Linnea's vehemence. "I know very little about your life back then. You are right, I do not know what choices you faced or what sacrifices you endured. Forgive me. I did not intend disrespect."

Linnea wrestled her emotions under control. She had not intended her words to be so harsh or her manner so combative. The old, unhealed loss was not Illona's fault. For an odd moment, she felt as if the room were crowded with phantasms of absent loved ones—Domenic, of course, and Marguerida, who brought off-worlder sensibilities to the discussion, Regis and even Dyan Ardais with his brutal adherence to the old order, Dani and his own children—Gareth and Derek and Regina-Javanne.

She brushed her fingertips along the younger woman's wrist, the gossamer touch of one telepath to another. The contact catalyzed a moment of rapport.

You are the daughter of my spirit. I have no wish to grieve you, especially at a time that should be an occasion of joy for us all. I take heart that you will not have to face the same painful decisions, and your daughters and their daughters will have even more freedom.

"We are both weary," she said aloud. "Go on, tell your beloved. After rest and thought, we will speak again."

After Illona left, Linnea remained in her seat, staring into the fire. The room felt somehow colder, shadowed.

She had deliberately mentioned only her son, Danilo Hastur, who had grown up in the most warm and loving family she and Regis could provide. In the end, Dani had refused the Regency and the lordship of Hastur in order to marry Miralys Elhalyn, whom he dearly loved. He seemed to be content with his choice, spending most of his time managing Elhalyn Castle and its estates, well away from the schemes and machinations of Thendara. Removed from the line of succession, neither he nor his family would ever be targeted the way Regis and his children had been.

Linnea closed her eyes, wishing she could as easily shut off the flood of memories.

I mentioned only my son, because everyone knows about him. His existence was not kept secret to protect his life.

Kierestelli . . . In her mind, she could see her daughter's face as clearly as when they had parted so many years ago. They had the same gray eyes, but Stelli's hair had been a brighter shade of copper. It was probably darker now—*no, don't think of that!* She remembered the promise of the Hastur beauty in the shape of her daughter's cheek, the long-fingered hands. Stelli had been tall for her age, graceful as a *chieri*, with a smile that lit her entire face.

The child had been conceived during the brief, intense time after the World Wreckers almost destroyed their world. Linnea had parted from Regis when Stelli was small, retiring to her family's holding at High Windward. She could not return to a Tower, not with sole responsibility for a child, but she had treasured every day, every moment. When she and Regis had reconciled about the time his grandfather died, he had offered her a chance to use her *laran* skills once more. What neither of them had realized then was that the danger to Regis—and to his family—had not ended with the defeat of the World Wreckers. Desperate to protect her, Regis had hidden Stelli from his enemies. He had told no one of the location, lest the secret be exposed and she be placed at risk.

How could Linnea blame him? How could she *not* blame him?

He went back to look for her, again and again, once the danger was past. Each time he returned, he looked as if a piece of his soul had perished.

Life goes on. Linnea had to believe that wherever Regis had taken Kierestelli and for whatever reason he could not retrieve her, she was safe and loved. Linnea had borne two more daughters, gone now to marriages of their own choosing, and she loved them with a mother's abiding love, but in her heart, she had never ceased to long for her firstborn.

I had no choice but to let her go. Is that why I am so troubled now when I have a choice about Gareth? The mind was a strange and capricious thing, the heart even more so.

Danilo Syrtis sent a message postponing their meeting, pleading the press of urgent business, so another day passed, a day in which Linnea devised a program of work that would be safe for Illona. She fulfilled her task with special care in repentance for her previous harsh stance. She had been justifying her own choices—and her own acceptance of the loss of her daughter. With proper precautions, Illona might serve in the relays or even do limited monitoring work.

Night was lowering when Danilo arrived. A haze of light clung to the western sky, quickly fading in the velvet hush of night that gave Darkover its name. Only a few stars glimmered through the streaks of cloud.

Linnea and Danilo sat facing one another by the fire. The glow of the embers reflected off his eyes. Linnea sensed nothing of his thoughts, but that was not unusual. Danilo had always been an intensely private person. He'd had to be, as paxman and lover to the most extravagantly public man on Darkover.

"I apologize for putting off our meeting," he said. "A matter arose that required my immediate attention."

"Is it something I might help you with?"

"Actually, it is very much your concern as well as mine. Young Gareth has not been seen in three days."

Clearly, whether or not he knew the man Gareth had gone off with, Danilo did not know of Gareth's plan. Briefly Linnea examined her conscience regarding the confidentiality of what she knew. Gareth had misled her, perhaps because he did not want to lie outright. Although she could not read Danilo's thoughts, she felt his anxiety as a shiver through her own bones.

"He's gone to Carthon with a man he says is known to you."

"Carthon! Of all the idiotic, irresponsible—! Whatever possessed him to do that?"

She took a sip of her honeyed mint tisane, giving him a moment to answer his own question.

"Something like this had to happen sooner or later." He shook his head. "Gareth will never be happy with a life at court where he has nothing better to do than stand around, surrounded by scheming popinjays. He's never been given any real work to do."

"And whose fault is that?"

"We all must share the blame, I'm afraid. It might have been better to keep him at Elhalyn when he was younger, where he could grow up learning to manage the family estates, but it's too late for that now. Here in Thendara, he faces a constant reminder that young men his own age like Domenic are already making their place in the world."

It's a pity Gareth has no calling for Tower work, Linnea thought. *He has the talent, certainly, but his heart would not be in it.*

"Carthon, of all places!" Danilo exclaimed. "Gareth is—well, he's a good lad under that foppish exterior, but he's had no experience in handling himself in a crisis."

Linnea frowned. Carthon might be rough and lawless compared to Thendara, but it had been a long time since the last formal war between the Dry Towns and the Domains. "Is that likely to occur? In Carthon?"

Danilo shifted in his seat and Linnea caught a flare of unguarded emotion. Her skin around her eyes tensed.

"I don't know," he said, not meeting her gaze.

"Then tell me what you suspect." *Or fear.*

He hesitated visibly, perhaps weighing the responsibilities of discretion against their history of trust. "It is possible—*remotely*—that the Federation has secretly returned to Darkover."

"What reason do you have to suspect this?"

"Very little, actually, besides the likelihood that it will happen sooner or later. Darkover's position in the galactic arm is too important to be abandoned indefinitely."

This was common knowledge, although Linnea rarely spared it much thought. Jeram had been training a cadre of young people, listening for any communications on the equipment at the old Terran Headquarters complex.

"No," Danilo said, as if sensing her thought, "we haven't heard anything direct, and Jeram believes the apparatus is operating properly. But . . . you know that Domenic has an odd form of *laran*. He can detect changes in the planet itself."

"Seismic activity, I believe," she agreed. The Regent-heir's talent had long been a subject of curiosity. No one was entirely sure what he could perceive.

Seismic activity, she repeated to herself, then caught Danilo's thought. "Impact tremors? As from a starship landing?"

"We don't know. Domenic says they're so faint, they must originate from a long distance. He can't determine exactly where, only the general direction—beyond the Dry Towns."

"Carthon?" *Blessed Cassilda, what have I sent Gareth into?*

Danilo shook his head. "We don't believe so. It could be something else or nothing. Even if it is a Federation ship, we don't know why they would not use the spaceport here. If this were an emergency landing, they might have been unable to contact us in the usual way."

"There has been nothing on the relays to suggest such a calamity. It is difficult to imagine a situation like that—the terror, the pain—without one or another of the Towers becoming aware."

"Doesn't that presuppose the *Terranan* possess enough *laran* to reach you? What if the disaster occurred in space?"

"Many off-worlders have a small measure of mental talent," Linnea explained. "We used to believe otherwise, but now we know that we Comyn are not the only ones with Gifts. Even though one individual may not be strong enough, many minds, when fueled by terror or desperation, can do extraordinary things."

Danilo nodded thoughtfully. "At any rate, I've asked my agent to look into the situation. It may be as we fear, or it may be nothing. Regardless, I'm not happy about Gareth . . ." His voice trailed off.

". . . getting in the way." She finished the sentence. "Making a mess of it? No, he has my confidence. I know he has behaved foolishly in the past, but he has worked hard to amend the shortcomings in his character. Think how he has applied himself in his studies—languages, as you advised, and matrix work with me. He may not yet have proven himself, but I believe he will."

A smile hovered at the edges of Danilo's eyes. "You see him with a grandmother's steady love."

"And you, having loved his grandfather, do not?"

"You know that I do." Danilo made no offer of a physical touch, no gesture of reassurance, but she caught the faint shift in tension around his mouth, the harmonics in his voice. "Do you want me to send someone after him? Caravans travel much more slowly than mounted men, and Cyrillon would stick to the main road."

Send someone after him? To drag him home in disgrace like a runaway puppy or a disobedient child? That would destroy the trust between them and likely ruin him.

"I thought not," he said. "However, if it will set your mind at rest, I can send a messenger to Cyrillon's house in Carthon. That way, we will know they have arrived safely."

"I don't think we can—we *should* do more at this time."

Danilo's gaze flickered, and Linnea wondered whether he was remembering how Regis had gone storming up to Aldaran Castle when Danilo had been taken prisoner there. Regis had been, what, sixteen? seventeen? and Danilo the same age, both of them younger than Gareth was now. If Danvan Hastur had dispatched men to bring Regis back, Danilo might not have survived. Worse, the Sharra uprising might have succeeded.

Regis . . .

A longing rose up in her, shook her deeper than any bodily hunger. She could do nothing for Gareth, but Gareth had gone on an adventure of his own choosing.

"Danilo, I have never asked you this," Linnea said, her voice breaking a little with the rush of unexpected emotion, "but if you do not know, I doubt any man living does. Did—did Regis ever confide in you? Did he tell you where he hid Kierestelli?"

Danilo was silent for a long moment. "He never did. I suspect it was for the same reasons he never told you, to keep her hidden and to keep us safe from extortion. What we did not know, we could not be forced to tell. Those were dangerous times for us all."

My daughter, my beautiful little girl! Where was she now? In some village or married off to some minor lord? Worn out with raising children or dead in bearing them?

No. I would have felt it if she had died.

"He never told me," Danilo repeated, "but he may have told someone else."

"Who was closer to him than you?"

"Lew Alton, in his way."

Linnea kept her features composed with an effort, but she could not entirely disguise the impatience in her voice. "What could Lew know? When Kierestelli was born, he was off-planet, representing Darkover at the Imperial Senate."

Perhaps Danilo had the right of it. He and Regis had known a different sort of intimacy than she had shared, from their boyhood friendship to being comrades in arms to the particular bond of male lovers. Regis—she knew very little of his early life. He had been fostered at the Alton estate of Armida during the formative years of his adolescence. He and Lew had renewed something of their old friendship after Lew returned to Darkover.

Linnea stood, her knees creaking. Danilo too looked tired. She bade him good night like the old friends they had become, shrugged her shawl around her shoulders, and made ready for the night's work. Try as she might, she could not shake free the thought,

What else could I have done? Regis was so frightened she might be seized by his enemies and used against him. I thought it was just for a little while, until it was safer. And now it is too late—no, it cannot be too late!

She paused in the stairwell to look out one of the slit windows. The wind had thinned the clouds, so that Liriel's peacock-hued radiance glimmered through the narrow opening. Linnea's heart lightened at the sight. Country people called it Evanda's Moon, after the goddess of mercy.

Do you look down on my daughter even now, O Blessed Lady?

Perhaps it was not too late, after all.

7

As the days passed, Gareth settled into the routine of the caravan. His body adjusted to the hours in the saddle, the rhythm of movement and rest, of meals and sleep and song. The mare turned out to have a mouth like leather and a gait that rattled Gareth's teeth with each step. He didn't care. For the first time he could remember, he was free, on his own. Anything could happen, and he rather hoped it would.

He had never spent time with men like these, rough-spoken and cheerful, handling the animals with competent ease. Sometimes one or another of them would sing a tune in an odd heptatonic scale. The words were not in Dry Towns dialect, but something far older. Gareth felt shy around them out of fear of drawing attention to himself. His accent, his bearing, even the reddish tints in his hair, any of these might betray him. From time to time, he caught Cyrillon staring at him, but the trader never confronted him with questions, leaving the daily interactions to his apprentice.

The hills grew more rugged, cut by eroded gullies. Now and again, they stopped at a village, where a few coins bought a hot meal and fodder for their animals. The caravan shrank in size as wagons left the main party when the roads branched, until the party consisted only of Cyrillon's own men and his two wagons. Gareth was the only stranger among them.

Two days away from Carthon, while winding through a narrow stream-etched gorge, an axle on one of the wagons broke. It took the better part of the afternoon to replace it with the spare. As the lowering sun cast the gorge into deep purple shadows, one of the horses pulling the other wagon began limping; a stone had lodged deep in the frog of its hoof. Gareth supposed they would go on without the horse and use one of the riding horses to pull the wagon, but Cyrillon said that there were wolves in these hills, and the poor beast would not be able to defend itself or run away. Rakhal spent a long time cradling the poor animal's foot on his thigh, and then walking the horse up and down, before advancing the opinion that if they bound the hoof with a poultice and rested the horse for a day, it would be fit to travel again.

"That is what we will do," said Cyrillon. "We cannot go much farther today."

They retraced their steps to the mouth of the gorge, where they had passed a little grassy dell. Gareth helped to unhitch and tend the animals. With his usual efficiency, Korllen set up camp, put on another pot of foul-smelling brew, a new and different one this time, and soon had the evening meal prepared.

After they had eaten, Cyrillon went off to make a circuit of the camp. He emerged from the shadows a short time later, his brow furrowed.

"What is it?" Rakhal asked.

"I cannot see or hear anything out of the ordinary, nor are the horses restless, yet something in me is not easy. We will set two guards tonight. Garrin, you take the first turn. Korllen will also watch, and then I will stand with Tomas."

"What about me?" Rakhal asked. "Am I to stay in the wagon with Alric, as if I were a child?"

Cyrillon's frown deepened. "We have had this discussion before, and I have not changed my mind."

Their gazes locked. Even without his starstone, Gareth sensed Rakhal's challenge and Cyrillon's determination. Finally, Rakhal muttered, "I hear and obey."

Gareth watched Rakhal head off to the horses, feeling as if he had inadvertently been party to a private battle of long standing. Withdrawing, he made his way to the latrine pits. On his way back, he lingered for a moment at the picket lines with the brown mare. She did not lift her head at his touch, but continued ripping up mouthfuls of grass.

Rakhal, silvered in the light of two moons, was combing burrs out of the tail of one of the wagon horses, quite unaware of his presence. Gareth searched his thoughts for something that might ease the lad's distress, but what was there to say?

"Those who love us want us safe, or as close to it as is possible in this life"?

Yet here he was, leagues from Thendara's walls, without the armed escort proper to an Elhalyn. He was the last person to offer platitudes to anyone else. When he looked again, Rakhal had melted back into the night.

When Gareth returned to the campfire to take up his watch, the cook was waiting for him. Cyrillon and the others were already asleep.

"I will teach you how we do this in the manner of the Dry Towns," Korllen said. "One of us must go out among the horses, on the perimeter, and the other stay here in camp. I will call to you like this—" he whistled through his teeth, "—and you must answer me, so that I know you have not fallen asleep."

Gareth tried several times to imitate the whistle, with little success. "Bah!" Korllen cried, "you sound like an asthmatic goat!"

"How about this?" Gareth cupped his hands over his lips and gave a two-toned *huu-huu!*

"That is well enough," Korllen admitted, stroking his beard, "although only a deaf *oudrakhi* would mistake that for a real rainbird. I suppose it is as good as any Lowlander can do. Now off with you, nice and slow around the outside."

Beyond the little circle of firelight, the world muted into a series of shadows. Gareth moved slowly as his eyes adapted to the multihued radiance from three of the four moons. The air, although rapidly cooling, was mild, and the only sounds were the soft grinding of the horses chewing grass, the occasional jingle of a halter ring, or the clink of a shod hoof against a stone. There was no sign of the wolves Cyrillon had mentioned.

"Thweet!" came Korllen's whistle from the camp.

"Huu-huu!" Gareth answered. The brown mare raised her head, ears pricked. He patted her neck. "Yes, I think it's a bit silly, too." She blew gently through her nostrils and went back to lipping the stubble.

Gareth completed his circuit and made himself comfortable, stretching out beside the fire. After a suitable time, he gave his rainbird imitation, to be answered by a distant whistle. The temperature was falling now, although he did not think it would rain. The banked embers gave off a seductive warmth. His muscles ached, thick and heavy, so heavy. . . .

With a start, he realized that in those few minutes, his eyes had closed. Had he actually fallen asleep? How long had it been? With a racing heart, he sat up.

"Huu-huu!" Gareth's hoot sounded louder and even less realistic than usual.

"Thweet!" came the reassuring whistle.

It would be better not to lie down again. After another interval, Gareth repeated his rainbird hoot.

Silence.

He blinked, wondering if he could have fallen asleep again and not noticed.

"Huu-huu!"

Although Gareth strained to catch the answering whistle, he heard nothing. Was Korllen playing a trick on him, teasing him for his lapse, poking fun at the newcomer? What should he do? Cyrillon and the others slept in the wagons and doubtless would not appreciate being awakened without cause.

An idea brightened Gareth's mind. He would sneak up on Korllen and turn the prank around. Moving as silently as he could, Gareth slipped from the camp. The orange glow of the fire receded behind him. He followed the same route as before, circling the horses. It was darker now, Idriel having set behind the ridge of the gorge. One of the horses blew out a gusty breath and stamped a hoof. Another shifted, restless. In his mind, Gareth saw their heads come up, nostrils flared wide, searching . . .

He halted. Adrenaline stung his nerves, enough to leave him uncertain. He realized then that he had left his sword back in the camp. Slowly he raised his hands to his mouth.

"Hoo-hoo!" Wavering, almost tentative, this time his cry really did sound like a rainbird.

Silence answered him. At that instant, a certainty swept through his mind. Beyond the single red oak, a handful of men crouched. With a rush of *laran*, even insulated by the amulet, he could smell the iron in their hands . . .

He dared not cry out to Korllen. If he made even the slightest sound, the intruders would be warned. They were hoping to use surprise as their advantage, so they would hold off their attack until they were closer.

Gareth took a step backward and then another. His boot came down on a stone and it shifted under his weight. To his ears, the clink sounded unnaturally loud, an alarm as shrill as any trumpet. Beside him, one of the horses shook its head, halter rings jingling. Gareth let out his breath.

Another step, and then a long stretch between the grazing horses, and then Gareth raced across the short distance to the camp. He scooped up his sword and, one-handed, jerked aside the heavy canvas drape of the nearest wagon.

"Cyrillon!" he hissed, trying to keep his voice low. "Wake up!"

"What is it, lad?" In the darkness, clothing rustled.

"Men to the south—Korllen's out there, but he didn't answer—"

"Did they see you?"

"I don't think so—"

"Hai-yah! Hai! Hai! Hai!" A series of cries, rising into blood-curling ululations, shattered the night.

An instant later, the camp seethed with struggling men. Bandits, a half-dozen at least, boiled out from the darkness. They seemed to come from every direction at once.

Cyrillon jumped down from the wagon, yelling. Steel clashed against steel.

Sword drawn, Gareth strained to make out an opponent in the near dark. Someone kicked the fire, sending up a cascade of sparks. The little space was briefly lit, but it was enough for Gareth to make out a lean, tall man in an ink-dark shirtcloak, wielding a curved sword. He swept toward Cyrillon, who was laying about with his own weapon. Gareth moved to help the caravan master, but he was too far away. The next moment, another bandit came charging out of the roiling shadows.

Years of training with the best armsmasters of the Comyn now flowed through Gareth's muscles. His body reacted faster than thought. He parried, using the other man's momentum to close the distance and batter away at his defenses. As they disengaged, circling, Gareth caught sight of a slender figure leaping from the wagon.

Rakhal!

The dying ember light reflected off a blade, a long knife or short sword, Gareth couldn't be sure. He had not a moment to spare as his own opponent came hard at him. He deflected the blow, but not before he had seen how the man's right shoulder hunched, leaving the opposite flank open as he spun away.

Across the camp, a shriek cut through the clamor of shouting and the ring of steel. It might have been Tomas, but Gareth could not tell. He dared not break his concentration to look.

The brightness of the fire faded quickly. In a moment, he would be blind. The bandit screamed and hurled himself at Gareth, blade whipping through the air.

Gareth stumbled back a pace, stunned by the ferocity of the attack. The other man's sword, visible only as a hair-thin line of reflected moonlight, blurred against the night. Ordinary vision was useless now. By luck or something more, Gareth caught the other man's blade in precise balance, flicked it to one side, and drove in. The edge of his own sword snagged on leather for a terrible moment before it bit into flesh.

The man screamed, this time a wordless animal roar. Gareth could not tell if he felt or only *sensed* the other man's body curl in on itself and crumple to the earth.

Light flared, bright and yellow. Someone had touched a torch to the fire and it went up like a miniature blaze. For an instant, Gareth faced no one.

Two dark-clothed bodies lay in the dirt. The man Gareth had wounded was still alive, struggling but unable to get to his feet. Tomas was down in the shadows beside the second wagon, his hands clasping one thigh that gleamed wet and dark. Cyrillon still fought, holding his own against a much smaller man. Rakhal ducked in and out, evading another bandit's sword thrusts, darting in to slash and run.

Two of them left!

No, a third attacker now rushed toward Tomas. Like the others, he wore a shirtcloak and loose pants tucked into boots, a wide sash and some kind of belt or baldric across his chest. With deadly intent, he moved toward Tomas, who was unarmed and unable to rise.

Fire shot through Gareth's nerves. The Dry Towner was too far to reach in a single stride. Before Gareth could take another step, however, the man pivoted with a swordmaster's astonishing grace.

The Dry Towner's sword swung around, but not before Gareth had brought his own up. Gareth's blade came alive in his hand, an extension of his own body. He felt the kiss of steel against steel, and in that instant, flowing through the joined blades, a sudden wordless awareness. His own body *knew* how the other man would disengage, the infinitesimal shift of weight to his stronger side, the curve of the lower spine, the barely felt weakness of the other knee. Like sunlight piercing cloud, Gareth surged into the opening.

The next instant, Gareth's vision snapped back to normal. He had broken the distance and was now within the circle of his opponent's guard. The other man's balance fractured; he twisted, struggling to bring his sword up. He was quick, but he had no room and no time. Gareth, his own blade already in perfect position, stepped forward. Overborne, the other man stumbled and fell to his knees, sword spinning free.

Again, that preternatural *sensing* swept through Gareth. He *knew* the instant before the other man slipped out a double-edged dagger. Before the blade had left its sheath, Gareth brought the edge of his blade against the other man's throat.

The other man's hand opened and the dagger, a *skean* fashioned in the style of the Dry Towns, dropped to the ground. Light flickered in the keen gray eyes, signaling a stoic acceptance.

"Hold, all of you!" Gareth shouted in Dry Towns dialect, "or he dies!"

He dared not shift his gaze from the man at his feet, but he heard the sounds of fighting die down.

Cyrillon called for Rakhal to help him gather their weapons. Someone built up the fire, and Gareth got a better look at the man he had just beaten, strong features with a hooked nose, well-trimmed beard, intelligent eyes. The man's age was difficult to tell. The flickering light cast deep shadows around mouth and eyes, the jagged scar across one high cheekbone, but there was no gray in the pale, braided hair. It was not, Gareth thought, the face of a man made desperate by poverty.

An outlaw, then? A bandit chief? What was he doing, raiding on this side of Carthon, still in Domains territory?

"Who are you who come upon us in the night like cowards?" Gareth demanded, still in Dry Towns dialect.

From behind, Cyrillon answered, "Do not ask a man to shame his house. Do what must be done, and quickly."

Aldones! They expect me to kill him!

And yet, if the fight had gone differently, it might be Gareth on his knees in the blood-spattered dust and this bandit holding the sword. Would this stranger have shown mercy?

From the other side of the camp, Tomas moaned in pain. Korllen was still out there, in all likelihood killed without a thought.

Gray eyes looked back at Gareth, unflinching. Without thinking, Gareth reached out with his unaided *laran*. During the fight, he had felt such a flowing unity with blade and opponent that it startled him now to sense nothing from the other man's mind. There was no telepathic presence, which was not surprising in a Dry Towner. Gareth sensed only a surge of emotion—fierce pride, admiration, and, yes, fear. But not fear of death, fear of the northern sorcery, the dawning suspicion that he faced not a human victor but a soul-devouring demon of the Comyn.

"What are you waiting for?" Cyrillon said in a voice gone tight with strain. "There is no honor in tormenting an honorable adversary."

What indeed was he waiting for? His steel was sharp, the blade touching the Dry Towner's neck just along the artery. A quick, light thrust and it would be over. No one would blame him. They all expected it. The defeated man himself was prepared to die. A man of the Dry Towns, even an ordinary man of the Domains, would not hesitate.

But, Gareth thought savagely, *I am no ordinary man. I do not live for myself but for my Elhalyn blood, and the blood in my veins is the blood of kings.*

As an adolescent, Gareth had been blinded by the notion of kingly power, and he was still paying the price of that foolishness. Now that he had a flicker of insight into what it truly meant to be the heir of Regis Hastur, he wanted nothing to do with it. Loathing rose up in him, but whether it was in response to the barbarity of the situation or to his own past actions, he could not tell. Even if no one at home ever learned of his decision here, *he* would know, and it would change him and everything that came afterward.

One Dry Towner had brought him to this point, a scarred and dusty man who would have not a moment's hesitation in taking Gareth's own life.

Quickly, before his nerve failed, Gareth withdrew his blade. Let Cyrillon deal with the situation.

Gareth stalked into the night, toward the horses. The sight of the Dry Towner, awaiting his death with stoic pride, now sickened him. His belly trembled, and if he was going to be sick, he preferred to do it in private.

He had not gone more than a few paces when he heard the sound of another man shuffling between the restless animals. He recognized Korllen's voice, and went to him.

The cook had taken a blow to the back of his head and was more stunned than hurt. Gareth, having slipped his sword back into its scabbard, pulled the older man's arm across his shoulders. Together they returned to the camp.

In the few minutes Gareth had been gone, the fire had been built up again and torches lit and set into the holders on the wagons. Rakhal knelt beside Tomas, bandaging his thigh. The face of the fallen bandit had been covered with a fold of his own shirtcloak, and the one Gareth had wounded leaned hard on another. The leader, as Gareth now recognized him, stood before Cyrillon, holding his sword in both hands in a position of offering.

They turned as Gareth and Korllen stepped into the circle of light. A flush swept across the Dry Towner's sun-dark skin.

"Will you, then, accept the sword of Merach of Shainsa, in payment of this debt?" the Dry Towner said.

"I don't want your sword any more than I want your life," Gareth said, still angry. "If you insist, then swear on your honor to never go raiding in the Domains again."

For an instant, the Dry Towner said nothing. Gareth sensed his shock. Then the Dry Towner, this Merach of Shainsa, made a deep, elaborate bow, touching his fist to his belly, heart, and forehead.

"Ancient wisdom tells us that only a fool returns to a battle he cannot win. The wise man lives to fight another day. May I know the name and house of the man who holds *kihar* over me?"

"I'm called Garrin, if that's what you mean. And you don't owe me anything. Just take your wounded and dead, and go!"

"Garrin." Merach said the name slowly, as if tasting its truth. He bowed again, an abbreviated gesture this time, and with a few decisive gestures, swept his party back into the night.

The boy Alric was soon scampering about, preparing hot water and bandages. Tomas and Korllen must be attended to, but the caravan master and his apprentice had escaped unscathed. Cyrillon drew Gareth aside. "You have no idea what you have done in allowing that man to live."

"I could not butcher him after he had yielded to me," Gareth said. His thoughts jumped and tangled with each other like maddened dogs. "Are these bandits so lacking in honor that he would attack us again or carry a blood feud against me?"

"Just the opposite." Cyrillon looked grave. "Don't you know who he was?"

Gareth shook his head. "Merach of Shainsa, that is all. Did he lie?"

"Merach is no ordinary Dry Towner, but a lord of Shainsa with kin ties to the Great House. I don't know why he was leading such a small raiding party. It must have been a matter of *kihar*, either his own or that of a member of his family. Now he owes you a debt that he can never repay." Cyrillon lowered his voice. "It might have been kinder to end his life, rather than leave him without any hope of regaining his honor."

The last part of their journey took longer than expected because of the two wounded men. Korllen recovered enough to resume his duties as cook by the second night, although his face tightened whenever the wagon wheels rolled over a rut. Tomas could not walk, but at least his thigh wound had not gone bad.

At the end of the third day, they crested the last hill. The sun, redder than usual in the lingering dust, slanted into twilight. Three moons clustered overhead like a pale bouquet. From his position near the front of the caravan, Gareth looked down on a wide plain, where Carthon squatted in a bend in the River Kadarin, a great jumbled heap of bleached rock and brick. In one direction, dusky shadows marked the foothills of the Hellers mountain range. In the other, a tenday's ride away, lay Shainsa.

At one time or another, Carthon had been occupied by either Dry Towns or Domains forces. Its dilapidated, much-broken walls and mixed architecture presented a face that was neither one culture nor the other, but an uneasy amalgam. In these days, its primary importance was as a meeting place and trading post, often used for outfitting expeditions.

Its markets were known for the filigree butterfly clasps prized by women in the Domains.

Cyrillon's caravan trudged through the outskirts, where other traders had already set up camp outside the city gates. One called out a greeting in Dry Towns dialect, and Cyrillon responded.

Teams of men stopped everyone seeking to enter the city. To Gareth, the guards looked outlandish and fierce, with their bearded faces, flaxen hair, and strongly arched cheekbones. They carried their swords and many knives openly, as if their manhood was measured in the number of their weapons.

Cyrillon halted his wagon and identified himself, greeting one of the men by name. Past the gates, the main road led them to the central plaza of the city. Even by Thendaran standards, the space was huge. An enormous structure of opalescent stone dominated the open area, surrounded by beds of brilliantly hued flowers. More fair-haired, visibly armed men patrolled in front of the double doors.

A train of merchants hauling sacks of grain and dried fruit in ponderous carts had preceded them into the square, adding to the riot of color and sound. Pedestrians clustered around several fountains, one of which was clearly reserved for the watering of livestock. In the haze of dust, Gareth could not make out much more than the general shapes of the stalls and spots of color—greens, purples, a dozen shades of brown and tan. Awnings shaded the fronts of shops. Canopied booths and blankets spread with trade goods and produce sprawled across the far end of the plaza. The air smelled of spices and alkali. Gareth felt as if he had stumbled into the pages of a romance.

Race Cargill, Special Agent, gazed out over the city of adventure . . .

When Cyrillon gestured a halt, Korllen retrieved his pack of personal belongings from the second wagon. Cyrillon handed him a battered leather purse that clinked softly, and the two exchanged a few words regarding travel to Shainsa. Rakhal led up Gareth's packhorse and held out the lead line. Gareth stared at the rope.

"This is the end of our journey," Cyrillon said. "By law and tradition, the care of a caravan ends in the center of the city of destination. Now I must see Tomas to his family and secure my goods and wagons."

Gareth took the mare's lead rope. Now he was truly on his own in this strange and mysterious city, where any moment might bring adventure. At the same time, he felt a reluctance to part with the caravan.

"A word of caution, Garrin of the Domains," Cyrillon added, with a sidelong glance that hinted for the first time of suspicions that *Garrin* might be an alias. "Carthon lies on the border between the lands you know and those where ignorance of custom too often leads to unfortunate consequences." He put a twist into the word, *unfortunate*, so that it might have meant *fatal* rather than *inconvenient*. "If you had arrived at Shainsa or Ardcarran, you would be obliged by the laws of those places to first pay your respects at the Great House. Here in Carthon, we tread a middle path, favoring neither Dry Towns nor Domains. We do not look kindly on those who would disrupt the balance."

Gareth followed the trader's glance toward the massive edifice of sun-bleached stone. That must be the Great House, empty during those years when the city had belonged to the Domains, but clearly inhabited now. Carthon might not be formally part of the Dry Towns, not yet anyway, but it would be wise not to borrow trouble.

"Thank you for the advice," Gareth said, and would have gone on, but Cyrillon waved aside any further thanks with the air of one who has done only what decency required.

Gareth opened his mouth to ask the name and direction of a reputable inn, but then realized that as a lens-merchant's apprentice, he would have been given local contacts, perhaps customers of his master. He stumbled through a farewell and then watched as Cyrillon turned the wagon and headed down one of the thoroughfares leading from the plaza.

The mare tugged at the bit, mouthing the metal. Thirsty, she had scented the water at the public trough. Gareth, like all Comyn, had been taught to tend to his mount before seeing to his own comfort. He loosened the reins and let the mare have her head.

The trough was broad and wide, a circle of stone around a central pillar. Seasons of wind had scoured away the carvings, leaving only a suggestion of decorative figures. Each rider first paused to give a few coins to a man sitting on a pile of cushions beneath a canopy. The man's face was so darkly weathered that Gareth could not guess his age, but the waist-long beard was pale yellow and the eyes as bright as steel. Such eyes missed nothing and forgave even less. A half-naked boy knelt in the shade, waving a wide, ribbed fan.

A man in the garb of the mountain folk walked up, leading a pair of mules. Their shoulders and flanks were dark with sweat. He spoke a few words to the bearded man, then dropped several copper rings on the blanket. The water-tax collector lifted his chin and made no move to sweep up the money. Muttering, the mountain man added two more. This time the fee was accepted and secreted somewhere in the collector's robes. All the while, the boy kept fanning, his rhythm as even as if he were one of the *Terranan* machines.

Gareth hauled the mare to a halt, no small matter as she was intent on getting to the water. He slipped from her back, took firm hold of the reins, and turned her slightly to approach the water-tax collector at an angle. She objected, but only for a moment. If he had tried to pull her in a straight line, as he had often seen inexperienced riders do, she would surely have set her feet, humped her back, and refused to budge. The old trick worked, deflecting her resistance and allowing him to present himself in a dignified fashion. The packhorse followed, placid as always.

"Estimable sir," Gareth said in Dry Towns dialect, "as your keen discernment has already revealed, I am a stranger to this city. Eager as I am to show all respect to your customs, I am in ignorance concerning watering rights."

Perhaps *rights* was not the properly diplomatic term when dealing with an official, but it was the best Gareth could manage. He had memorized the flowery compliments that his tutor assured him comprised the normal form of address to one of greater rank or influence.

The tax collector's expression did not waver. "For the beasts, ten copper rings."

Ten! The mountain man had not paid more than five for his two mules.

At that moment, Gareth noticed several men moving through the crowd, perhaps the very same who had questioned each party entering the city. He had no doubt that they were aware of him, too, and that there were more such men that he could not see.

Gareth affected a foolish little laugh, well-practiced in the court at Thendara. "Alas, this poor person has been deficient in the foresight to supply himself with such currency." Moving slowly, hands well away from the hilt of his sword, he poked two fingers into the purse he wore openly and withdrew a couple of reis. He wasn't sure of their exchange value in copper rings, four or five, still more than what he thought was reasonable.

The reis pieces clinked as they landed on the carpet at the tax collector's feet. For a moment, nothing happened beyond a faint deepening of the official's scowl. Then, with a movement so swift as to be almost a blur, the coins disappeared.

Keeping his own expression impassive, Gareth bowed and retreated, walking backward the first few steps until a boy with pair of dust-brown goats took his place.

The mare and the packhorse thrust their muzzles into the trough, gulping greedily. Gareth dipped his fingers. The water, although filmed with dust and grime, was surprisingly cool. Before the horses had drunk their fill, his own thirst threatened to overwhelm him. He offered a prayer of thanks—to which god, he wasn't sure—when the horses allowed him to lead them away.

The plaza was clearing out, the crowds noticeably more sparse. Vendors were folding up their booths. The water-tax collector appeared to have fallen asleep, lulled by the boy's fan. People still congregated in the area around the second fountain, some of them women. Some had the dark hair and modest dress of mountain women, moving quietly and talking among themselves as they filled their pottery jars. Among them, Gareth spotted other women who must be from the Dry Towns. They carried their heads proudly, swaying their hips to the bell-sweet clashing of their chains. Jewels glinted at their wrists and waists and dangled from ears only partly hidden by veils of butterfly-hued gauze. They cast sidelong glances at him and murmured phrases in Dry Towns dialect, speaking so low and rapidly, he could not follow their meaning. He caught the repeated word, *charrat*, perhaps akin to *chaireth*, stranger. They noticed him watching but did not pause in their errands. He had never in his life seen anything so beautiful and mysterious.

Gareth tied his horses to a ring set in a post of weathered pink granite. He dipped his hands into the fountain's clear water and drank deeply, over and over again until he could hold no more. Then he refilled his waterskins. The water gave him a burst of energy, but he was too excited to feel hunger. There would be time to seek out an inn and stabling for his animals, and the evening was yet young.

The cooling dusk turned the air sweet and mild. Never had he felt so daring. He had played at the adventures of Race Cargill, Terran Secret Agent, but now he was living an even more vivid tale.

A group of Dry Towns women approached the fountain, chattering. They seemed no less mysterious than at first glance, wrapped in layers of brilliantly colored veils. A gust of the freshening night breeze carried their musky-sweet perfume.

He could not take his eyes off their chains. By Dry Towns custom, each woman's hands were fettered with a metal bracelet on each wrist; the bracelets were connected with a long chain, passed through a metal loop on her belt, so that if she moved either hand, the other was drawn up tight against the loop at her waist.

Although Gareth knew that the Dry Towners chained their women in this manner, the reality shocked and fascinated him. He had grown up surrounded by powerful, independent women—both his grandmothers had been forces in their own right, and Domenic's mother, Marguerida Alton, had done more to shape her times than any ten ordinary men.

What kind of woman allowed herself to be shackled as the property of a man who was in all likelihood not her equal?

Repelled and curious, he strolled up to the nearest woman. A veil of pink translucent gauze, threaded with gold and blue, covered but did not hide her face. She met his gaze boldly, almost insolently. She had the pale, almost colorless eyes and flaxen hair of her people, and her exposed skin was lightly bronzed. With supple grace, she turned to dip her jar into the well. Drawing her chains through the loop at her waist so skillfully that they did not impede her movement, she swung the jar up to rest upon one shoulder.

Encouraged by the woman's direct manner, Gareth came closer. He caught a hint of her perfume, roses and musk. He wondered what her voice would be like, whether she would drop her gaze when she addressed him, whether she would smile in return.

Smiling, he greeted her in Dry Towns dialect, taking care to use the respectful mode.

The lady in the pink veil froze. One of the other women gasped aloud. A water jar crashed to the ground. It shattered, the sound unnaturally loud.

Zandru's demons! What have I done? His words had been impeccably courteous, even by court standards.

The next moment, he found himself surrounded by armed guards. By their elaborately gilded tunics and plumed helmets, they most likely served some powerful local lord. Their faces were grim, their hands ready on the hilts of their swords.

With a great swirl of veils, cries like the cooing of rock doves, and clashing of chains, the other women swarmed around the lady and hurried her away.

The foremost of the guards strode up to Gareth. Gareth was not short, but this man topped him by at least a head and was correspondingly broad in the chest. Gareth noticed a lacing of whitened scars over the man's upper arms and deep parallel grooves on one high cheekbone.

"What dust beneath the lowest gutter-sweeping offal dares to cast his eyes in the direction of the concubine of the Lord Yvarin?"

Gareth's guts clenched as he realized this Lord Yvarin must be the head of the Great House of Carthon. He had but an instant to reply before those swords left their scabbards. Above all else, he must do nothing to impugn the guard's honor.

He thought of the ambush, how easy it had been to jump into the fray. Then his sword had seemed a fluid extension of his body, both moving instinctively. He had had neither time nor need for thought. The fight had been upon him before he realized it. He had moved—acted—without considering the odds.

He had not faced three opponents at once, men who outmatched him in size and who clearly relished the idea of watering the dust with his blood.

I'm not here . . . You don't notice me. . . .

Although he wanted nothing more than to turn and run, or at very least to become invisible, he clapped both hands to the sides of his head, as he had seen traders do in order to exaggerate their astonishment.

"Truly, I am astounded, O most wise and venerable sir! I thought I was in the presence of a goddess, a dream sent as a foretaste of the afterlife for the faithful! Is she truly a living woman?" Some demonic spirit took over his brain as one phrase after another spilled out. "The most fortunate of men must be the Lord Yvarin, who may look upon such divine beauty whenever he likes! Oh, what have I done, to so presume? Such a vision cannot be suitable for ordinary men—"

The next idea that popped into his head was to beg the guard to put out his eyes, rather than have the memory of the High Lord's concubine besmirched by any lesser object. His tongue would not shape the words. There was an excellent chance the guard would take him up on it.

In Thendara, playing the fool had always succeeded because no one took him seriously. Here, it obviously did not lessen the gravity of his offense. The guards did not appear impressed with his performance. The scarred one frowned even more deeply. His enormous hand tightened around the hilt of one of his two swords.

Gods, what would Race Cargill have done? He wouldn't have gotten himself into such a mess in the first place, that's what!

Gareth's heart hammered so loudly, surely the guard must hear it. His breath rasped in his throat. He wondered if anyone at home would ever learn of the ignominy of his death. Still, he must fight, and most likely die, with what honor he could. He took up a fighting stance and reached for his own sword. If Avarra was merciful, it would be quick.

"There you are!" chimed a boy's high voice.

A figure in trail-dusty clothing darted between Gareth and the guard.

Rakhal?

Grabbing Gareth's arm, the apprentice threw both of them to the dust at the guard's feet, chattering away so fast that Gareth caught only a phrase here and there.

". . . noble and sagacious warrior . . . most merciful . . ."

"What's this?" growled the guard's voice from somewhere above Gareth's head.

". . . my unworthy brother," Rakhal rushed on, ". . . sun-touched, given to wild fancies . . . no harm in him . . . my dereliction of duty . . . allowing him to thus assault the sensibilities . . ."

"Boy! You are responsible for this scum?"

". . . generosity bestowed hereafter as in life . . ." Rakhal babbled on, launching into a discourse on the virtues of condescension to those less fortunate, and showed no signs of pausing even to draw breath.

"Eh, leave them, Sarn," came a voice from somewhere in front of Gareth, lighter and more nasal than that of the scarred guard. Over Rakhal's unceasing pleas, Gareth made out, "They're not worth the effort of cleaning your blade afterwards."

"You'd have to ritually purify it!" put in a third man.

A round of guffaws, echoed by other voices at some distance, answered him. Rakhal scrambled to his feet, leaving Gareth still prone.

"O most cunning and valorous servant of the Great Lord Yvarin, allow this humble person to rectify the grievous and utterly unpardonable actions of—"

"Out of the way, slave meat! And take that carrion with you!" sneered the first guard again.

Gareth dared raise his head, just in time to see the scarred man slip something into his folded sash. Rakhal hauled Gareth to his feet and pushed him toward the edge of the plaza. Gareth had only a moment to notice that not a single woman remained near the fountain.

Relief gave way to giddiness at still being alive and whole, and then to the sobering realization of how easily he had trespassed upon forbidden ground. What an arrogant idiot he'd been! Except for Rakhal's intervention and the guard's willingness to accept a bribe, the incident might have turned out quite differently.

"You! Stay right here! Don't speak to anyone! Don't even *look* at anyone!" With a parting glare that could freeze the Kadarin, Rakhal went to retrieve Gareth's horses.

Gareth trudged after Rakhal along a narrow street, barely able to see his own feet in the light of the widely spaced torches. The last of the day's adrenaline had faded along with the sun, and Gareth ached in every bone. The brown mare had taken a sudden dislike to the packhorse, laying back her ears and baring her long yellow teeth. The second time she tried to spin and kick, Rakhal seized her reins and walked her in a tight circle, cursing unintelligibly. A few moments later, the mare seemed to have forgotten her animosity and was quite content to walk quietly beside the other horse.

"Thank you for what you did at the fountain. I don't know what would have happened if—" Gareth stopped himself. He did know, he just did not want to think about it. Had this entire adventure been criminally reckless, venturing away from the safe, trammeled places he had known?

"You knew enough not to engage the guards. If you had, not even Nebran himself could have saved you. But you fought bravely on the trail, so no one can name you coward."

"You have very decided opinions for an apprentice."

"I know my duty . . . and my place," Rakhal said tightly.

A thought crossed Gareth's mind, a conclusion so obvious he couldn't think why he hadn't seen it before. Now it all made sense: Rakhal's self-confidence with Cyrillon, the easy way of giving orders, the faint edge of superiority that Gareth found irritating. "Your place? Are you Cyrillon's son as well as his apprentice?"

"No."

They proceeded along a tangle of ill-paved streets and finally to a district of wide, dusty avenues and sprawling compounds. Rakhal headed for one of these, no different from the others with its walls of mud brick and wind-etched sandstone. Sun had bleached the heavy wooden gates, so that even in the gathering dark, they shimmered, ghostlike. Torches burned in their holders, and a somber-faced Dry Towner, heavily armed, watched them approach.

Under the guard's watchful eye, the gates swung open. Beyond them, Gareth glimpsed a yard of raked sand, a rectangular house of white stone, and outbuildings, most likely quarters for servants, a stable for the master's personal mount or storehouses for the household goods, everything within the protection of the walls.

They entered the house itself through an intricately carved lattice gate. A pair of stout inner doors gave way to an open courtyard. Gareth, stepping inside, inhaled the sweetness of night-blooming vines. A fountain plashed gently. The noises of the town fell away, along with the cares of the journey. He glanced up at the sweep of stars and moons, now high in the sky, and felt as if their light shone clear through him.

In the few moments Gareth stood, drinking in the quiet garden, a woman had emerged from a doorway on the far side, silhouetted against the honey-warm light beyond. He could not make out her shape, beyond the full skirts and layers of veil. She moved toward them with the tinkling of chains. Rakhal went up to her, and the two exchanged hushed words. Gareth could not follow their meaning, only the urgency of their tone. At one point, Rakhal gestured in his direction. Gareth imagined the apprentice saying, *"He's got no more sense than a sun-addled* oudrakhi*! He'll get himself killed and bring shame to us all!"*

The woman disappeared into the house. Rakhal turned back to Gareth. "That settles it. You'll stay with us."

Gareth did not protest.

An hour later, washed and changed into a long Dry Towns robe, Gareth joined Cyrillon for the evening meal. The caravan master, resplendent in a shirtcloak of emerald-colored silk, reclined on a pile of cushions and gestured for Gareth to do the same.

When Gareth attempted to thank Cyrillon for his welcome, the trader cut him off, saying, "Hospitality first, business afterward." Gareth wondered what business Cyrillon meant, but a direct question, especially before the meal, would be the height of rudeness. In his years at the Thendaran court, he had learned patience if nothing else.

The woman who had greeted them, who must be Cyrillon's wife, offered platters of meat, chopped and rolled with dried fruit and savory spices, with pickled vegetables and flat bread. A second woman, slender and dark-eyed, moved silently by her side. Gareth could not get a good look at the younger woman's face through her veil. She moved with a gazelle's swift grace, although her chains glinted in the light of the lanterns. Except for an occasional soft clink, they made no sound. He supposed that most Dry Towns women went all their lives with fettered hands and became accustomed to them.

Gareth bent to his meal, trying not to stare at the women. They knelt a short distance away while master and guest ate. He thought of his own mother, of his young sister, chained into silent subservience—or Grandmother Linnea.

The Terranan were right to call us savages! Fire spread across his face and throat. He bowed his head, unable to eat.

Cyrillon gave orders for the food to be removed. The women took it away in that graceful, silent way and did not return.

"You will not smoke a water pipe, I know," Cyrillon said. "I could not stomach it myself for many years, but perhaps you will not mind if I indulge myself? It is men's business, forbidden to women. My wife and daughter will not disturb us."

"I would not have you deny yourself your usual pleasures on my account," Gareth said stiffly.

Cyrillon took up the water pipe and set about preparing to smoke.

Gareth tried not to cough on the pungent vapors. He wondered where Rakhal was. Most likely, it was not the custom for an apprentice to dine with his master when at home. Gareth found himself missing the camaraderie of the trail.

Gareth felt awkward, reclining in silence while his host smoked. He glanced in the direction in which the women had disappeared, wondering what they were doing—enjoying their own dinner, most likely, or gossiping about the men. What were they saying about him? Had Rakhal told them about the incident at the fountain?

"To you, a man of the Domains, this must seem foreign and exotic," the caravan master said, gesturing to include his compound and the town beyond, "but it is far more Domains than Dry Towns, and the wild lands of the desert are stranger still."

Gareth admitted that he had nothing to compare Carthon with. "Certainly, there are many Dry Towns customs here. I saw women in chains."

"The local custom offends you." Cyrillon paused for a meditative puff. "I have never been able to convince my wife to leave off her chains. I suppose she feels as naked without them as you or I would, were we to walk breechless down the main thoroughfare of Thendara in the dead of winter."

Gareth laughed, admitting the man had a point. The old saying went, *We are as the gods have made us.*

"As for my daughter, she is my only child and the ornament of my house. She does as she pleases."

"And it pleases her to wear chains?"

"Perhaps what she pleases is to be able to come and go, as secure as any woman can be from the predations of men. This way she draws no undue attention to herself, and any insult to her would surely be answered by whatever man holds the key to unlock those chains."

Was there a hint of mockery in those words?

"Enough smoke for today. A wise man is always temperate in his pleasures." Cyrillon took a final puff and set aside his water pipe. He disassembled it and carefully cleaned the mouthpiece with a cloth dipped in water, which had been laid out for the purpose.

"Now," he said, fixing Gareth with a humorless gaze, "to business.

You handle a sword exceptionally well for a mere lens-grinder's assistant. Do not deny it. I have seen men jab at each other with lengths of steel and call it sword fighting. More than that, you held back. You have been trained, and very well indeed, but I do not think you have ever killed a man. No ordinary man would have spared Merach as you did."

Gareth tried to summon a convincing story, but the only thought that sprang to his mind was that he had not planned to fight at all. That would raise the question why he carried a sword if he had no intention of using it.

Cyrillon grunted, as if Gareth's silence supplied the answer he had been looking for. "You speak the tongue of the Dry Towns quite well, you know. You must have had an excellent tutor. But he taught you the classical literary declension of the verbs *to be* and *to make.* A tradesman would use only the vernacular. Then, too, the color of your hair is not what one would find here in the lands adjoining the Dry Towns. I have never seen that tint of red except among the Comyn of the Domains. And if you will pardon my boldness in saying it, *vai dom*, you think entirely too much of yourself."

Again, the trader paused. From within the house came the sound of women's laughter and music, a flowing arpeggio played on a flute. Gareth's mouth dried up.

"Who are you, in truth?"

"Does it matter?" Gareth asked, the words emerging as a croak.

"It does if there is sworn blood between our houses."

"There is not."

"But there *is* something. No, I cannot read your thoughts. I am no sorcerer. Your eyes betray you, Garrin—if that is indeed your name."

An image sprang to Gareth's mind, of standing at a crossroads. He could cling to the disguise he had presented, in which case it would be best to not even attempt to explain the inconsistencies Cyrillon had listed. He could concoct another story, that he was the youngest son of one or another of the lesser houses. He knew enough of them to use an alias that could not be easily disproved. It was not unreasonable that such a person, with all the education of the Comyn but with no hope of inheritance, might seek his fortune in trade. This alternative story might sound more convincing, but was it honorable to deceive the man who had befriended him a second time? Was that not a betrayal of hospitality and of trust?

There was third choice. He could tell the truth.

And risk being sent back to Thendara under guard? Risk his parents and *Tío* Danilo, not to mention the Regent and the entire court, learning of his escapade? He knew what they'd say, and they'd be right.

He'd already thrown away any claim to respect when he'd followed Danilo and Domenic. It did not matter if they knew what he'd done. *He* knew.

He met Cyrillon's gaze levelly. "You are a keen observer and an even more perceptive judge of men. I am not an apprentice of any kind, nor is Garrin my real name. I am Gareth Marius-Danvan Elhalyn y Hastur. You are, I believe, acquainted with my father's namesake, Danilo Syrtis-Ardais."

Cyrillon's face tightened, but not before Gareth caught the flash of astonishment.

"I know nothing of your current business with him," Gareth hurried on, "only that you bring him information from time to time and that he has confidence in you."

"Clearly he must, if he has entrusted me with the safety of the Heir to the Crown." Cyrillon gave Gareth another of those piercing glances.

Gareth swallowed. "He does not know I am here. At least, I have not come at his behest."

For a long moment, Cyrillon did not move. Slowly the blood drained from his cheeks, although his expression did not alter, except for the pulsation of a vein in his forehead.

"Father of Sands! *Dom* Danilo's messenger told the truth! What are you doing here, then?"

"Does it matter?" Gareth said, miserable and ashamed. "What is to be done now?"

"We cannot change what has already happened, but at least you came through it safely." Cyrillon's color shifted toward normal as he spoke. "As for what to do now, there cannot be any doubt. You must return immediately to Thendara, Your Highness!"

Gareth forced himself to hold still, to accept the judgment. This was the only possible outcome of his escapade, to be sent home in disgrace. At least, he had enjoyed a brief time of freedom. Now he must pay for it.

"Yet how can this be accomplished?" Cyrillon muttered, clearly turning over the problem in his own mind. "There can be no question of your returning alone or, worse yet, remaining here when I depart." The light cast deep shadows in the furrows of his brow, giving him a sardonic look. "I may trade with the Domains, but in order to maintain the trust of the Dry Towns folk, I must keep to custom. As it is, my contact with your people makes me suspect in some quarters. But if a young man not related by blood were allowed the freedom of my household in my absence, that would have dire consequences. There are some—if word were to reach my wife's kinsmen, your—how do you say it in *cahuenga*? your *cojones* would be in grave peril."

Gareth felt the blood drain from his cheeks. "Then I must find an inn—"

"Of course, you must be my guest, and as long as I am here, there is nothing improper." Cyrillon seemed not to have noticed Gareth's protest. "It will take me some few days to arrange for your escort and assemble my own crew. Tomas will live and walk again, but not soon. I'll have Korllen, but I'll need another man to handle the *oudrakhi*. Then you will return to Thendara while I must be off for Shainsa."

Shainsa! If Carthon promised adventure, lying as it did on the border between the Domains and the Dry Towns, a mixture of the familiar and the exotic, then how much more exciting it would be to venture to that ancient city.

Gareth wrenched his attention back to the conversation. Cyrillon seemed not to have noticed the lapse and had gone on to discuss making arrangements for a suitable armed escort back to the Domains. Gareth was to remain here, within the walls of Cyrillon's compound, until his departure.

"I would not wish you or your family to be put to any inconvenience on my account." Gareth heard the stiffness in his own voice. "At the same time . . . if I am to return so soon, am I to see nothing of Carthon except the inside of these rooms? I am not likely to have another such chance again. Having come this far and risked this much, I very much desire to use these few days in exploring a city so unlike my own."

Gareth braced himself for a refusal. Even if Cyrillon said no at first, the trader might become amenable after another round of reasoned argument.

"True, you're safer here than you were on the road from Thendara," Cyrillon said, "and certainly safer than you would be in a place like Ardcarran. Perhaps a few days in the plaza district will convince you as no words can that there is nothing grander in Carthon than heat and dust."

Gareth could hardly believe his luck. "I would of course observe any restrictions you advise for my safety."

"You would give your word as a Comyn, *as a Hastur*, without even knowing what those might be?"

"I trust your experience and your commitment to my well-being."

"You'll do well enough as long as you keep to the better areas and don't speak to any woman wearing chains. It would be better, actually, not to even glance in their direction. I will send Alric with you as a guide."

"And not Rakhal?"

"Rakhal? Ah, here in Carthon, Rakhal goes his own way. We shall see little of him until it is time to leave."

The next morning, Gareth broke his fast alone, for Cyrillon had already gone about the day's business. Outside his door, he found a tray waiting for him, with a dish of grain porridge, much as he would have eaten in Thendara, and some pastries, dough that had been twisted, deep-fried, and then dusted with orange-scented honey crystals. There was no sign of the women, but Alric was waiting in the large chamber below. Shyly, but with obvious anticipation, the boy presented himself as a guide.

Alric led Gareth along the major avenues, past the Great House and the jeweler's guild, pointing out the bars of costly metal that protected the open windows, then through one marketplace after another. Almost everything Gareth could imagine was for sale here: carpets from Arcarran, bolts of woven *linex* and bales of the unspun stuff, filigree work, saddles from the Alton Domain, dried fish and pearls from Temora, salt and sulfur from Daillon. In the livestock market, horses and mules waited patiently beside lumbering *oudrakhi* and antlered stag-ponies. Gareth spent a few copper coins to sample the wares of the food stalls, purchasing spiced dates, cakes of an unfamiliar grain that had been parched and pounded together with slightly rancid butter, and skewers of sweet peppers, onions, and savory marinated meat.

The gathering crowds blended into a motley of color: the dusty browns of traders, blue and green woolen cloaks from the Domains, shirtcloaks worn to the color of sand, and once, to the blaring of horns, a Dry Towns lord—perhaps that same Lord Yvarin—and his retainers, arrayed in garish sashes and elaborately gilded tunics.

Through it all, Alric chattered away, mixing information and fabrication, much of which Gareth suspected the boy had concocted himself or picked up from street urchins.

They reached another square, windswept in the crimson noon. To one side, Gareth noticed a clutter of low buildings, shops of the poorer sort, a street shrine, and a little café. On the other side, dark opening mouths of streets led deeper into the town. The smell of the *jaco* roused an unexpected surge of homesickness.

Gareth tossed Alric one of the copper coins. "Here, go and buy yourself a treat. I'll be waiting there." He pointed at the shop. "I won't get into any trouble, I promise."

Alric looked dubious for a moment, but the temptation of an hour of freedom and the means to enjoy it won out. With a grin, he pocketed the coin and dashed out into the crowd. Gareth took a moment to drink in the sights and sounds, the rhythm of the market. He shaped his own thoughts, his posture, his facial expression to that of a person of no importance.

Just a dusty traveler, nobody of account . . .

Outside a shop, an awning cut off the worst of the sun's glare. A carpet, worn but surprisingly clean, had been unrolled in the pool of shade. A trio of men in flowing robes and head scarves were just getting to their feet, leaving a pile of cushions arranged around a low table. To sit outside would be pleasant, and besides, he would be in plain sight, where Alric could find him.

Gareth seated himself on one of the cushions. A wizened little man with skin like sun-darkened leather shuffled out and, in a querulous voice, demanded to see his money. When Gareth was able to satisfy him, the man returned with a chipped cup and dish of shriveled, lumpy confectionery. Gareth set the dish aside without tasting the candy. The *jaco*, on the other hand, was surprisingly good, strong and unsweetened, flavored with an unfamiliar but pleasant spice.

Voices drifted from inside the shop. Gareth heard the scraping of wood, a chair being drawn across a bare floor.

". . . water dispute . . . one of those little oases along the caravan route to Black Ridge," said one man, speaking Dry Towns dialect with an accent so thick that he seemed to have pebbles in his mouth. Gareth could make out only a phrase here and there.

". . . out beyond Shainsa . . ." said a second man, ". . . deep desert . . ." This one's voice was higher in pitch, almost reedy, but easier to understand.

". . . know the place . . ."

Race Cargill, Terran Special Agent, has penetrated the alien stronghold to discover a dastardly plot . . .

". . . *oudrakhi* herder, says . . . been cheated," the first man went on.

". . . strange folk out there, fierce . . ."

". . . the sons of fire demons, 'tis said . . ."

Little did the evil overlord know that his agents had been discovered and his schemes revealed . . .

"The waterseller . . . teach him a lesson," the storyteller said in such a tone that the others fell silent. ". . . a scuffle . . . the desert man calls upon his gods. Nebran? No, something stronger . . . sent a fireball that . . ." The man lowered his voice.

Gareth held his breath, straining to hear what came next.

"*Ate him?*" yelled one of the others.

Gareth came alert. His vision sharpened. The brightness of the day stung his eyes.

". . . burst into flames . . ." the storyteller said dramatically, ". . . disappeared . . ."

One of the listeners snorted. The other made a derisive sound, but to Gareth's ears, the disbelief sounded hollow, tinged with fear.

". . . mirages out there . . . heat and dust put things in a man's eyes . . ."

". . . didn't believe it . . . not the first time . . . I heard another such tale. Some details changed . . . but one thing is sure . . ."

"Nebran shield us!" one of the listeners cried, and all three mumbled what might have been prayers for protection or else curses upon an enemy.

Gareth's mouth went dry. The desert folk were said to be superstitious. Any sleight of hand, even sun glinting off a paring knife, might create an effect like magic in their minds. He knew as well as anyone how stories could become elaborated in the retelling. But . . .

He did not entirely believe his own reassuring thoughts. If what the storyteller had said was true, there was another, far more troubling explanation for the flash of light and the disappearance of the victim. An off-world weapon—a Terran blaster—could produce the effect the man had described.

Compact-forbidden weapons . . . in the hands of the Dry Towners? The prospect was too horrific to speak aloud, to even think.

How was that possible?

As far as Gareth knew, the Federation had never dealt with the Dry Towns, and it was beyond reason that the desert folk might have stumbled upon a cache of abandoned off-world weapons. Why would the Federation have returned in such a secretive manner? If their war was over, why not renew their old relationship with the Comyn?

The street was not completely deserted, but in that moment, the few men and veiled, chained women who hurried across it, faces averted, were all Dry Towners. Something in the antiquity of the place and the faintly acrid tang of the dust struck Gareth as profoundly alien from any other place he'd ever been. He remembered the old stories, the speculations that the Dry Towns had been settled by another colony ship, not the one that gave rise to the Seven Domains. Where had they come from—Wolf IV, where men once from Terra also interbred with the native races? No *chieri* blood flowed in their veins, but something far stranger. They could be anything, *do* anything.

A few minutes later, Alric came back, bearing a cone fashioned of fibrous bark and filled with bits of fried pastry. He grinned when Gareth declined his offer to share. They headed back to Cyrillon's compound.

Gareth was no longer eager to explore. He wondered if he'd imagined what he'd heard or had spun a perfectly innocent conversation into intimations of danger. He could return home, as Cyrillon desired, and make his report. Perhaps Mikhail would have returned by then. Certainly, no action could be taken until the Regent was consulted. Would the delay make a difference? Or would the additional time give whoever now possessed those weapons the chance to seize territory . . . perhaps even make an assault upon the Domains?

If they had blasters, what more might they have?

What if he was wrong? What if what he'd overheard were just wild tales, idle boasting? He could see it now, himself racing home to sound the alarm, then the hurried conferences, the meetings, the hasty mustering of a expedition force . . . the questions, the push into Dry Towner territory . . . The Dry Towners, quick to anger, ever jealous of their *kihar*, responding with contempt and suspicion . . .

Gods, he could set off a war.

"Lord Garrin?" Alric interrupted Gareth's churning worry. "Are you ill?"

No, but I will drive myself mad very shortly if I go on in this way. Then everything they've said about me being just another of those unstable Elhalyns will indeed be true.

"I'm well enough, lad," Gareth forced himself to sound casual. "I'm just not used to this heat. It's cooler where I live. We still have snow at night this early in the summer."

"Snow!" the boy exclaimed.

I should not be here, Gareth thought, and then, quite unexpectedly, *I know where I need to be. I know what I have to do.*

10

Alric, clearly disappointed when Gareth announced he had seen enough, took a circuitous route back to Cyrillon's house, undoubtedly to prolong the holiday. Having gotten his bearings by this time, Gareth knew the lad was dawdling but did not have the heart to press him. The delay gave Gareth time to gather his thoughts. He had some assets—a little money, the lenses, two horses, and his sword. He had no allies, no friends he could trust. He didn't know how he would manage on his own, but somehow he had to find a way.

They came to another square, empty except for a public well where women gathered in twos and threes, a few of them Dry Towns women with their fluttering, brightly colored garments. Their chains clashed musically, a counterpart to their quicksilver laughter. One in particular caught his attention with the strength and sureness of her movements. Like the others, she went veiled, and she carried a basket braced against one hip. Gareth slowed to a halt, watching her. He'd seen that same fabric, with its pattern of gold threads. The angle of the sun glinted off her veil, obscuring her face.

Cyrillon's daughter?

She made her way to one of the shops on the opposite side of the square. Gareth hesitated. Part of him wanted to follow, to see whether she was indeed who he thought she was, but another part of him held back. He'd already gotten into serious trouble by speaking to a chained woman.

While Gareth pondered what to do, Alric had come to a slouching halt, imitating the half-dozen or so men loitering in the area of the well. Although none of these addressed the women directly, their mutual interest showed in the women's lilting laughter and the occasional darkening in color of the men's faces. A girl in blue pirouetted, her veils fluttering around her, before turning back to her friends. Her posture, the carriage of her head and movement of her hands, revealed her awareness of the keen interest she aroused. The loiterers straightened up, pulling their shoulders back and sucking their stomachs flat. Gareth felt an immediate impulse to puff out his chest. One of the men started telling a joke in a loud voice. Scowling, the few mountain women in the crowd hurried away.

Just then, the woman emerged from the shop. She strode over to Alric with none of the flirtatious grace just displayed by the girl in blue. Her chains rattled as one hand shot out to grasp Alric's shoulder. At the same time, she shifted the basket on her hip to allow free movement of her other arm.

"What are you doing out here?" She shook him, but not roughly, only enough to emphasize her point. "Loitering around like those—" Gareth did not recognize the Dry Towns word, only its clear implication. "What would Father say?"

Alric flinched. "I was just—just showing Garrin—"

"You!" She released the boy and rounded on Gareth. "Haven't you caused enough trouble on your own account, without corrupting this child as well?"

He found his voice. "I *do* know you! You're Cyrillon's daughter!"

"We have occupied the same room at my father's house, you mean. But that does *not* constitute an introduction."

"I might as well ask why *you* approached *me*—" He reined in his temper. "Your pardon, lady. I would not have spoken to you had I known it was inappropriate."

"You are my father's guest. We are both under his protection," she said, more calmly. "This little scamp should have known better than to bring you to such a place. I can only attribute his lapse in judgment to your influence."

This square was much like any other marketplace, but no vendors had set up their stalls here. Its only feature was the well; the women came here for the water and to be seen by the men. Despite the warmth of the day, Gareth shivered. He pushed away the subtle residue of some unpleasant emotion—despair, perhaps—that lingered in the dirt. "Will you permit me to escort you home?"

"I am not going home. *You* are going home and taking Alric with you! And I do not need an escort." She held up her hands, to a gentle clashing of her chains. "I have all the protection I need."

Gareth managed to summon enough presence of mind to deliver an abbreviated bow as she turned, a swirl of pink and gold, and strode away.

Alric disappeared as soon as they arrived back at the compound, presumably about his own business, and Gareth saw nothing of the women. Cyrillon's affairs kept him elsewhere in the city. Gareth retired to his room, where he spent the next hours packing and repacking his possessions.

He felt the change in the air as the day drew to an end. Even without being able to see the sun lowering toward the horizon, he became aware of a scent rising from the earth, no longer the smell of dust and heat but coolness tinged with spices.

Gareth found Cyrillon just outside the central chamber. Cyrillon offered a formal greeting. Gareth, masking his impatience, returned the courtesy.

"Cyrillon, I must speak with you on a matter of importance."

"It is not our custom to engage in serious discussion before the evening meal. We will speak over smoke afterwards."

"I would rather say it now."

"What topic is so grave, it cannot be considered in a civilized fashion? No, do not answer, my young friend. I see this is indeed a matter that cannot wait. If it were as warm in your Domains as it is in the desert, your people would have learned to proceed at a measured pace. But since it is not, and you have not, let us satisfy your impatience. Accompany me to my personal office, where we will not be disturbed."

Gareth followed Cyrillon to a small chamber set well away from the shared areas of the house. High windows on two sides admitted light and a refreshing breeze. Below them stood cabinets with many small drawers, perhaps storage for scrolls. A low table bore writing implements, a beautifully wrought brass oil lamp, and several pieces of newly prepared vellum. Cyrillon dropped to one of the large cushions and gestured for Gareth to take the other.

"Now, my young friend, what has distressed you so?"

Gareth folded his legs under him and wished Cyrillon would stop calling him *friend.* The word was laden with mutual responsibility.

"I said I would return to the Domains as soon as a suitable escort could be arranged," Gareth began. "I request to be released from our agreement. I hope you will grant it. Regardless, circumstances have arisen that require another course of action, even at the price of my given word."

Cyrillon looked startled at first, then wary. "These *circumstances* must be dire indeed. You may be young and foolish, if you will pardon my saying so, *vai dom*, but you have never struck me as a man who holds his *kihar* in light regard."

No one had ever considered him a person of honor before. In a voice gone suddenly thick, Gareth said, "My own . . . *kihar* . . . is of no importance compared to what might be at stake for the Domains. Perhaps for all of Darkover."

"Dire indeed," Cyrillon repeated. "May I know these *circumstances*?"

"I overheard what I first thought were just wild stories from the lands beyond Shainsa, near a place called Black Ridge." Gareth went on to summarize what he had heard, along with his suspicion that beneath the bragging and tale-telling lay a kernel of truth. He finished by saying, "I pray to all the gods of both our lands that I am wrong. But so much is at stake, I must be certain."

"You mean to go to Shainsa yourself?" Cyrillon's usual equanimity dissolved. "Are you mad? Or simply suicidal?"

Gareth, remembering all the insinuations about *unstable Elhalyns*, winced. "I don't know! Does it matter?"

"What matters is that the Heir to the Crown of the Seven Domains cannot go wandering about the Dry Towns on a whim!"

"I'm well aware what is at stake!" Gareth's fingers curled into fists at his sides before he realized what he was doing. His skin crawled as if he'd fallen into a nest of scorpion-ants.

He forced himself to take a breath and lower his voice. "I could go back home and let you or someone else investigate. I could wait for news that might never come or might come too late. If someone out there is trading with the *Terranan* for Compact-banned weapons and I could have stopped them instead of crawling home like a wayward puppy, then on whose hands is the blood of those they might harm?"

He was talking too fast, his words and phrases jumbling over one another, probably making no sense at all. How could he expect to handle himself in Shainsa, with all its dangers, if he couldn't even govern his tongue here, where he was comparatively safe? What was he afraid of? That Cyrillon might disbelieve him, argue, try to stop him? Or that Cyrillon might let him go?

"The responsibility is mine alone," he said slowly, "to ascertain the truth or falsity of these tales. And to take whatever action I must."

So that was what it meant to be Comyn. The blood of Hastur flowed in his veins, as yet untested to be sure, but adamantine in its demands.

"I see why you do not wish to wait for further reports." Cyrillon nodded. "So would any man of honor act."

The words hung between them. For a long moment, Gareth dared not believe what he had heard.

"I would be—if you permit me to travel with you to Shainsa, I would be most grateful. But I will surely go there, with or without your help."

"In this matter, I must consider more than my own wishes," Cyrillon said after a pause, a pause in which Gareth imagined increasingly strenuous objections. "I have an obligation to *Dom* Danilo as my employer and as a friend of many years. Despite the formal termination of my contract with you, I bear a measure of responsibility for your welfare. I must also safeguard the means of supporting my family and must honor my other business obligations. However, as you yourself point out, some circumstances transcend law and custom."

Gareth felt ashamed that he had ever considered Cyrillon a man of superstition, a Dry Towns barbarian who kept his wife and daughter in chains and had no care for anything beyond the walls of his own compound.

"I am sorry to have placed you in such a difficult position," Gareth said. "It has never been my intention to cause injury to you, who have brought me nothing but good."

Cyrillon made a dismissive gesture. "Let us reason this matter out together. If the *Terranan* have returned, and in such a manner as to exempt them from the laws and Compact of the Comyn . . . that is bad, very bad indeed, not only for the Domains but for the Dry Towns as well."

The caravan master leaned forward. "These two lands are as night and day, as light and darkness, two halves balanced upon the edge of a knife. Up in your mountains and in your Lowlands, you do not see it, for the cities of Ardcarran and Daillon and, yes, Shainsa are far away. You know little of our customs, and we know even less of yours. The witchery and military strength of the Domains has kept the ambition and ruthlessness of the Dry Towns lords at bay and both lands at peace for many years now. But if that balance were to be overturned, if men whose very lives center on revenge and power were to gain access to off-world weapons, the consequences would be terrible indeed."

Gareth nodded, his throat too full to speak. He had braced himself for a lecture on his immature, irresponsible behavior; he had hoped for but not expected grudging acceptance. He had not anticipated the depth of the other man's understanding.

"I see that we understand one another," Cyrillon concluded. "Tomorrow I will speed my preparations, and we will depart for Shainsa on the day after."

Gareth closed his eyes, exhaling in relief.

"I have one condition, however. You are to tell no one who you are or your real objective in Shainsa. You will travel as Garrin, agent and apprentice to a Thendaran lens grinder. You will do nothing to expose yourself or any of my people to suspicion. Do I have your sworn word on this?"

"I will not reveal my identity or purpose."

"Then," Cyrillon said, "I presume we may dine together as friends?"

Gareth clambered to his feet and bowed, the full formal bow of a Comyn lord to an equal. "As friends."

Gareth and his host took their places on the cushions in the central chamber. Neither spoke much. Gareth had no heart for casual conversation, and Carthon itself had lost its romantic allure. He no longer imagined himself as Race Cargill, Terran Secret Agent. He felt like a bumbling imbecile confronted with a task beyond his capacity yet without any choice in the matter.

Cyrillon's wife and daughter glided into the room, bearing platters containing the same variety of little dishes as before. They set down the meal with the same silent grace. The daughter rose and, without a word, departed.

Gareth glanced at the shadowed arch of the doorway where she had disappeared. "I'm afraid I've offended your daughter, *mestre*. I saw her in the town today. She railed at Alric, but she held me responsible for his behavior. I don't understand what I did wrong."

Cyrillon's wife stirred on her cushion, and Gareth sensed her flicker of amusement. "Be kind, my dear," Cyrillon said, patting her knee. "He does not know our Rahelle as we do." He turned back to Gareth. "If you are distressed, you must by all means speak with her. Resolve the issue to your own satisfaction. Go, I give you leave!"

Gareth unfolded his legs and got to his feet. As he passed through the doorway, he heard a soft, feminine voice saying, "Are you sure that is wise, my husband?"

Gareth found Rahelle in the garden courtyard, sitting on one of the low benches under a trellised vine of delicate, moon-pale blossoms. She was playing a flute. He had heard that melody before, although he could not recall where. It must be a street tune or one of the songs the drovers had sung on the trail.

"Rahelle?"

She finished the phrase of music and lowered the flute. In the twilight, her veil glimmered like translucent silver. "You've found me. My father's doing, no doubt."

"I want to apologize."

The veiled face tilted, a gesture of consideration. "I am not so much offended by you as I am angry at myself. Alric wishes he had my freedom, although he does not understand how hard was the winning of it or how brief it will be. He sees only that I go places he wishes he might. He is so young, so willing to believe in the goodness of the world. To him, danger is an exciting tale, full of glory and flowery language. I hoped the ambush on the trail might have taught him otherwise. But to have taken an honored guest *there—!*"

"I saw no risk, save to a Lowland fool who does not know better than to address himself to a beautiful woman. Alric did no such thing, and the square was half-empty."

"*That place* was once the slave market of Carthon, when there was one. Slave-merchants from Ardcarran still come there to watch for pretty boys, who have not even a woman's means of protection."

"Protection?" Gareth echoed, taken aback by her casually spoken words. "How can you say that, you who go veiled and chained? The woman I was so foolish to speak to had three armed guards, but you had no one!"

"The retribution of a Dry Towns lord whose woman has been insulted need not be immediate to be a powerful deterrent."

Gareth thought again of his grandmother, of *Domna* Marguerida, of the *leronis* Illona Rider, and he wondered what they would say. "How can any woman allow herself to be treated as chattel?"

"So speaks the man who knows nothing of our ways!" she shot back.

"I think your mother grew up that way, so she cannot or dare not walk about as any free woman. But there are no laws, no Lord of a Great House, to enforce such things upon *you*. Surely your father does not demand it."

He was cut off by a ripple of laughter. "Do you think I wear *chains*?"

Rahelle rose and crossed the distance between them. Her hands came up so fast he could not see exactly what she did, only a flick of the wrists and then, in the dim light, a flash of metal. He felt the weight of the chain around his neck, the links digging into his flesh, pulling him forward and off his balance. In her hands, the edges of the cuffs gleamed. They were no longer locked upon her wrists but free in her hands. If she took another step, she could slash across his eyes before he could reach his own blade in defense.

Rahelle had spoken the truth. She did not wear chains. She wore a weapon as deadly as any dagger.

With a flick of the chain, he found himself free. Rahelle was already clicking the cuffs back into place and the chain into its loop on her belt.

"Lord of Light, can *all* Dry Towns women do that?"

"You forget, *vai dom*. I am no Dry Towns woman."

In the gathering dark, he saluted her. "So I see."

She was silent for a moment. "When I am in town, I go about my business in this manner without fear. I run errands for my mother. I visit my friends. I do all that is necessary. Except in this case," she added with a trace of self-censure, "watching out for my little brother."

"Your brother? I had not realized—"

"And when I am not in Carthon . . ." Rahelle folded back her veil.

Gareth stared down at her, the honey-gold hair tucked into a net of plaited ribbons, smooth skin over strong bones, full dark lips, eyes lowered. Then she lifted her eyes, and in the light of the torch, he saw they were blue, clear and unflinching, each ringed like a starstone set in gold.

Rakhal! What a fool he'd been, asking if she was Cyrillon's *son*!

"I am an idiot."

"Yes," she agreed, "you are. But it is not a fatal flaw, so let us go in and eat together. Perhaps my mother will relent enough in her disapproval to speak to you."

11

They left the wagons behind in Carthon, for the trail to Shainsa was too rough for wheeled vehicles. Just outside the city, Cyrillon's caravan joined with two other parties for protection. The caravan master set about organizing the laden horses and *oudrakhi*, great lumbering beasts with broadly padded feet and slit nostrils, well suited to desert travel. They had vile tempers, too, as Gareth found out when he led the brown mare past them, headed for the position Cyrillon had assigned him, and absentmindedly brushed up against the shoulder of a fawn-colored female.

Rahelle grabbed his arm and jerked him away just as the *oudrakhi* swung her long-jawed head around, her eyes glinting yellow. Enormous flat teeth snapped together just inches from Gareth's shoulder.

"They're not horses," Rahelle said.

"So I see."

The brown mare laid her ears flat against her neck and hunched her back, swinging her hindquarters in the direction of the *oudrakhi*. Recognizing the danger, Gareth tightened his grip on the reins and turned her sharply.

Rahelle fixed him with a quick, sideways glare, then went to scold the drover whose business it was to mind the *oudrakhi.* Gareth overheard a little of that lecture, the man grumbling a protest and Rahelle insisting that if his negligence endangered the *charrat* lens merchant—meaning Gareth—Cyrillon would hear of it.

By the third or fourth day, when the caravan had settled into a routine, Gareth had learned to avoid the *oudrakhi.* Rahelle gave him lessons in improving his Dry Towns dialect, although he would never be able to pass as a native speaker. Of the original crew, only the cook, Korllen, had come with them. Alric had stayed behind in Carthon. The other men kept to themselves.

Each day, Cyrillon called a halt for the noontime meal, and they rested in what shade could be found while their animals grazed or dozed. At night they pushed on, traveling from one watering place to the next. They carried water in skins slung across the packs of the *oudrakhi,* which could go a long distance without drinking. Even so, it would be hard going if they were to miss even a single oasis.

Gareth, wiping the sweat from his face, remembered the old tale. *When Zandru made the Drylands, the very bones of the world rebelled, refusing to be covered under the sand.* He wrapped his scarf around his face, leaving only his eyes uncovered.

The low, rolling hills with their cover of thorn trees and feathery spicebush eventually flattened out. Barren sands stretched to the horizon. Here and there, clusters of desert bracken dotted the dunes, and outcroppings of black rock, like massive burned bones, thrust upward. When they stopped to rest in the shadow of those black, uncompromising rocks, Gareth copied the posture of the other men, resting his head on his folded arms, and quickly fell into a light slumber. After a time, they went on.

Gareth rode side by side with Rahelle along a flat stretch where the soil was as white and crumbly as chalk. Dust caked the scrub. A faint alkali tang arose from the earth, scouring the inside of Gareth's nose and throat. He had not seen a living creature for the last hour, except for a bird of some sort, a desert *kyorebni* he thought, hovering high on the thermal air currents.

"You thought he was some street child my father had taken in out of charity?" Rahelle said when Gareth asked about Alric. "Or the fourth son of an impoverished family? Oh yes, he is my father's son, although not my mother's. He cannot inherit under the laws of either the Domains or the Dry Towns. I suppose that in your country, he might be legitimized, but even then, the house and business would not come to him. My father strives to make a place for him in the trade that will belong to my husband, when I acquire one."

Gareth's stomach gave a curious lurch. "You do not seem in any great hurry."

"Nor you, I might say, although I imagine that is not for want of matchmaking on the part of your people."

Gareth almost replied, *"Yes, I am considered a great catch, although for the same reasons I could not endure being caught."* To her, he was no more than a tradesman's apprentice. As such, he could expect to work hard, earn a decent living, but never aspire to anything more. He wished it were true.

"I am hardly in a position to consider marriage," he said.

"Mmmm. Your future employment would be enough of an attraction, even if your personal appearance were revolting to the eye, which it is not."

Gods, was she flirting with him? No, her expression was perfectly serious.

"The same is true for me," she said with a trace of wistfulness. "And so," rousing herself, "I am no more enamored of the prospect than you are. We both have indulgent families, but in the end, we will do our duty."

In the end, I will have no choice.

"So your husband will help your father with the caravan, learn the business, and then manage it on his own?" Gareth said.

"And my brother will have a place and useful work."

At last, they came over a low rise of dunes and looked down over the bed of a long-dried ocean. Nothing had prepared Gareth for his first sight of that plain of shimmering white, rising to pallid cliffs, or for Shainsa itself, like an incrustation of bleached and crumbling bones. The houses were tall, spreading buildings made of salt stone from the cliffs that rose behind the city. From this distance, the city had the appearance of immense age, but not the vigorous, ever-changing age of Comyn Castle and the Old Town. This was a brooding, sullen age, one that sank ever deeper into its own poisoned dreams.

He blinked, and the feeling lifted. The city below was ancient, certainly, and exotic, filled with strange and dangerous people, but it was not malevolent. Surely there must be many within those walls who lived with honor and decency.

They went down, through the outskirts and shanties inhabited by wretches too poor to pay the city gate fees, past pens and picket lines of livestock, and pans of sulfur and salt. Men moved about them, as sunbaked and colorless as the land itself. Alkali-tinged dust hung in the midday heat, tainting every breath. Gareth's lungs ached with it.

Inside the gates, they parted company with their traveling companions and set up camp on a broad unpaved square surrounding a common well. The well was very old, its stones crumbling into powder around the edges. The water tasted strongly metallic, but it was cool. Here they unsaddled their horses, unloaded the pack animals, and pitched tents for sleeping and shelters to protect their horses against the glare of noon.

A group of Dry Towners stood loafing by the common watering trough, watching the proceedings. They behaved as if the arrival of traders were an entertainment arranged for their own amusement, offering comments that in the Domains would have been outright rude. Gareth struggled to keep his expression bland, and Rahelle said in a low voice, "Such words break no bones and dishonor no one but he who utters them."

After a time, one of the onlookers strolled over to the camp. Cyrillon, who had been attending to the stowing of the baggage, went to meet him. Gareth caught only a little of their conversation, enough to understand that in an hour, half the city would know what goods Cyrillon had to sell.

Finally, the camp was arranged and the animals watered and given a ration of grain. Rahelle suggested to Gareth that they find a wine shop to quench their thirst, "and something to eat besides trail fodder. Come on, I'll show you something of the city."

They made their way through a series of merchant districts, past metal forges and dealers in rubies and other precious gems, and down streets lined by walls of sandstone and dried mud brick. Finally they emerged into an open, windswept square bounded on one side by a building of salt-pale stone. It was far larger than the Great House at Carthon, but it had no windows or beds of dusty flowers. It looked for all the world like a fortress. Four massive, sun-dark guards in livery of purple and gold stood beside the double doors.

"What place is that?" Gareth asked.

"The Great House of Shainsa, and do not inspect it too closely or you will arouse suspicion. The guards see threats everywhere."

A pair of fighting men could hold the front entrance for a long time, even against a direct attack.

"Lord Dayan, who now rules," Rahelle went on, "is said to be no worse than the rest, and certainly he is no fool. But they all have enemies, whether by blood feud or ancient quarrel, or simply the temptation of all desperate men to enhance their *kihar* by bringing down such a lord."

She led the way into a wine shop where red lanterns burned in the open windows. Gareth was used to Thendaran taverns, a bar and tables where men might sit to drink. This small, close room was lined with battered wooden benches. Cushions, many of them dingy with grime, were scattered over the stained, worn carpets.

"Here?"

"It doesn't look like much, I know," she said, "but this place has the best *tortugas* in Shainsa. Just don't use the green sauce if you're not used to spicy food."

Following Rahelle's example, Gareth lowered himself to one of the cushions. A few moments later, a girl with a tangled rope of hair down her back brought them two mugs, a pitcher of wine, and a plate of cakes dotted with seeds and salt crystals. Her chains clanked softly as she moved about, gathering up empty mugs and refilling pitchers. Rahelle gestured to the girl, who returned a few moments later with a wooden bowl laden with fist-sized fried pastries and a smaller ceramic cup of poison-green slime.

Gareth bent over his wine, which was surprisingly good, if a little sweet for his taste. The pastries turned out to be savory, not sweet, stuffed with spicy onions and beans. His eyes burned with the first bite, but the sensation of heat soon faded, replaced with a melting succulence.

As Rahelle did not seem interested in talk, Gareth contented himself with observing and listening as unobtrusively as possible. Perhaps in another day or two, he might feel confident enough to initiate a conversation with men like these, get them talking about the latest wild tales. Perhaps that might even lead to someone who knew more than rumor. For now, he must go slowly until he learned more of this city and its ways.

The following morning, when shadows still stretched long, a market sprang up in the brief coolness. Vegetables, dried fruits, pots of spices and sweet oil, and buckets of grain were laid out on blankets under coarse-woven awnings. Drovers clustered at the common well, watering their animals and gossiping. Servants in brightly hued liveries carried baskets of the day's purchases, rolled carpets, harness, pottery jugs, and bundles of precious wood.

A tall man wearing an elaborately plumed helmet approached their encampment. Twin baldrics crossed his ornate tunic, and he carried two swords and five visible knives. Cyrillon executed a formal Dry Towns bow, fist to belly, heart, and forehead. Gareth moved closer, curious.

"I am the one you seek, and these are my servants and apprentice," Cyrillon said, gesturing in Gareth's direction, "except for this one, who travels in these lands under my countenance."

"It is necessary for all who pass these gates to present themselves." The guard's eyes flickered over Gareth, clearly dismissing him as a person of no importance.

"When would it please Lord Dayan to receive these humble persons?" Cyrillon asked, his voice mild.

"The Glory of Shainsa commands you to appear at the third hour of this very day. May the grace of Lhupan and of Nebran shine upon your footsteps, for Lord Dayan will not be so merciful if you fail to obey his wishes."

Cyrillon made a warding motion and murmured, "A fire upon my eyes."

The guard responded with an abbreviated gesture of respect and then went about his business.

Cyrillon motioned for Rahelle and Gareth to come closer. "Continue with our usual preparations, but do not offer anything for sale. We dare not risk Dayan's displeasure by trading without his leave."

"What does he want?" Gareth asked. "Is this extortion, demanding a fee to trade here?"

"The great lords amuse themselves by interviewing newly arrived traders. They say it is to keep out dishonorable men, but really, it is to find out who is selling what and to make sure they have first chance at the best goods and at the lowest prices. We will of course present Lord Dayan with suitable gifts. Prepare a selection of your lenses, with perhaps one or two of your best quality but no more, only enough to appear respectful."

"I suppose that if he wanted to buy everything I had, I would have to sell it to him at his own price." Gareth said, thinking that would eliminate his professed reason for being here. He had not counted on having to acquire new trade goods. On the other hand, that might give him an excellent reason to ask questions, as a trader looking for curiosities to sell.

"Any of us thus favored must of course accept the offered terms," Cyrillon went on.

"We make up the lost profit," Rahelle added.

"Ah, but the lord who presses too hard soon learns that we traders are like the winds we follow," Cyrillon commented. "We can be bent, for such is the cost of doing business, but only so far."

Cyrillon did not add, for although no one stood near them, it was by no means certain they could not be overheard, that Shainsa was not the only market in the Dry Towns. Like her sister cities, Daillon and Ardcarran, Shainsa was heavily dependent upon imported food, leather, and other goods, much of them from the Domains. Over the ages, the armies of Shainsa had tried again and again to seize and hold Carthon as a gateway to the fertile lands beyond.

"I suppose," Gareth said, "that if you wish a man to trade with you, you must make it worth his while."

"Now you are beginning to think like one of us," Rahelle said. "Every man, no matter how high or lowly, has his own pride. Yes, even the beggars in the square and the herdsmen with their beasts."

"Even the women."

She glanced at him beneath dark, half-lowered lashes. "Even. So the lord who strips his subjects of their *kihar* and leaves them nothing but dreams of revenge will come, sooner or later, to eat the fruit of his deeds."

And that is as true in the Domains as it is here, Gareth thought. When the Comyn led wisely and used their *laran* with restraint, everyone prospered, but when they did not . . . there had been more than one peasant revolt in the turbulent Ages of Chaos. Whatever had happened once could happen again.

Of all the things he anticipated on this journey, standing in a Shainsa market square and discussing politics with a woman in the disguise of a trader's apprentice was not one of them.

Cyrillon set about preparing himself, changing his trail-stained clothing for a clean shirtcloak of fine *linex* trimmed with bands of intricately braided leather strips. Gareth, in the better of his two sets of clothing, presented a less imposing appearance, as did Rahelle. They followed Cyrillon across the square, where the morning crowd had already begun to disperse.

When they arrived at the Great House, guards in Dayan's now familiar livery stood beside the double doors. Cyrillon spoke to the one with the larger headdress, and after a moment the doors opened, and another guard escorted them inside.

Past an entrance hall that would have been almost impossible to take by force, they marched down a colonnade where men in robes of embroidered spidersilk paused in their conversation to watch them pass. To one side, an exquisitely carved arch afforded a glimpse of an interior garden courtyard, quiet except for the plashing of fountains. Gareth caught the blossom-laden scent under the shelter of wide-spreading trees. Here in the Dry Towns, little grew unless it was planted, except thornbush; this oasis was a treasure beyond gold. Gareth had not realized there was such wealth in Shainsa. Certainly, the exterior walls gave little indication of this opulence.

They came to Dayan's presence chamber, a hall of polished stone, glimmering with pink and gold iridescence. The air was dense with incense, and the room was dim. Guards, their eyes gleaming, hands alert on sword hilts, framed the three doorways, while servants glided about the perimeter like soundless shadows. Hassocks of supple leather, their sides lavishly ornamented with gold-thread embroidery, formed a crescent on the layers of jewel-toned carpets. There, a few men, as richly dressed as those outside, took their ease.

At their head, a man in a dark, austerely cut shirtcloak occupied the single chair. By some trick of light, his fair hair and sculpted beard glimmered like gold, or so Gareth thought until he realized the effect was due to tiny metallic threads intertwined in the natural hair. Even without the man's aura of power and the intensity of his gaze, there could be no question this was the current Lord of Shainsa.

At a flicker of the lord's eyes, one of the loungers rose and came toward them, an older man who, unlike the others, wore no sword.

"The Voice of Dayan," Rahelle whispered to Gareth.

Gareth had some experience with the flowery phrases and formal compliments so common in the Dry Towns. Now, hearing them exchanged between the Voice and Cyrillon under Dayan's watchful, almost unblinking gaze, each word seemed to take on hidden meaning. Gareth took pride in his knowledge of the undercurrents of power, growing up as he had as the target for every lordling's ambition. Here, although he understood the literal meanings of each speech, he caught only the surface of what was being said.

Cyrillon spoke for them all, offering the gifts they had brought. The Voice received them, exclaiming at Gareth's lenses. Dayan's gaze never left Cyrillon, not even to glance at the gifts. Neither he nor his courtiers took any greater notice of Gareth and Rahelle than of their own servants. Gareth sensed that he had been considered and dismissed.

The interview seemed interminable. Gareth's legs ached from the tension. Drawing on his experience at Comyn social affairs, he kept himself from betraying his discomfort. He kept his focus on the proceedings, tedious as they were, as a discipline. He knew nothing of the Lord of Shainsa, but he assumed that any man who could seize and hold power here must be both intelligent and ruthless. On the other hand, Cyrillon was an experienced trader, smooth-spoken and astute.

At one point, servants brought out trays of food and drink, *jaco* in tiny cups of translucent blue porcelain, balls of dried fruit pounded with nuts and sweet spices, and honey-glazed buns. Dayan accepted a cup and one of the pastries, then gestured for them to be offered to Cyrillon, watching with hawk-bright eyes as the trader took a sip and a bite. Gareth supposed that such men lived with the daily threat of poison, and it was an honor bestowed upon a guest to be the first to taste a meal.

Dayan signaled an end to the interview, and the Voice escorted them from the room. Dusk had gathered on the colonnade as other guests strolled or hurried by on their own business. The Voice presented Cyrillon with a small carved chest of spices and a porcelain medallion on a silk cord. On their way back to the encampment, Rahelle explained that the token was their franchise to trade as they willed, not only here in Shainsa itself but also throughout the lands where Dayan held sway.

"It is a good thing," she said, "and not often granted. I think he was pleased with your lenses and wishes to encourage greater trade in such things. We will do a good business tomorrow."

12

The next morning, even before Cyrillon had finished setting up booths to display his merchandise, a small assembly had gathered. He was not the only trader in the market square, nor were his the most sought-after goods, but word had evidently gotten around of Lord Dayan's favor. The medallion hung in a prominent place from one of the corner poles. As they opened for business, Gareth wondered aloud whether some of the buyers had come only so that they might be seen patronizing one of Dayan's favorites.

Rahelle laughed but did not disagree. As she had said, they were able to make up the lost profit by increasing their prices. Cyrillon was careful not to charge too much, however. No customer would be able to complain of an unfair bargain.

There was quite a bit of interest in Gareth's lenses, and at first he was worried that he would sell them all. Most had come to look rather than buy, though, and those who did buy selected only one or two pieces. As useful as they might be, the lenses were still luxury goods. Thanks to Cyrillon's tutelage, Gareth was able to negotiate in a creditable fashion.

The sun swung overhead, and the crowd dispersed as the day's crimson heat settled on the baked earth. Gareth, satisfied with the morning's work, helped to close up the booths. There was nothing to be done until the cooler hours. This might be an opportune time to see what he could learn in the city.

Cyrillon had lain down to rest, but Rahelle sat in the shade of the open-sided tent. Sitting cross-legged, she bent over a bridle strap. Gareth watched her manipulate the curved needle, dipping it in and out of the leather, drawing the waxed thread into a neat seam.

She looked up. "What are you staring at? Have you never seen anyone sewing before?"

"Of course. At home, my mother always had some piece of embroidery at hand, usually for cushions or tapestries. Nothing as useful as what you are doing."

"There speaks a man who has never had to count the holes in the linens. Embroidery isn't all for show. The added threads strengthen the cloth against wear, as do the bands on cuffs and collars. Or did you think they were mere decoration, that needlework has no other function except to amuse women who have no other occupation?"

To this, Gareth had no ready reply. He had never thought much about the contribution of the women to the household. "Are you not concerned that someone here will see you doing women's work?"

"Harness and clothing must be repaired, whether or not there is a woman to do it," Rahelle answered tartly, "and there is no unmanliness in caring for equipment. I am a dutiful apprentice, performing the tasks set for me by my master. Do you intend to stand there all day? There is a second needle in the mending case."

"I intend to find a meal and perhaps a little gossip." On impulse, he added, "Will you come with me?"

She shook her head. "Now that we have opened for business, one of us must stay here." She drew the thread underneath the last stitch and used a small knife to trim it close. "I don't like the idea of you going off on your own. You have a talent for getting into trouble. Be careful what you say."

"And what I do and where I put my feet. It's daylight—how dangerous can it be? I grew up in a city. I know what to watch out for."

Rahelle looked unhappy but said nothing more.

Gareth began by wandering through the outer areas, where a handful of other caravans had set up their camps. Most had finished the morning's business and now rested, still watchful, in the shade of their tents. He approached them with some confidence since he had listened to Cyrillon strike up a conversation with his fellow traders and thought he could do as well with the hirelings.

Traders, like other Dry Towners, rarely got down to business right away. Gareth offered greetings and comments on the livestock and the condition of the wells and roads. There followed conventional compliments and inquiries about where they had come from and what they might have to offer for sale or be interested in buying. Gareth let slip a hint here and there that he was curious about "unusual trade goods" and stories of strange happenings in the desert.

"What stories from the far lands are not strange?" one of the *oudrakhi* drovers said. "There the sun sucks the very marrow from a man's brains so that even the strongest sees visions."

"Do you mean heat mirages," Gareth asked, "or something more? Men vanishing in a flash of light, perhaps?"

The drover scowled. "It is unwise to speak about such things, lest the gods themselves take notice."

"I meant no offense," Gareth said lightly. "I collect tales to bring home to amuse the young children. They've grown weary of the same old stories told by the fireside."

"If it's tales you're after, let me tell you of the white *oudrakhi* with the three calves . . ."

The drover's tale was, as promised, amusing, although Gareth did not understand all the humor. With a little use of his *laran,* even unaided by his starstone, he was able to sense when the storyteller found something funny and then laugh appreciatively. Since some form of reciprocation was clearly expected, he offered one of the many story-songs from the Hellers about Durraman and his infamously decrepit and recalcitrant donkey.

Eventually, Gareth bade farewell to his new companions and made his way deeper into Shainsa. The city was a labyrinth, a series of open squares linked by crooked alleys. The sun-bleached walls turned blind faces to the unrelenting glare. Here and there, children with pale fleecy hair played in the shadows. A few old men drowsed on the stone benches. Their faces were as faded as their shirtcloaks, and many of them bore knife scars. What had they seen, and what could they tell? Gareth could think of no way to approach them.

He noticed a figure, hooded and robed in yellow, bent under the weight of a yoke from which hung two huge buckets. The figure went from one decrepit elder to the next, setting down the buckets. Curious but trying not to look conspicuous, Gareth watched the figure dip out a cup of water for each. Nothing was offered in return. The sight moved him unexpectedly, for he had not thought to find charity in the Dry Towns. Perhaps sensing his attention, the hooded figure turned to him, and he saw the symbol stitched on its breast, the same stylized representation of the Toad God Nebran as on the locket Grandmother Linnea had given him.

In the end, he went back to the Street of the Five Shepherds and the wine shops there. By this time, a scattering of red lanterns indicated establishments open for business.

Gareth selected one that seemed neither too run-down nor too elaborate, the sort of place a man with a few coins to spend might seek out. The interior was dim after the brightness of the street. A stale, musty tang hung in the air. Men sprawled on stained cushions or hunkered down in circles on the rough stone floor. From behind a curtain came voices and the clatter of cooking utensils.

Gareth lowered himself to the floor and turned to the nearest man. The fellow looked as weather-beaten and worn as any of them, slumped over a chipped pottery mug that was clearly empty.

"What are you drinking? Can I buy the next round?"

The man grunted. In the partial light, his eyes were gleaming slits. Gareth hesitated, unsure if this meant assent. Then he saw that half the men in the room had taken notice. A few stared outright, their faces unreadable.

"I don't understand, what I meant—" he began, then realized it was the wrong thing to say. He searched his memory for the words he'd heard in Carthon, "If you have no blood feud with my family, will you drink with me?"

What happened next was too fast for Gareth the follow. Men who only an instant before had sprawled about the room as if they lacked the will or energy to sit up straight now sprang to their feet. Several shouted out words Gareth did not recognize. The man Gareth had addressed whipped out a knife and slashed at his face.

Gareth twisted out of reach and scrambled to his feet. A line of fire shot across his cheek, and he felt a trickle of wetness. It was not a serious cut. The sting would pass in a moment. The danger lay in the meaning of the attack.

The man who had struck at him, the one he'd offered to buy a drink, sank into a fighter's stance. The foot placement was a little different from what Gareth's swordmasters had taught, but the intent was unmistakable. Around them, the other men formed a circle, intent, muttering.

Lord of Light! Without meaning to, he'd somehow insulted this man. He had been challenged, and if he did not answer or if he said the wrong thing, the room would turn on him like a pack of wolves on a wounded *chervine.* A man without pride, without *kihar*, was fair game; that was the first lesson he had learned about Dry Towns honor.

"Carrion-brained wearer of sandals!" the man spat. *Sandal wearer* was apparently as much a insult here as it was in the Domains.

One of the onlookers pressed a sword into the man's hand. Without thinking, Gareth drew his own blade. His heart sank even as his fingers closed around the hilt. The Dry Towner would spill his blood—or his guts, given the chance—without a qualm, and there was no way out. The crowd wanted this fight.

Some response seemed to be called for. Gareth tried to remember what the drovers had called their recalcitrant beasts. If he was forced into an exchange of insults, then let them be good ones.

"Filthy sand-swilling offspring of a bog-spavined *cralmac!* I will not sully my blade with your blood!"

One of the watchers hooted in appreciation.

"Then wither and die like the droppings of a *kyorebni* on the Plain of Fire!" Gareth's opponent narrowed his eyes and stepped sideways, circling. All appearance of intoxication disappeared.

Gareth adjusted his stance for the greatest advantage. His sword felt light and balanced. The quivering in his belly stilled. Heat swept through him. Every detail came into focus. Silvery adrenaline surged through his veins.

He caught the shift in his opponent's eyes an instant before the attack came. He pivoted, sweeping his own sword to catch the cut on the strongest part of the blade. The man lashed out with the knife in his other hand, closing quick and hard. Gareth jumped back, fueled by luck and instinct.

They engaged again, a flurry of quick jabs and parries. The man stumbled on the jutting edge of one of the floor stones and came up more slowly. He really was drunk, Gareth saw now, fighting by reflex in a style designed for a brave show and an early victory.

Gareth didn't want to kill the man. Was there no other way to end the fight? Every moment of delay only increased the possibility that one of them would end up maimed or dead. And why? Because one man was too ignorant to know what he was doing, and the other was too drunk or too in love with his own *kihar*? Was that worth a man's life? The waste, the obscene, futile *waste* of it infuriated Gareth.

They circled again, slashed and countered and broke apart. On impulse, Gareth stepped into the next opening, aiming not for a vital target but for the man's face. The tip of his sword flicked across the weathered cheekbone, almost by chance in the same place Gareth had been cut. Dark blood welled.

Gareth drew back, momentarily abashed by the anger that had driven him. His opponent raised one hand to his cheek and stared at his bloody fingers. The room seemed to hold its collective breath.

"Now," Gareth said, throwing away all caution, for what did it matter anyway? "Now you're as ugly as I am!"

The men froze, audience and combatant both. Even the noises from the kitchen fell away. The only sound was the buzzing of a single fly as it circled the unattended wine cups.

The other man threw back his head and laughed uproariously. Gareth stared at him, dumbfounded. The watching men relaxed, slapping each another on the back, and returned to their drinks. Within moments, the room returned to how it had been when Gareth entered. His erstwhile opponent, sword now returned to its owner, lowered himself to the floor and gestured to Gareth.

"One has only to look at you to see that the Double-Tailed Scorpion-Ant has graced you with his blessings. Ah, but I see you are already under Nebran's protection—"

Gareth's hand went to the neckline of his shirt, where Linnea's locket swung freely on its chain.

"—and so, as the Toad survives the drought and lives to snare the Scorpion-Ant, so all men of *kihar* must prosper. Come, come, sit with us. And if Nebran extends his blessings, the next round of drink will be paid for."

Returning his sword to its sheath, Gareth squatted beside the other men. As the conversation continued, he found it was unnecessary to say anything, only to nod in agreement and to slip the wine shop owner a coin or two when he arrived with pitchers of sour, watered wine.

Several mugs later, Gareth's opponent, even drunker than before, became effusively friendly. Gareth himself had downed more of the foul-tasting stuff than he had intended. When his new drinking companion asked what his business was in Shainsa, he shrugged and tried to look bored.

"I've taken a try at trading," Gareth said. "This and that, looking for something no one else has. Willing to go—" he gestured in what he hoped was the direction of Daillon and Black Ridge, "—out there to get it. *Unusual* trade goods, y'know. Things that go *boom* or *flash* or whatever. Y'know what I mean?"

His new friend, whose name was Rasham or Raseem or something like that, slapped his thigh. "To see things like that, one must be touched by the gods. And to be touched by the gods, one must be either very holy or else wanting very badly to leave this cursed life. You don't look holy. Do I?" He leaned forward, breathing heavily. The smells of wine and hideously bad breath washed over Gareth. The next instant, Rasham toppled sideways.

Suddenly disgusted at himself and the whole situation, Gareth disentangled himself and clambered to his feet. He gave the wine shop owner another few coins and shambled outside. He had wasted the rest of the day, almost gotten himself killed, received a cut that would surely leave a scar he'd have to explain to his hysterical mother, and now his belly threatened to spew forth all the cheap wine he'd poured into it.

Gareth could not make out any landmarks, only that the sun hung low in the sky, red and swollen, but where he was in relation to the square and Cyrillon's camp, he could not tell. As he made his way down the dusty streets, he tried to appear confident, so as to not present an obvious target for pickpockets. For a time, he could have sworn he was being followed, but when he turned to look, he saw nothing but shadows.

He got turned around and ended up in a twilit alley, hot and reeking with the gypsy glare of fires that burned, smoking, at the far end. The street was far from deserted, for at this hour, the city surged back to life. A wind sprang up, heavy with the smells of incense from a street shrine, unfamiliar spices, and rancid cooking oil.

Gareth felt a stirring, a breath across his neck. He turned. A Dry Towner, rangy and scarred, wearing a stained red shirtcloak, had come up behind him.

Gareth tried to pull himself into a posture of vigilance. He greeted the man with the formulaic, "I do not know your face. Have I a duty toward you?"

The man's eyes were as pale as ice. Lips twisted back from teeth that were surprisingly white. "No, but that can be arranged. I may have what you are looking for." He spoke clearly, but with a strange thick accent.

Gareth's heart gave a leap. "Let us find a place where we can speak freely."

"Not here." Pale eyes flickered to where a clot of men in ragged shirt-cloaks stood talking, voices low and hands on the hilts of their swords. "Tonight, when only Mormallor shines in the sky, come to The Place of the Silver Fan Ladies. Perhaps we will each learn something to one another's advantage." Again the man gave that rictus smile, and turned to go.

"No, wait!"

"There are things in the deep desert, things hidden in the Sands of the Sun, things beyond the power of men. Things sent in answer to our prayers. Things that will at long last grant us a holy victory over the witches of the north."

Aldones, the witches of the north *meant the Comyn!* The man was talking about war with the Domains.

"But—"

"Come alone. I will know if you are followed. Even the shadows have ears."

Without another word, the Dry Towner strode away.

By the time Gareth reached the traders' encampment, it was full night. The dregs of adrenaline had faded from his veins, leaving him queasy and shaken. Rahelle and Cyrillon sat around a fire of dried *oudrakhi* dung, such as they had used on the trail. The pungent odor rankled Gareth's senses.

Rahelle offered him mint-infused tea and a dish of boiled greens and grain seasoned with tiny seeds. Nauseated, he waved the food away and lowered himself to the ground. He was still a little drunk, the cut on his cheek throbbed, and his muscles had begun to stiffen after the fight.

"What happened to you?" she demanded. "What kind of trouble did you get yourself into this time?"

Gareth tried to make light of the duel, but the encounter still sounded like one hideous mistake after another. Rahelle glowered at him but said nothing. She was undoubtedly thinking that he was incapable of opening his mouth without endangering life and limb. In her mind, he would leave a trail of blood and mishaps wherever he went.

Why did he care what she thought? He could not remember a time when the people around him had regarded him with anything approximating respect. The only difference between then and now was that he was no longer cowering in the shadow of his disgrace.

Cyrillon, on the other hand, did not press Gareth for details. At the end of the tale, he nodded and said, "Seeing how well you fought on the trail, I do not think you were in much danger. You resolved the encounter and showed presence of mind."

I showed what an idiot I am!

"Next time," Cyrillon finished, "you will do even better."

"If you want my opinion, there shouldn't be a next time," Rahelle broke in. She looked as if she'd like to tie Gareth hand and foot to keep him from causing even more trouble.

"It is unwise to hold forth on subjects on which one has little knowledge and even less understanding," Cyrillon said.

She shot him a furious look but said nothing more. Gareth remembered how, after being told to remain in the wagon, she had fought alongside the men against the bandits. Now she dipped her head and began gathering up the dishes to scrub them clean in the sand.

"Drink the tea." Although Cyrillon did not add, his voice implied, *You'll need it.*

The aromatic tisane settled Gareth's guts. Stretching out on his blanket, he closed his eyes. He thought only to rest for a few minutes, while the tea finished its calming work.

After a moment of groggy confusion, he realized that some hours had passed. A sweep of stars glimmered across the night sky. Now fully awake, he slipped from the tent. The embers of several fires glowed dimly. Beyond, in the city, he made out dotted torchlight. He checked his weapons—sword and boot knife—and tucked the amulet containing his starstone inside his shirt.

Making his way back through the city, Gareth passed a street shrine, little more than a hut with a threshold dotted with offerings of dried flowers, figurines of soapstone or basalt, cracked pottery bowls, and a scattering of wrapped candies. Sheltered from the sun by a gable, a painted tile depicted the Toad God.

Was Nebran following him everywhere?

He reflected that he could ask for a worse patron among the gods of the Dry Towns. The Toad God might be squat and ugly, its spotted hide covered with warts, but at least its followers did some good in the world.

No, wait . . . Gareth paused, looking around, trying to remember if he'd passed the same shrine earlier in the day. He must have taken a wrong turn somewhere. Cursing silently, he retraced his steps.

Eventually, he found a landmark he recognized, a weapon shop with a distinctive sign, its emblem an improbably gore-covered sword. Everything, even the drops of painted blood, looked different in the night. Idriel had set, and Mormallor now hung solitary through the heavens, a tiny marble of pearly white.

At last he found The Place of the Silver Fan Ladies, a small plaza on the edge of the red-lantern district. Lights winked from second-story windows. A door opened, and a man stumbled into the street. Gareth caught a whiff of incense and the tinkling of some kind of stringed instrument before the door closed again.

Singing, the man staggered on his way. The plaza fell silent. Gareth hesitated, and then some instinct hurried him into the gloom of an overhanging eave, well out of the light. A moment later, he spied movement in one of the side streets.

Gareth had always seen well at night, and now his eyes adapted quickly. He was rewarded by the sight of a lean, tall shape moving with the calculated grace of a sword fighter. The figure paused, head turning slightly from one side to the other.

Gareth started to move away from his hiding place. Before he could take a step, however, three men burst from the darkness and rushed the first. Gareth could not make out anything about them, other than their size and the speed of their attack. His ears caught the clash of steel on steel and a *clink-clatter*, perhaps of some smaller weapon or a chain. With a effort, he forced himself to hold still.

Their voices were low, but he recognized the heavy accent of the man whom he was to meet. And from the others, he caught muttered phrases, a syllable here, a word there.

". . . Lord Dayan . . ." ". . . secrets . . ." ". . . tales out of . . ." ". . . the desert . . ."

And then, so quick and quiet he could not be sure over the pounding of his heart, "*. . . thunderbolt . . .*"

In a flurry of shadows, the men hurried away in the direction of the Great House. Gareth could not see well enough to tell if his informant went willingly, but that made no difference.

Lord Dayan's men were following me. I led them to him.

Gods, what was he going to do? What *could* he do? His head filled with thoughts of Dayan's torturers, from every tale of Dry Towner savagery he had heard as a boy.

They will have the secret out of him, if not by bribery then by force.

Lord Dayan had been looking for information about strange happenings—weapons—in the deep desert. That was why he questioned traders coming through Shainsa. He must have heard the rumors, even as Gareth had.

An image sprang up behind Gareth's eyes, the Shainsa lord sitting on his throne, the keen, hawk-bright eyes watchful and measuring. A proud man Dayan was, ruthless enough to seize and hold power here, with the ages-old enmity of all his kind against the Domains.

Now he had within his grasp the best—the *only* informant Gareth had been able to locate.

"Mother," Dani Hastur said in a tight, controlled voice, "you had something to do with this, didn't you?"

Linnea reached for the calm she had cultivated over the years, first as a very young Keeper, then as Lady Hastur, and now as Keeper again, and faced her son. She had, she thought, done well to make sure this conversation took place on her own home ground, the chamber of Comyn Tower reserved for receiving important guests. It was a small, gracefully proportioned room, its walls a mosaic of fine-grained granite and translucent blue stone.

Dani Hastur had never been at ease in the Tower. She needed no *laran* to see that. His normally relaxed features betrayed his tension. His eyes, a clear, pellucid gray that reminded her so poignantly of his father's, were troubled. He had come charging into the audience chamber to announce that his son had gone missing. His wife, Miralys Elhalyn, now slipped through the door and closed it quietly behind her.

"Gareth has been studying with me, yes," Linnea said, deliberately not answering the question. Her son and daughter-in-law had arrived in Thendara earlier than expected, and had dealt with the news of Gareth's absence worse than expected. "I have tried to give him what he would have learned in a Tower, not only the knowledge but the self-discipline to best use his talents."

"That isn't what I asked. I want to know if you had anything to do with him going off on some hare-brained scheme to who-knows-where." Although the words were terse, Linnea found herself responding to the pulse of love and concern beneath them.

"Will you not sit down?" She indicated the pair of well-cushioned chairs opposite her own. "Both of you?"

Dani recovered himself, guided his wife to the smaller chair, and sat. "I'm sorry I was rude, Mother. When we arrived, we found Gareth was not at home. The old retainer babbled some story about a secret expedition to the Dry Towns—what was I to think? Gareth's a good boy, you know that, but he's impulsive and easily influenced."

Weak-willed, he meant.

Linnea said nothing. Too clearly, Dani was thinking of that hideous episode from years ago. If Gareth's own father could not set it aside, what hope was there for those who did not know the boy as well?

"Easily influenced," Miralys repeated. Her voice, although low and pleasant, a lady's well-modulated tones, bore an edge of concern. "Gareth has always loved stories of adventure and daring. I—we couldn't help thinking of *Dom* Regis and all the wild things he did when he was young, like riding off to Castle Aldaran to rescue Uncle Danilo. Gareth's just the sort of hopeless romantic to run away on a whim."

She didn't add, although Linnea caught her thought, *But Gareth isn't Regis, and these times are different. He needs to prove himself serious and dependable.*

And, Linnea added silently, *who better to aid in a young person's rebellion than a doting grandmother?*

Her own grandmother, Desideria Storn, had lived life on her own terms, defying convention until the day of her death. *I come by it honestly.*

Gazing into the anxious faces of her son and daughter-in-law, however, she could not bring herself to laugh at their worries.

"Gareth confided in me, and when I could not talk him out of it, I provided him with the best help I could."

"If I had known he intended such a thing, I would have put a stop to it," Dani muttered.

"Which is why, since I am sure he was aware of your feelings, he did his best to make sure you did *not* know," Linnea said.

Miralys's taut expression softened as Linnea described the arrangements Gareth had made, a guide who was experienced and trustworthy, a credible disguise as a trader, "and such protections as I myself could give him."

Linnea deliberately omitted the possibility of contacting Gareth through his starstone. Few telepaths could manage such a thing over any distance, so it was a measure to be undertaken only in the direst emergency.

"At any rate," she concluded, "Gareth intends to return to Thendara before the opening of Council season. He is aware of his responsibilities. I would caution you, however, that if you greet him with censure, the most likely result will be that he will shut you out even more the next time he decides to do something like this."

"Next time!" Miralys cried.

"There will not be a *next time*," her husband said.

"But there *will* be a next time," Linnea corrected him, "and one after that, until the wild streak within him has run its course. We can reason with him, we can pray for him, we can try to protect him in the world, but we cannot turn him into an obedient puppet. Javanne tried, and we all know the result."

For a long moment, neither Dani nor Miralys spoke. A faint flush suffused Dani's features. As it faded, it left a film of sweat. His wife's pale complexion did not alter; she might have been marble.

"You are right, there is nothing to be done," Dani agreed, still looking unhappy. To Miralys he said, "Gareth is no longer a child. We cannot lock him up like a prisoner. How can he have a future on the Council, whether he is ever crowned or not, if he never learns to govern himself?"

"That is a question parents have been asking since the beginning of time," Linnea said. "We want to keep our children safe, and yet we want them to become men and women of conviction."

"I wanted to raise my children to think for themselves," Marguerida had once said, *"and now it is too late to change my mind."*

"I wish it were as simple as a youthful escapade," Dani said. "There is more at stake here than a youngster's adventure."

Linnea frowned. Her work as a Keeper kept her isolated from the daily politics of the court. Usually she preferred it that way. "What's going on?"

"I have reason to believe the Council is going to force the issue of Gareth's regency. I'd hoped to put it off for a season or two."

"Gareth's regency? Must anything be done? Surely, Mikhail is more than competent."

"Aye, that he is." Dani's eyes glinted very much like his father's, and Linnea reminded herself that he had grown up surrounded by schemes and alliances. "Half the Council would like his position to be permanent, and the other half want him replaced with someone they can manipulate."

"Gareth," Linnea said, unnecessarily.

"If not him," Dani said grimly, "then Derek."

"Derek? Surely not, he's too young." That was, Linnea corrected herself, the point. Derek had all the makings of a strong Warden of Elhalyn, but he had never trained for kingship. Did he even *want* the throne?

Mikhail was not Regis, or even Danvan Hastur, but in his own way, he was a true statesman, steady and yet imaginative. His judgment had always been sound, and he had been ably advised by his off-world wife. It would be a criminal act to reject his skills.

Gareth . . . Gareth was still unproven. In the time they had worked together in intimate telepathic contact, Linnea had detected in him flashes of passion, of vision and courage, of the same sense of responsibility and self-sacrifice that had driven Regis. What Gareth lacked was time to fully develop those qualities.

If Gareth were declared permanently incompetent, then the Council risked deadlock between Mikhail's partisans and those determined to have a puppet under their collective thumbs. In the end, Darkover might lose not only Mikhail and both Gareth and Derek, but Mikhail's very promising son, Domenic, as well.

The struggle could go on for years, draining precious resources and leaving the Comyn divided and vulnerable.

"When kinsmen quarrel, enemies step in."

Linnea was not without influence, as Keeper of Comyn Tower and a member of the Keepers' Council. She would not allow her grandsons to be sacrificed to any man's lust for power.

"I thank you, both of you, for coming to me with this," she said. "We still have time to make plans before the season begins. I will speak with the other Keepers, with Danilo Syrtis, and a few of the others. There is no pressing reason to abandon a Regency that is working so well. We are not so many that we can afford to exclude any member of our caste."

Dani and Miralys took their leave after agreeing to arrange a family breakfast in two days' time. After they had gone, Linnea returned to her private quarters. She intended to meditate, quieting her mind and gathering her energy for the arduous work ahead. Like a sleepwalker, she went through the motions of preparation. Miralys's words, *"There are so few of us,"* haunted her.

She drifted through her chambers, touching those few possessions she had brought with her from her life with Regis: a carved box with hinged lid in which she kept the butterfly clasp for her hair, a pottery cup, an old shawl. Each carried the distant imprint of his hand, offering her the box as a Midsummer gift, unclasping her hair and burying his face in it, sharing hot spiced wine on a blustery winter evening, wrapping both of them in the shawl.

Gareth was her student, her grandson, full of promise and tumult. But he was especially precious because the blood in his veins had come from Regis as well as herself.

"There are so few of us."

Linnea thought of the other children Regis had fathered, especially the daughter they had created together on a night of wild celebration. For too long, she had left those memories undisturbed. She had waited long enough.

Linnea's only lead to the fate of her daughter was Danilo's suggestion that Regis might have confided in Lew Alton. Lew had retreated to the monastery at Nevarsin, where he had found a measure of peace after a lifetime of torment. No one, least of all Linnea, expected that he would ever leave his sanctuary. He had survived two seizures of the heart, each one leaving him more frail. Linnea doubted he was strong enough to endure the mountainous roads to Thendara. Nor could she make the journey to Nevarsin, now that Illona was unable to perform an under-Keeper's work.

When Comyn Tower was reestablished several years ago, the relay chamber had been put to use again, making it possible to send telepathic messages to the other Towers. The relays, great matrix screens that were far more powerful than any individual starstone, amplified the *laran* transmissions over the leagues. Linnea still took her turn at the relays when her duties permitted, partly because Comyn Tower was still under-strength, but also for the sheer joy of speaking mind to mind.

The young worker serving this night looked up in surprise as Linnea entered the chamber. Brunina Alazar was fairly new to Thendara, having been discovered by Danilo Syrtis on one of his trips through the Venza Hills. Linnea had thought she might be one of Kennard Dyan's many illegitimate children, and hence kinswoman to Illona Rider, but Illona said not.

Brunina scrambled to her feet, almost oversetting the padded bench, and curtsied. "*Vai leronis!* I'm sorry—I wasn't expecting you!"

"Be at your ease, child. I'm not here to interrogate you. Illona says your work is excellent, and so I believe. What's the news this evening?"

Brunina handed her the logbook, with the most recent messages written out in her careful script. Most of them had to do with the upcoming session, matters to be discussed in the Keepers' Council, plus a few personal notes for the Tower staff. Linnea nodded. "This is very good. Do you enjoy this work?"

"Oh, yes!" Brunina's eyes shone. "It's like magic—to hear the voices of people I've never seen, from so far away, just as if they were in the same room!"

"I've always felt that way, too. Now I have some private business to conduct, and you have earned a rest. Go down to the kitchen and get yourself something to eat."

With a smile and another curtsy, the girl scooped up her shawl and fairly danced out the door.

Was I ever that young? Linnea settled herself on the bench, assuming a posture that would allow her to work, undistracted by tension, for hours. With her mind, she made a few small adjustments to the relay screens;

they had been attuned in a general way, so that any Tower worker could use them, but Linnea wanted the relay as responsive to her own thoughts as possible.

She focused her mind, setting aside all other thoughts except the lattice of linked matrix stones before her. When she closed her eyes, the pattern of brightness remained, a constellation she could feel as well as see. With practiced ease, she lifted her consciousness into that firmament. It was, as always, like immersing herself in an ocean of living light, connected to it from the depths of her being.

When she had reached the moment of perfect balance, she began to shape the *laran* energies, to hold in her mind a target.

Nevarsin . . . she called.

Linnea had visited Nevarsin with Regis, for he had studied at the monastery school, and the *cristoforos* there kept priceless records of many things. Now she pictured it in her mind, an ancient city built into the side of the mountain as if drawing its substance from the bones of the earth. Above it, set like a rough-edged gem at the edge of the never-melting glacier, rose the gray walls of the monastery itself. It was a hard place, a lonely place, a place to strip a man's soul bare. Why would anyone, let alone a tortured old man, choose such a refuge?

And yet, when Lew had returned to Thendara to help deal with the Trailmen's Fever, she had sensed a peace in him that she had no words for, not even in the wordless ecstasy of the circle.

Nevarsin . . .

Who calls? The mental voice had a distinctly masculine flavor. Linnea did not know him, but that was not surprising. Nevarsin was the most isolated of all the Towers. When the Keepers' Council had been only an idea in discussion, Nevarsin had sent but a sole delegate, Illona Rider. Illona had remained in Thendara, as under-Keeper to the newly reopened Comyn Tower and as Domenic Alton's consort. No other representative from Nevarsin had ever attended the Council meetings. The Keepers of other Towers attended one or another of the gatherings, but not Nevarsin. Even relay contact had been infrequent.

Who calls?

Comyn Tower, Linnea replied.

From Thendara, so far? Is aught amiss? The contact faltered as the Nevarsin worker recognized the characteristic mental signature of a Keeper. *Your pardon,* vai leronis. *I am Anndra MacDiarmid, matrix mechanic. How may I serve you?*

I wish to speak with Dom *Lewis-Kennard Alton, at the monastery. Please arrange for him to have access to the relay screens.*

Confusion tinged the pause that followed. Linnea sensed Anndra searching for a polite way to refuse. That in itself was odd. Her request was not beyond the customary courtesy extended between Towers. Lew might not be a member of the Nevarsin circle, but he was no stranger to matrix science, having trained at Arilinn. Even if he were out of practice, he should have no difficulty in understanding her question and sending a simple yes-or-no answer. If he did not know where Regis had hidden Kierestelli, then that would be the end of the conversation. If he did but could not explain, then she must find a way to travel the long miles to Nevarsin.

Had something happened to Lew? She drew in her breath, dreading the answer. He was old, worn beyond his years, and the climate of Nevarsin was harsh even in the mildest seasons.

Dom *Lewis is still alive, and as far as I know, in as good health as any man of his age,* Anndra hastened to say. Linked as they were, her instant of fear had been clear to him. *But he is in contemplative seclusion at this time, and we cannot ask the Father Master to make an exception.*

No, of course not. The balance of power between monastery and Tower must be as delicately nuanced as that between the various parts of the Darkover Council. Nevarsin's own Keeper was in a far better position to negotiate.

Then I would speak with your Keeper. Linnea searched her memory for the woman's name and realized how little she knew about the Nevarsin Keeper.

What was her name—Solana? Silvana? Silvestra?

Vai leronis, *I wish I could help you.* The poor man sounded frantic with apology. *Is there no one else who will serve or any information I myself might supply?*

It was not, after all, Anndra's fault that he could not help her, and he was clearly doing the best he could.

I fear that is not possible. I'm sorry to put you in a difficult position by asking you to carry my request to your Keeper—Silvestra?

Silvana. But she does not communicate with anyone outside.

Anyone? Ever? Even in the larger Towers, the society was confined. The intensity of the work necessitated both mental and physical recreation. Who could work in such demanding intimacy with the same small circle, tenday after tenday, year after year? Surely even the most reclusive Keeper must long to visit her family or those friends who had gone to serve at other Towers.

Linnea sent a pulse of mental pressure through the relays. Nevarsin's Keeper might well refuse her cooperation, but she would have to do it herself, not through a subordinate.

As the vai leronis *wishes,* Anndra relented.

Linnea sensed a shifting in the energetic patterns of the far end of the relay as Anndra withdrew. She settled in to wait, sustained by the currents in the psychic firmament. Now, as always, she felt as if she were dissolving, not a loss of self but a softening of the boundaries between her separate personality and the universe. Of all the miraculous gifts of her *laran*, this was the most profound, and the one for which she had the fewest words.

Time passed, and there came a stirring on the far end of the relay, a condensation of mental power. A trained mind now joined with hers, and not that of any ordinary *leronis* but a Keeper like herself.

Silvana of Nevarsin Tower? Linnea of Comyn Tower greets you.

For an excruciating moment, silence answered her. Through the intricate facets of the matrix screen, she sensed the Nevarsin Keeper's mind, the structured discipline, the barriers of self-imposed isolation . . . old fear . . .

Then came a blast of incredulity and fury.

Mother?!

Amazement swept through Linnea. *Kierestelli?*

She felt the recoil covering the long-distant echoes of familiarity, of yearning.

I am Silvana, Keeper of Nevarsin. I do not grant you or anyone else permission to call me by any other name.

Stelli, I had no idea—I looked for you for so long! I'd almost given up hope. That's why I wanted to speak with Lew Alton. I thought—I hoped—Regis might have confided in him where he'd hidden you. And here you are, after all these years!

Linnea forced herself to slow the torrent of her thoughts. She had been battering her daughter with her overwhelming joy. Her heart was so full, she could not have spoken aloud.

My sweet daughter, forgive my outburst. I am overjoyed to find you. When can we meet? Shall I travel to Nevarsin—or will you come to Thendara?

Silvana's reply came slowly, edged like steel. *I have no intention of leaving my Tower, nor are you welcome here.*

Not welcome? Linnea reeled. Surely she must have misunderstood. How could that happen when one mind spoke to another, when no deception was possible?

She tried to deepen the rapport below the level of deliberate thought, plumbing for the truth that underlay those harsh words. She found anger . . . bitterness . . . abandonment . . . grief. In the far dim past, she sensed a child's disconsolate tears.

He said he would come back for me, but he never did. He left me . . . he left me . . . *You never wanted me, you never cared . . . so why should I care now?*

Oh, my darling!

Never call me that!

Linnea flinched as if she had been physically struck. With a Keeper's discipline, she calmed the rush of sorrow and guilt, the reflexive denial, the bone-grinding fury at those who had created the need to rip a child from her family in order to safeguard her life.

Cautiously she formed a response, opening her own heartache first at the separation, then at the realization that no matter how many times Regis searched, he never found her.

The situation was so dangerous . . . your father's enemies had already kidnapped your cousin Ariel. If they'd taken you . . . if they'd harmed you . . . We had to make sure you were safe!

He left me there.

Ah, such bleakness in those few words.

He tried to find you, once it was over. Blessed Cassilda, how he tried!

Linnea felt a wavering in her daughter's animosity. Perhaps she, too, had faced difficult choices, impossible decisions. Almost, she could sense acknowledgment in the ripples of Kierestelli's anger.

Had it been so terrible, the place Regis had taken her? Linnea could not believe he would entrust his own child to anyone who would not cherish her as he had.

Linnea's chest ached. She could not feel her heart, only the throbbing emptiness where it had dissolved. She wanted to plead, *Come back to me!* but could not bring herself to break the gossamer moment.

Something lay between them, besides distance and outrage. Kierestelli—no, *Silvana,* as her daughter had renamed herself—had revealed her loneliness, her longing. It was a gift too precious to presume upon.

More might come, the slow accretion of such moments of honesty, of confiding, of guarded revelation. Linnea had rebuilt her life with Regis in such a fashion, minutes and tendays and then years of intimacy. Once she and her daughter had been so close, they might have mirrored one another's souls. Perhaps they might find their way back to one another, for she must be as strange to Silvana as this distant, angry woman was to her. Linnea realized that she could not, *must not* force the natural course of healing. This bridge must be rebuilt from both shores, and she was old enough to have learned patience.

Still, a feeling akin to grief passed through her. Regis was years dead, and Gareth gone off to the Dry Towns, risking things she could not acknowledge, and now Kierestelli—*no! Silvana!*—whose memory she had tucked into the farthest crevices of memory and dream, was now both found and lost again. How could one human heart endure so much loss?

I have made a life for myself, Silvana was saying, restless now and clearly eager to bring the interview to a close. *I have no desire to trade on my father's name or station in life. You have no claim on me, for you sent me away and did not care to find me after the danger had passed.*

You were always in my heart.

That is as it may be, but it buys no bread. I warn you, Mother, *do not attempt to force yourself upon me again. Now that you know where I am, I cannot unmake that knowledge. But we have nothing further to say to one another.*

Gareth reeled back into the shadows, heart racing. He racked his brain for anything he could do to prevent Lord Dayan from learning the truth of the rumors. He certainly could not storm into the Great House, demanding to see the man who had just been brought in. If he tried, he'd be lucky to survive five minutes, let alone to conduct his informant to safety.

Behind him, something moved in the shadows. His hand flew to the hilt of his sword. Before he could draw it, slim fingers closed around his arm. A voice hissed for him to hold still.

Rahelle. Rahelle, furious.

"What are you trying to do, get yourself killed?" Her breath brushed his ear. She was close enough to warm his cheek with the heat of her skin. The nearness brought an unexpected, fleeting *laran* contact. He felt the roil and surge of her emotions, her determination to protect Cyrillon, her fear that her few years of freedom were coming to an end.

"Go back," he muttered. "This is not your concern."

"Your worthless skin is indeed none of my concern. But it would reflect poorly on my father's honor if you were gutted and flayed for the amusement of the street rats of Shainsa while you are under his protection. Which is exactly what will happen if you keep behaving this way!"

Gareth peered in the direction of Lord Dayan's men, half-expecting to see them rush back, drawn by the vehemence of her whispers. Through gritted teeth he said, "I absolve your father of all responsibility."

"It was bad enough for him to take such an arrogant, stubborn, reckless—" she used a Dry Towns idiom that would have scandalized Gareth's tutor "—as far as Carthon. I have no idea what possessed him to let you come this far!"

"I said—"

She made a sound that was rude in three languages. "You wouldn't know responsibility if it were inscribed on a tablet of brass!"

A bubble of laughter tickled his throat. She was so sure, so righteous in her anger. And she was correct, or she would have been a month ago.

Gently he disengaged himself from her hold. "Some things are more urgent than honor, and more important than my worthless skin."

He heard her quick inhalation, sensed the quicksilver change from fury to astonishment. She had understood him, not the specifics of his meaning but the silent cry of his spirit.

Ever since I can remember, I have been a pawn to the schemes and ambitions of others, worth nothing in myself, he wanted to tell her. *For the first time, I have found something bigger than my concerns, and it has changed everything.*

How could he voice such a thing when it was so new, so cataclysmic an alteration, such an upheaval of all his previous life, that he could scarcely articulate it to himself?

They were standing barely a hand's length apart, shrouded in near-darkness. The sounds of the night city receded. He felt a butterfly touch on one cheek, the lingering warmth of her hand.

"Tell me," she whispered. In those short words, he heard her own hunger, her yearning for something beyond chains and veils and an impermanent boy's disguise.

He could not push her away or deny that longing. Memory flashed like dry lightning in his mind, and for an instant he was back on the trail to Carthon, scrambling for his life, and Rahelle was there, too, fighting as hard as any man.

The street looked empty, but Gareth could not be sure. "Where we cannot be overheard . . ."

She took his hand, strong warm fingers laced through his, and led him back to the Nebran street shrine he had passed earlier. Although no more than a crude hut with barely enough roof to shelter the few offerings, it was set apart from the other structures. No one but a ghost could approach without their knowing. They crouched beside the altar.

"In Carthon," Gareth said, "I overheard a story, perhaps not alarming to the locals, but to me it suggested that the Federation might have returned to Darkover, but not to the spaceport in Thendara. Out there, near Black Ridge."

"The *Terranan* . . . Are they weary of life or simply insane? No outlander can last long in the Sands of the Sun." She shrugged, a movement Gareth felt rather than saw. "Understanding waters no gardens. The desert will bury their bones, and it will be as if they had never existed. Why should you care? Have you kin-bond or blood feud with them?"

He brushed aside her taunt. "Not them—the weapons they carry. Weapons that can vaporize living flesh or stun a man into insensibility. Perhaps even worse things." After a moment, he went on. "Our Compact forbids the use of any weapon that does not bring the one who uses it into equal danger. It was not easy to convince the Federation to respect it."

Rahelle settled back on her heels. "Why should they? Why should any man willingly refrain from using his sharpest sword?"

"That attitude," Gareth retorted, raising his voice, "is exactly why such weapons must never fall into the hands of you Dry Towners!"

"I am no Dry Towner, as you well know, Garrin of the Domains! And if they did acquire such weapons, what evil would come of it, save to make them the equals of your people, who have always had the military advantage?"

He forced his rising temper under control. Was this how wars began, with words growing hot and hotter, insults traded, hands reaching for swords that were all too readily drawn?

"If we have learned anything in our long history since the Ages of Chaos," he replied, "it is that having weapons leads inevitably to using them. As the *Terranan* themselves found out at Caer Donn."

Rahelle's breath hissed between her teeth. "I thought Caer Donn was destroyed by fire."

"Not by any off-world weapon. By the unleashed force of the Sharra matrix, a—" how could he put it so she would understand the immense power? "—a weapon of the mind. The Compact exists not to protect us from blasters and needle-guns but from the much more terrible creations of *laran*."

"Bah! Witchery and superstition! Tales told by the credulous to explain such natural events as a mountain fire!" Even as she spat out the words, Gareth heard the quaver in her voice.

"No, it is true. My grandfather was there, and my uncle Danilo. And *Dom* Lewis Alton, who for all I know is still alive, up in Nevarsin. Do you see, if what I fear is true and the Federation has come back in secret for reasons of its own, the Comyn will not surrender to threat. Darkover could become a battleground far worse than Caer Donn."

"That's all very well, but does not explain what *you* are doing, sneaking about the city at this hour."

He might as well tell her, for all the good it would do. In the short time he had known her, he had learned how fruitless it was to argue with anything she said in that tone. "I was to meet a man who had more information."

"What did he say?"

"I don't know. Lord Dayan's men captured him." His throat closed up, half with hopeless dread, half with the simple impossibility of his situation.

"Dayan's men . . . So that's why he's been questioning traders when he never did before, at least not with such keen regard. He is no simpleton, and he loves power. He would not risk any other lord obtaining these weapons. He wants them for his own."

Gareth nodded, although in all likelihood, she could not see him. "That is my fear. And that is why I have no choice. I have to get there first."

"And stop him?" She snorted. "Who do you think you are?"

His name almost popped out before he could think. He clamped his teeth together, biting off his breath. "I can't tell you."

"Can't or won't?" Suspicion laced her tone.

"I have given my word."

Rahelle grabbed his shoulders, her fingers digging into his flesh, and gave him a sharp shake. *"Does my father know?"*

Gareth blessed all the gods of both lands that he was able to answer, "He has known since Carthon. Keeping my identity secret was his condition for allowing me to travel with him to Shainsa."

"So that's it." She released him with a little shove. "I couldn't understand why he let you come along. After you nearly got yourself killed the first day, I thought he'd want nothing more to do with you."

"I believe he was of that opinion . . . until circumstances changed."

"So he knows? About these weapons?"

"He knows only what I overheard in Carthon, my suspicions, and why it was vital that I find out more. Of tonight's debacle, nothing."

Cyrillon would not want to let him go further, not by himself. For a wild moment, Gareth wondered if Rahelle might agree to plead his case. He would have to convince her first, and that might be even harder than facing down her father.

He cleared his throat. "If what I suspect is true, our best—perhaps our only hope is to get there first and impress upon the *Terranan* the danger if Dayan obtains Compact-banned weapons. If we can, make them a better offer." Although why they had set down in the barren lands beyond Shainsa and not in Thendara, he could not imagine.

"Shht! I need to think!"

Gareth was so surprised by the force of Rahelle's command, he kept quiet. His eyes adapted to the near darkness of the shrine, illuminated dimly by the moonslight sifting in through the cracks in the crude roof. The world took on a dreamlike quality, where nothing seemed solid or quite in focus. He supposed the effect was due to how little light there was, at the physical limit of his retinas. He closed his eyes, touched the Nebran amulet on his chest, and tried to see the world through his *laran*.

At first, he sensed nothing through the psychic insulation other than his own body and Rahelle's nearness. Swirling currents of almost-heat, almost-color betrayed her agitation. He nearly gave up, for what was the point of trying to work with an insulated starstone? Yet there was something, hovering at the edge of his perception—

Rahelle shifted, rubbing her arms as she got to her feet, and the fleeting impression vanished. She paused, a silhouette against the glimmering lavender-lit street, and gestured for him to follow.

Together they hurried to the caravan encampment. Rahelle said nothing, except to cut off Gareth's attempt at a question. Clearly, there was no use trying to argue with her. He'd rarely encountered anyone, man or woman, as stubborn.

She drew him to a halt at a crumbling archway on the edge of trader's square. Just beyond, fires cast wavering circles of light. Men moved between them, to the sounds of murmured conversation, as they went about the tasks of the evening meal and the last of the day's labors. Gareth smelled grease and spices, evocative of many such times since he'd left Thendara.

Rahelle shoved him against one of the columns. "Stay. Here."

While she revealed the whole story to Cyrillon? Gareth shook his head. He owed the older man his honesty at least. He was going to have to explain his departure when he retrieved his horses, for he couldn't very well take off for the Sands of the Sun on foot.

He pushed himself away from the coarse-grained brick.

"You don't listen, do you? Do you want everyone in five camps to know where you're going and why? No? Then let me handle this."

Caught between being astonished and relieved, Gareth mumbled his assent. She left him, slipping through the shadows and fire-lit circles. In her absence, confidence deserted him. She thought him a fool, arrogant and incompetent, a danger to those around him as well as to himself. Why would she help him with the most far-fetched scheme he'd come up with yet?

And yet there had been that other moment, the sense of her own yearning, the kinship of spirit between them, the wordless sympathy. Perhaps she did not understand him, for why should she, but *he* had understood *her*.

Rahelle returned so quickly, she must surely not have had time to relate his scheme, let alone debate its lack of merit with Cyrillon. She was leading two saddled horses, her own mount and Gareth's brown mare.

"The *oudrakhi* would have been better for desert travel," she said as she shoved the mare's reins into Gareth's hands, "but you'd fall off or get kicked where it hurts most, and then where would we be? At least you can ride a horse."

Gareth fumbled for the stirrup. As he swung his right leg over the mare's rump, he encountered the thickness of rolled blankets as well as the usual saddlebags. Waterskins sloshed gently. He settled himself, slipping his sheathed sword into its place.

He didn't understand why she was helping him. If he asked, she'd likely repeat what she'd already said about defending her father's honor. But if he, Gareth, rode off on his own in the dark of night and perished in the sands or in any of a dozen other ways, who could blame Cyrillon? Who would even know? Rahelle had some other reason, perhaps one more personal. *Rakhal* the apprentice might act only as the agent of his master, but *Rahelle*, the girl who'd declared, *"Do you think I wear chains?"* had her own dreams.

Rahelle had already mounted and was reining her horse in the direction of the deep desert. Gareth set aside his speculations.

"Where are we headed?"

"The hill country about three days' travel in the direction of Black Ridge," she answered, adding, "Korllen's people come from a village there."

The brown mare tossed her head, sending the bridle rings jingling, and pranced a few steps before Gareth settled her into an easy, long-strided walk.

"And then what?" It occurred to Gareth that he himself had had no thought beyond racing out in that general direction. For all he knew, Black Ridge was a vast, uninhabited wilderness.

"There are only a few villages out there, not all of them permanent. Wells dry up, and then the herdsmen move on. The smaller villages are as hospitable as they are able, but they do not welcome travelers when they have barely enough water for their own animals. Your story about an argument over watering rights could have taken place only in the larger settlements. That's where we'll look first."

They went slowly, the horses picking their way along the dried ocean bed. In places, the ground was so pale, it glowed faintly, although that could have been a reflection of the light of the moons. The hoofbeats of the horses sounded hollow. Gareth was glad when they passed out of such areas and onto muffling sand, even though they made slower progress.

Rahelle called a halt just as the first crimson streaks appeared in the eastern sky. Ahead, Gareth made out the contours of what might be gently rising hills or dunes of coarse sand. The air smelled different here, dry with dust but free of the tang of the seabed.

They gave the horses a little water from the skins and a few handfuls of grain as well. Gareth walked about, loosening his muscles. The dawn light brightened. Now he saw the hills were deeply weathered, eroded by wind and heat, etched by the occasional spring downpours. Mounds of grayish-purple brushwood dotted the slopes, denser in the blind ravines and coves that had formed as the earth had been worn away. They headed for one of these sheltered places.

Rahelle hobbled her horse after loosening the saddle girths. "Get some rest," she told Gareth, and went to gather fallen branches. Within a short time, she had built a little fire. She half-filled a battered trail cup, added a handful of something dark and crumbly, and set it in the middle of the fire. Gareth's mouth puckered at the pungent steam.

Rahelle wrapped her hand in her folded head scarf, picked up the cup and gulped down half of it. When she held out the cup, Gareth shook his head. He'd had enough foul-smelling tisanes on the road from Carthon.

"You must drink," she insisted. "It will strengthen your blood against the heat."

"I'm strong enough," Gareth said, bristling at the unscientific assertion.

"You have known only the climate of Carthon and Shainsa, both places with cool shade and water. Now we venture where sun and dryness, sand and wind, test even the stoutest heart." She paused, her eyes narrowing. "It's better when it's hot."

Gareth sighed and took a gulp. The bitter taste of the tea crawled up the back of his throat, but he forced it down. Rahelle had already begun putting out the fire.

The hills dipped and rose, as if the land itself were a beast that had grown weary and lain down to rest. At night, Rahelle prepared the tisane again, downing her own portion as well.

With the coming of the second full day, a wind arose. It ruffled the mare's mane and tugged at Gareth's headscarf. At first he welcomed it, but the dry, dust-laden currents soon became irritating, and both he and Rahelle covered all but a slit for their eyes. The horses clamped their tails to their rumps and plodded on, heads down.

When the sun hovered overhead, Rahelle found a copse of spindly, wind-twisted trees that offered a spattering of shade. With a little of their precious water, she moistened a cloth to wipe the horses' eyes and nostrils. Hobbling them to graze on what dried grasses they could find, she curled up beneath the largest of the trees, draped her headscarf over a twig set upright in the gravelly soil, and went to sleep.

Gareth imitated her as best he could. Although he had become accustomed to sleeping on the ground, he could not get comfortable. It was too hot, with the wind hissing and howling overhead. The game of playing the noble hero was over; he had never been Race Cargill, Terran Secret Agent, and now he must face the hot, gritty reality of a fruitless and foolhardy self-indulgence.

Somehow, between feeling heartily ashamed of his daydreams and trying to argue himself into ignoring his many physical discomforts, he must have drifted off. His eyes were sticky with dried secretions, and Rahelle was kneeling over him, poking his shoulder.

They gave the last of their water to the horses before mounting up. Although the heat seemed no less, the sun hung a hand's length lower in the west.

Tracks marked the lowest paths between the hills, none of them fresh. Spinning clouds of dust arose and as quickly blew into nothingness. Once or twice, Gareth spotted movement on the flattened heights, flashes of white and tan against the sun-crisped grasses. They were desert antelope, Rahelle told him, fleet and shy. No horse could catch them, although they could be trapped where they came to drink.

The trail rose, following the slope of the pass. The horses grunted with effort, heads lowered, slowing. They were thirsty as well as tired. Gareth swung down and took the reins of his mount. After an appraising look, Rahelle did the same. They trudged upward in silence, saving their breath for the climb. The air turned thin, more so than Gareth would have expected. As the sun dipped toward the west, it blazed even redder than before.

At last they reached the summit, a broad opening between two hummocks of wind-scoured rock. They paused to let the horses breathe. Before them, the hills fell away sharply into an expanse of rutted badlands, marked here and there with darker patches of vegetation.

"That's Kharsalla." Rahelle pointed, and Gareth made out a cluster of buildings, much the same shade of tan as the earth, as well as livestock pens and a few swaths of green that must be irrigated garden plots.

Before mounting up, Gareth glanced the way they had come, down the wrinkled, sloping hills to the seabed beyond. The slanting afternoon light tinted the land the color of blood-washed chalk.

He froze, his breath catching in his throat. In the heat-blurred distance, billows of dust shot into the air. The dust obscured what created it, but Gareth did not need to make out the party of fast-moving riders. By his best guess, they were at least a day behind, and that was not nearly far enough. Rahelle, perhaps responding to his silent alarm, stepped to his side.

"Will we have enough time?" he asked her.

"At that pace, they'll kill their horses before they reach the first watering-hole." She sniffed. "Look at the dust trail. They're headed south. They will bypass this village."

A handful of ragged herd-boys spotted them before they reached the outskirts of Kharsalla and accompanied them, whooping in delight at the arrival of strangers. By the time they passed the livestock pens, a half-dozen men and women had gathered to meet them, all chattering excitedly. Their lilting dialect was so oddly accented that Gareth comprehended only its general sense. The women wore bracelets and belts of brightly colored wool, tied by braided cords instead of the chains of city dwellers.

The first concern of the villagers, after recognizing "Rakhal Sensar," was that something might have befallen Korllen. Rahelle reassured them that he was well and prospering. The villager's relief turned instantly to expressions of hospitality, with no further inquiry as to her business.

Rahelle bowed to the headman, Rivoth, and presented Gareth as "a man of Carthon," as if that explained any eccentricity on his part. The headman himself could not have been more than forty, but his skin was weathered, his hair the color of salt stone, and his eyes so pale as to be almost colorless.

Within moments, Gareth and Rahelle were ushered through the village and into Rivoth's hut. The women stayed outside along with the boys, who had taken upon themselves the care of the horses. From their chatter and the way they touched the horses, the animals would become pampered pets within a quarter of an hour.

They settled on the dirt floor of the hut. The interior was dim and, by some trick of construction, surprisingly cool. Rivoth offered tea and smoke. Gareth did not need the sharp glance from Rahelle to know that it was unacceptable to refuse.

In silence, the headman prepared the smoking apparatus on an ancient metal frame over a small fire. When the smoke was bubbling through the dingy glass bowl, he passed it to Gareth. Gareth bowed as deeply as his cross-legged position would allow, placed the mouthpiece between his lips, and inhaled as he had seen Cyrillon do. Hot, stinging smoke filled his lungs. An almost overpowering urge to cough seized him. At that moment, however, he remembered the exercises Grandmother Linnea had drilled him in, the repetitive deep breathing, the single-minded focus. He closed his throat around the smoke and counted heartbeats.

Three . . . four . . .

The urge to cough receded. The smoke flowed smoothly through him. His vision sharpened, and he felt his pulse reverberating through his skull. He exhaled, nodded, and returned the pipe to his host.

The headman beamed in approval. He took another long drag and then removed the apparatus from its stand. Gareth gathered that this was a luxury to be enjoyed only upon special occasions and that the headman had honored him by it. He noticed that the headman did not include Rahelle; even as Cyrillon's agent, Rakhal was a boy, not a privileged guest.

One of the older women entered the hut and set down a wooden tray with two cups of dark, steaming liquid. She withdrew without a word.

Rivoth gestured that Gareth should select a cup and then took the other. The infusion was pleasantly bitter but unexpectedly soothing along Gareth's throat.

For the next few minutes, no one said anything. The headman closed his eyes, a beatific expression on his face, clearly savoring the effects of the smoke. In his garbled-sounding dialect, the headman addressed Gareth, obliquely creating an opening for Gareth to state his business. Gareth paused, pondering how to begin. Until that moment, he had expected Rahelle to negotiate for a guide. She, or rather her father, was the one with ties to this small community. But apparently apprentices had insignificant stature compared to exotic strangers.

"I am a lens merchant from Carthon." Gareth tried to stick to the truth as much as he could. "I heard a story in Carthon—men seeing bright flashes, out by Black Ridge, you understand? Lens can be used this way?" He gestured using a lens to reflect sunlight.

"Yes, yes!" The headman nodded vigorously. "Good sand to be found at Black Ridge! Good sand make good lens!"

"Maybe so. Or it could mean nothing." Gareth shrugged. "Others had heard this story, so I must find out the truth of it first."

"Ah." Eyes bright as bits of steel glinted in the weathered face. "You need guide and fast road through sands?"

"Yes, yes exactly!"

"Fast road. Safe road."

The headman clapped his hands twice, and a young man ducked into the hut. Gareth recognized him from the crowd that had greeted them.

"This Adahab, first son," the headman said.

Adahab touched the fingers of his right hand to belly, heart, and forehead. He listened solemnly while his father spoke, asked no questions, and offered no demurral. From his expression, he was being offered the highest honor in being chosen to guide the man of Carthon and Cyrillon's apprentice wherever they might choose to go. He maintained his composure until Rivoth dismissed him, then he backed out of the hut. A moment later, Gareth heard his uplifted voice crying, *"Tajari kihara! Emell-tajari kihara!"* and did not need a translator to understand that the prestige of the young man and his entire family had just received an enormous boost.

At Rivoth's insistence, they rested until sundown. The headman tried to offer them his own hut, but Gareth, seeing Rahelle shake her head, concocted an explanation that required them to remain with their horses. Within a short time, barely enough for Gareth to finish his excuses, the young people had constructed a shelter of sorts, open on two sides to admit the fitful breezes yet providing a modicum of shade. Their blankets had been unrolled at the other end, the gear stacked neatly at the foot of each. The horses were already tethered at one end and had clearly been watered and groomed. The mare's coat gleamed, and every mote of sand and dust had been polished from her saddle and bridle, yet not a single article of tack had been misplaced. The saddlebags and blanket roll, even the case containing the lens samples, were exactly as Gareth had left them.

Although he was sure he would not be able to sleep, Gareth stretched out on his blanket. The horses lipped at the few remaining kernels of the fodder that the children had laid down for them. A fly buzzed, and the mare snapped at her flank.

Idly, he thought of the riders from Shainsa. Even now they might be pushing on toward Black Ridge. He should not indulge this lassitude. Too much was at stake.

At his side, Rahelle murmured something and turned over without rousing. She was weary; he would let her sleep just a little longer.

Beneath the blanket, the earth radiated heat like the bricks of an oven. It seeped, gentle and relentless, into Gareth's muscles. His eyes closed. One of the horses blew softly through its nostrils, clearing the dust. In the distance, a baby cried until a woman began singing to comfort it.

"Garrin."

He sat up so suddenly that his senses whirled for a sickening moment. His skin felt gritty with dust and dried sweat. But it was cooler than when he'd fallen asleep.

Rahelle squatted, tying her blanket with deft movements. She flashed him a grin before carrying it to her saddled horse. The brown mare was loaded, ready to go except for the blanket on which Gareth lay. And Gareth himself.

"You shouldn't have let me sleep so long." Grumbling, he got to his feet. A headache pulsed in one temple, and his mouth felt as if he'd been chewing on chalk.

"Might as well," she said. "We weren't going anywhere. And there were appearances to maintain," meaning that she, as a mere apprentice, would be expected to prepare everything.

Outside, the crimson orb hung a hand's width above the line of the western hills. The sky to the east bore a faint indigo cast. A vitality infused the village, the shouts of children at play, the lowing of hungry animals, the air redolent with the smells of onions frying, of grain simmered with garlic and dried meat, and something pungent as wine.

It seemed the entire village had gathered to see them off. One of the older women held out a dish, pale wood polished to a sheen like an ocean shell, with thin pancakes wrapped around a mixture of shredded meat and eye-wateringly hot peppers. Following Rahelle's example, Gareth ate his portion and licked his fingers to demonstrate his enjoyment. The woman blushed, bowed, and scurried away.

Adahab had already saddled his own mount, a gray *oudrakhi* so gnarled and decrepit in appearance, it looked as if it could not walk from one end of the village to the other. He led a second beast on a rope halter, this one laden with cloth-wrapped bundles and leather sacks that bulged and sloshed.

Gareth accepted the brown mare's reins from the small, tousle-haired boy who looked up at him with wondering cerulean eyes. An impulse stirred, the kind of spontaneous urge to action he was beginning to trust. He untied the lens case. As he peered inside, it occurred to him that its contents represented more than the worth of the entire village and all its herds and pastures. He selected two lenses of moderate quality, suitable for simple telescopes, the sort that might be useful in a place as remote as this, and handed the case to Rahelle to secure once more to his saddle. She flashed him a smile.

When Gareth placed the lenses in Rivoth's hands, the older man stared at them. The children murmured among themselves. One or two ran to the women, who sent up a ripple of cries like birds penned and then set free all at once.

Rivoth's stillness made Gareth feel uneasy. Had he erred in the gift? Were the lenses too costly or too paltry? Had he in his ignorance presumed that these unsophisticated people would have the slightest notion what to do with the bits of polished glass? He had no way to tell.

Yet Rahelle had *smiled.*

At last the headman looked up. His eyes, that washed-out blue, seemed to have too much white in them. He lifted the lenses to his lips, his face once more falling into shadow. Then Gareth understood the magnitude of what he had given. The monetary value of the lenses was nothing compared to what they would bring to the life of the village—a way to see across distances, to receive advance warning of storms and raiders. A way to save precious lives.

They set off in the twilight, a climb into the darkening hills and then a brief descent as crumbling earth gave way to sand. Adahab took the lead, as confident as if it were full day. The horses followed, stepping in the hollows made by the broad padded feet of the *oudrakhi.* Here and there, rocks jutted upward, dark jagged prominences against the paler sand. A fanciful notion seized Gareth, that they were treading a thin and treacherous crust over a vast range of mountains, of which only the highest peaks could be seen. At any moment, the crust might give way, and they would plunge to their deaths.

He looked up, turning his face to the coolness of a stray breeze. A wash of multihued light, shading from mauve to silver, suffused the sky. As he watched, the light dimmed in the fall of night that had given Darkover its name. Piercing bright in the dry desert air, a thousand pinpoint stars flared. For an instant, Gareth saw them as individual stars, yet too numerous to count. Then they blurred into a vast milky veil. He understood intellectually that from Darkover's position he was seeing the galactic arm side-on, but it seemed to him that the heavens teemed with light. Farther than any human eye could see, a thousand thousand suns filled the night with cold eternal fire. Even the two moons, one a slender crescent, could not outshine the mass of stars. The sight of them left him breathless. The stars glittered, but whether solely with their own light or as seen through his sudden tears, he could not tell. He thought, *This will remain when I am dead.*

"Garrin?" came Rahelle's voice, sweet as starlight.

He tore his gaze from the glory overhead. "I'm well, just . . ." Where were the words to describe the moment of awe and humility? ". . . astonished."

"I, too, never tire of the night sky. In Carthon, there is too much moisture in the air to see it properly." She was quiet for a moment.

Around them, the glimmering sands stretched as far as Gareth could see. It muffled the sounds of the horses' hooves.

"I suppose that the gods did not want us to weary of such a gift," Rahelle said, "so they set it out here, where only the most hardy men venture."

"Or the most desperate." It was a facile comment, unworthy of the fading awe. "I might have lived my whole life without seeing it."

"Every land has its own beauty. I have seen only a little of yours, just Thendara and the road to Carthon."

She sounded wistful, and Gareth wondered what she longed to see: the never-melting glacial ice of the Hellers, the lush country around Lake Mariposa, the rich Plains of Valeron, the Temora sea coast, perhaps his own family's home at Elhalyn Castle. He thought of all the places he had been and those he had never seen, and an unfamiliar pang shot through his breast.

Let me take you there! Let us explore those places together! Why would he even think such a thing, let alone offer it to a woman who by her own admission faced no future beyond a marriage in chains? If he survived this adventure, his own destiny was perhaps more luxurious but no less confined.

They continued at a pace the horses could sustain, more slowly than they had traveled on hard ground. Although Gareth discerned no landmarks, Adahab seemed to know exactly where he was going. Perhaps he used one or another of the constellations as guidance.

The temperature fell, and Gareth and Rahelle wrapped themselves in their cloaks. In the lead, Adahab and his *oudrakhis* formed dark, ungainly silhouettes against the star-studded horizon. They trudged on in near silence except for the hiss of dislodged sand and the occasional snort of the horses clearing their nostrils.

After some hours, Adahab halted in order to water the horses from the leather sacks. Gareth had not realized how thirsty he was until he smelled the water.

"Drink," Adahab urged. "We ride through the night. Sleep in the day."

Imperceptibly, the dimmer stars faded from the eastern sky until only the brightest remained. One of the smaller moons was setting. They had traveled all night through starlight and sand.

Adahab brought the *oudrakhi* to a standstill in a valley formed by dunes to either side. The horses halted, their heads low. Gareth sagged in the saddle. Behind him, Rahelle said nothing. The light was strong enough now that Gareth could make out Adahab's expression, the lift and tilt of his head, the quick flare of his nostrils as if casting for a scent. Gareth smelled nothing beyond dry air, dust, and the bodies of the animals. Then their guide gestured, pointing off to one side. They kept to the lowest route, and within a short time they emerged from between the wind-heaped dunes into a grove of lace-branched trees.

Moist air swept through Gareth's senses. A moment past, he had been surrounded by the rolling dunes, without any clue this little oasis existed. Tucked between the dunes, it would surely be hidden from anyone who did not know its location. A man might ride by and not realize it was there.

At the heart of the grove, shade pooled around a stone well that was so broken and weathered, Gareth could not guess its age. Off to one side sat a shrine of similar antiquity. Gareth was not surprised to see the eroded emblem of Nebran. On the sand before the altar lay a tattered ribbon, bleached colorless, wrapped around a few withered stalks.

Adahab tapped the *oudrakhi's* shoulder. When the great beast halted, grumbling a protest, he jumped lightly to the sand. He knelt before the shrine, touched his fingertips to his forehead, then to his lips and again to the emblem, leaving behind a smear of moisture. It was, Gareth realized, as much an act of faith as of reverence, faith that the precious water would be restored, that life would continue even through the most desperate times. Without thinking, he curled his fingers around the amulet Grandmother Linnea had given to him, the locket that enclosed the starstone that was like a second heart, the touchstone of his *laran*. Moved without understanding, he slipped from the mare's saddle and repeated the ritual. When he straightened up, he saw Rahelle watching him intently.

Adahab clapped Gareth on the shoulder. "Now we drink. Horses first, then men, then," with a sniff, "*oudrakhi*." By his tone, he implied that the ill-tempered beasts required regular reminders of their place in the world. "Then eat. *Then* sleep."

The water was cool and surprisingly good; the metallic edge added to its refreshing character. Gareth would have traded the finest *firi* imported from Vainwal for a single goblet from this well.

The hypnotic peace of the night journey faded with the coming of full sun. After the animals had been tended, Gareth sat hunched over a cup of Rahelle's foul-smelling brew. He could not shake the feeling that across the expanse of sand, catastrophe loomed ever nearer. He should be doing something . . . planning an ambush for Dayan's men, figuring out exactly how he would locate the Federation agents and what he would say to them, how he would convince them not to have anything to do with the Dry Towns . . .

"You are troubled." Adahab softly interrupted Gareth's rumination. With a jerk of his chin, he indicated the way they had come.

Gareth nodded and downed the last of the tisane, barely tasting it.

"Shainsa*'imyn*!" Adahab gestured with his left hand in a way Gareth gathered was extremely derogatory.

It took Gareth a moment to understand Adahab's meaning, that just as there were conflicts and differences between Domains and between city and country folk, these villagers who lived under the harshest conditions scorned the city dwellers, or at least the great lords.

"They think themselves masters of the sand but know nothing of the true desert," Adahab said.

"I would not dismiss them lightly," Gareth said. "They may not be as wise as your people in the ways of these dry lands, but they have weapons and know how to use them."

"Swords and whips, the tools of the *kifurgh*—what are they against sun and open sand? Can they force water from stone? Or friendship from the village tribes?"

"Yet your people helped us at the request of Cyrillon, and he is a man of Carthon."

"Cyrillon is a trader, yes, but throughout the Sands of the Sun, he is also known as a man of honor and a true friend. He pays his debts, unlike the Shainsa*'imyn*, who take what is not for sale." He lowered his voice, glancing surreptitiously at Rahelle, who had busied herself scouring the dishes with sand and then wiping them with a cloth. "Water, goats . . . children. Where do you think the slave markets in Ardcarran get them? My cousin," meaning Korllen, "brings the money Cyrillon pays him. And we in turn pay off the raiders who would take our little ones."

Gareth met Adahab's fierce blue gaze. If Dayan's men did arrive in the village, they would receive a polite welcome but not a hint that Rivoth had seen, let alone given aid to, two travelers. Nor, Gareth suspected, would any of the other villages on the border of the Sands of the Sun. They would take special pride in deceiving the intruders. He wondered if the Federation agents, whom he remembered as arrogant and closed-minded, would fare any better.

For four nights they traversed the sands, arriving each dawn at a hidden oasis. One was nearly dry, another befouled by the twisted, desiccated carcass of a small wild *oudrakhi*, or what the desert *kyorebni* had left of it. They drank and watered the animals from the contents of their leather sacks and rested as best they could in the shade.

On the sixth day, the first light revealed the land rising into a series of ridges. Gareth was no geologist, but the stone looked as if it had once been a volcanic flow, rare on Darkover, that over uncounted millennia had bleached to the color of ashes. Along the base of the ridges, dark green clusters gathered like beads on a string. A haze blurred their outlines. He reckoned there to be a half dozen such oases, some no more than a few scrub bushes, others the size of villages.

"Nuriya." Adahab pointed to one of the larger spots, filling a gap in the ridge. He clapped his heels to the sides of his *oudrakhi*. Without a protest, the decrepit-looking beast quickened its pace. The horses, too, seemed eager to press on, although they had traveled many miles that night. They must smell water and fresh forage ahead.

Gareth nodded to Rahelle as she reined her horse beside his. She gave him a tentative smile. "Nuriya, I take it, is the name of that village," he said. "Do you know it?"

"Only by name. I've never been farther than Kharsalla. That's as deep into the desert as my fa—as Cyrillon ventures, and then only for Korllen's sake."

"I think they owe a great deal to Cyrillon. He is an extraordinary man."

"He has always revered the virtue of charity. We in the Dry Towns speak of the compassion of Nebran, but we do not practice it overmuch." Absently, she transferred the reins to one hand and rubbed her wrist with the other. "*Kihar* is for men, so kindliness is left for the gods."

"And justice? And compassion?"

"These things can be sought, but are they to be found in the world of men? Or is it folly to even try? My father believes we must, but what can he do? Give a little alms here and there, employ a desert man who sends his pay home to his family? Send bits of information, tales and half-truths, to Thendara? What good does that do?"

In her voice, Gareth heard the resonances of outrage, of desperation. *What of the children taken from their homes to be scullions and playthings?*

she seemed to ask. *What of the people left broken and starving so that great lords like Dayan or Evallar of Ardcarran can live in luxury?*

And I, he asked himself, *I who have never known anything but privilege and ease, I who have done nothing to earn it, what is my part in all this?*

The answer lay before him, shimmering slightly as the risen sun heated the sand.

"Is justice to be had?" he said aloud. "I do not know, but if we do not try, it will not happen."

"And you are the one to do it?"

For that, he had no answer.

As they neared Nuriya, Gareth noticed bright pennons rippling from poles and a team of men unloading lengths of milled wood from *oudrakhi.* They dismounted and led their beasts to a watering hole with a painted emblem indicating it was for animals only. A man, as weathered and wind-burned as any desert dweller, was watering a pair of *oudrakhi,* their saddles gleaming and clearly new, their halters bedecked with gaudy tassels and bits of faceted colored glass. He grinned at them in a friendly manner, revealing a gap between his discolored teeth.

When the *oudrakhi* drover led his beasts away, Rahelle edged up to Gareth, pretending to adjust the girth on the roan. "Where would villagers this far out get the money for saddles and banners, not to mention wood?"

"There's new wealth here, that's sure," he murmured in reply.

Adahab's gaze flickered over the same unusual details. "Come, my friends. If your horses have finished, let us go and drink. Then I will introduce you to the headman . . . if he still is headman here."

Gareth and Rahelle followed him to the stone well designated for human use. A handful of children and a couple of women surrounded it, dipping out jars of water. The children were thin and round-bellied, clad in knee-length shirts worn to the color of mud. They darted away as Gareth and the others approached, eyes huge in their pinched faces. One of the women was gray haired and bent, and the cords attached to her wrists were so frayed, they looked as if the merest tug would snap them. The second woman, barely out of her teens, tossed her head and glared at the new arrivals. Her cheeks gleamed as if her face had been oiled. With insolent languor, she balanced her jar against one hip. Water sloshed over the copper-inlaid rim. As she strode away, her chains clashed as they slipped through the ring on her metal-link belt.

Adahab took out his cup and offered it to Gareth. The water was cool enough, but the now familiar acrid tinge rankled. Whatever was going on in this village did not lessen the plight of those most in need.

They passed into the open square at the heart of the village, where Adahab stopped in front of a hut. It was larger and looked to be of better construction than many of the others, although there were no signs of repairs.

"The headman here is Cuinn," Adahab told Gareth. "He knew my father long ago, but they have not had any dealings since before I was born. Still, loyalty and mutual obligation endure long in the desert."

A man emerged, spare in frame but with an air of authority. His hair had a dull sheen that suggested it had been bright as polished gold in his youth, before the years had darkened it. The skin around his eyes tightened when he spied the strangers.

Adahab presented greetings from his father. As the headman listened, his features relaxed, reflecting an innate good humor. "Yes, yes, by Lhupan the Compassionate, who walks the sands in a stranger's guise, we open our guest dwelling to you."

Gareth made a gesture of respect. "The generosity of your people is an ornament to the heavens."

"Hospitality is ordained by the gods as a blessing to those who give as well as those who receive."

They exchanged a few more salutations along those lines, and then Cuinn himself conducted Adahab and his party to the guest dwelling. This turned out to be a hut of sun-baked bricks much like the others, providing protection against sun and wind. Adjacent to it was a pen and shed for livestock, both quite dilapidated.

The interior of the hut consisted of a single room with a dirt floor. There was no means of heat or cooking, except for a circle of blackened stones outside the door. Once Gareth would have scorned such accommodations as being unworthy of even a donkey, but now, when he expressed his thanks to Cuinn, the depth of his own gratitude surprised him. Such a village, existing on the very margins of civilization, had devoted a portion of its scant resources to maintaining a shelter for the needs of strangers.

Once they had unloaded the horses and brought the blankets and saddlebags into the hut, Adahab turned to Gareth. "My friend, here I take my leave of you. I shall return in five days to guide you back across the Sands of the Sun, unless you send word to me at Duruhl-ya that I am needed later. Or sooner."

Startled, Gareth returned the gesture of leave-taking. He could not mistake the glint of eagerness in Adahab's eyes as the younger man swept from the hut. A moment later, Adahab mounted his decrepit gray *oudrakhi* and kicked the animal into a reluctant trot.

"I take it Duruhl-ya is a neighboring village," Gareth asked Rahelle, who was arranging their bedding on either side of the hut.

"Yes. The name means 'unfailing dew.'" Rahelle did not look up. "I think he is courting a woman there."

The hut suddenly seemed too small. Although they had shared a campsite many times on the trail, sleeping within the same walls carried a new degree of intimacy. Anxious to break the tension, Gareth suggested that they begin their search by touring the village. Maybe they'd hear something about the water seller story.

Surrounded by a cortege of curious children, they strolled through the village. Women sat under awnings in front of their huts, weaving or pounding grain. Some had the same shy curiosity as the children, but others were narrow-eyed. All wore some form of chains.

They had almost completed a circuit of the village when a party of riders approached from the direction of the Sands of the Sun.

"Yi-yi-yi!" came their ululating cry.

The children ran up, shrieking with excitement. The leader rode a horse so scrubby and stunted, it was barely the size of a *chervine.* The carcass of an animal was slung across the horse's withers. Gareth had seen that white and tan pattern, although from afar. This must be a desert antelope.

"No horse can catch them," Rahelle had said.

The lead rider laughed, wheeling his horse to show off his prize. The legs of the antelope flopped against the horse's shoulders. The sun gleamed on its hide, except for the swath across its forequarters, where the skin was raw and blackened.

Gareth had seen injuries like those, but never in real life. Tri-vid tapes from the Federation Headquarters, the ones *Tío* Danilo had insisted he watch, had pictured just such wounds.

The rider reached into his sash and held an object overhead—a short handle, a blunt but unmistakable barrel. Sun glinted on polished durasteel.

A blaster.

16

What in the name of all the gods was the Federation thinking? Had they completely abandoned the Compact? Or did Sandra Nagy and her Expansionist Party intend to leave behind all respect for local law and custom?

It is ill done to chain a dragon to roast your meat, ran the old proverb.

As ill done as to give devices of such destructive power to those who had no tradition or training in their wise use.

The smell of the charred flesh filled Gareth's nostrils. The blast had scorched the antelope's bones. He felt the utter chill where its life spark had been. It had been extinguished so quickly, yet in such a conflagration of searing pain, that the instant of agony lingered still.

Gareth had assumed, had come prepared to confirm, that the Federation had been careless in its display of its weaponry. It had not occurred to him that carelessness might extend so far as to give those same armaments to the villagers.

"I must speak with Cuinn immediately," Gareth said to Rahelle. "He must know where the Federation landed, where the blasters came from."

"He will not tell you." She sounded utterly certain. When he gave her a questioning look, she curled her lip. "You? A stranger from Carthon? Look at this place! Can't you see the link between these *Terranan* devices and the recent improvements? Why would these people share the source of their wealth?"

"If they will not tell me freely, they will find Lord Dayan's men far less understanding."

The rider with the antelope moved off toward the center of the village. The sounds of celebration receded.

"Men can be violent," Rahelle agreed, "but not as harsh as the desert these people battle every day of their lives."

Images flashed across Gareth's mind—men in sand-pale rags scrambling over dunes . . . an eruption of dust rising so high it blanketed the crimson sun . . . sand melting like wax, fusing into sheets of opalescent glass as far as the eye could trace . . . the village going up in plumes of greasy smoke, the hills melting into piles of cinder-dark slag. . . .

He blinked, and the pictures dissolved. Around him lay a living village, huts and goats and children, looms and firepits.

"Then I'll have to persuade them," he said.

Cuinn listened, his face impassive, as Gareth presented his case. "Lord Dayan's men are only a day or two behind us," Gareth concluded. "They want these weapons, and they mean to seize them if necessary. For this reason alone they have crossed the Sands of the Sun."

Cuinn's expression was even more guarded than before. "We are not afraid of them."

You should be! Gareth thought, but held back the words.

"Perhaps it is you and not the sun-weapons that put Nuriya in danger," Cuinn added darkly.

"I did not lead Lord Dayan's men here!" Gareth said so hotly that Rahelle put out a restraining hand, as no apprentice boy would dare to do.

"If they come, we will deal with them." Cuinn added in a less belligerent tone, "You meant well by your warning, man of Carthon. Your intentions are honorable, even if you have little understanding of the desert and the strength of its people. We are not easily deceived," he used the phrase that implied *cheated in contests of wit and wiles.*

Cuinn's gaze flickered to the hills, then returned to Gareth. "Be at ease with us tonight. The law of guest hospitality still holds in these lands. Tomorrow you had best return to where you belong, since you find these men of Shainsa so intimidating."

Gareth knew when he had been summarily dismissed. He bowed, touching his fist to his belly, heart, and forehead, and withdrew. Rahelle followed closely. When they were out of earshot, he turned to her. "Any idea what to do now?"

"It would be unwise to attempt to go back across the Sands of the Sun without Adahab to guide us, and he said he would not return for another five days. We should make our way to one of the other villages and find out if they too have these *Terranan* weapons."

Rahelle's practicality made sense, but Gareth felt a tremendous resistance to moving on. There might or might not be Federation weapons elsewhere, but he knew for certain such devices were here.

Cuinn had glanced up at the hills, no more than a tiny jerk of his eyes, but enough to betray his thoughts. For all his confident words, the headman had looked worried.

The Federation base is up there, Gareth thought. And he had a single night to find it.

After the men finished skinning and preparing the antelope carcass, removing certain veins and tendons according to custom, the women rubbed the meat with spices and set it in a stone-lined pit. The roasting was accompanied by a frenzy of preparation, chopping and soaking and grinding and mixing, all of it unfamiliar to Gareth. He didn't recognize any of the dishes. If Rahelle did, she said nothing as they took their places with the other men in the wide circle.

The women carried out the roasted meat, carved into thick slices and surrounded by mounds of dark dried fruit, some kind of slimy-looking vegetable paste, and balls of sticky boiled grain. They laid the platters on the ground and took their places behind the men. The circle fell silent. With painful slowness, an elderly man rose to his feet, assisted by two youths. He raised his voice, and in a dialect so archaic that Gareth could barely understand it, chanted a prayer of thanksgiving.

Cuinn signaled for the meal to begin. Around the circle, groups of five or six men clustered around each platter. Cuinn and the other villagers took out their own personal knives to slice off slivers of meat. Gareth followed their example. Placing a morsel of antelope meat in his mouth, he found it tough but intensely flavorful. The balls of grain were firm enough to be easily picked up, but the vegetables were too spicy for comfort.

About halfway through the meal, Cuinn stood up and began a song-chant, deftly improvised around a fixed structure. In it, he extolled the virtues of the hunters and their prowess at arms. Hoots of approval from the audience punctuated his delivery. With each repetition of the refrain, the villagers roared even more enthusiastically.

"We are the men of the sun, of the sand!
Red is the dawn, and red the river!
Our strength is a knife honed by drought and storm!
Like the god of the well, we will rise again!"

Red the river . . . red the blood of their enemies . . . Gareth did not like the sound of that at all. *The god of the well* must be Nebran. Toads were said to survive dry seasons by burrowing beneath the mud. The rest of the verse needed no translation.

The celebration turned increasingly raucous after the women withdrew. The feasters passed round-bellied skins around the circle. When one came to Gareth, he lifted it to his lips before he caught Rahelle's expression of warning. He tipped it back, pretending to drink. Enough remained on his lips, burning like liquid fire, to convince him of the drink's potency.

In his years at court, Gareth had perfected the appearance of drunkenness. He knew he had little head for anything stronger than ale or watered wine. He also knew that men like Octavien Vallonde deliberately plied him with much stronger liquors in order to render him more malleable. Surreptitiously, he glanced around the circle to see how the others responded to the drink. In this way, he noticed he was not the only one who lifted the skin with every appearance of enjoyment but did not swallow. The other man was Cuinn.

The villager who'd carried back the antelope showed no such restraint. His face flushed in the reflected glow of the fire. Every few moments, he or one of his friends burst out in coarse laughter, shouting out bits of tales and jokes. Someone would begin a song and others would join in for a verse or two, usually a variant of the victory song.

Every aspect of the feast showed Gareth how poor these villagers were, how marginal and precarious their existence. They lived surrounded by potential catastrophe. A season without rain, a well that failed, predators that decimated their flocks, raiders or disease—any of these things would mean the end of their tiny community. No wonder they celebrated the rare bounty of the hunt with such intense abandon. No wonder Cuinn would not speak of the blasters, for fear of losing their tenuous advantage.

"Sing for us, man of Carthon!" one of the men called.

"My songs are too poor for such an occasion," Gareth protested.

"A song!" the others shouted. "A song to praise our brave hunters!"

"A tribute to the *kihar* and prowess of all Nuriya!"

"Nuriya, Jewel of the Sands!"

Gareth let them go on in this manner while he racked his brains for a suitable song. He had a fairly good voice, but most of what he knew was in *casta*, the language of the Comyn. The respite paid off, for he remembered several of the ditties sung by Cyrillon's men on the road to Carthon. The melodies were strong and simple, the words a patois of Dry Towns dialect and *cahuenga*, and the subjects frankly bawdy. Such songs would never be performed for the Elhalyn Prince. His parents would have been scandalized, and so he had been delighted.

He performed three of them, slurring his voice and making up nonsense syllables when he could not remember the exact phrases. With any luck, he'd sound like a drunken stranger from far-off Carthon. As he'd hoped, his singing elicited generalized merriment, both at what the men could understand of the lyrics and at his own bumbling rendition.

By this time, the women had come back and taken away the remains of the food, most likely to share it among themselves. A few of the men staggered away from the circle, but most of them remained, drinking and singing, and telling stories.

One of those who left, quietly and unobtrusively, was Cuinn. Gareth marked the direction the headman took. He waited for a moment when he could follow without being noticed. Luck was with him, for two or three of the village men began a dance outside the circle on the side opposite from where Gareth sat. Kicking and whirling, staggering and howling in laughter, the dancers drew all other eyes to them. The audience called out encouragement as each dancer strove to outdo the others.

Gareth crawled backward away from the circle. Once past the circle of firelight, he stood up and threaded his way between the clusters of huts. There was no sign of Cuinn. Gareth hurried, caught by a sudden fear that he'd lost his quarry. His own footsteps, leather over bare soil, sounded overly loud.

At the base of the nearest hill, Gareth halted. What if he'd made a mistake and Cuinn had taken some other route? Or been about some perfect ordinary business within the village?

Then I will have to go on alone. It would be insane to wander into those hills at night. The chance of stumbling on the Federation base was slim, especially compared to the risk of some mishap, a fall most certainly, or an encounter with a predator. He didn't know what kind of beast might hunt here, but the antelope must have natural enemies besides the villagers.

Behind him, a pebble rolled over hard dirt. It was the faintest sound, one that Gareth might not have heard, had he not been straining for any sign of the headman. He froze, not daring to breathe. The sound had come from behind him, but how far? In what direction?

Laughter erupted from the celebrants around the fire. Whoever was following Gareth might advance another step or three, the sound masked by cheering. Ordinary senses were useless. Gareth slipped his starstone from the Nebran amulet and reached out with his *laran.*

The village took on a completely different appearance. Pinpoints and globes of living energy flared, most likely mice and sleeping children and beasts in their pens. The bonfire of activity behind him must be the circle. He probed the motes of brilliance, separating human from animal, animal from the dying embers of harvested plants. The villagers gave off only the unfocused mental chatter and emotional surges of those without *laran*, but behind him . . . like the single ringing of a bell, sweet sound and color and the smell of a meadow after a storm . . . a flicker of warmth . . .

He knew her. He would have known her anywhere.

"There!" Rahelle whispered, so close that her breath touched his cheek.

Slipping the starstone back into the locket, he looked where she pointed. Shadows wavered, dark shifting upon dark, in a fold of the hills.

There was no use trying to convince Rahelle to stay behind. He thought of a dozen reasons why it was too dangerous, knowing she would interpret them all as insults. The truth was that he could not stop her. The harder truth was that without her keen sight, he would not have noticed the man-sized flicker of movement against the hills. So they went on together. He tried not to think what might happen, tried not to see her as Rahelle but as Rakhal, tough and resourceful.

They had not gone far into the hills, following the erosion gullies, when the village passed out of sight behind them. The trail led steeply upward, cradled between the jutting ridges. Fortunately, the night was clear and the skies unclouded. Once or twice, Gareth heard a cry from above, most likely a desert owl.

The hills were not entirely bare, as they had appeared from a distance. Curling grasses lined the trail to either side. Things rustled in their dried stalks, perhaps the natural prey of the hunter aloft. The smell of the earth shifted as they climbed, here and there hinting of moisture, of things still green, of the honey-musk of ripe seed-heads.

The moons set, casting the ash-dark hills into near darkness. Only a few stars glimmered in the west, while from beyond the eastern ridge, a faint intimation of light tainted the sky.

Gareth tripped over an unseen obstacle, most likely a rock, caught himself, and kept going. One foot and then the next, he climbed. Climbed and stumbled, stumbled and climbed, until he realized with a start that he could see his feet.

At last they came to a crest, a flat place before the trail dipped downward. Dawn, red and oblique, sifted into a wide valley floor ringed by sharply rising walls. Much of it was hidden by the outcropping below. There was no sign of the village headman.

Gareth took in the sight, his thoughts racing. His first impression was of a crater, although as far as he knew, Darkover had no significant volcanic activity. It might as well be a natural formation, weathered by the passing of many seasons in such a way as to now appear like an enormous bowl.

They started down the trail, slipping on the loose pebbles, until they came around a shoulder of splintered rock. Below them, the basin now looked broad and flat. Shadows stretched from the eastern rim except where, not too far distant from the wall on which they stood, strings of yellow lights glared from poles. A field of actinic brightness surrounded arch-roofed buildings, sheds, and tall stacks of crates. . . and what surely must be the smallest, ugliest starship in creation.

No distinctive insignia marked the craft, at least none that Gareth could see. Its outer surfaces looked dull, in places blackened or deeply scored, as if it had been raked by the claws of a celestial predator. It squatted in the middle of an irregular patch of fused sand.

Like most others of his caste and generation, Gareth had gone through a spasm of space fever. He'd visited the Thendara spaceport, properly supervised of course, and watched the great Federation ships take off. On one memorable occasion, he and his escort had been permitted on board. The captain had given him a sheaf of beautifully rendered images of the various types of craft capable of planetary landings. Although that had been some years before the Federation withdrew from Darkover, Gareth remembered their sleek, functional lines and impeccable maintenance.

This craft hardly looked big enough for a crew, let alone any cargo. It reminded Gareth of one of those short-coupled, muscular horses of the Valeron Plains that could turn on a spot no bigger than the span of his hand, and launch itself from standing to a full-out gallop within a single stride.

Quick. Agile. And, by the look of it, without the luxury of tending to appearances.

A few men moved between the crates, the buildings, and the opposite side of the ship, where the hatch must be located. None of them wore uniforms.

Rahelle murmured under her breath, "So you were right about the Federation landing here."

He found his voice. "That's no Federation ship."

"What is it, then?"

"I don't know. I need to get closer."

"*We*."

Argument would have been useless. He closed his eyes, prayed for patience, and said nothing.

Rahelle touched his arm and pointed below, drawing his attention to the trail and the places where rough protrusions of rock provided cover. They would still be exposed from time to time, but chances were good the off-worlders would not look in the right place at the right time to see them.

To go any farther would entail a criminally irresponsible risk. He ought to return the way they'd come, race back to Nuriya, locate Adahab, and get himself back to Thendara. He ought to be anywhere but here.

Although Rahelle posed a dilemma, her presence steadied him. She held herself so still, hardly breathing, and yet in his mind, she was like one of the oases they had passed across the Sands of the Sun. At the very edge of his mental awareness, he sensed the steady beating of her heart, the glow that was her spirit. He remembered staring up at the swath of stars on clear nights, and if he held his gaze very steady, he could just barely discern the pale wisps of distant galaxies. The instant he looked directly at them, they vanished from his sight. His *laran* perception of Rahelle was like that. He dared not look directly at her for fear that she, like those glorious, unreachable stars, would vanish.

Instead, he reached out a hand, bone and blood, nerve and sinew. He touched small, strong fingers, and felt them tighten around his own.

He went down, crouched and gliding, to the first of the outcrops. She followed like his shadow. Here they paused, studying the men at their work below.

After another step and then another, voices sounded below, indistinct. Gareth thought the men spoke Terran Standard, but he could not make out the words. He was gathering himself to slip down to the next lookout point when three men emerged from behind a piece of landing apparatus shaped like a stubby paddle. Two of them were clearly off-worlder, and both wore one-piece, dark brown garments. One was unremarkable in stature, but the other resembled a bloated spider with spindly, elongated legs and massive shoulders. The blue-tinted pattern over his hairless skull might have been a fuzz of hair or a tattoo.

The third man was Cuinn.

By his posture, the headman was not at all pleased with the conversation. He accompanied his words with a gesture that indicated an urgency, a matter of *kihar*. The thin-legged man gave no sign he'd understood either words or hand movements. He turned to his fellow, who consulted a palm-sized instrument, perhaps a dictionary or translation device. Gareth had heard about such things from Lew Alton's friend Jeram, who had once fought with the *Terranan* and then stayed behind when they left.

The discussion went on for some minutes more. Cuinn grew visibly more agitated, yet the off-worlders seemed as oblivious or as uncaring as before.

What were they saying? Gareth itched with curiosity. He considered and as quickly discarded the notion of using his starstone. Rahelle would demand an explanation, and he doubted that even with the gem's capacity to amplify psychic energy, he would be able to pick up much of value. Cuinn might not be a city Dry Towner, but his people must have sprung from the same roots, and no one had ever reported them having any *laran.* The only reason Rahelle had even a trace of psychic ability was through her paternal Domains ancestry.

As for the off-worlders . . . Watching the casual arrogance of their stance and the way they persistently ignored the increasing intensity of Cuinn's demands, Gareth was not at all sure he *wanted* to sense their thoughts.

Cuinn reached into the front folds of his tunic. Gareth's muscles tightened reflexively. His body recognized, if his mind did not yet, the shift from words to action. An instant later, two more off-worlders stepped from behind the landing apparatus to flank their leader. One wore the same dark-brown garment, but the other was dressed in trousers and sleeveless vest, both bulging with pockets. Wide belts of some glossy material circled their waists, and from these hung a variety of what Gareth assumed were tools . . . except for the blasters beside their right hands. Clearly, they expected trouble.

The village headman paused. The off-world leader barked out something in Terran Standard. Cuinn reached into the folds of his shirt and drew out a blaster. He moved slowly, holding it muzzle downward. With his other hand, he pointed to the chief off-worlder, then to the weapon, and finally back toward the hills where Gareth and Rahelle crouched.

He can't know we're here, Gareth told himself. *He must mean the village.*

The guards shifted ominously. Gareth could almost see the way their eyes narrowed and smell the adrenaline in the air. One of them curled the fingers of his right hand around the handle of his blaster.

The off-worlder conferred with his interpreter. Cuinn repeated his gestures, this time emphasizing them with a step toward the hill, then turning to point again at his blaster and that of the two guards.

Blasters. He's got one, and he wants more.

Rahelle's fingers tightened around Gareth's arm. He dared not speak aloud.

The translator consulted his device again. His voice was too low for Gareth to catch any more than a muted rumble. Then the leader turned to face Cuinn. Head high and spine rigid, the villager held his ground.

The off-worlder no longer looked vaguely comical, but as eerie as a gigantic scorpion-ant and as deadly. He took his time replying, and when he spoke, it was with a few words only.

Gareth needed no *laran* to sense Cuinn's answer, delivered as much in the single step he took toward the leader as any verbal outburst. Did this off-worlder not realize he was driving a man of pride and dignity, perhaps the only things of value Cuinn possessed, to the brink? Or did he simply not care?

Rahelle saw it, too. She cursed softly under her breath.

A stillness like the shadow beneath a storm front spread across the scene below. The off-world leader tilted his head, a movement so slight and so compelling, it fractured the quiet. Moving with catman-like speed, the two guards bracketed Cuinn. The next instant, one had relieved the headman of his blaster and the second stood ready to restrain him.

Whatever these strangers might be, Cuinn was no fool. He remained still, a statue of frost and flame. In Gareth's imagination, the air around Cuinn shimmered with his outrage.

The off-world leader was speaking again, more rapidly now, and gesturing, although in an unfamiliar pattern. He sounded to Gareth like a courtier making a speech, but one that conveyed the threat of power and the will to use it, not idle mouthing of words.

Cuinn was no underling to be cowed by a show of strength. Anyone who understood even a little of the customs of the Dry Towns would have known better than to try intimidation. Gareth would not have been surprised if Cuinn had hurled himself at the off-worlder, armed only with his own teeth.

Cuinn made no such move. Wiliness and the slow nurturing of revenge were said to be highly prized by the Dry Towners, and he must have been steeped and seasoned in those ways. He might be dismissed, but he was not beaten.

There would, in the words of the *Terranan*, be hell to pay.

The off-world leader seemed oblivious to the grudge he was creating. Gareth saw unbridled self-assurance in the way he addressed himself to Cuinn, not as one proud man to another but as someone so superior that he could dispense with common courtesy.

He sees a savage, ignorant and superstitious, with no more effective weapons against blasters than a few stones and a sling. So had the Federation once regarded the men of the Domains. That was before Sharra, the immensely powerful matrix stone that had ravened through the hills at Caer Donn, leaving the city itself a blasted ruin . . . and brought down a starship.

After that, the Federation had scrupulously enforced the Compact. These off-worlders had no experience of weapons more advanced then their own.

Hence, *ignorant savages.*

Gareth ducked behind the rocky shoulder just as Cuinn turned and, with infinite dignity and even more menace, headed back up the trail.

Rahelle tugged at Gareth's arm. As soundlessly as he could, he crept back. He hugged the rock until he had put it between himself and the trail.

Cuinn made no effort to conceal himself as he climbed. He moved quickly, with the assured step of a man in full command of his own destiny. Grit crunched beneath his feet, and pebbles went tumbling down the trail. Air currents swirled in his wake.

Head against the porous black rock, Gareth waited until the last sounds of Cuinn's passage died away. "He's going to do something." Gareth slid forward and hazarded a glance at the off-worlders' camp. "I wish I knew what."

"I agree. He will surely exact revenge for the insult to his *kihar.* Any Dry Towner would, but more so a headman."

"Cuinn and his people pose no threat. What could they do? Throw stones at a starship? Go up against blasters with knives? Or does a headman's *kihar* render him suicidally stupid?"

"You Comyn!" Rahelle scoffed. Gareth stiffened before he realized she meant the term loosely, to mean *men of the Domains.* "You think bashing one another is the only way to settle a matter of honor!"

"What then? Refuse to trade with them?"

"For food or other goods? That would be an idle threat. But for water . . ."

Water was life.

"I thought the people here observe water-truce, even as the folk of the Hellers set aside their arguments when a fire is to be fought."

"Cuinn would not withhold water, not even from his most bitter enemy. But he may well ensure that these strangers wish he had."

Gareth shook his head. The spaceship must have its own supplies of water and food, but Cuinn might not know that. It would be far safer for everyone if the off-worlders left Darkover. He wondered if he could convince them. So far, he hadn't been able to accomplish anything he'd set out to do, except walk like a rabbit-horn from the cookpot into the fire.

"We can't stop Cuinn." Gareth posed it as a statement, not a question, and heard Rahelle's sigh of agreement. "But I might be able to talk sense into the off-worlders. I speak passable Terran Standard. It's not exactly a brilliant plan, but I can't think of a better one."

She got to her feet and stepped out on to the trail.

"Not you."

Rahelle set her jaw, her eyes stony, and Gareth remembered how she had fought alongside the men during the ambush on the Carthon road, despite her father's prohibition. In his memory, she lifted her chin and demanded, *"Do you think I wear* chains*?"*

He had never in his whole life wanted anything so desperately as to keep her by his side.

"Someone has to bring news. To your father, and he to my people in Thendara. There's no one else I can trust."

She glared at him as if to say that wasn't a fair argument. He didn't want to fight with her. It would feel too much like lying about how he truly felt. After a moment, however, she nodded. "I will return to Nuriya and ensure that word of the situation is sent to my father."

"My sword—take it with you. If anything happens—" He wanted to say, *It's yours*, but no woman, not in the Domains and certainly not in the Dry Towns, could own a sword.

"I'll keep it for you." She wasn't agreeing to go to Carthon.

He took her by the shoulders. "Do not come back for me."

"What makes you think I—"

Unable to think of any other way of silencing her, he covered her mouth with his own. Her lips were full and smooth, taut. Something gave way in her, and also in him.

Laran flared, washing his senses in blue-white fire. He needed no starstone; he *was* a starstone. Heat chiseled the moment into crystalline perfection, all pretense burned away, leaving two minds and a single heart.

She pushed him away and skittered backward, trembling like a leaf in a Hellers gale.

No, please, I didn't mean—!

He could have borne it if she were disgusted or bored or simply appalled by him. That she might be *frightened* paralyzed him with horror.

She gave him a long look, then whirled and darted up the trail to Nuriya.

After a long moment, he tore his gaze away and forced himself to focus on the encampment below.

He went down, stepping cautiously on the patches of wind-blown grit and making sure that those below had ample time to see him. He wanted his arrival to be open and unconcealed.

They had clearly spotted him, as he intended, for the spindly-legged leader and his bodyguards arranged themselves near the perimeter of the camp. As Gareth reached the bottom of the hill and moved on to the flat basin, a third guard stepped out to block his path. This man would have been impressive in any venue, towering above Gareth's height by more than a head, and he was armed with a blaster and a braided-leather whip. He kept his hands so that his fingertips brushed both weapons. Slit eyes regarded Gareth from a moon-pale, moon-round face, a face that reflected not a trace of good will.

Gareth halted and called out in Terran Standard, "I'm a friend!"

The words produced a visible reaction, although not from the guard, whose demeanor remained as unyielding as before. The others regarded him with surprise and curiosity.

"I'm not armed, except for a small knife in my boot." Gareth raised his hands well away from his body.

"Who are you? What are you doing here?" the leader asked.

With the exception of his identity, Gareth had already decided to stick to the truth. "Garrin of Carthon. I'm here with a warning."

"Let him come."

The guard glided around to Gareth's back, moving with surprising speed for his size. All Gareth felt was a series of soft nudges that followed no particular pattern, yet he had no doubt that they would have revealed any hidden weapons, even a toothpick. There was a slight tug on his boot as the little knife slipped free and then a pat between his shoulder blades. Taking that to mean he had passed inspection, he approached the leader.

Had he thought this man comical? Compared to those eyes, so black they seemed all pupil but alight with cunning and suspicion, and that mouth framed by lines of vigilance, the awkwardness of the rest of the leader's body seemed trivial. Blue tattoos, like blurred hieroglyphs, spread over his bare scalp.

One corner of the leader's mouth tightened, infecting his expression with the ghost of a sneer. He seemed to be asking, *Why would I heed a warning from someone like you?* He would never ask aloud, not this one, would never commit himself. He ruled by keeping his options open, by making only those threats and promises he could keep.

"I'm listening."

"I have given you my name and purpose. Is it not customary to offer yours?"

The almost-sneer deepened. "For a village man, you learn fast. I didn't think any of you spoke Standard this well. Too bad, I could have used you," with a flick of dark eyes toward the man who had acted as translator, "earlier."

"I'm no Dry Towner," Gareth said, shaking his head for emphasis, "and Cuinn, the headman with whom you spoke, does not know I am here."

The translator shifted closer. "Local politics?"

"Have their uses," the leader replied. He turned his attention back to Gareth. "Carthon, you say?"

Gareth nodded. "On the border between the Dry Towns and the Domains . . . where the Federation had their base."

The gambit provoked a flare of emotion, quickly suppressed, from the leader's mind. *Surprise? Fear?* Gareth couldn't be sure, only that the off-worlder was not at all happy about the possibility of encountering the *Terranan* authorities.

They set down here to avoid being noticed. That means whoever they are and whatever they're doing here, it can't be legal.

Were they outlaws? Fugitives? Deserters? A rebel faction?

"Look," Gareth said, trying to sound earnest and a little desperate, "I don't care who you are or what you're doing here. But you're the one who gave Cuinn those blasters, and that's going to cause more trouble than you can imagine, not just for my people, but for yours."

The off-worlder did not correct Gareth's use of the plural, *blasters*, thereby confirming Gareth's fear that there was more than one.

"I'm Poulos of Windhoven, Capella IX, captain of the *Lamonica*. Let's talk." The leader jerked his head toward the largest of the ground structures, then headed in that direction with a jerky but surprisingly rapid pace. The translator followed, and then Gareth with the guard a quarter pace behind.

Gareth had spent enough time on the deserted Federation base to recognize the building as a prefab, quickly assembled and taken down. This one, and the row of similar structures beyond, was of sand-colored, slightly translucent material. It looked old and worn, perhaps surplus or a discard. Just inside the door, a cramped chamber functioned as an entryway and holding area. Gareth felt a little thrill as he entered. He sniffed, detecting a faint, unfamiliar smell, a little like the recycled air at the Headquarters Building. There were no windows, although three parallel luminescent strips ran the length of the ceiling to cast a harsh, slightly blue light.

Rows of stacked crates filled the back of the building, the smaller ones piled several layers high. The crates had seen rough handling, but they bore no insignia or identification markings beyond scrawled, unfamiliar symbols. Gareth didn't think the spacecraft could have contained all of them, unless it was a shuttle, going between this base and a larger ship in orbit.

A crude office occupied the center, consisting of a worktable, an assortment of chairs, and a bank of apparatus, perhaps communications devices or computers, Gareth couldn't be sure. The cups of brown liquid were recognizable, and the smell of stale coffee hung in the air. The guard halted on the perimeter, from where he could observe the entire office area.

Poulos of Windhoven lowered himself into the largest and most comfortable-looking of the seats with an ease that suggested it was his habitual place. He reached for the nearest cup, took a sip, frowned, and set it down again.

"Now, Garrin of Carthon, let's hear more about this *trouble.* Go ahead, sit."

Gareth settled into the nearest chair, a folding contraption that proved as uncomfortable as it looked. The translator perched on a third chair and bent over his device, perhaps making a recording.

"Darkover isn't one uniform culture, any more than the Federation is," Gareth explained. "We have our factions and alliances, even within a single territory. Out here, where there's nothing but sand, the only people you've encountered are poor and powerless. About the only things of value they have are a few goats, their knowledge of the land and its water sources, and their pride."

Which, he did not add, *you have sorely offended.*

Poulos blew out through loosened lips. Gareth wondered if he was remembering another place and another people for which that was true. "That—" he used an unfamiliar word, most likely from his native tongue rather than Terran Standard "—wasn't thrilled at having his toy taken away. I'll give it back after he's had a chance to cool off. Believe it or not, we're not interested in antagonizing the locals. Cooperative arrangements are mutually profitable. They get their blasters and we get . . ."

"Anonymity."

Poulos lifted his massive shoulders in an approximation of a shrug. "Let's say, an absence of hassle, plus a few extras like fresh meat and a water supply. Oh, we'll get what we want, regardless. We just prefer not to have to fight for it. Too much work, too many things that can go wrong, and for what? To convince a bunch of peasants that their gods can't hurt us? Or are you here to tell us we should be afraid of their little pig-stickers?"

"*Not them,*" Gareth said with such firmness that the translator looked up sharply and the guard took a step closer. "Rumors fly across the desert like sandstorms. Word's gotten out. There's an armed party on their way, Lord Dayan's men from Shainsa. They suspect someone out here has gotten hold of advanced weapons, and they mean to acquire them. They're ruthless and canny. They've been at war with my own people on and off for a century. So listen to me when I say they're desperate for an advantage, and this would give it to them."

"Well now," Poulos broke in as Gareth paused for breath, "isn't this nice? You want us to believe these old enemies pose a threat, so we'll take care of them for you? Is that it?"

Gareth's face went hot. "I wasn't—"

"Listen, son, I don't disbelieve you. You want the advantage for your own side. It's only natural." The off-worlder captain's tone did not alter, but his eyes narrowed. "Maybe we can cut a deal, depending on how things go. The old Federation spaceport lies in your territory, I believe. That might interest us—"

"You think I want blasters for *myself*?" Gareth blurted.

Lord of Light, Grandfather Regis would burst into flames at the idea!

"I didn't mean—" Gareth stammered, wishing he didn't flush quite so easily. "I wasn't expecting—It's just that we do not use such things. They are dishonorable! For obvious reasons, we cannot permit the Dry Towners to obtain them, either."

"Maintain the balance of power, eh? Sounds like an admirable goal." The captain waved one long-fingered hand in a careless gesture. "I don't care if you chop each other up for tonight's dinner, so long as we don't get drawn into it." At Gareth's expression of revulsion, he added, "All I'm saying is you people need to sort out your own affairs. We won't interfere."

"You've already endangered the peace and made yourselves a target by arming the Nuriyan villagers with blasters!"

The translator gave a sound like muffled laughter.

"Calm down," Poulos said. "Take a deep breath. Want some cold coffee?"

"You need to get those blasters back, any that are still out there, and get off this planet!"

"No, sonny, we don't need to do any such thing. Look, you're a decent enough kid, and clearly you've had enough exposure to modern technology to recognize a blaster, but give us a little credit here. We gave away a few that are so obsolete, you can't even get parts for them. The capacitors might hold one more recharge, maybe two at the most. As for these *Lord Dayan's men*, our perimeter defense is more than adequate. If they get too pesky, we've got a few surprises that make blasters look like party favors. I'd rather not waste the ammo, but as you see, there's really nothing to worry about."

Gareth stared at the off-worlder. Should he tell him about the catastrophe at Caer Donn and what *laran* weapons could do? No, he'd only sound even less credible. He'd already made a thorough mess of things. The way the present conversation was going, he wouldn't be able to convince a drowning man of the existence of water. Time, he needed more time to establish trust and try another tactic.

"I feel like an idiot, running up here to warn you." He allowed himself to slump a little. "I mean, *look* at all this! What do you have to worry about? Zandru's hells, you come from the *stars,* and we're just a little backwater planet with nothing anyone wants."

"Well, the location does offer a few advantages," Poulos remarked.

"If you say so." Gareth stood up, wiping his palms on the thighs of his pants. It wasn't difficult to sound eager. "I don't suppose I could peek inside the ship? It's probably the only chance I'll ever have . . . No, I guess not." He sighed. "Look, I can't go back to the village. They'll know I've talked to you. I needed a guide to get across the Sands of the Sun, but now he's gone, and I'm stuck out here. I could work for you—I could translate. Maybe I can help Cuinn calm down, explain things to him. He'll have to listen to me if he knows I'm with you."

The translator said, "He's seen the camp. And he looks healthy enough. We could use another strong back."

Poulos rubbed his tattooed scalp and considered for a long moment. "What the hell, why not? You may regret the offer, kid, once Offenbach's done with you, but I'll give you a try. You'll bunk and eat with the rest of the crew. Deal?"

Gareth let his features relax into an expression of relief. "Deal."

"First thing, though," Poulos said with a grimace, "I don't suppose you know how to make a decent cup of coffee?"

Kierestelli.

Trembling, Silvana pushed her stool away from the relay screen. The legs of her stool scraped against the unadorned stone floor. The fire had died down. Outside, winds howled down from the glaciered mountain slopes to batter Nevarsin Tower. She felt the faint vibration, as if through her own bones.

She shivered, she who was never cold.

Kierestelli.

She thought she would never hear that name spoken by human lips. For all these long years, ever since her *chieri* foster father had bidden her farewell at the borders of the Yellow Forest, she had been *Silvana.* Silvana, Woman of the Forest. Silvana of no family, no origin, nothing except her extraordinary *laran* talent. Only later did she become Silvana of Nevarsin Tower, *leronis* and Keeper.

Nevarsin had been a refuge but never a home. Yet where else could she have gone? It had been past time for her to leave the Yellow Forest. She had read that truth in the fading of the season, in the grave expression in Diravanariel's pale eyes, and in the increasingly strong bond between herself and Lianantheren, first-born child of the *chieri* Keral and the human David Hamilton.

Even now, so many years later, she remembered Lian, as graceful as a willow, as resilient as the tall, blue-flowered grasses of spring. Lian's eyes had been the color of rain, of silver, of dawn. But she could not bring to mind the shape of mouth or hands, the color of hair, the blush of cheek, the music of voice.

Had they been in love? Did they know what passion was, beyond the unsettling and exciting sensations when they were together? Did it matter for two young creatures raised as they were, without others of their age?

Now that she had lived with humans, she understood such feelings were the natural and healthy accompaniment to the hormonal surges of adolescence. Human children learned of sexuality and love in slow stages. They stumbled and blushed, flirted and sighed, touched with eyes and hands, and then with lips and bodies. They made mistakes, chose poorly, wept as if their hearts had truly been broken, mended with the next fair cheek or bright glance, and began again.

Sometimes, she thought as she watched the youngsters who came to the Tower for basic training, they gained as much from what went wrong in love as from what went right. Eventually, they learned that a comely appearance or a noble family name or even the way ardor masqueraded as intimacy counted far less than the quality of another person's character and most of all, the sympathy of temper and of mind.

If she and Lian had followed their youthful inclinations, if they had become lovers, she would not have suffered any lasting harm. Lian, on the other hand, this most precious treasure of the people of the Yellow Forest, the first *chieri* child to have been born in many human lifetimes . . .

Lian would have changed, polarized, body and mind and heart's desire forever fixed. Bonded too young, anchored to maleness in response to her own femaleness, Lian would never have had the chance to grow into full *chieri* maturity. Would never be able to choose who and what he or she might become.

Lian had walked with her to the boundaries of the Forest. The leaves had cast gold-hued dapples across their path. For a moment, she had imagined the sky was weeping flowers for her, for them both. Lian had not touched her during their journey, not even the slightest brush of a finger. Her skin felt as if it were starving. David Hamilton had come with them, his eyes watchful, his expression somber.

They had reached the edge of the sentinel grove. Beyond, trees stood widely spaced and solitary. Lian had held back and would not meet her eyes. She'd thought, *Not a word for me, my heart, not a glance? Am I as dead to you as I once was to my parents?*

She'd shifted her pack across her shoulders and turned her back on the person she had once believed was the touchstone of her soul.

"Kierestelli," David had said. "Beloved daughter of my friend. When you see him, tell him that we hold him ever in our hearts."

I will not see my father, she had thought in a sudden flare of anger. She had set her lips and said nothing.

"Of all the men of the Seven Domains, we hold Regis Hastur in the highest honor," Diravanariel had murmured, the words like running water over stone.

At any other time, she would have drunk in those phrases, let them nourish her spirit. As long as she had lived among the *chieri* and felt herself cherished by them, had seen the joy her very existence brought them, she had been able to forget the agonizing truth at the center of her own life.

Her father, that same Regis Hastur, had brought her to this place and left her with these people. She had understood at the time that he did so for her own safety. The world of men contained those who would harm the helpless and innocent, most particularly the children of their enemies. And Regis Hastur, the man who could have been king, had many enemies.

He had brought her here, and he had promised he would come for her when the danger was past. Season after season, she had watched for him, and still he had not come. He had sent no word, no token, no messenger. From her mother, whose love she had never before doubted, there had been only silence. Eventually, she had been forced to acknowledge the truth.

They had forgotten her. They no longer wanted her. The son her mother carried had taken her place in their hearts. Either that, or they were both dead. In the end, the difference did not matter.

Then had come the day when she herself must leave the people who had become her own, whose love had given her a measure of peace. She had been a fool to trust in their constancy. Who in all the wide world could ease this second betrayal? As she set her feet toward the path and the meadow beyond, she had glanced back. A moment was enough, and that moment changed everything.

Wetness gleamed on David's cheeks. *Chieri* did not weep, but in their bearing she saw such grief, it put her own to shame.

Lian had looked up, hair falling like a cascade of tears around that perfect face. Rain-gray eyes caught hers. A thought like the distant, rippling notes of a harp touched her mind.

I will never cease to love you, Kierestelli.

And now, years later and leagues away, in this Tower she had made into her fortress, that same name reverberated through her.

Kierestelli.

She had known that her mother, Linnea Storn, still lived, now Keeper of Comyn Tower. News might reach Nevarsin slowly, but it did come. Her brother, Dani Hastur, had grown to manhood, set aside his heritage, married for love, and fathered a son of his own. In time, Regis had died. That news had come swiftly, but not even for her father's funeral would she expose herself. Nothing she could do would bring him back. He had long since ceased to be an adored parent.

After all this time, when she believed herself safe from the past, her mother had found her.

Without thinking, Silvana went to the table beside the door. Dried fruit, butter toffee, and nuts rolled in crystallized honey were arranged on a platter, beside a pitcher of sweetened mint-water. *Laran* work drained the body's energies, sometimes dangerously. She wasn't hungry, and that was a bad sign. Shock and fatigue could be a deadly combination, especially when combined with cold. She scooped up a handful of dried apples and forced herself to chew them well. The tart sweetness flowed over her tongue. She ate a few nuts and a piece of the candy. Her trembling eased. She felt steady enough to make her way to her own chambers.

The authority of a Keeper within her own Tower was absolute. No one had ever questioned Silvana's desire for privacy, even when it bordered on reclusiveness. She had once felt safe, her barricades inviolable. Now that her isolation had been breached, now that the worst had happened, she did not know what to do.

Would Linnea accept her rejection? Would she tell anyone else? Would Nevarsin Tower soon find itself the center of Comyn attention?

Silvana lowered herself into an armchair beside the empty hearth of her sitting chamber, acutely aware of the vulnerability of these stone walls. She was no stranger to gossip and power struggles, to ambition and alliances and petty jealousies. Tower society might be small, but it was in every way a microcosm of the larger world.

They will not leave me in peace. The long-lost child of Regis Hastur is found, they will say. And then some will whisper that I have a claim to the Domain of Hastur . . .

Her heart drummed against her ribs. She wondered in a wild moment if it might batter itself into bloody pulp.

The room, once a haven of calm, now closed around her like a cage. Every furnishing and ornament, all the things she had collected so carefully over the years, each one a thing of grace and simplicity, took on a sinister aspect. They altered in her sight into instruments of torture, such as had been used during the Ages of Chaos.

I don't belong here. I have never belonged here.

Silvana had never been one to wallow in self-pity. Such abuse of the spirit was unknown among the *chieri*. She had seen its devastating effects in many she encountered in the human world, the people of Nevarsin village as well as travelers. Those injured in mind sought healing at the Tower, little suspecting that they themselves were the origin of so much of their own misery. In her care of such unfortunates, she was never less than scrupulous, for in all her *laran* work she never allowed herself the slightest self-indulgence or lapse.

This was no time to relax her own standards of integrity. The question she posed to herself now was whether, having been discovered, she should continue in her role as Keeper. She had been taught, and had accepted wholeheartedly, that the Towers must function apart from the distinctions of rank and privilege. No Comyn lord, not even Hastur of Hastur, had the right to influence the work of the circle. That principle had been established only after a long and bloody history. During the

Ages of Chaos, when kings and great lords commanded their own Towers, the land itself had been torn and poisoned. Fiery death had rained down from the skies, and generations of beasts and children had been twisted into monsters—

Silvana jumped to her feet and paced the width of her room. Her thoughts, usually so calm and rational, jumbled together like fractured shadows. What was wrong with her? The sorrows of the day were more than enough for any one person to bear—why must she manufacture more?

If the Comyn lords, descendants of those ancient war leaders, learned who and what she was . . . if they came after her, sought to draw her into their power schemes . . . what then? Even if she refused, even if they accepted her refusal, her identity—her name, her parentage, her history—would be public.

Regardless of her parentage, she was a trained Keeper. She had not ceded her conscience to any other person. It was no one else's concern who her parents had been, whether she possessed the Hastur Gift, that she had grown up among the *chieri*, what work she did, or what dreams she cherished.

Silvana came to a halt, facing the mullioned window that overlooked a garden courtyard. She turned her attention inward, felt the strong bones of her body, the balance of nerve and muscle, the flow of her blood, the slowing rhythm of her heart. Below her feet, the stones of the Tower hummed with the accumulated psychic imprints of a millennium of Gifted minds. Panic receded, but not caution.

Now that her initial shock had abated, Silvana felt a resurgence of confidence. She could drive away those who would invade her sanctuary. Even though Keepers were no longer regarded with almost religious reverence, she could disable or even kill any man foolish enough to lay hands upon her without her consent.

If by some chance, however, they should learn where she had passed those years, who had sheltered her . . . if they were able to backtrack her path, what then? The odds were minuscule, but even the slenderest risk was intolerable. Once the larger world had been alerted, she would not dare to contact her old friends, not even to warn them. If she were to do so, it must be now.

To leave now, to bolt like a brainless rabbit-horn, to abandon her responsibilities as a Keeper, none of this was rational. She could be wrong; she prayed to Aldones, Lord of Light, father of her fathers, that she was indeed wrong.

She could not live with the consequences if she were right.

In her early years at Nevarsin Tower, Silvana had rarely ventured outside unless some duty required it. As she had risen in the ranks of matrix workers through under-Keeper to her present rank, she had found less and less reason to do so. The ancient stone walls had become a welcome barrier, screening out the village and the world beyond.

It took her only a short time to give instructions to send to Arilinn for one of their under-Keepers, claiming an emergency, and to prepare and pack those few possessions she deemed necessary. Over the years, she had maintained the aloofness of a Keeper so well that no one questioned her leaving the Tower at an hour when the rest of the *leroni* were resting. Matrix work, including relay communications, tended to be done at night in order to minimize distractions from the unfocused psychic emanations from the village population.

The sun was well up but not yet at its highest point when Silvana made her way along the narrow, twisting streets of the city. Wearing a cloak of ordinary brown wool, worn boots on her feet and a pack slung over her back, her head bowed and shoulders hunched, she looked like any other mountain-bred woman. The cloak and boots had been a gift to the Tower from a smallholder in payment for saving his wife and babe during a difficult birth.

Today was a market day. The stone-cobbled streets carried a stream of farmers, their carts piled with wild greens, onions, and ice-melons, fur traders leading laden *chervines*, country folk anticipating a day of merriment, housewives intent on the best price for cooking pans and needles, and a troupe of ragged musicians.

Silvana slowed her pace, wary of drawing attention to herself as someone leaving the village when all others were heading in. She tugged the hood of her cloak over her distinctive copper-bright hair. The crowd swirled around her. She noticed the round, apple-blush cheeks of the children, the musical voices of the women, the call and response of the vendors—

"Fine *chervine*-kid wool! Soft as baby's hair!"

"Nuts! Pitchoos and hazels! Who'll buy my fresh roasted nuts?"

—and a dozen small acts of kindness. A boy barely older than a toddler stooped to pat an old dog lying at the feet of its master, a seller of ribbons. A grizzled horse dealer fed an apple to a pony. A young woman, visibly pregnant, helped an elderly man up several steps and into a doorway.

A strange feeling, part amazement and part regret, arose in her. She had not seen as much of the community in all the years she had lived here as she had in these few minutes. She had not expected it would be so difficult to leave.

These people were not her enemies, but they could never be her friends. She had served them with the Gifts of her mind—*laran* healing, the manufacture and delivery of fire-fighting chemicals to safeguard the forests on which so many of them depended, and speedy communications along the relays. But she had never known them or they, her. They were good and simple and without influence. Her early experiences had taught her all too well the powerlessness of good will in the face of determined evil.

That thought propelled her through the markets, down the steep, walled streets, and past the outskirts of the village. Only then did she allow herself to glance back. Beyond the village, the *cristoforo* monastery clung to the everlasting ice. A trick of the wind carried the sound of bells calling its denizens to prayer. She wondered if Lew Alton was among them and for a moment regretted not bidding him farewell. They had visited but rarely during the last few years, due to his declining health, yet he would grieve her absence. Not too much, she hoped.

The trail followed the contour of the mountains as it dipped toward the valley below. Silvana settled into a brisk traveling pace. The boots were too big for her, and she had briefly considered sandals such as those the monks wore. An impulse had led her to solve the problem with two pairs of thick socks. Very soon, she realized what a lucky choice she had made. The trail, although as well traveled as any in this part of the mountains, was littered with small stones. When she had lived with the *chieri*, she had never worn shoes; she would have danced down the trail. Her years of Tower work had turned her feet soft, so she was grateful for the cushioning layers of wool and leather.

She thought, *I have become a creature of stone and fire*, and wondered how her foster kin would receive her.

Her doubts did not linger. The mountain winds, redolent with the sweet wild smells of spring, blew them away. Clouds scudded across the sky that was somehow much larger and deeper than it had been in Nevarsin. She threw her head back to watch a hawk hovering on the thermal currents, and her spirit soared to meet it.

Her muscles ached from the unaccustomed exertion, but her bones hummed in contentment. Memory sharpened. She remembered which plants would nourish her and which to avoid. For the time being, however she dared not delay.

The day wore on. The land grew more rugged, the vegetation wild and twisted. Shadows pooled in the folds of the hills, chill as winter nights. In the distance, a wolf howled. At least she was well below the tree line, so she need not fear the giant flightless banshees. But she was growing weary, and fatigue would make her more vulnerable to the cold.

Silvana crouched in a copse of tangled, willow-thin yellowbark saplings and considered her situation. Night would soon be upon her, and she found herself reluctant to light a fire. She could draw upon her Keeper's discipline to avoid hypothermia, but that would use metabolic energy at an accelerated rate.

In the Yellow Forest, she had never been cold. The seasons had shifted like dancers in a round, green to gold to silver to green again, each with its own harmony.

She laid one hand on the nearest trunk. *Friend*, she thought, using the *chieri* word.

She slipped her pack off her shoulders and settled herself in a cross-legged posture. Her knees twinged, then eased. The muscles in her lower back relaxed. She closed her eyes, breathing deep into her belly to focus her thoughts. Her awareness of the world narrowed to the bark, its texture and density, and then the living wood inside. As if flowing through her own veins, she felt the movement of the sap, the slow yearning for warmth and light, the sure and intimate intelligence of the soil, the minute droplets of water bathing the roots, the steadfast bedrock. Moisture and minerals rose, molecule by molecule, into the budding leaves. Tiny creatures, insects and worms and things invisible to the human eye, transformed the debris of last year's leaf-fall into humus.

The borders of her human personality dissolved. As effortlessly as drifting into sleep, she found herself in communion with the tapestry of soil and water and living things. She knew the weight and texture of such a unity, so like that of a working matrix circle. Instead of human minds, each focused through a starstone and then gathered, harmonized, woven together by herself as Keeper, these streams and currents were purely natural in origin. No tree required a starstone to amplify its essence; no bird labored under a lifetime of anxiety every time it spread its wings. No mariposa ever attempted to dominate its fellows.

Distantly, as if it were happening to someone else, Silvana felt wetness in the corners of her eyes. She had come home to a place she had forsaken so long ago, it had vanished from her thoughts. Her body, however, and the deep sure workings of her dreams, and the core of herself from which arose the power of her psychic Gifts, these had not forgotten.

Although she had always been able to sense things she could not see and touch, her *laran* had woken fully during her sojourn with the *chieri*. Trees and stones, sky and brook and wolf had been her teachers, her companions. She had learned reverence for the balance of fast and slow, hot and cold, light and dark, life and death. No wonder the work of a Keeper had come so easily to her, she who had danced in the forest. Sometimes, her time there had seemed like a dream, too beautiful to be real. Now she realized, as her awareness shifted and she came back into her separate self, that the forest years had been the enduring reality and the years of stone and fire, only a fleeting apparition.

She folded her hands in her lap and studied her surroundings with new perspective. The copse and hillside, once bleak with the coming of night, abounded in resources. Everything she needed was here. She no longer felt cold or stiff. A gossamer web of life-energy surrounded her, filled her, bound her in harmony to the living world. It also shielded her from any unwelcome presence. A passing fur trapper would see only brush and rock.

The last shimmer of color had almost disappeared from the jagged western horizon. Night folded its cloak across the face of the world. A hush arose from the hills, a stilling of the wind. The clouds thinned to reveal the vast milky sweep of the galactic arm. A hundred hundred suns burned like lightning pinpoints, their numbers beyond human reckoning.

Somewhere out there lay Terra, ancient and legendary, and the worlds that made up the Federation, Castor and Ephebe, Wolf and Thetis. The assassins and schemers and far-off battles diminished to fleeting inconveniences. She must be careful not to underestimate them, for flesh itself was all too fragile, but neither would she accord them the privilege of controlling her through fear.

She was a grown woman, a Keeper . . . a daughter of Hastur. She would face life on its own terms.

19

Even before she reached the outskirts of the Yellow Forest, Kierestelli sensed the change in the trees. For most of her journey, she had slipped through thicket and grove, shaping herself into harmony with the natural landscape. Now she sensed a withdrawal. Hillside and forest turned opaque, and chill winds brushed the edges of her awareness. Dry leaves crunched beneath her feet, when only a day before she had passed without a sound.

She slowed her pace. There was no point in pushing harder, insisting that the forces guarding the heart of the forest give way before her will. She was the supplicant here, returning without any expectation that the home she had left was still hers.

This part of the forest filled the hollow between the hills. The trees grew taller here, their trunks gnarled with age. As she went on, their tops intertwined to form a canopy, imperfect and shifting in the wind.

It is as all life, each part flowing into a greater whole, she thought. *None of us is truly separate.*

She halted, tipping her face to catch the dappled sunlight. Motes of brightness flickered behind her closed eyelids. For a moment, she felt as if she floated in a sea of softly effulgent lights or perhaps of living stars. The intimation of chill receded. As if from a distance, she caught the chiming of sweet notes, a harp's laughter, the ripple of a snowmelt stream, a riot of songbirds after a rain.

Overhead, leaves rustled. Shafts of sunlight glittered on motes of forest dust. As quickly as the rays appeared, they vanished as the branches shifted. Their warmth lingered like an afterimage in Silvana's mind. It cradled her, lifted her up, sustained her. In her imagination, the trees inclined in salutation, then parted before her. She hesitated.

"So you have come back to us." The words came in a low voice, the *casta* archaic but perfectly clear in the way an ancient chant would be understood in spirit as well as syllable.

Between one pulse of her heart and the next, a *chieri* emerged. The figure was, as all those ancient people, tall and slender, androgynously beautiful. Gray hair fell halfway to narrow hips; the only garment was a sleeveless tunic that looked as if it had been woven from tree bark and moonlight. Colorless eyes met Silvana's without a hint of emotion.

No welcome, no censure, no curiosity. Only the immense gift of recognition.

She raised her fingertips to her forehead and said, in the language of the *chieri*, "Foster father." The word actually meant *Nurturer-of-children-who-belong-to-the-race.*

"The river flows in only one direction," Diravanariel answered, keeping to *casta.*

"All water is one," she answered. "Did you not teach me that truth yourself?"

A chuckle answered her as a second figure stepped from behind the largest of the trees. "You must concede the point, Dirav. There's no hope when she starts quoting your own words back at you."

"Uncle David!" All dignity fled, she rushed into the *Terranan* doctor's arms.

As he drew her tight against him, she felt the thinness of his flesh, the withering of muscle, the brittleness of bone. Very much like one of these ancient trees, he retained surprising vitality for a man of his years. She pulled away, looking up into his smiling eyes, saw the lines of laughter bracketing his mouth, the mass of silvered hair, and thought, *My father might look like this, had he lived.*

"You're all grown up," he said, smiling even more deeply.

"These many years since. Now I'm Keeper at Nevarsin Tower!" To her own ears, she sounded like a child greeting a beloved uncle, bragging about her achievements.

"It does not surprise me." He pressed dry lips to her forehead. "We're all very proud of you."

We? Her gaze flickered to the *chieri*. Diravanariel stood like an island of immobility against the constant play of dappled light.

"Why have you returned?"

"She's only just arrived!" David protested. "Give us a little time to catch up before getting down to business, or she will suspect we of the forest have lost all notions of hospitality."

Silvana walked over to the *chieri*. She knew better than to touch him, uninvited, but she held out her hands. "You welcomed me when I was a small child and had no choice in the matter. Is there no place for me in your heart now that I am grown and come to you freely?"

"Child, you will always be cherished among us. More is at risk than any one individual, no matter how beloved. I speak for what is left of our people and those few and fragile new lives we guard. Have you forgotten how perilous is the world of men? I ask again, *Why have you returned?* What danger hunts you this time, and will it follow you into our midst?"

Silvana lowered her hands. Where was Lian? Had something happened . . . or was Lian's absence a way of preventing their reattachment to one another?

If I see Lian, if what once existed between us has not changed . . . I may never want to leave . . .

"If I had any awareness of such danger," she said tightly, "I would never have come. I am a trained Keeper. There is not much of importance that escapes my notice."

Diravanariel's posture softened. A stray curl of breeze lifted the moon-pale hair. One slender six-fingered hand brushed hers with a touch as delicate as a butterfly wing. She felt as if the entire forest, trees and sky and ferny undergrowth, distant birds and small furred creatures, flowers and sun-bright meadows, wrapped her in a homecoming embrace.

In a voice suddenly thick, she said, "My mother found me. I don't want to be found. I didn't know where else to go."

David drew in his breath. In that faint, sharp sound, Silvana sensed a riot of questions. He asked none of them, however. He had lived a long time with the *chieri.* Instead, he slipped one arm around her shoulders. She felt his desire to reassure her, but it was not for him to offer her refuge. It came to her then that in order to be welcomed, she must be equally prepared to accept refusal. Diravanariel was right; no personal need, no matter how great, must be allowed to place the entire community at risk.

Still, it was good to see these two again, the *chieri* who had taught her, given her so many gifts of mind and spirit, and the man who had kept alive her own human identity. She stepped back from them, signaling her acceptance that this brief greeting might be all she received.

With a tilt of the head, Diravanariel led the way deeper into the forest.

The *chieri* did not cluster together the way humans did. Perhaps once, in their long-distant past, they had lived in technologically sophisticated cities, but no longer. With the passing of ages and their withdrawal to the planet of their origin, they had forsaken the trappings of civilization for the simplicity of the natural world. *If we are all there are or will ever be,* they seemed to be saying, *then let us live each day in joy.*

Some *chieri* lived in caves or in houses in thickly growing trees. Diravanariel's extended family constructed shelters woven from naturally fallen branches and fabrics spun from bark fibers and downy feathers. Such a dwelling might last a handful of seasons or be abandoned to wind and water when the desire to commune with a different part of the forest arose.

Silvana followed her foster parents into a little clearing, barely ten paces across. Among the thick boles of the trees, she spotted a half-dozen structures of white and glimmering gray, ridged along the center of their roofs to facilitate runoff of rain and snow. The largest one looked as if it easily contained several chambers the size of her own at Nevarsin. Although there was no sign of a fire, for cooking or other purposes, two waist-high looms had been set up. A *chieri* sat cross-legged before the nearer loom, dressed in a long, loose robe. Pale hair rippled like a cascade of living starlight with the movement of the shuttle. At the approach of Silvana and her friends, the weaver stopped work and rose, a single movement of breathtaking grace. Soft lips curved into an expression of delight.

"Star maiden, daughter of my friend! How it brightens my eyes to see you again!"

"And you, S'Keral." Silvana's hands flew through a gesture of respect. She had not used it since she'd left the forest.

Keral took a step to meet her, and the fabric of the robe flowed around the curves of breasts and belly. The touch of fingertips to fingertips flashed through Silvana's mind. Telepathic sensations rushed through her, the complex patterned texture of Keral's personality, pleasure at their reunion . . . the intense and abiding joy at the new, utterly unexpected life.

When David had come to greet Silvana, Keral had remained behind in the sheltered nest, pregnant again. For the two of them to have produced Lian had been a miracle beyond imagining. Not even the *chieri* language, so rich in the nuances of joy, had words to describe what a second child meant to their entire race.

For a long moment, Silvana stood there, just barely touching the *chieri*. Tears blurred her physical sight, intensifying her inner vision. The feeling of overflowing abundance saturated her. Every twig, every bud, every seed lying dormant in the soil, every creature drawing new sustenance from the rich decaying leaf-fall, all sang to her, lifted her up.

How could a single event, one impending birth, so transform the entire world?

Silvana's mind stretched wider. In that fundamental unity, Diravanariel's people were linked to every other *chieri* gathering. Here and there, like motes of sun-drenched brightness, she sensed the shimmering auras of fertility. It seemed that the Hellers themselves, their peaks rising like snow-shrouded giants, echoed their delight.

She wanted it to go on forever, this bliss that was at its heart an affirmation of love, of connection, of mutual joy.

I want to stay. I want to never leave you all again.

"We have never been separated." Diravanariel had glided soundlessly to her side. Those words, spoken with the tender intimacy of a parent murmuring to a beloved child, swept away all other thought. "You have always been here with us."

How could she have been so blind? In her childish grief, she had felt herself expelled, ejected. Forsaken. In truth, the change had been one of outer appearance only, like taking off one garment and donning another, stone city walls exchanged for trees, *laran* circles for dancing beneath the moons. The bond had not waned. She had carried it with her, although she herself had barricaded the memory of it in a distant corner of her mind. She would never do so again.

The rapport faded from the peak of intensity. Silvana came back into herself, her limited, separate human self.

David brought up a seat with a back support and placed it beside Keral's loom. With a smile, he offered it to Silvana. "Lian made it for me when I began having difficulty sitting on the ground. Or rather, getting up from the ground."

Lian. Just to hear the name spoken aloud pierced her. A dozen questions pressed the boundaries of her thoughts.

Where was Lian? Not here, with David and Keral? Had something happened?

She forced her mind to stillness. Keral gave her a measured look, kind for all its unflinching directness, and said nothing. Dirav sat comfortably on the bare earth, looking up as three other *chieri* emerged from the forest. Silvana did not know them nor they, her, and they were shy and curious. David inquired about Silvana's life since leaving the Forest, her work first as *leronis* and then as Keeper, and the strange *chieri* listened intently. Keral resuming weaving, humming softly.

As if moving through the steps of a formal dance, one or another of the *chieri* left the group and returned with platters of food, fruits of many sorts, vegetables, and the thick, honey-sweetened nut paste Silvana had loved as a child. Dirav began a lilting ballad—a sweet song in a very old dialect. The other *chieri* joined in, their voices weaving counterpoint to Dirav's steady melody. They sang of taking leave of the many worlds where their kind had walked, of distant stars no more than a blur in the galactic mist, of turning away from cities whose towers covered half the sky, of laying down wars and their terrible weapons, weapons of mind as well as matter . . . of coming home.

Home to these forests under the crimson sun.

Home to earth and snow and the long twilight of their race.

Day wore into dusk. The song ended, replaced by another, this time a chant of welcome. With the thickening of the shadows, however, the temperature fell. Silvana shivered a little.

"You'll stay indoors with us tonight," David said. "These old bones don't tolerate the cold nearly as well as when I was younger."

Dirav made a gesture of approval, and the gathering began to break up. Silvana went to bid her foster parent good-night. Together they strolled around the perimeter of the settlement.

"You have grown well and strong," Dirav said. "For a time after you left us, we feared the world of humans might change you."

"I do not know if I am better or worse than I would have been had I stayed." She was what she had become, what humans and *chieri*, each in their own time and manner, had made of her.

"And wise as well, to understand that we never step into the same river twice."

"No." She could not resist a smile. "There is one thing I would like to know."

"Ask, then."

"Did my father—did Regis ever come looking for me? Or did he just forget about me?"

Dirav regarded her, pale eyes glowing with their own inner moonlight. "He came."

"But—" She bit her lip, caught in a torrent of feelings, relief and outrage and things she had no words for. "I never knew."

You never told me!

"I myself closed the Forest against him. After a time, he stopped coming."

"After a time? How many times?"

"Many."

A wave of strangeness rushed through her, as if the world had just shifted on its axis, so that the sun now rose in the west. So few things in life were certain—death, next winter's snows . . . and that her father had abandoned her.

Why? howled through her. Because evil men still menaced the innocent? Because of the memory of her half-brothers, slaughtered in their cradles simply because they were the children of Regis Hastur? Because children do not thrive in isolation and Lian needed someone of a similar age?

Because they loved me too much to let me go?

Did the reason matter? Did any of it matter—yes, it did. Linnea, weeping in the night for her lost daughter, mattered. Regis, returning again and again, quartering these hills in vain, mattered.

And she herself, growing to womanhood and building her life around a core of bitterness, her grief mattered, too.

She looked inside herself for righteous fury at those who had stolen life and family from her and could not find it. There was no selfishness in Dirav or Keral or any of them. Only the long slow decline of a dying race. Only the hope and joy brought by a single human child. Only love.

If I had returned with my father, she thought, *I might never have become a Keeper. My bloodline alone would have made me too valuable, for reasons having nothing to do with my own happiness. Perhaps I might have forged my own path . . . but I would not be here now, in this place under the stars.*

"I must think about this," she murmured. Greatly daring, she slipped her fingers into the crook of Dirav's arm. Together, they ambled back to the clearing.

Fairy-soft lights flickered inside the dwelling shared by David and Keral. Leaving her boots neatly arranged beside the door, Silvana slipped inside. The air was warm and smelled of conifer needles and herbs. Patches like *laran*-charged glows illuminated the interior. The walls were patterned in tapestries of spider-silk and translucent blue snowmoss, providing both insulation and beauty. The effect presaged the ancient Comyn style, only without the use of stone.

At the far end of the chamber, Keral and David stood talking to a *chieri.* At Silvana's entrance, the newcomer turned to face her, more beautiful than memory . . .

Lian.

Silvana's heart caught in her throat. Lian's hair bore hints of red among the moon-pale strands, like living embers still aglow. Silvana had forgotten the silvery lights in Lian's eyes that made it seem as if she were gazing into some distant place, a realm of heart and soaring spirit. She had forgotten, too, how tall Lian was, although not as tall as Keral, and how gracefully made.

Keral's lips curved in a smile as he crossed the distance between them and held out hands, palm up, in invitation.

No, Silvana realized. *Not* he, for the movement had brought Lian more fully into the light and now, through the gossamer fabric of Lian's tunic, Silvana saw the roundness of breasts and hips . . . the faint swelling beneath the slender waist.

The next instant, her fingertips met Lian's palms. The touch dropped them into rapport. The barriers of years and distance, of gender and the scars of living, all vanished. It was as if they had never been apart, an intimacy even closer than that which Silvana experienced when working in a matrix circle. This closeness needed no artificial enhancement of mind energy, of thought and emotion. Each flowed into the other.

For the briefest instant, Silvana felt a wrenching of her own hope, her own unacknowledged desire. She had indeed been Lian's childhood heart mate, and in some corner of her own thoughts, she had expected the bond to be lifelong and mutual. Lian had grown into a fully functional adult, capable of the depth of attachment necessary for the Change. But not with her, not as the male who might have been her lover.

The sorrow lasted only a fraction of a heartbeat. Lian radiated both contentment and delight to such a degree that Silvana felt herself swept up, carried away, incandescent with happiness. Laughter, sweet as a mountain stream, rang out. She could not tell whether it was her own or Lian's, and she did not care.

As the rapport faded, a dozen thoughts leaped into Silvana's mind. She felt awkward again, a little embarrassed at having expected that although *she* might have changed, Lian had remained as they had parted.

I have never ceased to love you, Kierestelli, Lian said, speaking mind to mind.

"My heart friend," the words sprang from her mouth. "Nothing is as I imagined it."

Not the constancy of her father's love, not her mother's grief at their separation, not the secret hopes she had harbored about returning here. Perhaps not even who she was, what it meant to be a Keeper . . . and her place among the Comyn as the daughter of a man who could have been king.

She had kept herself apart for so much of her adult life, how could she know?

"No," Lian said. "It is better."

Silvana caught a vivid impression from Lian's mind, a kaleidoscope of images and sensations, a strange *chieri*, tall as all those people, but strong, with a quintessential masculine beauty like her father's, hair like a river of iridescence, dancing together with Lian, dancing in ecstasy beneath the four moons . . .

She found herself gasping, dazzled into breathlessness by the shared memory. Tears stung her eyes, and her heart ached, though not with sorrow.

David put an arm around each of them, ever and always human. "Take a little time with us, Stelli, as much as you need. Talk, rest, think things through. Wander through these woods. You're safe among those who love you."

20

At the end of Lian's last day, the two of them hiked high into the mountains. Silvana carried a blanket and a little food in her pack, for she was not sure how late they might lie out under the stars. The meadow where they used to play as children was smaller than she remembered, but she could not decide if that was because the entire world had been bigger then or because the trees were slowly encroaching on the open space.

The day's warmth clung to the grass. When she lay down on it, forgoing the blanket, the smell of honey and fresh green rose up. It would linger on her skin, in her hair, evoking memories of childhood's long, dreamy days.

They lay side by side, silent and still, an arm's length apart, while the light drained from the sky. Silvana felt as if she were floating in a cloud-lake spun of twilight and the sounds of night-rousing birds. Her mind and Lian's had been in light rapport, so subtle and sensitive that she could sense the beating of the baby's heart.

In a way, it is my child, too.

Yes, dearest heart friend, as it belongs to all of us. As we belong to one another.

Sadness hovered on the borders of Silvana's thoughts. Her sojourn, like Lian's, was nearing its end. No one had to tell her that. She simply knew that she could not stay, not because she was not welcome but because her life had a different shape, a different rhythm.

When she met Lian's gaze, she looked into the mirror of her own soul. They were not the same, but each embodied the best blending of human and *chieri*. Each had been conceived on a night when differences had fallen away, when there had been no boundaries between lovers.

Lian looked away, up to the stars that even now had grown from pinpoints against the lavender dusk to a veil of brilliance. Already the temperature was falling.

Silvana rolled on to her side and propped herself up on one elbow. Lian looked so peaceful, wanting nothing more than what this glorious night offered, but Lian was half *chieri* and had been raised in harmony with the forest. She, on the other hand, was entirely human, had come to the trees in fear and confusion, and had spent the better part of her adult life trying to maintain her distance from her own people. Certainly, she had done everything she could to prevent her family from learning her whereabouts.

She had to go back. She knew it, and she also knew that she could not take the peace of this moment, the joy of her psychic bond with Lian, with her. A dozen questions buzzed around her mind like angry bees, none of them worth asking. The ones Lian would answer, she already knew the response to, but the ones she could not figure out—*What should I say to my mother? Can my life as a Keeper ever go back to what it was before?*—no one could tell her.

A ripple passed through the serenity of Lian's mind. "You are troubled, heart friend."

"It is the human condition." She smiled in gentle self-mockery. "We are always between one thing and another, always wanting whatever we do not have. I don't know why I thought it might be different here. I have changed my location but not what lies within me."

"You had not come to terms with your past—why you came here, why you left—in your time in the Tower?"

She shook her head. "I learned to examine my thoughts and motives in every area of my life except this. Now I know that my father came back for me, it has eased the bitterness but given me no new direction.

I am a Hastur, daughter of a king, but I don't know what that means. Do I have responsibilities beyond those I have taken on for myself? What do I owe Darkover? My mother? The Comyn? And what do they owe me? It's very confusing."

"Confusing, yes. Humans and all things that pertain to them are, or so my father has taught me." Cloth rustled on grass as Lian shifted position, easing the weight of the baby. "This is a time of change for all of us, my people as well."

"Two new children—"

"Much more than that. Yes, my people rejoice because we now have hope when before there was none, but it cannot be more than a slim one. I spoke of the change that has come over our entire world. The—" Lian used a word that meant, roughly, *Those-who-show-the-earth-disrespect*—"changed Darkover when they removed their ships, but they are not gone."

Despite herself, Silvana glanced skyward. She saw nothing amiss among the stars, but what did she expect? "They still walk other worlds, I suppose, and fly their ships between them." She wondered if the *Terranan* were still engaged in the war that precipitated their withdrawal.

"They do."

"How can you know that? I have heard nothing of them over the relays." She wondered whether her mother had contacted Nevarsin Tower for this reason.

"We used to roam the stars," Lian said in such a way that Silvana knew the reference was to the *chieri* of the distant past. "In the end we returned here, to the world of our origin, and for a long time we gave no thought to everything we had learned and built. But the knowledge was not lost. Since the time of the—the time when you and I were conceived, some among us have delved again into the old learning."

"Darkover must never again be vulnerable to those who would pillage our resources," Silvana murmured. Her own father had stood against the World Wreckers; must she as a Hastur now answer a renewed threat?

"What must I do?" The question came as a whisper, as if she were hoping not to hear the answer.

"Dear one, I am not saying those evildoers have indeed returned. But there are others . . . up there, passing . . . and setting down far across the sands. Dirav bade me speak to you of this. It was felt that you might hear it more clearly from me."

For a long moment, neither spoke. Lian was waiting for her to reach her own understanding.

"That is the reason I must go back. So that I will be ready." Silvana heard the bleakness in her own voice and dismissed it as self-indulgent. She was an adult, Comynara and Keeper. She was also Hastur, although as she had said, she did not yet know what that meant. But she would.

She peered up at the stars, like powdered gemstones strewn across a black velvet cloth, and wondered which of them was a starship . . . and what that ship might bring to Darkover.

When Silvana and Lian returned to the dwelling of Lian's parents, Dirav was waiting. They settled around a fire made fragrant with chips of resinous wood. The flames burned with a soft blue-green hue. Keral took out a harp and sang, a wordless sweet-sad melody that Silvana remembered from her childhood. It seemed to her that the trees themselves grew quiet, listening. She drifted effortlessly on the lilting tune, her *laran* senses as vivid as sight or hearing, touch or taste. As the song died into silence, she found herself alone with Dirav. The others had withdrawn.

Dirav held out one hand and dropped a ruby-tinted crystal into hers. The instant it touched her skin, it came alive. She started as a twist of light flared in its depths. She held it up so that the fire's light shone through it. It glowed with its own crimson luminosity. On closer inspection, she made out not just a single shimmering light but a multiplicity, reflection upon dancing reflection. Each had its own pattern, its own rhythm. It was as if a dozen—a hundred and more—Gifted minds had imprinted on this single gem.

She lowered the crystal and met Dirav's gaze. *How is this possible?*

"When your people came to Darkover millennia ago, my people taught them the secret of the starstones, where to mine them, how to key them to individual minds, and how to build them into higher-order matrix screens."

Silvana nodded. Some of this was the history every Tower novice learned.

"The blue starstones are the best suited to human *laran*," Dirav went on, "but they are not the only type. Others can retain the imprint of a personality or even the incarnation of an elemental force."

Like Sharra, the Form of Fire.

"And this, this is the rarest of them all. We call it a heartstone."

Silvana closed her eyes, focusing her inner senses on the stone. She felt it resonate with her mental touch, but there was none of the amplification of *laran* characteristic of a blue starstone. She might, by force of will, channel her *laran* through it, but it was made for some other purpose. She relaxed her focus, inviting the stone to guide her, to tell her how it worked . . .

. . . and found herself linked to other minds, *chieri* minds, as if in a circle . . . many more than she had ever experienced . . . some in this very forest, others in mountain fastnesses. She had no sense of the effortful concentration of matrix work. Instead, ease suffused the unity, giving it a responsiveness and fluidity beyond any human circle. In this unity, distance no longer existed. Nor time, she suspected.

This is the technology we once used, shimmered through her consciousness. *And now, in time of need, we remember.*

With an effort, Silvana detached a part of her thoughts from the *chieri*-unity. Her vision doubled into overlapping images of what she saw with her physical eyes and what she felt with deeper, surer senses. "Time of need?"

"Others," Lian had said. *"Up there, passing . . . and setting down far across the sands."*

Cool, slender fingers closed over hers. "You may have occasion to call upon us. Just because we have withdrawn to the planet of our origin does not mean we have forgotten what we once knew during those times when we were equally at home in the vast reaches of space."

Was that what the heartstone was for?

Firelight gleamed on silver-gray eyes. "One of the things. But it is not good for a human, even one accustomed to our ways and trained in *laran* as you are, to spend too much time in its depths."

Reluctantly, Silvana withdrew her mind from the stone. The loss of contact felt as if a telepathic damper had just been turned on, as if part of her that had been vividly awake had been severed from her. How easy it would be to plunge back into that greater consciousness, that merging, and lose all track of time.

With trembling hands, she drew out a square of insulating silk from the pouch she wore on a cord around her neck, wrapped the heartstone, and tucked it beside her own starstone. The heartstone emitted a pulse of warmth, gently muted, and then subsided to a state that was neither inert nor completely quiescent. The ruby-touched unity hovered just at the edge of her *laran* senses. With it, she would never be truly alone.

When she let out her breath, she admitted to herself that she did not know what she would have done if it had not been safe to keep the two stones in such proximity. She did not think she would have had the strength to set the heartstone aside.

Dirav, watching her, gave a gesture of approval. She had passed a test. Had she been anything less than a trained Keeper, she would have succumbed.

"In time of need," he said aloud, implying both a promise and a warning.

"In time of need, and only then," she agreed.

21

Captain Poulos had not exaggerated his warning. From the moment the mate, Offenbach, had taken Gareth in charge, he had been assigned one physically strenuous task after another. He could not remember having worked this hard in his life, and he seemed to have been given the heaviest lifting. The reason for this had become clear during one of his infrequent breaks. One of the other crew, an older man with a potbelly and a hooked nose, explained that the *Lamonica* couldn't afford to upgrade its artificial gravity, and despite a program of exercise, prolonged time in space weakened both muscle and bone. They'd been a long time looking for a safe port, meaning one where the Federation Spaceforce wouldn't find them. They'd gotten weaker, but their cargo hadn't gotten any less massive.

"Local labor, that's the thing. Cheap, and the gravity don't wear 'em down none," Potbelly had concluded, spitting a wad of something brown and foul-smelling. It narrowly missed Gareth's feet and landed with a squishy sound.

Local labor, indeed.

Toward dusk, Gareth lowered himself to the ground in a rough circle with the rest of *Lamonica's* crew. They sat outside, relaxing in the breeze that sprang up with the lengthening shadows. It wasn't much cooler than the rest of the air and carried a bitter tang, but it was better than the stale, heavy air of the prefab structures. Gareth had not yet had the chance to go inside the ship itself, but he understood from the other men that the air there was even worse.

Gareth rested his forehead against his folded arms on his knees. He wished he had the privacy to take out his starstone and attempt a little *laran* healing on himself. Grandmother Linnea had taught him only the most basic monitoring, but with the proper motivation, such as aching in every joint and muscle, he was sure he could figure the rest out.

"You're all right," Potbelly said to Gareth, punching him none too gently in the shoulder.

"For a native," one of the other men quipped, but without malice.

"If you off-worlders are so superior," Gareth groaned, "you can carry my share tomorrow."

"Shy-oot up, Taz," one of the others said.

"*Shy-oot?* Where'd you learn to talk like that?"

"Gods of space, not another of Robbard's bad jokes! Spare the poor boyo!"

"Spare *you*, you mean!" The repartee went back and forth, with no one having much energy to take it beyond a few enigmatic jibes.

"What's in those crates, anyway?" Gareth spoke up when the pauses lengthened. "Rocks?"

"Nothing you need to know about," Robbard said, an edge in his voice.

"Leave the kid be," said Taz. "It's just a question. If you'd been hauling several times your sorry weight all day, you might want to know it was worth the while."

"Kid doesn't *need* to know." Robbard squinted against the sun, low against the line of western hills. "Captain wouldn't like it."

Gareth kept his head down. "I didn't mean anything."

"Robbard's right," Potbelly said. "It's safer not to ask. Curiosity's not too healthy in certain lines of work, if you take my meaning. If Captain Poulos wants you to know, he'll tell you."

Offenbach stuck his head out of one of the smaller structures. "Grub!"

With the others, Gareth collected a packet of food cubes and a cup of some synthetic material. He shook his head at the offer of a ration of space grog. One whiff convinced him of its potency, and he had no intention of impairing his faculties. The food cubes foamed up into thick paste on contact with the air. Some of the crew scooped it up with their fingers, others took out metal spoons. Gareth found the concoction flat and unappetizing, although he assumed it was nutritionally adequate. The roasted antelope and spiced grain he'd eaten at Nuriya faded into a dream that had happened to someone else.

He drew out a cup from the water cask, then paused. It looked and smelled safe enough, although with the alkali reek characteristic of oasis water. He'd been drinking it all day without a thought.

"Something wrong?" Taz appeared at his elbow.

"N-no. I was just wondering. This water's local, isn't it?"

"You think we got fuel to burn, carting around our own water? Nah, we get it dirtside."

Gareth shrugged. Water was heavy, as he'd learned from their trek across the Sands of the Sun. "From the village?"

"Gods of space, that's awful stuff!" Taz twisted the valve and filled his own cup, took a mouthful, swished it and spat it out. "You couldn't give it away on a decent planet!" Frowning, he regarded Gareth. "What's it to you where it comes from?"

"I was just curious. I wondered what the villagers had given the captain in exchange for the blasters."

The spacer's suspicious expression eased. "Now you're thinking like one of us! Everything's a bargain, you see. The secret's all in knowing what the other giz wants and how much he'll pay. This bokk-piss masquerading as water, the yokels think it's so valuable! They're too dumb to realize it's this *place* we need."

He means Darkover, an ideal base and staging area now that the Federation's no longer here to enforce its laws.

Gareth broke the pause that followed. "Do you go into the village for water? Won't there be trouble after the way Captain Poulos sent the headman away?"

"Nah." With a roll of his eyes, Taz indicated a cleft in the inner rim of the rock wall, perhaps a mile distant. "This's from a well off yonder. Don't you worry none about the locals getting to it. We know how to protect our own. One of them tries—*zap!*—he gets one nasty surprise."

"Why didn't you set up camp closer to the water?"

"Too close to the rocks." Taz made a sucking sound through his teeth as he squinted at the sharply eroded hillside. "Winds ain't exactly friendly."

Gareth nodded, thinking of the unpredictable air currents in the Hellers Range, which had made mapping and exploration by aircraft impossible. Whole sections of those mountains remained uncharted, at least by human explorers. Several of Darkover's nonhuman sentient races, the shy arboreal trailmen and the *chieri*, found sanctuary there. The *chieri* were probably extinct; no one had seen a living specimen since Keral ventured from the forests to aid Grandfather Regis against the World Wreckers.

"Besides," Taz went on, "it ain't like the well is far, not by space measure. We haul it back in a crawler, but we've only got the one, so we load it up good. We'll need to fill up tomorrow, most like. Want to come?"

Gareth managed an expression of eagerness. "If the captain can spare me."

In response, Taz took another draught, swished and spat, then downed the rest of his cup. From this, Gareth deduced there was little chance he would not be needed.

As if to emphasize his doubt, a warning klaxon blurted out a series of short, ear-rattling blasts. The other men went about their business, finishing the meal and an assortment of personal tasks, including lining up at the ultrasound unit that substituted for bathing.

Gareth remained, watching the shuttle rise in billows of superheated dust. The shuttle dwindled to a pinpoint of reflected brightness against the purpling sky. Now that he knew how to look for it, he found the starship, smaller than pearly Mormallor but larger than any of the stars. The *Lamonica* itself never landed on a planet's surface. It wasn't built for the descent through the atmosphere. Instead, two shuttle craft alternated shipside and dirtside. In addition, each was capable of low-altitude flight.

Meal and sanitation accomplished, the crew headed off to their barracks in one of the smaller prefabs. Gareth had thought that they, like the characters in tri-vids or the stories he'd heard about Darkovan outlaws, would stay up half the night drinking and gambling, or at very least sharpening their weapons. But there was nothing to drink beyond water and the small ration of space grog, these men didn't fight with knives, and the unrelenting gravity left them exhausted. They didn't even set a watch; that was accomplished by mechanical instruments. Gareth wondered what *Dom* Mikhail or *Tío* Danilo, both of whom had served their time in the City Guard, would say to that.

Although his muscles ached, Gareth wasn't tired enough to sleep. It was almost full dark, and he could hear none of the usual night noises. From the center of the camp, the lights on their poles emitted an occasional crackle, and various other machinery hummed or clicked. He tried to imagine what it must be like in space, encased in tons of metal, all of it cold and noisy.

He thought of seeking out Captain Poulos again, before it got too late, and trying once more to convince him. By his calculations, Lord Dayan's men could not have been more than a day or two behind. Why hadn't they shown up? The villagers could not have mounted an effective resistance, and Cuinn might well have welcomed them as powerful allies, as instruments of revenge.

Maybe the Shainsa party hadn't made it across the Sands of the Sun. Maybe they'd tried for the shorter route and missed the watering places, or had ridden their horses to exhaustion and death. Gareth, having grown up with people who treasured their horses, shuddered at the idea, but he was enough of a realist to know that not every culture, or every man for that matter, felt the same. To some, horses were no more than a means of transport, disposable and interchangeable, whose lives and suffering counted for nothing. Horses . . . and people.

He wondered if he had been one such, or might have been. Or still was. He'd bolted from Thendara with no care for the worries he would cause, the anxiety he'd bring to the people who loved him. He thought of his parents arriving to find him gone. Of *Tío* Danilo's expression.

He'd been as thoughtless and irresponsible as everyone believed he was. Nothing had changed since he was fourteen; no matter how hard he tried, it never would. *You can't build a castle out of eggshells,* after all. He'd thrown away the small measure of respect and trust he'd earned, and for what? For some overblown notion of duty? More like self-delusion!

The threat he'd so romantically envisioned, the raiding party from Shainsa, was never going to materialize. There was nothing left for him, no justification for prolonging this whole misguided escapade. He saw no other choice than to return to Nuriya tomorrow at first light to beg for a guide across the desert.

"You. Boyo." The giant guard had approached so silently, he emerged ghostlike out of the shadows. Without taking his eyes off Gareth, he tilted his head toward the shuttle.

Poulos had summoned him.

When Gareth and his escort entered, Poulos and Offenbach were bending over a crate at the far end, its lid partly open. Like the other crates, it was not made of wood but of some synthetic material. Scuff marks stood out pale and rough on the dark gray surface.

The mate reacted to Gareth's arrival, blaster in hand as he straightened up. Gareth froze. Adrenaline swept away any trace of curiosity as to what was in the crate. Whatever it was, it wasn't worth what a single look might cost him.

Poulos said, "As you were," and Offenbach lowered the muzzle of his weapon.

"Secure that," Poulos told his mate, meaning the crate. "We'll finish up later. It's time for a chat with our new recruit."

A few moments later, Gareth found himself as before, standing on the other side of the battered worktable from the seated captain. Offenbach slipped out the door, but the guard remained. Also as before, Gareth had no doubt that any suspicious behavior on his part would be promptly and unpleasantly terminated.

"I hear you're a good worker," Poulos said, his tone light. "But then, this is a primitive world. Such places offer little quarter for slaggards."

Gareth almost laughed aloud, thinking how many in Thendara held the opinion that he was exactly that, an overbred, spoiled *slaggard.* Instead, he assumed his most helpful expression. "I did my part."

"No problems with the crew?"

Gareth shrugged. Then, since more was clearly expected, he added, "I get along. I think they like me well enough."

The captain picked up a slender metal rod from the tabletop and ran it through his fingers, turning it this way and that. Gareth didn't recognize it; it could have been anything from a pen to a miniature weapon to a medical instrument. Whatever it was, he sensed the threat implicit in the way Poulos handled it.

Poulos said, again in that casual tone, "Then you wouldn't object to making your status with us permanent."

It was a statement, a demand, with no room for demurral. Gareth's throat closed up.

Click . . . click . . . went the metal rod against the table surface.

"I didn't expect an offer," Gareth said.

"I wasn't planning on making one. You posed quite a problem, sonny, breaking into camp like that. If you were a villager, which clearly you're not, I'd have no worries. By your own story, you're from elsewhere, and your Terran Standard is too good for you to have learned it from a book."

The clicking stilled. Poulos held the rod so tightly, the skin over his knuckles bleached white. "You've got a faint accent, although I can't quite place it. But I'll lay you a hundred credits you got it from someone in Spaceforce."

Gareth thought, *Jeram.*

Slowly Poulos opened his fingers and tilted his hand so that the rod rolled onto the tabletop. "I figured maybe you were just what you appeared. Maybe not."

Meaning, *Maybe you're Spaceforce yourself, a sleeper, a spy.* Zandru's demons, why had he ever thought it romantic to be Race Cargill, Terran Special Agent?

"So you see, it's much to your advantage to accept this . . . opportunity of a lifetime," Poulos said. "The aforementioned lifetime being yours."

Gareth swallowed hard, acutely aware of how his larynx worked beneath his skin. The metal rod gleamed, slick and bright and entirely too pointed.

Poulos laughed. "Green-eyed gods of space, sonny! I'm not asking you to sign your name in blood! Or bring me your grannie's scalp! Just stay in camp, preferably in plain sight, keep up the hard work, and get ready for one hell of an adventure! You comprehend?"

"Yes . . . yes, sir."

"Good, then. Get your sorry ass out of here. No nonsense about sleeping under the stars, either. You'll bunk with the crew." *Right where we can keep an eye on you.*

Gareth knew when he'd been dismissed. He hazarded a bow, the abbreviated nod of one of superior station to someone who must be acknowledged but never as an equal, and felt a small thrill when Poulos just smiled.

Between the snoring of the other men, the stuffy, odd-smelling interior of the barracks, and his own emotional state, Gareth didn't sleep at all well. He tried to convince himself that his only recourse—the only rational option open to him—was to play along, gain the captain's trust, and wait for an opening to get away, but he could not quiet the sense of impending disaster. It must be nerves, nothing but the notorious Elhalyn nerves, and not the Aldaran Gift of precognition.

The next morning, he stumbled into daylight along with the others and stood in line for his share of the soggy gelatinous mess that was breakfast, along with a cup of coffee. He'd never liked coffee when *Domna* Marguerida had offered him some of her precious hoard, and that had been far superior in quality. This stuff could be used to disinfect a banshee's nest. He gulped it down and tried not to think what it might be doing to his stomach.

There was no question of his going along on the water-haul crawler. Taz, who was the driver, had been alerted to Gareth's situation. He grinned from his seat in the narrow cab and sketched a salute in Gareth's direction as he guided the vehicle in the direction of the well. Robbard and Potbelly had gone along, leaving Gareth with the other two crew, the mate and the captain, and the captain's ever-present guard in camp. Gareth still hadn't learned the giant's name and was beginning to suspect he didn't have one.

"Don't worry, kid," said one of the other men, a rat-faced fellow with a long, barely pronounceable name that had been abbreviated to "Viss."

"Cap'n don't work us too hard, times like this. No point in it, see? Time takes as long as it takes, otherwise we'd just be shoving crates from one end of camp to the other, see?"

Gareth didn't see, although as the morning progressed, he managed to piece together enough of the other man's comments to deduce that another ship was expected to rendezvous with the *Lamonica*, at which time bargains would be struck and goods exchanged. Just when he'd heard enough to conclude that Poulos and his men were indeed smugglers, Viss would make a cryptic comment that implied piracy might also be involved. In the end, it didn't matter. What mattered was the willingness of Poulos, or any of his men, to do whatever was necessary to keep their presence here hidden from Federation eyes.

Around midday, Taz and the others returned with the crawler laden with filled casks. The work of unloading them more than made up for Gareth's easy morning. He and Robbard wrestled them into place beside the old casks.

Robbard wiped his forehead and took the cup hanging from the flimsy metal rack. He filled it from the cask they'd just set up and downed the water in one long draught. Rivulets ran down his jaw and neck, dampening the front of his shirt. With an appreciative belch, he wiped his mouth with the back of one hand, then held out the cup to Gareth.

The smell of the fresh water filled Gareth's head. Until that moment, he hadn't realized how thirsty he was. He'd been sipping the dregs from the old cask all morning, until he couldn't get the acrid taste out of his mouth. Even so, something—some nudge of instinct perhaps, or some tendril of incipient rebellion—held him back.

The brief hesitation was enough for the other men to crowd in front of him. There seemed to be an unspoken custom that no one drank from the new casks before the men who'd unloaded them. Robbard had taken his share, and now Gareth seemed willing to forego his own turn.

"Gods of space!" Viss said, in between gulps. "Thought I'd go alky on grog."

Taz poured a cup of water over his head. "This place could dry up a sun-slug."

"When this run's over, I'm shipping off to Thetis," said Potbelly.

"Gonna soak me in them waters for about a month. Figure it'll take that long just to rehydrate."

"Prune you!" said Viss, and everyone laughed.

Offenbach had emerged from the main building, watching the unloading of the casks. He strolled over.

Potbelly held out a cup. "Want a free sample?" The mate shook his head, clapped the other man on the shoulder in a friendly way, and turned back to the office.

"He doesn't drink the same water?" Gareth blurted.

"Sure he does, except when he shares the captain's." At Gareth's puzzled look, Potbelly lowered his voice. "Poulos doesn't like to mention it, but he's got, you know . . ." with a waggle of his eyebrows, ". . . so some quack put him on distilled water, no grog, no nothing, and now he swears by it. Bitch of a nuisance, but he's the cap, so we do things his way. Better him than me, right?"

The other men, having drunk their fill, began returning to their tasks. Robbard lingered, cup in hand, watching Gareth. "Well? What are you waiting for? An engraved invitation?"

Gareth eyed the line of casks. Affecting an insouciant shrug, he filled a cup from the old cask. The water was from the bottom of the cask, almost thick enough to be called sludge. Turning away, Robbard shook his head at the incomprehensibility of dirtsider taste. *Locals can't tell the difference anyway, so why waste decent water on them?*

After the water casks had been arranged, the men had drunk their fill, and a few other camp tasks been attended to, there wasn't much to do. Poulos remained indoors, along with Offenbach and the moon-faced guard. The rest of the crew divided their time between sleeping, repairing their personal gear, and grumbling.

The afternoon pressed thick and heavy on the bare earth. Even the shuttle looked as though a layer of dust had settled over it. Gareth drifted about the camp, pausing here and there but careful not to give the appearance of eavesdropping.

"Kid, you drive everybody crats if you don't settle your down bones," Viss called out, as Gareth ambled by for the tenth time. Viss slumped against the shade side of the barracks, along with Taz and Robbard. It looked as if they'd been engaged in a game involving six-sided dice, although Gareth didn't see any sign of money.

"Sit," said Taz. "Tell us about the local women."

Robbard made a sound halfway between a snort and groan. "For all the good it'll do us."

"We can dream, *ni*?"

Viss watched while Gareth folded his legs and settled beside the men. "Spill."

"They're Dry Towns women," Gareth said. "What else is there to say?"

"Gotta give us more than that! You passed through the village, didn't you?" Taz said.

Robbard made an expression of barely contained aggravation. "We haven't so much as peeked over that rim." He blew out a breath through loose lips. "Captain's being a stickler."

"But what I don't get is *why not?*" Taz said, his tone growing more animated. "Sure, while Cap'n wanted to keep on their good side, I can see the sense in it. Locals, you never know what they'll take the wrong way. Look at their women through the wrong eye and *bam!* you've got a war on your hands. Right, kid?"

In his mind, Gareth saw these men rushing back up the trail over the hills and charging down on Nuriya. He didn't know the level of hand-to-hand fighting skill of either the spacers or the village men. Even if they were roughly equal, the results wouldn't be good. That assumed Robbard and the others didn't carry off-world weapons . . . or the villagers didn't have more blasters. Even so, it would be all too easy to smash livestock pens or huts, and the Nuriyans lived close to the edge of survival. At least Rahelle wouldn't be there.

"Crat!" Taz snorted. "Ain't seen a woman since that mining colony on Bellatrix and they don't hardly count! It's not as if we were gonna *hurt* 'em. Just want a little fun! Desert women know how to have fun, don't they?"

"Not what *you'd* call fun," Gareth said, trying to manufacture an expression of disgust. "Shriveled up things, uglier than toads and worse smelling. They'd as soon skin and roast you as look at you."

Taz and Viss exchanged glances. Gareth's gorge turned sour as he realized they had taken the implication of cannibalism seriously. He did not want to find out why. His story might fall apart within moments of testing, but with any luck, he'd managed to discourage their interest.

Robbard heaved himself to his feet. The sun had dipped halfway behind the ridge line, and the slanting light bathed his face in an unhealthy flush. "Don't know about you, but I'm about gabbed out. If those women are anything like this sink of a planet, you can have them all, tied up with a ribbon. Uhn!" Wincing, he rubbed his belly.

"You okay?" Taz said.

"Sure. Should of known better than to drink so much, all in one go. A little lie-down'll see me right again."

Gareth watched as Robbard lumbered to the barracks entrance. Although the spacer looked steady enough on his feet, Gareth remembered that horses could get sick from drinking too much when they'd gone too long without. But horses weren't men. Men didn't get colic.

Neither Taz nor Viss seemed to be ill, but the heart had gone out of their talk. They no longer seemed to care about the village women.

As for Gareth, he was content to sit here, watching the lengthening shadows, when his companions shuffled off to their bunks. A soporific warmth clung to the earth. His muscles felt heavy. The sounds of the machinery receded, distant and dull. He bent his head, resting his forehead on his folded arms, and closed his eyes . . .

. . . and opened them to the sound of Offenbach shouting. By the fading western light, he guessed he'd been asleep for an hour. The air was noticeably cooler.

"Hai-yi-yi!" A shriek, shrill as a raptor's cry, shattered the dusk.

Gareth scrambled to his feet as a mounted horse raced past. Hooves pounded over the bare earth, throwing up billows of dust. His eyes streamed tears so freely that he could barely make out the attackers. There was a second rider . . . a third, all of them screaming at the top of their lungs and brandishing spears. Shouting came from the barracks.

The horsemen galloped between him and the building that housed the captain's office. They circled, swerving and changing direction. Gareth was reasonably certain they hadn't spotted him. He could rush them—and do what? All he had was the little knife he'd been allowed to keep, utterly useless in a fight. His hands ached for a sword.

One of the riders sprinted into Gareth's field of vision, wheeled his horse using knees and balance, and hurled something. The next moment, dust erupted like a fountain in front of the barracks door. A figure stumbled through the wall of dust—Gareth thought it was Viss, rather than Taz—and fell to his knees, clutching his belly.

Gareth rubbed his eyes and regretted it the next instant. His lids burned as if someone had thrown a handful of pepperspice in his face. With an effort, he wrenched his hands away. Through streaming tears, he glimpsed the center of the camp. A spear clattered off the metal side of the crawler, an instant before another landed between two water casks.

Gareth darted along the side of the barracks and hauled Viss to his feet. Retching, the older man half-fell into Gareth's arms. Gareth dragged him back into the open barracks doorway. The reek of vomit filled the room. His stomach clenched in rebellion. When he released his hold, Viss bent over, knees folding. From the far bunk, Taz struggled to rise, then fell back. In the gloom, Gareth couldn't see any reaction from Robbard or Potbelly. There was nothing more he could do here. He ran out of the barracks.

Shouting, two figures emerged from the office building. Gareth couldn't make out their words over the cacophony of war cries, neighing of the horses, pounding hoofbeats, and the muffled yelling from behind him. One of the figures, by his size and the controlled power of his stride, was most definitely the guard.

The guard raised his weapon and took aim. A bolt of searing light pierced the layers of dust. A horse screamed and reared. Only by a feat of athletic skill did the rider cling to its back. Apparently the horse had not been hit, only startled, for the next moment, its rider urged it into a hard gallop toward the office building.

The rider drew back his arm, readying his spear. The guard shifted his weight, settling deeper into his firing stance, and brought his blaster around.

"No!" Gareth darted forward, sickened with the certainty of impending, unstoppable tragedy. His warning blew away on the dust.

A second rider barreled past, so close that only a lucky reflex saved Gareth from being run down. The rider joined the spear thrower, the two of them sprinting for the office building. Gareth raced after them.

He slid to a halt just as the beam from the guard's weapon shot out. A shriek of inhuman agony drowned out all other sound. With tears still flooding his eyes, Gareth couldn't make out who'd been hit. He heard shouting in Dry Towns dialect, a high keening cry, then the syncopated beat of a horse's retreating gallop.

The guard stood half a pace in front of Poulos, Offenbach at the captain's shoulder. The guard still held his blaster at the ready in both hands. Danger radiated from the stillness of his posture. A few meters away lay the rounded form of a horse. Its legs splayed out from its immobile body.

Someone whimpered in pain.

"Robbard! Taz! Viss! Where the hell are they?" The captain's gaze lit upon Gareth, his face a mask of fury.

Gareth gestured back toward the barracks.

Poulos jerked his chin toward Offenbach, who headed in that direction at a near run. Then, to the guard: "Keep an eye on him."

The guard shifted his blaster to point directly at Gareth. Gareth dared not move other than to breathe. A trick of light glinted off the guard's eyes, as uncaring as obsidian.

Poulos strode over the fallen horse. Gareth heard another sound of excruciating pain. Was the rider, pinned beneath his own mount, still alive? The moment stretched out as the rider's cry faltered, then rose again. All the while, Poulos watched, impassive.

Do something! Don't let him suffer like this! In the guard's unrelenting glare, Gareth dared not speak.

Offenbach emerged from the barracks and hurried over to the captain. "Taz and Viss are sicker than rats. Robbard's dead. Lakrin—" that must be Potbelly's real name, "—he's barely breathing."

The guard's vigilance heightened. Nothing moved, not even the air in Gareth's throat. Then, with a curse in a language Gareth didn't know, Poulos lashed out with one boot. The kick landed with the sound of leather against flesh, of splintering bone, and then there were no more tortured moans.

Poulos inhaled, the air hissing between his teeth. A little of the raging tension went out of his massive shoulders. "Let the kid bury Robbard. It's got to be done right away in this heat. The others—" with a flicker of his gaze toward the guard, who gazed back impassively, "do what you can for them. Offen, we'll need a specific, if you can analyze the agent."

Offenbach nodded. "I'll do my best."

Poulos responded with a brief, almost invisible hunch of one shoulder as he pivoted and headed back to his sanctuary. Offenbach, grim faced, followed him like a shadow. The guard waited for a long moment before lowering his blaster.

Gareth swallowed. "It was the water. That's why the captain didn't get sick."

"He knows, sonny. He knows."

Something in the guard's words, spoken ever so softly, chilled Gareth to the marrow.

Gareth halted at the door to the barracks. The stench from inside hit him like a physical blow. In his death throes, Robbard had clearly fouled himself. The smell added to the general stink, a mixture of vomit and sour sweat. Gareth's mouth filled with bile-tasting saliva. Gulping hard, he fought against his body's reflexive need to purge itself.

"Steady, kid." Surprisingly gentle, the guard touched Gareth's shoulder.

They went in. A tube of yellow-hued lighting ran along the center of the roof, casting a sickly illumination over the interior. Bodies stirred on two of the bunks. Neither Robbard nor the fourth man, Lakrin, moved. The guard checked them and then pulled the blankets over both bodies.

"Oh, god . . ." the nearest man moaned in a voice so raw it was unrecognizable.

Gareth bent over the feebly writhing man. It was Taz. He'd never looked robust, but in the last hours his body had shriveled in on itself. He struggled to lift his head, then fell back, retching dryly.

"Come on," Gareth said, slipping one arm beneath the sick man's shoulders, "let's get you out of here."

The guard nudged Gareth aside and picked up Taz without visible effort. Gareth folded up the pads from the unoccupied bunk and took them outside. In a few minutes, they were able to lay both sick men in the open air.

Twilight washed the sky in hues of mauve and deepening purple. Nightfall, when it came, would be swift. For the moment, there was enough light to work by.

Gareth knelt beside Viss, who was in worse shape than his comrade. His swollen tongue protruded from his mouth and his breathing was rapid and shallow. His skin felt dry and hot to the touch.

"He needs water and hydration salts." The guard squatted on his heels, surprisingly limber for a man his size.

"I think there's a little water left of the old supply," Gareth said. "It should be safe. I drank it and I'm all right."

The guard's moon-round face remained impassive. Gareth could not sense anything of his thoughts or emotions. Either the man had unusually strong natural psychic barriers or else he came from a race that had no *laran* at all. Finally, the guard rose and disappeared into the barracks. From this, Gareth understood that he was to care for the two sick men while the guard took care of the corpses.

There was no use protesting that he had no experience in healing, certainly not patients as dreadfully ill as these. He would simply have to do whatever was necessary.

The dehydration must be addressed first. Gareth used his own cup to carry water. Crouching beside first Viss and then Tas, he lifted each man's head and steadied the cup for him to drink. By Evanda's blessing, both were able to swallow. Gareth didn't know what he could have done otherwise.

One at a time, the guard dragged the bodies from the barracks. He'd improvised a sledge from the disassembled rails of a bunk and what looked like a long-tailed coat. He disappeared into the gathering dark.

Offenbach came out and took a sample of the contaminated water. He paused for a moment to watch Gareth. Gareth kept doggedly to his work, although each cup drained the small amount of water left in the old cask still further. The guard returned, took a tool like a spade from one of the storage sheds, and left again, all without a word.

After a time, Gareth decided that Viss and Taz had drunk as much as was prudent. The water had turned slimy, and he feared it might harm as much as help. He found a pile of wadded-up clothing in a cabinet just inside the barracks door and tore the most worn of the shirts into strips. These he wet and began washing the faces and hands of his patients. He hated to leave them in their vile-smelling clothes. His initial burst of energy had faded, and doubts circled like *kyorebni.* Should he venture back into the barracks in search of clean garments? Or set to work washing up the mess inside? His gorge rose at the prospect, but perhaps if he didn't *think*, if he just *did it* . . .

Then one of the men—Gareth thought it was Taz—groaned and shifted to his side, and everything came clear. The barracks room didn't matter. Clean clothing didn't matter. What mattered was just getting these two men through this night.

Gareth lowered himself to the ground beside Taz and cupped the side of the other man's face with one hand. Taz jerked away, muttering incoherently. His skin no longer felt hot but clammy and alarmingly cool. The physical touch catalyzed a rush of sensations, fleeting and jumbled. Gareth bit back a curse. He felt as if he were half-blind and half-deaf, when he needed to be at his sharpest.

He glanced around for any sign of the guard's return and saw nothing. Offenbach had not emerged from the headquarters since he'd collected the water sample. Taz and Viss were too far gone in delirium to pay attention, or so Gareth hoped.

It took Gareth a few tries to find the clasp, but at last the Nebran locket popped open. Blue-white light flared as the starstone tumbled into his open palm. For an instant, it felt as if an answering light sprang up within his core. Brilliance filled him, even as a twist of light filled the crystal.

Gareth settled beside Viss, straightening his spine as he had been taught. *Your body is your foundation, your springboard, your anchor,* Grandmother Linnea had told him more often than he could count. *Make it strong and steady, so that petty discomforts will have no hold over your mind.*

Petty discomforts . . . Systematically, Gareth turned his attention to how he was sitting, the balance of his torso as it rose from his pelvis, the lift and fall of his chest, the position of his head, the suppleness of his neck. He was holding tension in his abdominal muscles again. Grandmother Linnea would scold him if she were here. Visualizing his breath descending along a channel of light directly in front of his spine, he felt his belly soften. Nodes of *laran* energy ignited inside him like a chain of miniature suns.

In his loosely closed hand, the starstone radiated warmth. He focused on it, knowing that his body would remain poised and energized. Behind his closed eyelids, he could still see the play of light in its faceted depths. He opened his mind and felt the psychoactive gem enhance his own abilities. And yet, he noted curiously, it was as if the stone were more mirror than amplifier.

Once he had established the flow of *laran* through his starstone, he directed it to the man lying before him. At first, he visualized the rough outline of a body. Then, as his mind penetrated more deeply into the patient's energy fields, he sensed a network of luminous strands. Some were thick cords, others no more than gossamer threads. Colors pulsed along them. . . .

Gareth noted patterns corresponding to internal organs. Red hues darkened into browns and grays, ugly shades reminiscent of stagnation and deterioration.

If only he knew more, knew what to do! Seeing what he saw, he did not think Viss would recover on his own.

Trained or not, competent or not, it was up to him. There was no one else.

Aldones, Lord of Light, what must I do? Sweet Evanda, Cassilda of the blessings! I've messed up everything I've turned my hand to, but don't punish this man for my shortcomings! Show me how to help him!

There was no answer. Of course, there was no answer.

He searched out the darkest, dullest channels. A tracery of charcoal filaments wove together, loose as a fisherman's net. The more he focused on them, the more their overall distribution became clear. He was not seeing blood or lymph vessels, nerves or bones or sinews, but a tapestry composed of millions of faintly glowing motes . . . living cells?

There, a voice whispered in his mind, or perhaps it was only his imagination, *go there . . .*

He didn't have the faintest idea how, except to trust to the instinct that had been bred into his lineage since humans landed on Darkover.

Let the light guide you . . .

The starstone ignited in response, burning even more brightly until his own body filled with blue-white flame. He opened the gates of his mind and let the energy pour out, seeking its own path.

For a wild and terrifying moment, fire raged through his inner senses. He lost all orientation, all connection with his body, his starstone, and the man into whose energy body he had ventured.

Down . . . This way . . . Seek . . .

He grasped the telepathic commands as a lifeline, grasped and held. And found himself once more floating above a web that ranged in hue from orange to barely luminescent gray, marked here and there by patches of black. As he watched, more threads dwindled and the dead zones enlarged. He heard—he *felt*—dying intestinal cells and, fainter yet deadlier, irreversible damage to kidney . . . liver. . . .

Down, the voice had urged, so *down* he went. Down between the flickering strands, down into a sea of particles that blurred and shifted so quickly he could not follow the changes. Infinitesimal energy surges, like motes of invisible lightning, buffeted him. Fear curdled within him, gelid and enervating, fear that he would become lost, shredded, torn apart, unable to return. In the back of his thoughts, he remembered the admonitions against unmonitored *laran* work, the dangers an untrained telepath posed not only to others but to himself. Whatever the risk, it was too late to pull back now. He lowered the last bulwarks of his mind and let the light take him.

In that moment, he became the light, and it became him. Exuberant, extravagant, unquenchable, it obliterated all awareness of himself as a separate entity. Boundaries melted. He had no thought of what he must do or how. The surging brilliance carried him, suffused him . . . penetrated the cells of the dying man.

Sparks flared as light answered light. Tendrils of brightness, of the very stuff of life, infiltrated the knots of blackness. Molecules combined, neutralizing toxins. He had no knowledge of the processes he was witnessing, only the deep intuitive sense of *rightness.*

Metabolic fires ignited as biochemical reactions built into a cascade.

Fluids surged through vessels, drenching tissues, a flood that carried away the ashes of dying cells and swept clotted debris from kidney tubules. Muscle membranes repolarized; nerves shimmered with electrical charge; synaptic gaps danced with transmitters. Diaphragm muscle fibers tensed and ribs lifted; air rushed through bronchioles.

Currents of air and blood caught him up, tossed him this way and that. Images sped by, too many and varied, too overwhelmingly fast for recognition. Flashes of color battered him. Within moments, he lost all sense of orientation.

The light that had sustained him wavered. Senses in disarray, he tried to grasp stability. He found none, and each effort only intensified his desperation.

Pull out . . . came the voice, so faint and distant he could barely make out the syllables, . . . *before it is too late* . . .

Pull out? he echoed dazedly. *How?*

Out . . . back . . .

All contact ended.

Alone, he was alone in a maelstrom of dark and light . . . ripped and shredded into a thousand bits of wispy nothingness . . . Brightness flared, wavered . . . nausea rose in storm-whipped waves . . . muscles spasmed. . . .

Help me . . . he thought, and then thought itself left him.

He slammed into something hard. The impact shocked along bones and bruised flesh. Lungs fought for air, but his breath had been knocked out of him.

Gasping, he pushed against the hardness. He found himself on his hands and knees. One hand curled around something small and sharp-edged. Yellow lights overhead cast a sickly illumination. He made out a man on a makeshift pallet beside him.

The man stirred. "Garrin?"

Garrin? In a rush, the last few days came back to him.

He opened his fist. The starstone glinted with its own inner light. Moving clumsily, he managed to wrap it in its layer of silk and put it back into the locket. His hands were shaking so badly, it took all his concentration to manipulate the clasp, but the movement seemed to help steady his vision.

"Viss? You're better?" His mouth formed the words, although his tongue felt as if it were coated with sour-tasting slime.

"Some. Gods of space, kid, what happened to me?"

What happened to you? What happened to me*?* But he knew the answer. In a fit of insanity, he'd accomplished a deep *laran* healing, one beyond the scope of all but the most powerful matrix workers. Even without Grandmother Linnea's repeated warnings, he ought to have known better than to attempt such a thing without a monitor safeguarding him, mind and body. Only by the wildest stroke of luck had he and his patient survived. Whether he had sustained any lasting damage remained to be seen.

Meanwhile, Viss was tugging at his sleeve. "Taz, Lakrin . . . Robbard . . . they okay?"

Gareth shook his head. Robbard and Lakrin were beyond help, but Taz might need the same cell-deep cleansing.

Blessed Cassilda, I can't go through that again!

Viss seemed to not have noticed that Gareth hadn't answered. With a sigh, he shifted onto his side, facing away from Gareth, and fell asleep.

Dizziness lapped at Gareth's senses. He struggled to remember what he should do . . . food, yes. Linnea had insisted that he eat after a *laran* session . . . and moving around, to stabilize those parts of his brain. . . .

But Taz . . .

Food first, he told himself sternly. *You won't be able to help anyone if you fall over in a faint.*

With an effort, Gareth managed to get to his feet, although he was none too steady. In the process, he remembered something Robbard had said during the last meal, about keeping packets of sweets for the natives. The last thing Gareth wanted was to put something in his stomach, and he had never been overly fond of candy, but it would be better than nothing.

The stench that greeted him at the barracks door almost brought him to his knees. He clung to the frame, unable to force himself to go in. His only other option, he thought dazedly, was to beg something to eat from headquarters.

He jumped at the sudden weight of a hand on his shoulder, losing his balance and almost falling against the guard's solid bulk.

"Boyo."

With heightened sensitivity, Gareth felt the guard's mixture of curiosity and suspicion and deeply masked kindness.

"Viss . . . he'll be all right." Gareth was babbling, making no sense to himself, praying that he didn't sound as incoherent to the guard as he did to himself. "I need to eat . . . and then see about Taz. He wasn't as bad . . ."

The grip on his shoulder tightened for a moment. Then the guard released him and turned away. Breathing heavily, Gareth leaned against the doorframe.

Move, he thought, but his legs would not obey. Tears brimmed up in his eyes, further distorting his vision. Savagely he told himself that if he gave up now, he would be throwing away any hope of saving Taz. It did not matter that these were not his kin, his own people. What mattered was that he was the only one who could reverse the poisoning. So he stayed on his feet.

A few minutes later, the guard reappeared. He brought two of the packaged meals, steaming hot, and a glass bottle of distilled water from the captain's own supply. At the sight, Gareth's knees folded under him. His hands stopped trembling enough for him to spoon the food into his mouth. After only a few mouthfuls, he felt a tremendous, overpowering hunger. His body recognized what it needed and demanded sustenance. The water tasted flat but sent a shiver of pleasure through his belly. He devoured one of the meals and drank all the water. By the time he handed the empty bottle back, he was feeling stronger and cautiously hopeful that if Taz needed a similar healing, he would be able to do it.

"You sure were hungry." The guard sucked air through his teeth. "Good to go?" Gareth clambered to his feet in response. "When you're done, you can get to work cleaning up in there," meaning the barracks. "I left disinfectant and some other stuff for you. Just stay in camp, you hear? You're a good kid, and it'd be a shame if you got into trouble. Take my meaning?" The guard disappeared into the headquarters building.

Gareth couldn't think past tending to Taz, praying he'd have the strength for a second healing. Whether or not he was successful, he wouldn't have any resources left, certainly not for escape.

Viss was sleeping quietly, his chest rising and falling in deep, easy breaths. Taz had been in better shape to begin with, and he'd been able to down more of the uncontaminated water. Even so, his skin felt cold and slick with sweat. He shuddered when Gareth touched the side of his face.

Gareth settled himself, cross-legged, beside Taz. The starstone brightened as he cupped it in his bare palm. A breath lifted him into a near-trance. This time he knew what he was looking for. The memory of the interlacing webs of energy was still fresh in his mind. He wasted no time casting about. As before, he directed his own mental energy into the dying tissues and sensed returning vitality flare up in response. He was relieved to find the damage was not as extensive as with Viss. Taz would have survived without intervention, although his kidneys and liver might have been impaired.

It was not until Gareth withdrew into his own body that he realized he was alone. The voice that had guided him through healing Viss had not spoken to him again. For a dizzying moment, he wondered if the voice had been real or only a figment of his own desperate need.

No, he thought as he touched Taz's forehead, still cool but no longer damp, *I didn't imagine it.* He'd reached out, begging for help, and something . . . *someone* . . . had answered.

Gareth, like most of his generation, referred to the four primary gods of the Domains—Aldones, Evanda, Avarra, and Zandru—as figures of speech. He didn't for a moment believe in any supernatural being that could or would answer personal prayers. Yet *someone* had guided him through the healing.

The most likely explanation was that Grandmother Linnea had left a residue of her personality and knowledge in his matrix stone, perhaps because she had handled it as his Keeper. Another possibility was that in the extremity of the moment, he'd managed to access buried memories of what she'd taught him about *laran* healing.

Yes, that must be it. What else could it have been?

Carefully, he rewrapped and replaced the starstone in the locket, then tucked the amulet inside the front of his shirt. Weariness drenched him. Hunger gnawed at his edges but did not threaten to overwhelm him as it had before. Even so, he was steady enough on his feet.

Gareth found the second of the prepackaged meals where he had left it, although it was no longer hot. He sagged against the outside of the barracks to eat. The food steadied him but did not entirely lift his fatigue. Instead, he felt the full impact of having expended so much mental energy in such a short time.

I'll rest here . . . just for a minute. His head dropped forward. Dimly, he felt the packaging slip from his limp fingers.

He roused some time later, although he could not have said what had woken him. The camp lay utterly still under a sky that lacked even a hint of western brightness. Stars spread across the heavens, piercing the dry desert air. Of the four moons, only Idris had risen.

Taz and Viss still slept. By the regularity of their breathing and the resilience of their skin, both were doing well. Gareth went to the door of the barracks. Some of the smell had dissipated, but the muck would be harder to clean when fully dried. He'd best get to it.

He found a large plastic bottle labeled as disinfectant, as well as a bucket and a bag of cloths and a large, coarse-bristled brush. Sighing, he told himself that if he had been permitted to enlist in the Guards cadets, he would have been assigned similar duties and been expected to perform them regardless of the hour or his own inclinations. Besides, the work needed to be done, and there was no one else around to do it. Taz and Viss were well enough where they were, but only for a time. The night was chilling rapidly and they'd fare better inside.

Gareth set to work, beginning with the area around Robbard's bunk. Before long, he'd skinned his knuckles and stubbed his fingers more than a few times. The disinfectant stung his abraded skin. His eyes watered at the smells and the slime, or perhaps from the images that flickered across his mind, fractured impressions of a man struggling to breathe, retching and purging as his body fought to rid itself of the poison.

Gareth sat back on his heels, brush hanging from one limp hand. Two men were dead, criminals perhaps but not evil men, and now no one would know, no one who remembered them or cared for them. They would never come home, and it would be as if they had never existed. . . .

His chest heaved, but not with the effort of resisting the waves of nausea. Within him, a great sobbing wail gathered, pushing out through his throat, pouring out into the night. He hunched over, leaning into the brush on both hands, scrubbing and weeping and scrubbing, as if he could scour away the terrible, senseless loss. His nose ran and his eyes burned and his throat ached as if flesh could not contain his grief. He couldn't understand why he felt so strongly. He'd barely known these men.

He went on from one patch of filthy floor to the next, from vomit-spattered bunk frames to compact footlockers, each marked with the owner's initials.

AT . . . L . . . JV . . . RE.

The letters, in the Terran alphabet, brought him up short. So Robbard had been a first name, a personal name. *E* must stand for a family.

Gareth crouched beside the lockers of the two dead men, running his hands over the initials. He picked them up, stacking one on top of the other, and got to his feet. They were surprisingly light. Perhaps the dead men's other possessions remained on the starship. The best thing to do would be to take the lockers to Captain Poulos.

"Captain? Captain Poulos? Offenbach, are you there?" No one answered when Gareth set down the lockers and rapped on the door of the headquarters building. He knocked a second time with still no response. The door itself had been secured.

Gareth started back toward the barracks, thinking to leave the boxes there until morning, when he realized that the crawler was missing. He rushed over to where it had been parked with a growing sense of dread.

Poulos, Offenbach, the guard—gone!

Gareth halted on the scuffed and empty site. In the depths of a *laran* healing, he would not have noticed a herd of banshees stampeding through the camp, let alone a crawler leaving it.

In the next heartbeat, he realized where they had gone. And why.

Gareth reached the hills at an adrenaline-fueled run. Between Idris and the stars, there was barely enough light to make out the trail. His feet pounded up the slope.

The trail steepened, following the folded contours of the earth. He stumbled on the rough footing, once or twice almost going to his knees. Fire bathed his lungs. His heart thrummed. Heat radiated from his body, but the wind of his passage dried his sweat almost as quickly as it dampened his skin. He pushed himself even harder.

He tripped on a stone the size of his hand and went sprawling. Somehow he managed to catch himself on his hands. The impact knocked the breath out of him. He sat back on his heels, rubbing his hands. His whole body rocked with the force of his breathing.

Wiping his hands on the thighs of his pants, he clambered to his feet. Tiny bits of gravel had embedded themselves in his skin. The abrasions stung as they bled.

Gulping in one breath after another, he took his bearings. His headlong rush had brought him much farther than he'd expected. Below him, yellow lights marked the off-worlder base. When he peered at the trail above, the top of the ridge seemed almost within reach.

The hills around him lay so still, he felt as if he were the only living thing in the world. Above him, the stars had faded. Idriel hung low on the horizon.

If he had not been listening to the velvety silence of the night, he might have missed the sounds from the other side of the ridge top. Over the hammering of his heart, he caught the whine of a motor, the grinding of metal treads on loose rock.

Without a second thought, he scrambled off the trail. A moment later, a pair of headlights appeared where the trail cut through the top of the hill. They seemed to hover for a moment before descending. The trail curved away, taking the crawler out of direct sight, but the noise of its approach grew louder.

Gareth flattened himself against the boulder. He told himself that the passengers could not hear the beating of his heart over the sound of the engine. They were not searching for him. They had no reason to believe he had left the camp.

But as soon as they arrived, they would know differently.

The crawler was almost upon him now. He smelled its exhaust. Just as it passed, he heard a voice—Poulos, he thought—but could not make out the words. Then the vehicle was descending toward the camp and he could breathe again. He was shaking, his hands clenched so tightly that his fingernails dug into his abraded palms.

Slowly he got to his feet. A hint of pastel light touched the eastern sky. At least he knew where the crawler and its riders were. With that thought, the sense of urgency that had been blanketed by the near encounter returned in full. This time, however, he kept control of himself. He climbed steadily and deliberately, not in headlong haste.

Shortly after Gareth began his descent on the far side of the ridge, the village came into view, bracketed between two arms of dark rock. He stumbled to a halt. His muscles went lax in horror.

Even in the ebb of night, he could see the village, or what remained of it, burning.

Lines of flame marked wooden structures, sheds and huts, and the rails of livestock pens. Here and there, stone walls created blots of darkness. Nothing moved against the brightness.

He plunged down the trail, half-flying, half-tumbling. Pebbles sprayed out from under his feet. He slid and slipped but somehow kept going.

Dark Lady Avarra, may I not be too late!

No, there *was* someone below . . .

Gareth pushed for more speed. He burst on to the flat and sprinted for the village, speeding through the outskirts. He passed a few of the poorer huts, distant from the rest, that appeared to be intact.

He rounded what was left of a livestock pen. Half the railings had fallen away and the rest were burned nearly through. Goats darted this way and that, bleating piteously. The largest rushed at him, then skittered to a halt and reared on its hind legs. The fire cast weird reflections on its eyes. Its pupils were so dilated, they looked round. Incensed, Gareth aimed a kick at the nearest post. His foot collided with fire-weakened wood. The post shuddered but held. A second kick, and the rails on one side broke into burning fragments. The goats bolted through the opening. Something on the other side screamed.

Another goat . . . a horse or an *oudrakhi*? Or—*please, Dark Lady, no!*—a human? The sound was so distorted, he could not be sure.

The well, where was the well?

Anyone able to get out of danger would already have done so. There might be wounded . . . he'd need water.

Another frenzied sprint brought him to the center of the village. The stench of charred flesh hit him like a physical blow. A pall hung in the air, a smothering psychic miasma, the residue of terror and pain. A lungful of smoke provoked a coughing fit.

That pile at the very place where he'd feasted with Cuinn and the others . . . that lumpy sprawling heap . . . was bodies.

Bodies . . . he forced himself closer . . . charred and twisted, but not by natural fire.

Blasters . . . they'd used blasters *on the villagers!*

Gareth doubled over in a renewed spasm of coughing. The last dregs of the adrenaline that had fueled his race over the hills vanished, leaving a sickly, roiling chill in his guts. Ignoring the pain, he balled his hands into fists and pressed them over his mouth.

This was all his fault, his! He had been unspeakably arrogant and puerile, picturing himself off on a great adventure—*Race Cargill of the Terran Secret Service!*—heedless of the consequences. Now his friends had paid with their lives.

Stop it! he raged at himself. This was the worst indulgence of all, wallowing in self-pity instead of taking action, as if his ego were more important than those who might still be alive. He sent a promise to whatever god might be listening that whatever happened, whatever good he might be able to accomplish, he would claim no credit for it.

Nausea crested. Somehow he resisted the wave of retching. Then it receded. Letting his hands fall at his sides, he inhaled sharply. The fires had almost burned themselves out, and the eastern sky was visibly brighter. At least, stone and sand and bare earth could not burn. The survivors, if there were any—

As if in answer to his thought, a figure emerged from behind one of the buildings, dragging another. Gareth called out. The figure straightened up and turned toward him.

It was Rahelle.

For a moment, Gareth didn't recognize her beneath the cloth covering her nose and mouth. He ran up to her, grabbed her by the shoulders, and shook her, dislodging the cloth. He found himself shouting at her, barely coherent accusations, demands for explanation, words jumbled with relief and fury.

She made no attempt at a reply, but hung there in his grasp, trembling. Her lack of resistance at first fueled his outrage, then extinguished it. He saw the wetness shining on her cheeks, and all anger fled. What had happened here was not her fault.

Rahelle pulled away. He had not the strength to hold her.

She could have been one of those bodies in the center of the village. If anything had happened to her. . . .

"Is there anyone else a-alive?" he stammered.

She shot him a quick, hard look. "They're just outside the village perimeter. The smoke's not so bad there." Her voice had a husky quality, most likely from the smoke.

"Who—" he broke off at a spasm of tickling in his throat and pointed toward the pile of bodies.

"Some of them are human, yes, but not all. One of our horses is there, your mare, I'm afraid. She panicked and ran into the path of an off-worlder weapon. Her body was too heavy to shift, so I left her. The others ran off with the *oudrakhi*."

You've done all this by yourself? His throat closed up around the words. He glanced down at the body she'd been dragging, a woman.

Rahelle stooped to lay one hand on the woman's chest. "She's still breathing. I think she's the wife of one of the headman's sons."

Gareth picked the woman up, slipping her slender form across his shoulders. Rahelle led the way past a few smoldering huts.

Dawn and lingering smoke turned the air into a luminous haze. It would have been beautiful except for the circumstances.

The survivors huddled together, Cuinn at their center. The headman looked dazed. A hugely swollen lump, blackened and oozing blood, marked one side of his forehead. No one made a sound as Gareth and Rahelle approached. Mothers clutched their children to their breasts. Soot streaked their faces and clothing. Their eyes had a glazed expression of incomprehension. An older man took the unconscious woman from Gareth's arms and sank to the sandy ground, cradling her and stroking her hair. Then several of the babies burst out crying.

Gareth stood for a moment, torn between gratitude that this many villagers had survived and impatience at their near-stupor. Someone had to see that the wounded were properly tended. Something broke open in him, a dam giving way, and he fired off a string of orders. He sent the younger men back into the village to search for anyone else still alive, to begin salvaging what they could—food, implements, clothing—and others to fetch water and anything that could be used as bandages.

Staying alive through the next few days would be the easy part. He didn't think Poulos would come back, unless it was to search for him. Even so, the villagers couldn't stay here. They'd lost too much and were too few to rebuild a community, even supposing they could recover their livestock. But without horses or *oudrakhi*, the trek to the next village would be perilous. He wished he knew more about survival in the desert. If it hadn't been for Adahab, he'd never have reached Nuriya.

Adahab had promised to return in five days, now four. . . . There was hope, after all.

Meanwhile, Rahelle went to each of the remaining villagers and gently questioned them about where and how badly they were hurt. The grandmother who'd served as village healer had perished, and the woman Gareth had carried died before regaining consciousness. Two of the smaller children looked so stunned, so hollow in their eyes, that Gareth feared they might never recover their wits.

By midmorning, the fires had been extinguished and a few goats rounded up, so there was a little milk for the children. The stone-walled huts had survived, some in better condition than others, but at least there would be shelter enough for everyone. Best of all, the well was intact.

The men set about cutting up the dead horse. They worked without speaking, doggedly finishing what must be done. Since he had no skill in butchering, Gareth helped with the burials, dragging the dead outside the limits of the village. When he returned with each new body, it seemed that the ones he had laid out had sunk into the sands, as if the sand itself were a living thing, cradling the twisted forms. By the next morning, it would cover them. Perhaps there were rituals to be followed and prayers to be spoken, but Gareth did not know them. The Comyn followed the old tradition of burial in unmarked graves, with family and friends sharing remembrances of the departed, each one ending with, "Let this memory lighten grief."

After a short time, Gareth no longer smelled the charred flesh. He had become inured to the reek. Each one of these bodies had been a living person, a man or woman or child that he might have spoken with, laughed with . . . He was grateful for the silence, for the weight of the physical burdens, for he had no memories to offer up to lighten grief.

All but one of the women had rallied, organizing the children, laying out the wounded on pallets improvised from scraps of salvaged blankets. Where they had found cooking implements and food, Gareth didn't know. When a younger woman shyly offered him and Rahelle cups of gruel, he noticed that her string bonds dangled, broken, from her wrists.

Gareth and Rahelle sat together in the dwindling shade beside Cuinn's hut. His cup, thick-walled unglazed pottery, was blackened and chipped. The gruel itself tasted burned, but it was hot. Rahelle sipped, pursed her lips, and set her cup down on her lap. Gareth felt much the same way about the taste.

"You should eat," he said, as much to himself as to her. His muscles throbbed with weariness. When had he rested last? The few hours' sleep he'd gotten last night had long since vanished. He forced himself to take another swallow.

She arched one eyebrow as she glanced in his direction, then returned her focus to the cup. "Don't tell me what to do."

"I've already discovered the uselessness of that. You never listen to anyone. You were supposed to be on your way back to Shainsa and your father! Do you have any idea how dangerous it is here? You could have been *killed*—"

"And I suppose *you* were so much safer at the *Terranan* camp? What if they'd discovered who you are? You have just as much to hide as I do!"

"*Who I am?*" he snapped, hearing the irrational temper in his own voice. "What do you mean by that?"

"Only that *someone* has to keep you out of trouble!"

"Who appointed you my Keeper? I was doing just fine without you!"

At her look of incredulity, a bubble of something like laugher burst open inside him.

Her gaze faltered. "I *did* leave. I rode to Duruhl-ya. Adahab agreed to guide us back, but he needed another day to finalize his betrothal contract. The return took me longer than I expected. I should have passed the night at Duruhl-ya, I suppose. As it was, it was past sunset by the time I returned. I saw the fires . . ."

For a long moment, they sat in silence. Gareth found his voice. "I couldn't stop them."

Another pause, then: "Why did they do it?"

"Cuinn poisoned the well. Two men died."

Rahelle drew in a sharp breath. Gareth closed his eyes, resting his head against the rough stone of the wall. He felt her fingers, strong and slim, twine through his. The contact brought a rush of inexpressible comfort.

I thought you were gone, safely away from here. His arms ached to hold her, although he was painfully aware of the risk carried by even this touch of hand on hand. Her best hope for safety lay in her disguise. Unlike the Comyn, Dry Towners did not tolerate *lovers of men.*

Gently, he loosened his fingers from hers. As she stirred, he felt the leap in tension in her body. She scrambled up, listening intently. Her ears were sharper than his, but now he caught it, too—the muffled bawl of an *oudrakhi.*

By the time Gareth had clambered to his feet, a handful of villagers were already gathering toward the desert side of the village. Following them, Gareth said to Rahelle, "Adahab has returned earlier than promised."

"I don't think—"

Dust and sand rose in low, desultory billows that did not conceal the approaching horsemen. The party was clearly in desperate condition. Their horses plodded, heads sagging, feet stirring up yet more dust. Just in front of them paced an *oudrakhi*, straining at its lead line and now and then letting out a vociferous complaint. Gareth thought it belonged to the village and had run off in the attack. The riders must have found it and realized that it would surely lead them to water.

Dust caked the hides of the horses and the clothing of the men. They had covered their lower faces with scarves, desert-style. Even so, Gareth could not mistake the quality of their gear or the swords that hung scabbarded from their saddles or across their backs.

Within moments, riders and villagers met. Gareth nudged Rahelle into the center of the villagers, so that the two of them would not stand out. There was none of the usual excitement at the arrival of so many strangers, no murmurs of curiosity, no children darting out for a better look, none of the welcome Gareth had received. These people were still in shock and not yet come into the fullness of their grief. They feared more of the same.

The foremost rider pulled his mount to a halt and dropped the *oudrakhi's* lead line. One hand resting on the hilt of his sword, he used the other to loosen his scarf.

"I am Hayat, son of Dayan, High Lord of Shainsa! Who speaks for this place?"

Son of Dayan? Gareth didn't remember having seen this man among the courtiers in the presence chamber. With luck, Hayat wouldn't know him, either. The man at Hayat's right side, however, looked familiar. His gaze lit on Gareth, and the muscles around his eyes tightened in recognition.

Gareth knew that unflinching regard, those gray eyes. When he'd last seen this man, fire and shame had flushed the Dry Towner's sun-dark cheeks.

"Ancient wisdom tells us that only a fool returns to a battle he cannot win," the other man had said. *"The wise man lives to fight another day."*

And so Merach had.

Merach, sword arm of Dayan of Shainsa. Merach, whose life Gareth had spared in the ambush on the road to Carthon.

The villagers drew together, murmuring under their breaths.

"Well?" Hayat demanded. "Has the fire stolen your tongues as well as your wits? What happened here?"

No one stepped forward to answer him. He clenched his hands so tightly around the reins that his horse, weary though it was, threw up its head and jigged sideways in protest. His lips drew back from his startlingly white teeth and his brow furrowed. Gareth had seen that expression many times at the Thendara court, usually on the faces of men with little control over their tempers, men who expected instant obedience but lacked the ability to accommodate themselves to reality. Then, such a display of ill temper had either amused or annoyed him. He had been sufficiently above their position that he had nothing to fear. He knew they vented their frustration on those without rank or powerful protectors, but he had not cared enough about the servants and underlings, not to mention dependent family members, of whose lives such men made a misery.

Should he step forward now, drawing attention away from the villagers, who had not yet regained their full senses after the attack? Should he attempt to masquerade as one of them, or would Merach identify him as the trained swordsman of Carthon?

While Gareth hesitated, Merach nudged his horse closer. "Look around you, Lord Hayat. Surely these people would give you answers if they were able. There is no rebellion in their faces. They are but ignorant country folk, sturdy enough for simple work but without sophistication."

Hayat grunted in response. The strain in his features eased. He let the reins slip a little through his fingers, and the white horse drooped its head. "I suppose *you* in your superior wisdom can tell me what happened?"

"I would not presume to inform the great lord of what he surely has deduced from the evidence of his own eyes. He has already recognized that the burn marks could not have been made by any ordinary fire."

Gareth let his breath out, unaware until that moment that he had been holding it. One of the babies whimpered fitfully.

"The demon-fire weapons," Hayat muttered. Then he gestured to his men. "Dismount! The horses need water. You and you," pointing to two of his men, "and you two," then to Rahelle and one of the older village boys, "tend to them. And the gear as well, sand-rats. If so much as a bridle ring is missing, or there's a single hair of my horse's mane out of place, I'll take it out in strips of your hide."

There was a brief scurry as the Shainsa riders dismounted and removed their weapons from their saddles. Rahelle and the boy led the horses off toward the well.

"You there!" Hayat indicated Gareth with a flick of one finger. "Step forward. The rest of you, prepare a meal. My men are hungry."

The women, startled into action, started hurrying back toward the center of the village. Gareth hunched his shoulders and hung his head, trying to look as bewildered as the others, as cowed by the presence of so many armed men. Merach would not be fooled . . . but Merach had already had a chance to betray Gareth and had not.

"Your Magnificence," Gareth mumbled and made as if to prostrate himself as he'd seen men do in Shainsa.

"Oh, get up!" Hayat snarled. "If I wanted to see the back of your head, I'd have ordered it severed from your body. I want to see your eyes when you speak to me, so that I know you're telling the truth!"

Gareth made a show of reluctantly, fearfully raising his face.

"You seem to have some small measure of wit," Hayat said. "Do you have a tongue as well? A name?"

"G-Garrin, great lord."

"Garrin, is it? Tell me what happened here. Who attacked this village? Where did they come from?"

"I'm sorry, great lord. I don't know." Gareth kept his features blank. So Lord Hayat thought he could read truth in another man's eyes? It was more likely that Dayan had given his son command of this mission and then sent Merach along to keep him out of trouble. Doubtless it had been Hayat's idea to ride straight across the Sands of the Sun, regardless of the risk to the horses.

"You *don't know*?" Hayat demanded with scornful incredulity. "How can you not know who did this to your own village? Are you, after all, an idiot? Or do you suffer from periodic blindness as well as deafness?"

"I-I was not here." Gareth held his hands out from his body to show his undamaged clothing. "I had gone looking for an *oudrakhi* that had strayed." Pointedly, he turned his head in the direction of the beast that Hayat's men had followed.

"Is there *anyone* in this dust hole of subhuman halfwits who knows? Where is the headman?"

"Great lord, he is wounded—"

"I did not ask after his health!" Hayat struck Gareth backhanded across the face. "I asked where he is! Or is your hearing as defective as your wits?"

The blow staggered Gareth. When he raised his hand to his mouth, he felt the slickness of blood. One of Hayat's heavy rings had split his lip open.

He stared at his fingers in incomprehension. He'd been injured before, sometimes by accident on the fencing field or from his own inattention or mischance. But never before in his memory had a man deliberately struck him.

When Hayat drew back his hand to strike again, Gareth flinched. He did so without thought, although even as he sank to his knees, it occurred to him that appearing to be more overwhelmed than he actually was would not be a bad strategy. If Hayat thought he was too cowed to even speak, it might be worth the beating that he was about to receive.

"Lord." Gareth heard Merach's voice. "There is no need to sully your hands on vermin such as this. Your perspicacity will surely reveal the dwelling of the chief."

Gareth remained as he was, crouched in the dust, until the fading footsteps told him that Hayat and his retinue had moved off. He got to his feet, but not quickly in case one of them was watching. Affecting a limp, he headed for the center of the village.

By the gathering of riders around Cuinn's hut, the headman had not moved from where Gareth and Rahelle had left him. A woman's wailing cry rose above the voices of the men. Gareth heard Hayat's imperious tones, then a hoarse rumble in reply. He pressed through the little throng of villagers.

". . . curses upon the outlanders . . ." That sounded like Cuinn. ". . . owe them nothing."

"The gracious and compassionate Lord Hayat means to avenge your people." Merach's voice rose above the others. They fell silent, even the wailing woman. "Will you permit this outrage to go unanswered? Now that you have gained such a powerful protector? Think of your children, if not yourself!"

"I will not greet another dawn . . ." Cuinn's voice receded to an indistinguishable mumble. Gareth could no longer understand the headman's speech, but the sense was all too clear. Even without *laran*, Gareth had not the slightest doubt that Cuinn was telling the entire story of the blasters and where he had gotten them. Cuinn would rather see such weapons in the hands of men whose rank and honor he respected, than remain with those who would destroy an entire village. It was revenge of sorts, delivered in the belief that Hayat and his riders were mighty enough to overcome the off-worlders' defenses.

Clearly, Hayat thought so, too. He strutted from the hut, giving orders to his men to establish a perimeter guard and prepare for battle the next day, but his bearing was not the empty bluster of a coward. He truly believed in his victory. No one would have dared to stand against him in Shainsa. So far, Merach had ensured his success on this expedition.

But none of the Shainsa party, not even Merach, understood what they faced. They themselves had in all likelihood raided and burned, taken slaves or destroyed whole villages. The smoking ruins of Nuriya and the desolation of its inhabitants were not beyond their experience. Confident of victory, they would go up against blasters with swords.

The gathering dispersed, with the villagers salvaging what they could and tending to the injured. Two of Hayat's men erected a pavilion, and the rest went about commandeering the best of the remaining huts. Gareth stayed out of their way. He felt torn between his outrage at the burning of the village, his own desire to see Poulos and his forces suffer for what they had done, and the foolishness of any assault on the base. He reminded himself that there was more at stake here than simple retaliation. If by some twist of fate, Hayat prevailed, that would place the blasters in the hands of the enemies of the Domains.

As horrific as their burning of the village had been, the off-worlders were not the worst threat to the Domains. The real danger came from those same weapons in the hands of men such as Hayat. Gareth had no real hope of dissuading Hayat from making an effort to obtain blasters, whether by force or persuasion, yet he had to try. Failing that, as he most likely would, he must do whatever was necessary to prevent an alliance between Poulos and Hayat. Perhaps he could sow suspicion, create a rift, but he had no idea how he might accomplish that.

Carrying himself like a man treading a path between two looming catastrophes, he approached the pavilion. The cloth roof provided shade, and the flaps on two sides had been drawn up to admit what little breeze there was. A pile of blankets, wool woven in distinctive Shainsan patterns, covered the floor. Hayat had stretched out on the blankets, head propped on one hand, a cup held in his other.

The Dry Towner on guard outside blocked Gareth's path. He was one of the riders who carried his sword across his back, hilt just behind his left shoulder. A bandolier holding an array of knives crossed his chest. "Get lost, sand-rat. Unless you're looking for a beating."

"Please . . ." Gareth insinuated a fawning tone into his voice, as he had heard so many times from those seeking favors from him at court. "I beg a word with the great lord . . ."

The guard scowled, clearly skeptical that a villager could have anything of interest to say.

"Let him approach, Ward," Hayat called. "He'll furnish a moment's amusement, if nothing else."

In the shade of the pavilion, Gareth dropped to his knees. It surprised him how naturally he prostrated himself, he who had never before been required to bow to a superior.

"Well?" Hayat's eyes glinted as he drawled the question. "I hardly think you're here for more punishment, so what's this about?"

Gareth took a breath, reminding himself that it was best to stick to the truth as much as possible. "These off-worlders, the ones the headman spoke of . . . they will not welcome a native emissary. You will be leading your men to certain death if you try. Yes, once they were willing to bargain—a few of their weapons in exchange for a secret base. But that pact is broken now. They insulted Cuinn's honor and in return, he poisoned the well from which they drew their water."

By Hayat's reaction, Cuinn had not revealed that part of the story.

"Two of the off-worlders died, and others sickened. Their leader ordered this attack—" Gareth gestured to the smoke still rising from the smoldering remains of wooden structures. "They have weapons much more powerful than blasters, and they will not hesitate to use them. If they destroyed a village to prevent Cuinn from revealing their presence, do you think they'll hesitate to eliminate anyone else who might tell the tale?"

Gareth stumbled to a halt. He'd already said more than was prudent. His tongue had run away with him.

Hayat did not dismiss Gareth but studied him for a long moment. One corner of his mouth twitched. Merach stepped out from behind one of the tent sides. Hayat's gaze flickered to his adviser and then back to Gareth. "How exactly do you know all this?"

"I've been—I've seen the base."

"More than just *seen*."

Gareth hung his head. "As you say, great lord."

"Humpf! Merach, what do you think? Is it worth whipping the truth out of this one?"

"His story does explain what we've seen here. It would do no harm to approach this base as friends and allies, rather than as conquerors, just in case the rest is true. If this one has had dealings with these off-worlders, he might be useful to you, lord."

"And best remain unwhipped?"

Merach inclined his head in acknowledgment. "For the time being."

"I don't trust him," Hayat continued. "He's not like the others. He has eyes in his head and a tongue in his mouth." He looked as if he'd like to change that but did not want to cripple a useful tool.

"He looks familiar, this Garrin," Merach said. "I've seen him before . . ."

Gareth bowed again, this time to Merach, carefully keeping his face averted. "In Carthon, my lord. I believe we passed in the plaza when I was about business for my master."

"Carthon," Merach repeated, a trace too smoothly. "Yes, it must have been. A trader, as I recall."

"You're a long way from home," said Hayat.

Gareth hung his head deeper.

"In Carthon, he might have had dealings with the *Hali'imyn*," Merach said. "Perhaps even learned their tongue, what is it called? *Chasta?*"

"I have often spoken that language," Gareth murmured. "I know a little off-worlder talk, as well. That is how I know what I just related to Your Magnificence."

Hayat grunted again. Then, after a moment's reflection: "He might serve as a translator. Yes, that's it! Merach, you're worth your weight in rubies! Take the sand-rat away and make sure he doesn't run off. Find out what else he knows. We'll take him with us tomorrow and see if he's telling the truth. If not, he'll make a good example to show these *off-worlders* I mean business."

Merach laid one hand on Gareth's shoulder and propelled him, firmly but not too roughly, in the direction of Cuinn's hut. When they were out of earshot of the pavilion, Merach said, "I would let you go in payment of my honor debt, but that would ensure your death. Hayat would think you guilty of deceiving him and would not rest until he placed your severed head on a stick. He enjoys the hunt."

Gareth lifted his head to meet the other man's gaze. "I did not do what I did in order to extract payment at a later date. You owe me nothing. What I said to Hayat was true, all of it. If he tries to threaten the off-worlders or even if he doesn't, if they even *think* he does, they'll eliminate you all. You have no idea how powerful their weapons are."

"Demon-fire."

"Not demons. Off-world technology."

Merach made a dismissive gesture, as if the origin of the weapons did not matter, but his expression remained serious.

"Hayat's used to having his own way with his father's warriors to back him up," Gareth blurted. "He'll go riding into the *Terranan* camp, not caring who he offends, acting as if he's entitled to whatever he wants. Swords are useless against the weapons down there. He'll get himself and everyone who follows him killed." At this, Merach's eyes narrowed slightly, and Gareth knew his point had hit home. "Look, I may not have said this in the best way. Hayat won't listen to me, but he does listen to *you*."

"A man's sword is but one tool in the service of his *kihar*," Merach said, in the manner of one reciting an oft-heard aphorism.

No man of honor is ever truly disarmed.

They had reached Cuinn's hut. Someone had replaced the charred wooden door with a blanket. "Remain inside," Merach said, sounding genuinely regretful. "It's for your own safety. If Lord Hayat sees you wandering about the village, he'll be certain you are up to no good." *Then not even I can save you.*

"I won't run off." Gareth grasped the edge of the blanket, creating an opening wide enough to slip through sideways. The smells of burned wood and sweat, of pain and grief, flowed from the darkened interior. He turned back to Merach. "I will go with you tomorrow. To do what I can to prevent another slaughter. I meant what I said about the dangers of having anything to do with the off-worlders."

"What is Hayat to you, that you would commit yourself to his service?"

"I would not see him—or any man—slaughtered for no reason other than his own ignorance," Gareth replied. "The killing would not stop with his own death. Lord Dayan would retaliate. He would be bound by honor and kin bond to do so."

Merach inclined his head, his eyes hooded. "Indeed. He would send an army to avenge the death of his son and heir."

"He'd stand as little chance as Hayat. The violence would escalate until nothing could stop it. Look at this village! Would you see all of Shainsa reduced to *this*?" Gareth broke off, his mind filled with images of wildfires ravening across the Hellers, of the fertile Plains of Valeron a vast reach of ashes, of Thendara itself a splintered ruin—

Without waiting for Merach's response, Gareth strode into the hut. The darkness blinded him until his eyes adjusted. His heart, which had been hammering against his ribs, slowed.

A figure in a long dark robe and headscarf crouched beside the bed where Cuinn lay. For a moment, Gareth thought he looked upon Avarra, the Dark Lady who ushered the dying into the peace of death, but she was only an old woman in widow's black. She dipped a cloth into a basin of water, wrung it out, and wiped Cuinn's forehead.

The woman looked up, her eyes like blots of night in the pale oval of her face, and returned to her nursing. The headman rolled his head from side to side, murmuring incoherently. Gareth leaned against the wall beside the door and slowly slid to the floor.

There was nothing to do except wait. Wait and hope that Rahelle had had the sense to get to her horse, wherever she had hidden it, and escape to Duruhl-ya.

His own chances for survival were almost nonexistent. If he could, he would make another attempt to dissuade Hayat, but he didn't think he'd be any more successful. Merach was a man of sense and intelligence, but even he would not overtly defy his master's son.

The old woman finished her task and left. Hours passed. From time to time, Gareth got up and stretched. He slept fitfully, rousing when the woman returned. She brought not only a basin with fresh water but a jug and a plate of smoke-smelling boiled grain for Gareth. She repeated her bathing, but this time Cuinn lay as one already dead. For a time afterward, Gareth heard the sound of Cuinn's breathing, and then he did not hear it.

When the woman came back the third time, it was night. She halted just inside the blanket curtain, sniffed twice, and withdrew. A few minutes later, two of the older village boys took away Cuinn's body.

Alone, Gareth lost all sense of the passing of night. He could not bring himself to lie down on Cuinn's empty bed. His mind, which had been so full of doubts and questions, went blank. He did not feel calm, he felt empty, empty of purpose, empty of grief.

Eventually, he slept.

The next morning, one of Hayat's men—Ward, Gareth thought—came to tell him to prepare to leave. Gareth was given a few broken fragments of bread, probably from the Shainsans' own supplies, and was allowed to drink and to wash his face and hands at the well. A sort of altar had been set up beside the well, a few pieces of partly burned wood on which someone had drawn a crude picture of a toad in charcoal. One of Hayat's men knelt there. His eyes were closed, and his lips moved soundlessly. He'd placed a piece of dried fruit beside the dried flowers on the altar.

Without thinking, Gareth raised one hand to his amulet. If he pretended to be a devotee of Nebran, but failed to offer even a single prayer for protection, someone might well take notice. He still had a few coins tucked in the folds of his belt; Hayat's men might be rough, but they were not thieves. He placed a small copper piece beside the other offerings and settled on his knees in imitation of the other man. He had no idea what the proper prayers might be, but no one questioned him. Perhaps there was no set procedure and men simply offered up their hopes and worries. Kneeling there, moving his lips, his eyes closed against the ruin of the village and the flat, uncompromising light, Gareth felt an unexpected sense of calm creep over him.

He startled alert at the sounds of horses, of men calling to one another, and shouted orders to mount up. He clambered to his feet and shuffled over to the knot of riders. Someone had caught a couple of the village horses and was leading them back . . . *Rahelle!*

Headstrong, stubborn woman! Gareth was too furious to look directly at her. He'd sent her away—she was supposed to be safe! Instead, she'd wheedled herself into becoming Hayat's horse boy.

Hayat himself was in a fine, fiery mood. He laughed loudly as he made his white horse prance and spin on its hindquarters. A handful of village children watched, silent and round-eyed. Merach sat quietly on his neat bay, wasting neither his breath nor his horse's strength on idle show. He looked over at Gareth, his gray eyes somber.

He knows this is no holiday parade. Perhaps there was hope if Merach had believed the warning.

Ward indicated that Gareth should mount a speckled gray mare. There was no saddle or pad, only a rope halter. The lead line had been looped under the noseband, through the beast's mouth, and then tied into reins. They started off and soon were climbing into the soot-dark hills.

Gareth struggled to maintain his seat. He'd ridden bareback on a few occasions, but always on a horse with a smooth, round back. The mare's spine stuck out like a ridge of knives. As the trail became more steep, Gareth took hold of her mane to keep from sliding. By contrast, the saddles used by Hayat's men had thickly padded seats for comfort. As they neared the crest of the hill, it occurred to Gareth that going down would be much worse, with nothing between his tender parts and the mare's bony withers. Rahelle, Gareth noticed, perched on her horse with apparent ease. At least she kept to herself in her horse boy disguise. None of Hayat's men looked twice at her.

Merach, in the lead, raised one arm to signal a halt. Hayat nudged his horse beside the bay. Gareth tried to imagine what the base must look like to men who had never seen a spaceport before. The sight clearly excited Hayat even further, although he had sense not to gallop downhill the rest of the way.

"Lord Hayat, if we can see them, can they not also see us?" Merach said.

Gareth caught Hayat's expression, a glint of frustration quickly smoothed away by reason. He was intelligent enough to realize that a measured advance was his best hope of a friendly welcome.

He'd probably prefer an open fight, Gareth thought. He couldn't see men moving in the camp below, but he had not the slightest doubt that Poulos knew the riders were there, as well as their numbers and weapons. Poulos was not such a fool as to dismiss the possibility of retaliation from the village.

Hayat started once more down the hill. He kept the white horse to a measured pace, with Merach next. The trail forced the riders to go single file. The horses dipped their heads, picking their way on the uneven surface. No one attempted to converse. The only sounds were the clopping of the hooves, the skitter of dislodged pebbles, and an occasional snort or whisk of a tail.

It was just as well for Gareth that they descended slowly. He kept sliding on to the mare's withers, and then, when he could stand the pressure no longer, he would grip the thin ribcage with his knees until his thigh muscles burned. Before long, he was alternately bruised and aching. His hips felt twisted half out of their sockets.

They were about two-thirds down the hill, with the base camp in plain sight, when Merach cried out a warning and pointed. Hayat came to a stop. The horses crowded together. For a moment, Gareth could not make out what was happening, but then a gap opened between the rider in front of him and Merach's horse. He saw a commotion at the base of the shuttle. There seemed to be too many men, even assuming Taz and Viss had recovered.

One of the men, Offenbach most likely, ran for the office building. A mass of glowing brilliance, whiter than any natural flame, ignited below the shuttle. Rumbling, hard-edged thunder rolled out from the valley. The rock beneath Gareth's horse shook. Pebbles and dust tumbled downhill. The white horse whickered in terror. Behind Gareth, another horse tried to turn around. It slipped on the rock, and only the skill of its rider kept it from falling. Gareth's mount stood, head down, placidly oblivious to anything but a chance to rest.

The sound increased, quickly rising to deafening loudness. The shuttle no longer rested on the ground; there was a distinct gap beneath it. Then it rose, at first slowly but gathering speed with each passing moment. Within moments, it had cleared the crater on its way into space.

"Hai!" Hayat exclaimed. "Victory is mine! See how the cowards flee before me!"

Hardly fleeing, Gareth thought.

He struggled to make sense of the scene below. Surely the smugglers had not abandoned their base, not with the buildings intact, the lights burning, the crates in their stacks . . . no, there were gaps here and there. He might not have noticed, had he not hauled them into place himself.

Two men emerged from the headquarters. One he would have recognized anywhere—Poulos.

With the massive guard at his back, Poulos took up a position facing the trail. By the angle of his upper body, he was staring at the Dry Towners. Both he and the guard held unfamiliar weapons, forearm-long cylinders with handgrips like elaborate basket hilts. Gareth's skin prickled, although he did not think the off-worlder knew he was among them. He hoped Nebran or whatever god these Shainsans prayed to was listening. He wished there were some way he could make Rahelle leave, although that was impossible now.

Hayat had the sense to realize that the men below were not only aware of his presence but were ready for trouble. With a glance at Merach, he nudged the white horse downhill again. The horses, picking up the tension of their riders, flicked their ears unhappily.

By the time they reached the bottom of the hill, a third man had joined Poulos and the guard. Gareth did not recognize him, although he'd met all the men in the camp. The three carried the rod weapons in plain sight and with an ease that spoke not only of familiarity but of supreme confidence. These men had nothing to fear from horsemen armed only with swords. Gareth thought of the poisoned well and of the value Dry Towners placed on cunning and deceit. Perhaps the odds were not as uneven as Poulos clearly assumed.

On the other hand, Poulos had fired the village.

Hayat shouted out a reasonably polite greeting, which had no visible effect on the off-worlders. Poulos remained immobile, his face set, his gaze never faltering. When Hayat continued, rattling out the traditional phrases that every Dry Towner would know, still Poulos did not respond. Offenbach shifted uneasily; perhaps he understood a little or wanted to take out his translator device but dared not put down his weapon. At last, when Hayat was on his fourth or fifth iteration and growing visibly impatient, Poulos jerked his chin in Offenbach's direction.

"Ask him what the devil he wants."

Offenbach said something in Dry Towns dialect, so broken and ungrammatical that if Gareth had not known what the spacer intended, he might well have guessed wrong.

Hayat turned to Merach with an expression of disdain. "What sort of mumble-mouthed uttering is this?"

In the pause that followed, Gareth kicked his horse forward. "Magnificent lord, if I may—"

"May *what*?" Hayat's temper was barely under control.

"—now act as translator?"

"Merach, your opinion?"

"I do not believe he will play us false, my lord. He has no reason to love these outlanders." Merach meant, *After what they did to the village.*

"Go on then, wretched boy! But at the first sign of trouble, I will have your hide flayed from your bones."

Gareth bowed as best he could in the saddle. He had not expected Hayat to agree so readily. He weighed and discarded the idea of riding up to Poulos. A man on horseback had psychological as well as tactical advantages, but he did not want to needlessly antagonize the off-worlder chief. Poulos would be sensitive to the indignity of having to look up to someone he regarded as having lesser status. Praying his knees would not give way under him, Gareth leaned over the mare's neck, dragged his right leg over her rump, and slid to the ground. Fire shot through his inner thighs and hip joints. He clung to her mane, forcing himself to take deep breaths. He did not need to feign hesitation in approaching Poulos. He could barely walk.

The off-worlder's eyes narrowed as Gareth halted, well beyond arm's reach, and bowed.

"Traitorous little sneak. What are you doing with *them*?"

Gods, this wasn't going to be easy.

Gareth tried unsuccessfully to still the quivering in his legs. Now that he was this close, he was certain he'd never met the unfamiliar spacer. He said, using Terran Standard, "You destroyed the village."

"So now you've brought the local police force to set things right? I didn't mark you as that stupid. Naïve, but not stupid."

Gareth took a breath. He would gain nothing by responding to insults. "These men have nothing to do with the villagers. They're from Shainsa, across the desert, and their leader—the one on the white horse—is the son of the lord of that city. He was greeting you in the respectful way of his people. Perhaps the words do not translate properly without cultural connotations."

As Poulos considered this, his expression became a little less belligerent. "What does he want, then? The same deal as I had with the villagers? Tell him, *Not a chance.* I made that mistake once already."

"It would be better to speak to him yourself. If I may translate . . . ?"

"The kid does speak their ling'," Offenbach said.

"Will you know if he messes up?" Poulos muttered, not taking his eyes off Gareth and the Dry Towners beyond him.

"In anything essential, I think so. Not in the finer points, though, and I might make even worse errors. The translator doesn't handle regional variations well, and it's set for the village dialect."

Poulos made a sound deep in his throat. "All right, then. But first tell him, that chief of theirs, at the first sign of trouble, they're all fried. Dead. Got it?"

Gareth bowed again and went back to Hayat, to whom he bowed even more deeply. He was getting used to all this scraping and found to his surprise that the movement helped to loosen his back.

After a few exchanges, with Gareth shuffling back and forth, the talks progressed enough for Poulos to permit Hayat and Merach to come closer, unmounted. By slow steps and subtle prompting, Merach managed to convince Hayat to suggest that although the Shainsans sought a trade for weapons, they had far more to offer than had the villagers.

"News travels quickly across the sands, and there are many who would seek to take the fire-weapons for their own," Gareth translated Hayat's words. He did not add that the attack on Nuriya would only fuel the desire to obtain the means of such destructive power. Then he explained, "Lord Hayat says he is a great warrior among his people, capable of dealing with such—I believe the word he used is *stable sweepings*."

"Protection, eh?"

"They're offering to deal with the locals so you won't have to be bothered, yes." Gareth turned back to Hayat. "Magnificent lord, I do not think the off-worlder chief is willing to give away the sun-weapons after the treacherous manner in which the villagers repaid his generosity."

"Perhaps he might consider an exchange," suggested Merach. "Among Shainsa's many riches are goods such as our gold filigree that is without compare in the Dry Towns. These off-worlders appear to be traders, and traders know the value of craftsmanship. Even everyday items can become precious commodities when no one else has access to them."

"Precious commodities, hmmm." Hayat tugged a ring off the little finger of his left hand. It was no doubt the least of his personal ornaments, being worn on the least of his fingers, but he would not offer a blade to an outlander, not even an eating knife.

Poulos examined the ring carefully. Although he kept his expression impassive, Gareth detected his keen interest in the way he turned the ring over, testing its weight in his hands, running his fingers over the gold. The ruby would be of excellent quality, or the son of the Lord of Shainsa would not have worn it.

When Poulos looked up from his examination, he was smiling. "I believe this discussion is worth pursuing. I propose a trial period, beginning after the conclusion of my present business. Until I am certain we can trust one another, however, I will not commit to a trade for weapons." He held out the ring.

After Gareth had translated, Hayat refused the ring with a munificent smile and bade Poulos keep it as a token of goodwill. "May this be the first of many gifts we will bestow upon one another."

Poulos slipped the ring into a pocket and suggested that the party set up their own camp on the edge of the base, well away from the crates. "Take your rest. The water's been made safe, and there's enough for your animals as well."

At this point, the discussion came to a halt as a shuttle appeared overhead and began its descent. The air vibrated unpleasantly and a wind sprang up. Hayat's white horse jigged sideways, ears flicking, tail wringing. The other horses snorted and circled as their riders wrestled them under control.

"*You*," Poulos shouted to Gareth over the din of the shuttle's engines, "get over to the barracks!"

Outrage flickered across Hayat's features, but it faded when Merach directed his attention to the shuttle, looming ever larger overhead. The insult Hayat's *kihar* had suffered at this peremptory appropriation of a member of his party would have to wait for satisfaction.

As Gareth hurried away, he glanced back at Rahelle, who was already occupied with managing the restive horses. He wished he could think of a way to bring her with him, but a horse boy could not desert his responsibilities at a time like this.

Tucking his head, Gareth broke into a shambling run. Whirling air currents from the shuttle stirred up clouds of dust. He ducked through the open door into the closed-in dimness of the barracks. The walls shook with the roaring of the shuttle. The air still smelled of disinfectant, but less strongly than before. Taz was sitting up, slouched against the wall. He lifted his hand in greeting and pointed to the other bunk.

At Gareth's approach, Viss lifted his head. He said something, but his voice was so soft, Gareth could not understand him over the din.

Gareth raised his voice. "Do you need anything?"

Viss made an ineffective effort to roll up on one elbow and made a gesture of drinking. Gareth found a cup and a plastic bottle of water. He poured out a cup. The water looked and smelled all right, but without using his starstone, he couldn't be sure. Poulos had said the water was now safe, so perhaps Offenbach had found a way to neutralize the poison. He glanced at Taz, who nodded encouragingly and pointed to the bottle beside his own bed.

Gareth slipped one arm under the sick man's shoulders and held the cup to his mouth. Viss gulped down most of the water, then lay back with a visible sigh.

The racket from the shuttle died down. A horse neighed. The barracks felt closed-in, a prison. Gareth wondered whether he'd find the guard on duty outside.

"Offen said you'd gone," Taz commented.

"I came back. How do you feel?"

"Ah. Weaker'n a Vainwal mud-puppy. But I'll be around for the next rainy season."

"Mud-puppies? On Vainwal?" The reference reminded Gareth of Nebran. "The Dry Towners worship a toad god."

"Resurrection myths. Every planet's got 'em." Viss broke off into coughing.

Gareth chuckled, although the situation was hardly humorous. Here he was, discussing comparative religion with a space smuggler, when Hayat might be concluding his deal.

"The shuttle took off," he said, "and another one landed."

"Customer," Taz said, as if that explained everything.

"For what's in the crates?"

Taz slitted his eyes as he returned Gareth's stare, as if to say, *What else?*

Viss broke into another fit of coughing. Gareth didn't like the sound of the cough, wheezy and congested. He'd heard of men contracting pneumonia after inhaling their own vomit; it was said to be very bad.

Viss said, "You were in my dreams . . ."

"You were pretty sick—" Gareth protested, uncomfortably aware that Taz was listening and might remember his own healing.

". . . surrounded by blue light. . . like an angel . . ."

"You must have been hallucinating." Gareth shook his head, hoping he sounded reasonable. "All I did was get enough clean water into you so your body could get rid of the poison."

"Yeah, don't go making the kid here into some kind of hero," Taz drawled. A note in his voice clearly indicated he didn't think much of anyone who would run out on his comrades in the middle of a crisis.

The accusation stung. "I went over the hills. To the village. Do you know what happened? Poulos," Gareth almost spat out the name, "burned them! Women, babes, old people, everyone! They live on the edge of the desert, just barely surviving. Now they have nothing, those that are left!"

"Forget them—"

"Don't tell me to forget!" Gareth could not remember ever being this angry. He knew it wasn't rational to take it out on these two men. They'd had no part in the decision. They'd been lying here, too sick to even lift their heads, while the village burned. "Listen, if you'd been there—"

"No, *you* listen, kid. Or weren't you here when me'n'Viss almost took the Starry Walk? I could've sworn you were."

Gareth refused to be sidetracked. "If Poulos had the sense of a rabbit-horn, he would have known that Cuinn would never let such an insult go unavenged." He shut his mouth, appalled that he was about to *justify* the poisoning of the well.

Taz sighed. "Kid, it don't matter. It's too bad about the villagers, but when all's said and done, that's the way of it. On these backwater planets, if it isn't one thing—warlords or plague or simply being in the wrong place at the wrong time—then it's another. Better they learn right off not to mess with us. They hit us, we hit them back harder. This ain't no business for soft hearts."

Gareth's chest pounded with the beating of his heart. His breath came as fast and hot as if he'd just run all the way from the village. In a way, in his mind, he had. What kind of men were these, friendly enough one moment and callous the next? What kind of business did Taz mean, that attracted such men?

"What in the seven hells is in those crates?" Gareth said.

Taz shot Gareth a stony glare that said men had died for asking that same question. Viss was silent except for the phlegmy noise of his breathing.

Gareth gulped. "Sorry. None of my business."

"Captain decides you're in, he'll tell you. I have to say, that's not looking too likely at the moment. Not that I'm not grateful, mind. Took care of us right proper you did, when you could've run off. But . . ." Taz shook his head, leaned back against the wall, and closed his eyes.

". . . like an angel . . ." Viss murmured. Gareth wished he would shut up.

Gareth went over to Robbard's empty bunk. It had been stripped of bedding except for the pad. He sat down, braced his elbows on his knees, and rested his face on his hands. And tried not to think about what might be happening outside.

It occurred to him that he didn't have to stay in the barracks. Neither Taz nor Viss was in any shape to stop him. He could sneak out . . . and then what? Single-handedly disarm both the Shainsa party and the off-worlders?

He would simply have to wait, wait and reflect how very poorly prepared he was to deal with any serious problem.

Raising his head, he said, "If there's a chance Poulos will keep me on, I'd like to know what's in store. Okay, you can't tell me what's in the crates. How about those shuttles—there's more than one, right?"

"Used to have three but lost one out by Ephebe when a deal went bad." Taz, evidently deciding this was a safe enough topic, warmed to the story. "Not that it was any great loss, mind. Eygen—that's our engineer, and she's spent so much time in micrograv her bones can't take dirtside, so she don't never leave the *Lamonica*—Eygen had patched that thing together so many times, you could've opened a—" and here he used a term Gareth didn't know "—shop with it. General rule's to keep one onboard, one dirtside. When we got us a customer in orbit, they take turns, like."

"So they're never in the same place at the same time," Gareth said.

Defensively, that made sense. Without backup, a ship without landing capability couldn't afford to have cargo or crew stranded, without any means of reaching them. He could no longer hear the shuttle's engines and wondered why Poulos had come "dirtside." Perhaps whatever was in the crates couldn't be entrusted only to crew.

"Ephebe," he repeated, turning the name over in his mind. He'd heard of it before, something about a Federation intervention there. "Wasn't there some big military action at Ephebe?"

"Yep." Taz sucked air through his teeth. Outside, men were shouting to one another. "Bad for the locals but good for business. Now there're a dozen Ephebes, more every day. Gods of Hyades, what a mess! I'll be just as glad when I can cash out and find me some nice little planet nobody's ever heard of."

If you found us, then someone else will find you, Gareth almost said. Then two parts of his thoughts meshed. The *Lamonica* had been at Ephebe, Ephebe, which the Federation had felt a need to subdue . . . *"good for business . . ."*

"Weapons!" Gareth exclaimed. "You're weapons dealers—smugglers—selling to planets that rebel against the Federation."

"I never said that. And neither did you."

Gareth caught a wash of emotion from the other man's mind, and it was confirmation enough. No wonder Poulos had set down in a remote location, well away from the Domains . . . which might still have radio contact with the Federation.

Just then, a figure appeared at the door, silhouetted against the brightness outside. It was the off-worlder Gareth didn't know.

"You work," the crewman said.

Gareth got to his feet. "I understand Terran Standard," he said in that language.

". . . an angel . . ." Viss murmured.

The spacer frowned. "What's wrong with Viss?"

"I don't know. His cough sounds bad."

The crewman hesitated. For all Gareth knew, the two were friends as well as shipmates. "We'll take him up on our last run. The Castor Sector ship has a medic. So the sooner you stop yammering and come with me, the sooner he'll get help."

"What needs doing?"

"Loading crates on the shuttle." The crewman glared at Taz, as if Taz had created a work crisis by deliberately getting sick. Taz slumped even farther on to his bunk.

Gareth followed the crewman, whose name was Jory, to the stacks of crates. There were only three of them with himself and Offenbach. Taz and Viss wouldn't be fit for work for a while yet. Offenbach drove the crawler, with Gareth and Jory loading and unloading the crates at either end. The crates themselves had indented handholds, which made handling them easier.

Poulos stationed himself inside the shuttle, directing the stowage of the crates. He kept glancing in the direction of the Dry Towners, although they were some distance away.

One of the riders took off at a jog for the ridge trail, most likely to fetch their pack animals and provisions, along with Hayat's pavilion. Rahelle had gotten the other horses unsaddled and hobbled; one at a time, she was leading them to the water area. Merach was on his feet, hand to sword hilt, alert. Hayat, on the other hand, reclined in the shade cast by his horse, propped on a saddle draped with its own blanket. He couldn't have been comfortable, but there was a certain dignity in his pose. Once, this might have been all the luxury a rider of the desert might desire.

Halfway through moving the stack, Offenbach looked terrible. He was sweating heavily and had gone gray around the mouth. Jory was also having a hard time, although he was younger and more fit.

Gareth finished carrying one of the crates up the ramp to the shuttle and walked over to where Poulos and the guard stood. "Offenbach needs a rest."

"I didn't hire you as a medical consultant."

"With respect, sir, you did when you asked me to see to the sick men."

"Transit windows don't accommodate themselves to our wishes. Can't afford to slow down now." Poulos glanced overhead, beyond the hazy sky. "Offen! Take a break! The kid and Jory'll carry on."

"Captain . . ." Gareth moved closer and lowered his voice. The guard glanced in his direction, then returned to surveying the Dry Towners. "Hayat knows what's in the crates."

"What do you mean? Who told him—did *you*?"

"I'm not that much of an idiot," Gareth retorted. "I figured it out myself, and if I did, Hayat has, and if he hasn't, Merach has. They know you aren't carrying fine carpets or perfumes, not out here where no one has the money to buy such things. The way they think, there's only one type of trade goods worth all this safeguarding and only one reason to destroy the village." He paused to let Poulos fill in the rest of the argument for himself.

Poulos bent closer to Gareth. "You're only half right. Most of this stuff isn't for guerilla fighting on the ground. It's replacement parts for shipboard weapons, bound for the Castor Sector. We've only got enough hand weapons for ourselves and a few crates of outdated blasters for trade, and most of those are almost out of charge."

"So the ones you gave to Cuinn—"

"—were little more than fancy trinkets. Usually the trade works great. The chief fries up a few game animals and then mounts the blaster on a stick for everyone to bow down to, and nobody realizes it's out of power. But Cuinn got greedy . . . and you know the rest." Poulos let his breath out in a sharp exhale. "Nothing to be done about it now."

"Hayat won't take that for an answer. He'll think you're trying to trick him."

"Then you'd better pray to whatever shriveled-up gods there are out here that he never finds out." By his tone and the shift in his posture, Poulos indicated the conversation was at an end.

Back and forth, back and forth, Gareth and Jory carried one crate after another to the crawler, then Jory drove and Gareth hung on to its sides for the slow, rocking trip to the shuttle. Then they'd reverse the procedure. Gareth had never thought of himself as strong, but he was able to take the greater part of the weight of each crate. Even so, Jory began to flag.

The stack of crates dwindled. One of the last was in bad shape, its surface scuffed and worn. The crates might have been designed to withstand hard usage, but this one had seen more than its share. In the process of moving it, Jory's hold slipped and the crate fell on one corner. As Gareth bent to straighten it, he saw that one of the latches had come undone. The lid was so badly warped that he couldn't close it without unfastening the other latches in order to reposition the lid. A layer of clear material, most likely meant to cushion shock, did not obscure the lettering on the boxes inside.

Cepheid X light pistols.

Whatever those were, Gareth would have wagered Comyn Castle itself that there were more of them in other crates.

"Not that way. Let me do it." Motioning Gareth aside, Jory leaned hard on the lid. He secured the latches, first the nearest, then the one diagonally opposite.

The crawler took an eon to reach the shuttle, or perhaps it only seemed so. They found Offenbach slumped on the ground beside the shuttle ramp. His breathing was labored. Poulos was giving orders for takeoff in a voice gone hoarse with weariness.

Gareth squatted on his heels beside Offenbach. The thought came to him that one way or another, when off-worlders and Darkovans came into collision, people died. The early years of contact with the Federation had been filled with accidents and misunderstandings. He'd been taught so much political history and had understood so little of the human cost. None of his tutors had mentioned burned villages, children with empty eyes . . . or men like Robbard or Viss.

Offenbach licked cracked lips.

"I'll bring you some water."

Gareth found several of the plastic bottles and filled them from the casks. There wasn't much left, for the horses had drained the supply. As he neared the shuttle, he noticed the crawler heading his way, carrying the guard, Offenbach, and Jory. A rumbling issued from the shuttle. Engines whined, and the elongated nozzles on the lower part of the craft began to glow.

"Hop on board!" Jory shouted over the increasing din. He slowed the crawler for Gareth to grab the hold bars. Until the shuttle attained sufficient altitude, conversation would be impossible.

Gareth helped Jory settle Offenbach in his own bed in the headquarters building. Offenbach was breathing somewhat better now. Gareth thought he would improve with rest.

Since Offenbach was too exhausted to safely pilot the shuttle, as was the original plan, Poulos had gone himself.

"I can tell you, he wasn't happy about leaving Deeseter behind," Jory told Gareth, "even if there really wasn't any choice, not with them—" meaning the Dry Towners "—out there."

Deeseter? So that was the guard's name.

With Taz and Viss out of commission and Offenbach down as well and now Poulos gone . . . It wasn't a good situation, but Gareth didn't think the smugglers understood just how vulnerable they were.

"Think Taz'll be on his feet soon?" Jory squinted up at the red-hued sun, now slanting well toward afternoon. He and Gareth, having finished getting Offenbach settled, stood at the headquarters building door, looking toward the barracks.

Gareth shrugged. He seemed to have become the camp healer, although he had no particular expertise. He took a conservative guess. "Tomorrow?"

"Good. If he can drive, we'll send the two of you out in the crawler to get more water."

"It may not be a good idea to wait," Gareth said. With his glance, he indicated Rahelle leading two horses to the water area. The smugglers hadn't counted on how much water horses needed, even these desert-bred animals. It would be dangerous to risk running out of water at a time when anything could go wrong. Gareth said as much aloud.

Jory did not answer at once. His brow tightened, and he began chewing on his lower lip, then caught himself and stopped. It was one thing to carry out the orders he'd been given as temporary leader, and quite another to have to make unexpected decisions himself. Jory wasn't stupid; he clearly understood both Gareth's point and the risks of sending off most of the able-bodied men.

"You got a better plan?" Jory asked.

Yes, pack up and get out of here! Find some other planet!

Aloud, Gareth said, "Let me see if Taz is able to sit up. If he can drive, that'll leave you and Deeseter on guard here. Offenbach, too, once he's rested."

Jory rubbed the side of his nose. "Yeah, it'll be one less thing to worry about if we're stocked up. I don't like the idea of waiting until the captain gets back. You sure you can handle it? After hauling those crates today?"

A sudden inspiration burst upon Gareth's thoughts. "I'll need help."

"From where? The rocks?"

Gareth gestured toward the Dry Towner's camp.

"*Them?* Are you crazy?"

"No Dry Towns warrior would lower himself to manual labor, but there's the horse boy. He looks tough enough." Gareth reflected that if he did manage to get Rahelle away from Hayat, it would be because Merach, not Hayat, thought it was a good idea.

"Aren't you forgetting that he's *their* horse boy? I don't like the idea of owing those local warlords any favors."

"Hayat didn't object when Poulos ordered me to the barracks. I can say that the captain needs both me and the horse boy." Gareth shrugged. "This sort of thing happens all the time as a way of establishing dominance. I don't think Hayat will refuse, but if he does, we're no worse off than we are now. I'll figure out something else or I'll do the work myself. But if he concedes, he'll be less likely to challenge us on other matters."

Jory agreed this would be a good thing and told Gareth to try. Gareth headed off toward the Dry Towners' camp, where Hayat's pavilion had already been erected. The side panels had been lowered. Hayat must be inside, taking his ease in shade and privacy. Merach and one other stood guard.

As Gareth approached, Merach came alert, hand to sword hilt. Gareth halted and bowed, a shade less low than he had before. "Lord Merach, I've come for the horse boy. The off-world captain claims his service."

The door panel jerked open. Hayat poked his head out. "Whatever for? He doesn't have any horses to be tended."

"Great lord, the horse boy is needed to carry barrels of water."

Merach stooped to murmur, "Remember, my lord, that two of these off-worlders died from the poisoned water." In this way, he reminded Hayat that the smugglers were under-strength.

Hayat nodded in comprehension. He waved his fingers in the direction of the water area. "Very well, then."

Gareth bowed several times as he backed away. Rahelle had finished watering the horses and was leading them back to the Shainsa camp. He saw the subtle wariness in the way she carried herself, as if she were warning him off or bracing herself for some new crisis. Then she lowered her head and kept trudging.

"Rakhal!" He broke into a run.

She paused for him, scuffing the dirt with one foot. He halted an arm's length away, flushing in memory of the last time they'd spoken. There was so much he wanted to say, and none of it found words.

For a fleeting moment, she met his eyes. Her posture did not alter. She still looked for all the world like a village horse boy, except for that clear, uncompromising gaze.

He cleared his throat. "You're to help bring water from the well. The off-worlders need another strong back."

"This is your doing, isn't it?" Rahelle frowned. "Couldn't you let well enough alone? Hayat is jealous enough of his *kihar* as it is. Likely he will see such a demand as a personal affront."

"He's given his permission."

She straightened up from drawing circles in the dust with her foot. One of the horses rubbed the side of its head, itchy with dried sweat, against its leg. "There will be a price. He won't easily relinquish anything he considers to be his."

"Listen to me," Gareth said, quelling the impulse to grab her by the shoulders. "You're absolutely right. Hayat's accustomed to getting his own way, but so is Poulos. Neither of them truly appreciates the destructive power of the other or the willingness to use it. This bargain they've struck is liable to fall apart at the slightest thing going wrong . . . and something will go wrong."

She blew out her breath. "It always does. That's the first rational thing you've said."

"When that happens," he rushed on, "there won't be any safe place in this entire valley. The least dangerous place, however, is going to be with the off-worlders. I'd rather have you here, with Hayat's men coming at us with swords, than over *there,* where Poulos and his people are going to be aiming their blasters."

Rahelle's cheeks went pale. In the intensity of the moment, in his fervent desire to make her understand, Gareth caught a flickering image from her mind . . . the village in flames.

Why didn't you keep going? he wanted to ask, and then realized he knew the answer. Now here they were, each trying to protect the other.

He lowered his voice. "I never wanted you to risk yourself for me."

For a long moment, she made no response. Her lips pressed together as if she were trying to refrain from speech. Then: "You've made a thrice-damned mess of it."

"Yes." Seeing her startled reaction, he rushed on. "I've done everything wrong. But I have to keep trying."

"Then," she said with another of those astonishing glances, "we will try together."

Taz was not only sitting up but was looking for an excuse to get out into the open air.

"Spend enough time on a spaceship, and the last thing you want to do dirtside is lie in bed and stare up at them same gray walls."

Taz drove the crawler, remaining in his seat while Gareth and Rahelle filled and lifted and stacked the barrels of water. Rahelle worked steadily, without complaint, although she strained visibly to lift the filled barrels.

The horses had made a muddy mess around the water area, but it had mostly dried by the time the crawler returned. The sun had disappeared behind the western ridge, and the long, slanting shadows had gone from purple to black. The strings of yellow lights glared against the darkness and the black rock. Jory, watching from that side of camp, came out to help Taz back to the barracks. Rahelle did her share of unloading and stacking the barrels without a word, then trudged back to the Shainsa camp.

A packaged meal waited for Gareth at the barracks. Sitting on Robbard's bunk, he opened it, but he hardly tasted the food. Viss was snoring on one side of him and Taz on the other. He intended to rest here for a moment before checking in with Jory and Deeseter. Maybe Poulos would be back soon . . . maybe with more men . . . maybe with the announcement that they were leaving. . . .

Gareth sat up with jerk and scrubbed his knuckles across his eyelids. Zandru's demons, he hadn't meant to fall asleep! Hopefully, it hadn't been too long or too deep. If he did that, he might wake up with Hayat's sword at his throat . . . or not at all.

He heard the sounds of a heated discussion even before he entered the headquarters building. Deeseter's bulky form, silhouetted against the artificial light, blocked Gareth's sight. Offenbach was arguing in that slow, relentless way of his, punctuated by Jory's raised voice.

"I say let them all go blow each other up and leave us out of it! How long does the captain expect us to—" Jory broke off.

"It's me," Gareth said as they all turned toward him. "What's the watch schedule for tonight?"

Jory glanced at Offenbach, and in that flicker of a movement, Gareth understood Jory's dilemma; he had been given command but felt deeply uncomfortable about taking precedence over Offenbach, who had always been his superior. Offenbach wasn't challenging Jory; it was Jory's own lack of experience that undermined his confidence.

"Two and two," Jory said. "You and me, Offen and Deeseter."

Gareth nodded. It made sense to pair the two strongest of them with the weakest.

Then Jory said, "Captain says you can have a blaster—" and something broke loose in Gareth. A burst of reflexive horror left him shaking and nauseated.

"I . . ." he stumbled. "I wouldn't know how to use one."

"Have it your own way." Jory shrugged. "Me, I'll be sleeping with mine under my pillow, ready to go."

Deeseter, who apparently had a collection of weapons from every planet he'd worked on, provided Gareth with a long knife, serrated along its outer curved edge, and a long staff. Gareth had practiced with a staff much like this one, although without the curious markings that looked like dried blood snaking around either end.

They began their watch. Jory went quiet, focused. Gareth tried to imagine himself as someone else—no, not Race Cargill of the Terran Secret Service—maybe the best of his sword instructors. One grim old guard had taken part in the Battle of Old North Road, just before the Federation left Darkover. He wouldn't answer Gareth's questions about what that was like, but sometimes Gareth had noticed the look in the old man's eyes, and then he'd have to watch out because the next bout would be in earnest, nothing held back, no quarter given. What happened next would not be a lesson in technique but a lesson in survival. Just as this night was.

Gareth's initial rush of adrenaline faded, rather more quickly than it would have if he had not already been so tired, although he started at every night sound. He managed to find a place of balance between dry-mouthed, heart-pounding alertness and sleepwalking. He would be ready. He hoped.

Near the end of their watch, Gareth asked Jory what the discussion with Offenbach was about. Jory's expression darkened. He said, with a flicker of his eyes toward the fading stars, "Things're heating up. We sell, the customers buy, that's all." From the thinly masked emotion behind his words, that was not all. Gareth did not need *laran* to see how deeply worried the off-worlder was.

If things were "heating up," if there was outright conflict between the smugglers and the rebels they supplied . . . if the Federation followed the rebels here . . . Gareth let out an explosive breath. The Shainsa lord and his followers would be the least of their troubles.

We will fly that hawk when his pinions are grown, Gareth reminded himself, although in this case, the hawk might well turn out to be a dragon.

Light seeped across the eastern sky. The shadows pooled like half-melted snow along the base of the hills. Gareth finished the watch with a sense of relief and amazement. He'd fully expected Hayat to take advantage of the absence of the captain.

"That's it, pal," Jory said, yawning. "Shuttle should be back any minute now. Go get some sack time while you can."

After returning the weapons to Deeseter, Gareth headed back to barracks. Taz grumbled at being woken, but Viss opened his eyes and sat up. He seemed a little groggy, but his breathing was easier. Gareth threw himself down on the bunk he now thought of as his own without even taking off his boots. He slipped out the knife, holding it by his side, and closed his eyes . . .

"Hey, kid." Someone shook Gareth's shoulder with annoying persistence.

Gareth swam up to consciousness like a diver moving through warm mud. Grit burned his eyes, and something thick coated the inside of his mouth. His muscles responded sluggishly, every movement provoking some new twinge. The knife was still in his hand, a reassuring solidness. He swung his feet over the side of the bunk and glared up at Taz. They were alone in the barracks.

"You was sleeping like a—" Taz used a term Gareth didn't recognize. "You'll be happy to hear Viss is once more among the upright. Not that he can tote anything heavier than his own sorry self, but it's a start. Offen says the shuttle's on approach. Time to earn your keep."

Gareth bent over to replace the knife in its boot sheath. He paused, the hilt still in his hand, unsure whether he'd heard anything outside or only felt a prickle of adrenaline, excitement laced with fear. He glanced up at Taz, who looked unalarmed.

Gareth surged to his feet, bringing his knife up to ready. Taz turned, but too slowly, for Gareth was already moving, pushing past him, jerking open the door.

The camp looked quiet and still. The sun was full up, and only a gossamer hint of purple lingered in the western sky. Overhead, a mote of brightness shimmered: the approaching shuttle.

"Kid!" Taz laid a hand on Gareth's shoulder. Gareth almost lashed out with his knife. Heart pounding, he pulled himself back. "What's gotten into you?"

Gareth lowered the knife. "Nerves, I guess."

"This place'll do that to you. Work you so hard, you don't know if you're dreaming. *That's* real enough."

Following Taz's gaze, Gareth craned his neck to look up. The vibration in the air increased, now barely audible. They watched as the point of brightness enlarged. The shuttle engines whipped the air into miniature dust storms. As the noise of its approach increased, Gareth thought of his first sight and sound of a shuttle in flight, on his return to the base after the village had been destroyed. He remembered that same unnatural thunder, that same sense that the earth itself was being tugged from its moorings. He thought of the arrogance of men for whom such power was an everyday thing, as ordinary as an eating knife. As the shuttle neared its landing place, it occurred to Gareth that if Hayat were going to seize the base, this might be a good time, under all that racket and dust. The shuttle set down without incident, however, leaving Gareth feeling a bit foolish.

Poulos descended. Offenbach greeted him; the two men exchanged a few words and then proceeded to the headquarters building. Gareth and Taz joined the others, sitting with their backs against the wall of the barracks but with a good view of the rest of the base, waiting to load the shuttle again.

Before work could begin, Hayat strode up. He wore two swords, still sheathed, and was accompanied on one side by Merach and on the other by the man Ward, each of them similarly armed. Hayat halted in front of the headquarters building, clearly expecting Poulos to come out to him. He had the stance of a man accustomed to controlling the situation.

Within a few minutes, Gareth and the others who had been lounging by the barracks had formed a rough half-circle around the Dry Towners. Neither Hayat nor his cortege paid them any visible notice, another nice touch. Hayat could hold his own in the Thendara court.

Poulos must surely have realized what was going on, but he waited another few minutes to emerge, thus making it plain that he did not answer to the whims of the Shainsa lord. He waited by the door, gesturing for Hayat and his men to enter. As they did so, Poulos rattled off a string of orders to his own men, dispersing all of them except for Gareth. "You, with me. I'll need you to translate."

Inside, Offenbach looked up from a bank of communications equipment. He nodded to Gareth. Poulos, moving with studied casualness, took his place in his own chair with the desk between him and the Dry Towners, leaving Hayat to stand like a supplicant. Hayat, to his credit, gave no sign of being perturbed in the least. He crossed his arms over his chest and looked down at the off-worlder captain.

"I have secured your base, as agreed." Hayat paused for Gareth to translate, and in this way gained a measure of control over the encounter. "Now it is time for you to fulfill your part of the bargain." He paused again, this time for dramatic effect.

Gareth heard Hayat's words and for the first time hesitated to turn the phrases into Terran Standard. He had already incurred the displeasure of Poulos by rushing down to the burning village. He'd worked to rebuild his credibility since then, although he understood from his own painful adolescence that such memories lingered long after the offense ceased to have any significance. The harder he tried to prevent the Dry Towners from acquiring high technology weapons, the more likely it became.

It would be so easy to lie, to fabricate some offensively arrogant statement in place of what Hayat had actually said, something that would inflame the off-worlder's suspicions. What Gareth really wanted to say, he had rehearsed in his mind a hundred times.

Don't trust anything Hayat says! It's a devil's bargain. He'll take your weapons and turn them against you!

But the opportune moment had already passed. Hayat's scowl deepened and Merach shifted to a subtly more vigilant posture.

Poulos glared at Gareth. "Well? What did he say?"

Gareth translated. Poulos looked as if he were considering the matter carefully. "I don't think our friends here have really done much to defend the base, do you? After all, once we took care of the village, I haven't seen anything even approximating a threat. Let's see what he says to that."

Hayat listened, expression impassive, as Gareth interpreted. "Ha!" he exclaimed, gesturing and grinning. "That is because we have dealt with them all! Is this not the work of skilled and dedicated warriors? And are such men as we not worthy of our promised rewards? Or is your captain a man without *kihar*, who says one thing with his forked tongue and intends another in his coward's heart?"

Gareth cleared his throat. "Lord Hayat says his men have neutralized any threat before it became apparent to you. He repeats that he is entitled to what you promised. Sir, we have no way of verifying the truth of his assertions, or his intentions, should you hand over the weapons. Is it wise to arm these men, who serve no master but their own lord in Shainsa? Is it—"

Poulos cut him off with a gesture. Gareth's plea had been a forlorn hope at best, but the captain had the right of it. Hayat was no fool and would surely perceive that Gareth had spoken more words than had been uttered. Even a loose translation could not be so verbose. Hayat would suspect . . .

Fool! Fool! Son of an addlepated, spavined rabbit-horn of a fool!

Now Poulos was rising, a bland smile on his face. Gareth had seen such smiles before, and never had any good come from those who wore them.

"Tell the desert lord that he has made his point. I see he is a man who keeps his word, as I shall keep mine. I will have my own people carry crates of these weapons to Lord Hayat's camp. He may select whichever ones he pleases, as many as he pleases, and test them to his own satisfaction."

"But—" Gareth blurted.

"Who is giving the orders here, Garrin? You or me? Say further that I regret he may not keep the crates themselves, as they are necessary to a trader's business. Say it!"

As Gareth repeated the speech in Dry Towns dialect, he felt Poulos glaring at him, as if daring him to deviate in any small point. Offenbach, too, was listening, and he understood a measure of the dialect. In a rush of homesickness, Gareth thought of the trust between Mikhail Lanart-Hastur and his son, between them both and Danilo Syrtis, even between Danilo and Cyrillon Sensar. They were bound not only by common purpose but by their mutual regard, by loyalty and integrity. These smugglers were not statesmen. They lived in a world of shifting opportunist alliances. Poulos had lied about the light pistols. Hayat owed no allegiance to anyone but himself and possibly his father.

Gareth could not entirely conceal his reaction as the meeting broke up. Hayat said, "This creature disapproves. If I were you, I would strike off his right hand to teach him respect."

"What did he say?" Poulos asked Gareth after the Dry Towners had departed.

"Nothing of any importance."

Offenbach went out to the Dry Towner camp to supervise the opening of the crates. Poulos deliberately held Gareth back at headquarters, and Gareth seized the chance to speak again.

Poulos waved aside Gareth's concerns. "It's really of no importance. We carry a supply of these weapons, trade goods for such occasions as this. In case you hadn't noticed, we know how to deal with the natives."

Gareth shook his head in disbelief that Poulos meant to play the same trick on Hayat as he had on Cuinn, giving him blasters that would work for a short time only. Hayat was no downtrodden village headman.

Poulos reacted to Gareth's expression of dismay. "Buck up, Garrin. Everything'll work out. Look—" he pointed to the camp and the crawler already beginning its return journey. "They're happy, we're happy. Hell, even the Castor Sector folks are happy, and Zhu knows they've little enough reason. There's nothing here dirtside worth worrying about."

Gareth did not at all agree, and he agreed even less when, a short time later, Hayat and a couple of his men rode for the Black Ridge trail, whooping and brandishing their blasters.

Hayat and his men returned to the base late that day. Even from a distance, Gareth could see they had ridden their horses into a lather. They bypassed their own camp, galloping straight for the center of the base. Hayat's furious shouting rose above the sound of the excited horses.

By the time Gareth reached the headquarters building, Poulos had come out and was waiting calmly. Deeseter stood, arms crossed over his massive chest, just behind his commander.

"Fork-tongued one who copulates with dead *oudrakhi!*" Hayat wheeled his wild-eyed, panting horse. "He who uses deceit to trick an enemy has earned his victory with cunning. But he who forswears a bargain is without honor!" He hauled on the reins, drawing the sweating, prancing animal to a standstill, and aimed the blaster at the off-worlder's torso.

Nothing happened. No beam emerged from the barrel of the weapons. Poulos stood there, as outwardly unperturbed as before. One by one, the other Dry Towners fired their blasters, with no more effect.

Poulos had taken a crazy chance. Either that, or these blasters, like Cuinn's, had already been nearly exhausted.

Hayat hurled the useless blaster to the ground. It skidded, coming to rest beside the smuggler captain's booted toes. Poulos stooped to pick it up. He brushed the dust off and turned the weapon this way and that, as if he were examining it. He raised it, sighting along the barrel, but with the muzzle pointed directly at Hayat.

Sweet Cassilda! Gareth thought with a rush of horror. What if the blasters had not been drained? What if Hayat and his men had only operated them improperly?

What if Poulos now intended to give the Shainsa lordling a lesson?

Hayat must have realized this, too. He no longer forced his horse into display but sat frozen in the saddle. Merach suffered no such paralysis; he urged his own horse forward, although such a gesture would have been of little use against a fully charged blaster.

With a smile that did not reach his eyes, Poulos tilted the blaster to the sky. "My friend, you have every reason to be displeased. My abject apologies for the malfunction. Please accept my assurances that to the best of my knowledge, the blasters were in perfect working order when I delivered them to you. Such devices were not intended for use under primitive conditions. Rough handling and exposure to dust can misalign their settings. I will personally supervise the testing of the replacements to which you are, *of course,* entitled." Poulos handed the blaster to Deeseter and sketched a bow in Hayat's direction.

"Ah, Garrin, there you are. Collect the other blasters. I assume you know how to handle them, in case they still have a little power."

"Captain, this is a dangerous game!"

Poulos waved the objection aside. "And convey what I said, leaving out the reference to *primitive conditions.* It would not do to antagonize the locals needlessly."

Before Deeseter could stop him, Gareth placed himself directly in front of Poulos. "Yes, Hayat might be willing to listen *this time.* He won't be happy, and he won't trust your assurances. He'll test the new ones. We both know that the same thing will happen. What then?"

Poulos returned Gareth's stare without the slightest waver.

"Captain, please!" Gareth begged. "Call the deal off!"

"There is nothing whatsoever to worry about," Poulos said in a voice laced with the chill between the stars, a voice that reminded Gareth this was the man who had ordered the burning of Nuriya. "I believe Lord Hayat and I understand each other better than that. We have just established who has the power in this relationship, that is all. Your opinion is of no interest to either of us. Now follow your orders . . . without commentary."

It was no use, Gareth thought. It was never going to be of any use to reason with Poulos. The smugglers saw Darkover as an insignificant but convenient way station. If every man, woman, and child from Temora to the Wall Around the World were to disappear, they would regard the tragedy as the removal of a source of annoyance. What a fool he had been to waste his breath trying to make Poulos see sense!

Fighting a rush of disgust for his own naïveté, Gareth turned back to Hayat and translated, summarizing the words of the off-worlder captain. Hayat demanded to know how long the testing would take and when he would receive functioning weapons. Poulos promised him, through Gareth, that the blasters would be ready the following morning. It took no *laran* to recognize Hayat's lingering suspicion. His flushed face and scowling brows were proof enough.

What was the old saying, said to date back to the years of Darkover's founding? *Fool me once, shame on you. Fool me twice, shame on me*? Hayat clearly had no intention of suffering a second humiliation.

By the time the sun had set, leaving a veil of purple light across the western sky, Gareth had resolved upon a plan. He'd stayed in the off-worlder base far longer than was prudent, trapped by the hope that he could prevent the Dry Towners from acquiring blasters. The events of this past day had convinced him that Poulos had no intention of giving away fully functional weapons, so the situation had altered. Gareth had allowed himself to be caught up in that, too, when the smart thing would have been to leave the two parties to their own folly. If Poulos was so certain of his own invulnerability that he failed to recognize the threat, then he deserved whatever happened next. As for Hayat, Gareth had had his fill of Dry Towner arrogance.

The only thing holding him here was Rahelle. If she tried to run away and was caught, Hayat would have no qualms about whipping her to within an inch of her horse boy's life. And if Hayat discovered she was a woman . . . that fate was too horrific to contemplate. They must escape together.

Through the gathering dusk, Gareth kept watch on the Dry Towner camp, hoping to catch Rahelle as she took the horses to water. He was counting on the Dry Towners keeping to the rhythms of a desert camp, the tradition of sleeping by day and waiting for the coolness of twilight for more active tasks. Although he watched, he caught no sight of her.

"Hey, kid!" Taz called out from the direction of the barracks. "You gonna eat?"

"On my way."

He'd have to find another way to reach Rahelle. Not only would he not leave without her, he needed her help with the horses. If they could make off with two and scatter the rest, they might stand a chance. They could make it over the ridge on foot, but not across the Sands of the Sun.

Time was running out. They must make their escape tonight, before Poulos handed over the next set of blasters. If he couldn't talk to Rahelle soon, he'd have to wait until dark and then sneak into the Dry Towner camp. Meanwhile, he had to act normally.

Taz and Viss hunkered down outside the barracks, finishing their supper. Idriel, brightest of the four moons, shone like a solitary jewel in the lingering twilight. At Gareth's approach, Taz grinned and held out a meal package.

"Fresh from the kitchens of—where did we pick this lot up, Viss? Vainwal?"

The other smuggler snorted. "You dreamer! More like some dump beyond the Outer Hyades."

"Well, wherever it's from, eat up, kid."

Gareth stood to eat, leaning against the wall and glancing surreptitiously in the direction of the horse lines. The food, once strange and tasteless, had become familiar. Although not particularly appetizing, it was filling. With a shiver of homesickness, he remembered dinners at Castle Elhalyn when he was a child. He had taken for granted the fresh seasonal vegetables, ale so dark it looked black, nut-studded breads still hot from the oven . . . Even the meals he'd eaten on the Carthon trail seemed more appetizing than this synthetic pap. He set down the meal package, still half-eaten.

"Not want the rest?" Viss inquired hopefully, just as a muffled sound brought Gareth alert.

Gareth's hand shot out, unconsciously commanding silence. Holding his breath, he slipped out his one weapon, the boot knife. The sound came again, so faint that if he had not already been keyed-up from watching for Rahelle, he would surely have missed it.

His *laran* senses came fully alert, even though the amulet insulated his starstone. As if a veil had been ripped from his eyes, he saw through walls and around corners—

Hayat's men crouched in battle readiness. Idriel's light glinted on their drawn swords. They carried shorter blades thrust beneath their sashes as well. Merach gestured silently toward the headquarters building—

Dry Towners rushed into the center of the camp, Hayat in the lead. Their war cries sounded like the howling of demented wolves. Even sprinting as fast as he could, Gareth was too far to intercept them. Behind him, Taz shouted curses.

Hayat and the man at his heels reached the door. One of the others, in rear guard position, spun around to face Gareth. Gareth dodged and swerved out of reach of the Dry Towner's sword. By luck, he caught the oncoming blade on the edge of his knife. Steel whined as it slid over steel. The impact rattled his teeth.

Gareth disengaged with a sideways lunge. Out of the corner of his vision, he saw the door swing open. Hayat rushed inside.

The Dry Towner redoubled his attack on Gareth. Training and instinct fired Gareth's response. He swerved without thinking. His opponent lunged forward, sweeping his curved sword in a diagonal arc.

This time, Gareth misjudged the angle. The slashing edge came within a hair's breadth of his unguarded side. He twisted sideways and almost lost his footing.

From inside the building came more shouting and the sounds of fighting. Someone shrieked, an inarticulate scream. Agony resonated through Gareth's *laran*. His mind reeled with it.

The momentary lapse was enough for the swordsman to close with him. Gareth tried to deflect the attack with his knife, but his defense was too slow, too late. He felt the prick of the sword tip at his throat.

Glowering, the Dry Towner raised his arm so that the slightest pressure would drive the point into the soft tissue between Gareth's collarbones.

Gareth forced himself to stand still. He held his arms well away from his body, although he did not drop his knife.

The base fell suddenly, sickeningly quiet, except for Merach's voice, shouting out orders, and someone moaning in pain.

Gareth kept his gaze fixed on his captor's eyes. He caught the momentary flicker as the man's attention was distracted.

In one movement, Gareth stepped sideways, brought up his knife to the level of his throat, and pivoted. He threw all the strength of his legs into the movement. The sword tip left a trail of fire across the front of his neck, but the sharp pressure vanished.

Gareth's knife clanged against the flat of the sword. Momentum carried the two blades around in a circular sweep. Gareth managed to keep control for a critical instant before tenuous contact gave way and the two weapons flew apart. He clenched the knife hilt through the jarring impact and release. The sword, propelled by Gareth's blow, swung wildly to the side.

Darting inside the arc of the sword, Gareth took a long step and brought his knee up. His roundhouse kick caught the Dry Towner on the side of the thigh. It wasn't a disabling blow, but the pain caused the man to bend over. His knee buckled. His grip momentarily relaxed. Gareth came down on the foot he'd used for the kick, stepping even deeper through his opponent's defenses. A hard punch to the solar plexus sent the man to the ground, gasping and coughing.

Gareth snatched the hilt of the sword from the man's inert fingers. It was different in both length and balance from the ones he'd trained with, but it settled into his hand as if it belonged to him.

The Dry Towner was fighting for air and holding his thigh. He wouldn't be getting up any time soon. Gareth rushed past him toward the headquarters building.

Before he reached the door, an ear-splitting crackle lanced through the air. A blotch the color of charred ashes appeared on the outer wall. More shouting followed, the words indistinguishable.

Reaching the door, Gareth spotted Merach standing just out of sword's reach. Jory was on his knees by a pile of crates. Bright blood drenched the front of one pants leg. He held a blaster in both hands, aimed at the struggling pair a little farther inside.

Offenbach was on his knees as well, with Hayat standing behind him. With a grip on the off-worlder's hair, the Shainsa lord bent Offenbach's head to expose his neck. Hayat held his sword precisely across the big blood vessels.

Poulos? Where was the captain? And Deeseter?

"Let him go!" Jory bellowed, his voice hoarse. "Or I'll fry you all! I swear it!"

Jory might well have just sealed the mate's death, Gareth thought. He'd spoken in Terran Standard, which none of the Dry Towners understood. Aldones knew what Hayat thought he'd said. By the amount of blood and the speed at which he was losing more, Jory had only a short time before he passed out. The Dry Towners were only waiting for a signal from Hayat to rush him.

Gareth still had a moment's grace before anyone noticed him. He could rush in and probably get himself killed, along with Offenbach and Jory, who wasn't going to survive without care. It would be a glorious ending, but he didn't want glory. He wanted a way out of this impasse, and he couldn't see one.

Where in the seven frozen hells was Poulos?

Gareth closed the distance to fighting reach with Merach. Merach reacted, blade at ready, but as Gareth had anticipated, he did not make the first offensive move.

"Hear the off-worlder!" Gareth held his own position and called out in Dry Towns dialect. "He vows on his honor to kill you all unless you release his comrade!"

Merach's response was to settle deeper into his fighting stance. Gareth felt the Dry Towner gathering his energy into a still center, a center from which he would explode into a lightning-quick attack. Hayat had but to give the word.

Hayat smiled, a smile that sent a chill up Gareth's spine. "Say this in the tongue of the barbarians! Say that he will watch his man die before him. Say that the *kyorebni* of the sands will scatter their bones, and it will be as if neither of them had ever walked the earth."

Jory wavered on his knees. Although laced together for support, his hands shook visibly. His face had gone the color of chalk. He blinked hard, fighting to keep his eyes in focus.

"It's no good," Offenbach said in a choked voice, forcing the words through the twisted angle of his neck. "I've sent the message. The shuttle's been warned off. They'll blast the whole camp from space. Garrin—tell them—"

No, Gareth thought, *that's a lie. Even if the ship has such weapons, Poulos will try to rescue his crew first. He values his men. That's why he burned the village in retaliation.*

Gareth wanted to tell both parties exactly which of Zandru's hells awaited them. Instead he said, using Terran Standard, "It's no use bluffing. Hayat doesn't care about the shuttle. And if we don't end this stalemate, Jory's going to bleed to death."

"Jory . . . stand down . . ." Offenbach said, just as the blaster tumbled from Jory's limp fingers and Jory himself slumped to the floor.

"There is your answer," Gareth said to Hayat. He knelt to place his sword on the floor in the respectful manner of surrendering a weapon of honor. "You have won, great lord. Surely this man's death adds nothing to your glory," meaning Jory. "Will you allow one of his comrades to tend him?"

Hayat propelled Offenbach forward with a thrust of one knee. The off-worlder sprawled face down on the floor. "Go, then. He fought bravely. As for you . . ."

The air between Hayat and Merach shimmered like a heat mirage. Without warning, Merach crumpled to his knees, his muscles lax.

Two translucent figures took shape. Each lifted an arm to aim at the Dry Towner lords. A hissing sound accompanied a flare of pale light as the visual distortion faded, revealing Poulos and Deeseter.

Hayat turned toward Poulos, sword raised. Deeseter pivoted, training his weapon on Hayat. Hayat froze.

Offenbach scrambled to his feet and to the desk. Wrenching open a drawer, he removed a flat box with the snake and staff emblem of *Ter-*

ranan medicine. He knelt beside Jory and wrapped the oozing wound in a wide elastic belt. Gareth would have liked to see more of the healing technology, but the confrontation before him was not yet ended.

"This is a neural disrupter on its lowest setting," Poulos said to Hayat. "It's not lethal. Your man will come around in a few minutes . . . as long as you cooperate."

"I am the son of the Lord of Shainsa!" Hayat snarled. "I do not bend to the whims of thieves!"

"I would not say that to a man who holds such a weapon aimed at me," Gareth replied mildly.

"I challenge this leavings of a diseased scorpion-ant to a duel by *kifurgh*!"

Even as Hayat issued his challenge, Poulos disappeared in another near-invisible rippling of the air. An instant later, he solidified behind Hayat, one forearm slipping into the angle beneath the Dry Towner's chin. With the other, Poulos dug the muzzle of the neural disrupter into Hayat's temple skin.

"Drop. The. Sword." With each word, Poulos administered a little jab, so that Hayat flinched visibly. The sword clattered to the floor. "Offen? Tell me Jory's alive."

"Got to him in time, Captain. He's lost a fair amount of blood, but nothing we can't replace. The Castor ship's got a supply of synthetic serum."

"Garrin, tell this dust beetle it's his lucky day." Poulos did not relax his grip as Gareth did so. "Now you listen to me, little man. *Nobody* threatens me or my people, least of all some trumped-up backwater bully like you. You wanted a deal, you got a deal. Here it is. You'll get your weapons when and how I say you do."

He paused while Gareth interpreted. "Understand?"

Hayat gave the slightest nod. Gareth thought he looked about as terrified as a man could be without soiling himself. On the floor, Merach groaned and began moving weakly.

"What did I tell you?" Poulos said. "Now you and my friend here," meaning Deeseter, "are going to take a little stroll around the base. You're going to collect your men and take them back to your camp. And you're going to stay there until *I* say you can leave."

Gareth repeated the smuggler captain's words, thinking that as soon as Hayat recovered from his fright, he would not remain as cowed as he was now. He might not try another assault on the base, and he might well depart under the cover of night. That might be the best solution, and Poulos would not object. But Rahelle would have to go with them, unless she managed to slip away.

Gareth wrestled his thoughts back to the present moment. He had thought the smugglers unrealistically confident. Now, barring a massed attack by an army from Shainsa—unlikely, given the difficulties of so many men and beasts crossing the Sands of the Sun—the advantage rested with the off-worlders and their technology.

Poulos released Hayat to help Merach to his feet, although he still watched them closely. Offenbach went to the radio equipment, slipped on a listening device, and established communications with the ship in orbit. Gareth caught only a few phrases that indicated Offenbach was making arrangements for the Castor Sector ship to furnish medical treatment to Jory. There was a long pause while Deeseter escorted the Dry Towners out of the headquarters building.

"Should I go with them—" Gareth began, but Offenbach was signaling frantically as Poulos hurried over to the radio.

Poulos slid into the place Offenbach vacated and grabbed the listening device. His face tightened into a scowl.

"Offen?" Gareth said in a low voice. "What's going on?"

"Shhh. Captain's call."

"I see," Poulos said. "No, you're right. Start countdown to leave orbit. We'll dock soonest." He touched a series of panels on the controls, then set down the listening device.

"Damn those Castor Sector idiots! They must have stirred up one big wasp hole to get themselves tracked this far."

"Or they've got a spy onboard," Offenbach murmured.

"No honor among thieves and rebels, eh?" Poulos said, sardonic. "Guess we're the last honest men left."

"Evacuate, Captain?"

"Evacuate and sterilize. If we get lucky, we'll be gone before the sharks arrive, so they won't come looking for us."

28

Poulos issued a string of orders, getting his men onboard the shuttle, along with communications equipment and a few things Gareth didn't recognize. The crew responded with a speed and efficiency that surprised Gareth, some racing off to the barracks, others to the headquarters building.

They've done this before, Gareth thought as he watched the intense, almost silent frenzy. *They've had to leave everything behind on short notice.* No wonder the crew had so little attachment to this place or its inhabitants.

"You." Poulos gestured to Gareth. "Bring the natives here, and make it quick."

Spurred by the undercurrent of urgency in the captain's tone, Gareth raced out of the base. He had no difficulty finding the Dry Towner's camp by the small fire. Where they'd found anything to burn, he didn't know. Perhaps they'd brought it with them when they returned from their first foray.

Hayat got to his feet, looking as if nothing would give him greater pleasure than to disembowel Gareth on the spot. Behind him, the other men came alert. Gareth spotted Rahelle at the edge of the camp, near the horse picket lines. Her eyes gleamed in the near darkness.

"The captain of the off-worlders requests your immediate presence," Gareth said, bowing and trying to sound as deferential as possible.

"So now he's ready to redeem his honor?" Hayat sneered. "Tell him you found me indisposed. He can wait until morning."

Gareth allowed his own anxiety to color his voice. "Great lord, he said to come at once. There is other news. After you left, a message came from the ship in the heavens. I think the off-worlders mean to evacuate the base as soon as they can."

"So much the better, may they soon meet the fate of all cowards. But this may be a ruse. Why should I believe what you say? Why should I not whip the truth of you?"

Gareth had no need to dissemble his reflexive terror. "Because it would cost you nothing to find out for yourself?"

Merach spoke up. "Lord Hayat, if this off-worlder intended to cheat you of your rightful part of the bargain, would he not have departed without warning? I think this must be bad news indeed to cause him to abandon the—" he used a term like the *cahuenga* word for *temporary fortress*. "Men who are made desperate are often distracted and therefore less careful of their own advantage in other matters."

"Very well, Merach, you've made your point. You and you—" Hayat gestured to his two most fit-looking men, "—come with me. And you, boy," to Gareth, "pray to Nebran that your captain has not deceived you as well."

As Gareth turned to follow Hayat back to the base, he searched the place where Rahelle had been standing, but she was gone. For the first time, his only desire was to go along with events as they unfolded. The smugglers would soon be gone. Even if Poulos gave Hayat another set of barely usable blasters, the charges wouldn't last long. The Dry Towners would head back to Shainsa. Cyrillon was most likely still there and could provide cover back to Carthon . . .

A sense of relief washed over Gareth as they passed the outer perimeter of the base. Even though things had not gone the way he expected, it was going to be all right. He just had to stay calm, follow orders, and keep his head down.

Back at the base, Taz and Viss grunted under the weight of a long rectangular box while Offenbach shouted from the crawler for them to hurry. Jory lay on a stretcher, still unconscious.

Poulos and Deeseter waited in front of the headquarters building, a few crates at their feet. They'd just finished unlocking the lids. Gareth watched them remove the topmost packing material and open the inner boxes. In the glare of the yellow overheads, Gareth made out the shapes of blasters. There must be tens upon tens of them. Poulos had lied about possessing so many.

Without preamble, Poulos pointed to the opened crates. "There they are, the blasters we agreed on. All fully functional."

Was this the truth, and had Poulos lied about that, too?

So many working blasters in the hands of the Dry Towners!

Before Gareth could translate, Hayat approached the nearest crate, his gaze flickering between the off-worlder's face and the tightly packed weapons.

Poulos gestured impatiently. "Take what you want. All you can carry." He clapped Deeseter on the arm. "Give Taz a hand with the stretcher. I need Offen on the shuttle. Well," he glared at Gareth, "what are you waiting for? Tell him!"

"Captain, it's too much, far more than Lord Hayat expected," Gareth said dazedly. "He'll suspect a trick."

"Then tell him I have no use for them where I'm going. The shuttle's already on countdown. I can't afford the extra weight, and I can get more, easily enough. He's welcome to whatever he wants."

"Should I tell him you're leaving?" Gareth struggled to take in what he'd just heard.

"Hell's goblins, boy! Tell him anything you want! Just make sure he knows to get as far away from here as he can. In a little less than an hour, Terran time, this whole place is going to be slag. You got that?"

Gareth stared at the smuggler chief. There was no deception in the off-worlder's face nor in the emanations from his mind. He meant to destroy the base, rather than leave behind any trace of its presence.

Just how powerful were the ship's weapons?

"Got it?" Poulos repeated.

Gareth nodded.

"Okay, kid. You've probably figured out this next part. I've got to get my people out of here. The shuttle won't handle your added weight, and

I can't come back for you. Besides, I don't think you want to go where we're headed."

Gareth stared at him, unable to summon a response.

"Look," Poulos went on, "we haven't always seen eye to eye, but you're a good kid, so I'll give you this: Get clear of this base but stay away from any place that has a space port. I know there's one up toward the big mountain range. When the sharks catch up with the Castor Sector ships, they'll like as not decide the rebels have set up a base there. The way things are going, they'll bomb first and ask questions later."

Gareth rocked back on his heels, stunned. "But Darkover's a Class D Closed World—"

Poulos cut him off with a hard-eyed grimace. "All that talk means nothing any more. Nobody's protecting anyone except themselves. Besides, half the ships with the old Fed ID are sharks."

"Sharks?"

"Privateers. Arms runners like us but with a whole lot more firepower—planet-killing firepower—and no reason not to use it if it'll get the job done. Most of 'em are just glorified pirates. They know, just like we did, there's nothing worth looting here. But there is a hefty bonus for wiping out a rebel stronghold."

Poulos clapped Gareth on the shoulder. "So here's to clear skies for both of us, kid. Now tell that dirtsider chief what I said and get yourself out of here."

Heart pounding, Gareth stumbled through the translation. Poulos lingered just long enough for Hayat to reach into one of the crates. Then he was gone, loping toward the shuttle.

The sound of the engines built into the now-familiar roar, but the Dry Towns lord paid no attention. He stuck four or five blasters under his sash and bellowed, "Bring the pack animals! Saddle the horses!"

Gareth raced back to the camp to deliver Hayat's orders. He had to shout to make himself heard over the din of the shuttle's take-off. "Lord Hayat says to hurry! Break camp! Ride for Shainsa!"

The Dry Towners responded slowly. Clearly, they saw no reason for hurry. Rahelle was struggling to keep control of the horses, which hadn't gotten accustomed to the noise or the winds, laden with coarse black dust.

Gareth glanced back at the base, still bathed in alien yellow light. Already, the sound of the shuttle was becoming fainter, more distant. He didn't know how much time remained or how wide an area Poulos meant to destroy.

And the Feds, or whoever they were, pirates as Poulos said or proper military, would they bother to determine that the Thendara spaceport hadn't been used in years? Would they care?

If only there were a way of getting a message to Mikhail or Domenic—if Jeram could contact the Feds on the radio equipment at Terran Headquarters, explain to them—

In a fractional moment, Gareth knew he could not simply run away. He'd never reach Thendara in time, but he could warn these men.

Merach, apparently recovered from the nerve disrupter, was supervising the folding of Hayat's pavilion.

"There is no time for delay!" Gareth urged him. "The off-worlders mean to blast their camp from space. Lord Hayat—you know how he desires these weapons. He will linger, taking more and more of them. He will give no heed to the danger."

"Why would the off-worlders do such a thing?"

"They too have enemies. Why else would they have hidden their base out here, so far from any settlement?"

Merach grunted in agreement, enough to be heard over the fading sound of the shuttle.

"Please—we have only a little time."

"By your *kihar*, this is true?"

By my word as a Hastur, or anything else you want me to swear by!

"Lord Merach, I have no honor, but by *yours*, it is."

"Then we will leave at once." Merach vaulted on the back of his own horse, took the reins of Hayat's, and shouted for the men to follow him as if they were in battle. Then he booted his horse into a gallop toward the base.

Gareth ran to Rahelle. "Get out of here, do you hear me? Even if you have to run away!"

She did not answer.

In front of the headquarters building, Hayat's men were digging through the crates. They'd piled up the blasters, those they hadn't stashed under their own belts. There was no sign of Hayat or Merach, although the sounds of a heated argument came from inside the building.

"Take what we have, great lord," Merach insisted, "and live to fight another time!"

The sounds of crashing glass and cursing answered him. Gareth rushed to the headquarters door. The lights had been left on, bathing the interior in a cold-edged brilliance. The place looked as if it had been ransacked. Hayat was using a metal bar, most likely from the rack that was lying in pieces nearby, to pry at the lid of another crate.

"—not be bought off with toys that break when put to use!" Hayat muttered.

Merach noticed Gareth's arrival. "The rest of your men are here, lord. You have no further reason to tarry. Let us take what we have. If we use these weapons sparingly, they may yet be of service. And if the *charrat* has not spoken the truth, you can always return and take what you wish in safety."

"Better a small treasure than none at all, you mean? I know my father sent you to keep me in line, so now I suppose I must take the coward's part."

"Your father, great lord, sent me to make sure you came back in glory."

With a snort of disgust, Hayat threw down the length of metal. On his way out of the building, he halted in front of Gareth.

"As for you, I see that your off-world masters have cast you aside. I have no use for you, either. What is there for you to translate now? Who else are you going to deceive?"

"I didn't—" Gareth bit off his protest. No simple villager would dare to talk back to a powerful lord. It was too late to call back those words, too late to cringe or hang his head.

Eyes narrowing, Hayat peered into Gareth's face. "Who are you? You fight like a noble, not a slave. Where did you learn the tongue of these off-worlders?"

Hayat grabbed the hair on top of Gareth's head and twisted, forcing

Gareth's head back at a painful angle. "What have you to say for yourself?"

Gareth closed his eyes, bracing against what would come next. Hayat would be neither quick nor merciful. Not even the truth would appease him.

"My lord, we dare not linger," came Merach's calm voice. "We already have enough fire-weapons."

"My father will be pleased!" Hayat's voice took on darkly triumphant harmonics. "As for this one, whoever he is, spy or outlaw or madman—" he released Gareth's hair and seized the Nebran amulet, "—he has no right to wear a token of decent faith."

The chain dug into the back of Gareth's neck for an instant, then snapped. Even through the layers of insulation, Gareth felt a jolt of disorientation as the starstone left his body. He scarcely heard the Shainsa lord's next words or Merach's response. His body felt icy and thick, as if he'd been trudging naked through a Hellers storm. His knees folded, and an instant later, he slammed into the hard earth.

As if across a vast distance, he heard Hayat yelling for the horse boy to bring his mount. Something hard nudged his ribs, but he could not tell if it was his own heart, hurling itself against the cage of his chest, or something from outside.

Someone was shouting . . . the voice, he should know that voice.

"He's hurt! Can't you see that?"

"Leave them both!" someone else snarled, a voice like a distant thunderstorm.

"Garrin . . ." said a woman's voice, echoing down a tunnel as long and chill as the Kadarin River.

The world swirled away from him in a hurricane of gray and white and silver-blue light.

"Garrin? Garrin, are you all right?"

The voice had been pestering him for what seemed his entire life, waxing and waning, threading through the dense fog of his mind.

"Can you hear me? Garrin! What's the matter?"

Someone was cradling his head, looking down into his face, trying to hold his gaze. He thrashed, seeking escape.

His thoughts blew away like the glittering crystals.

It's threshold sickness . . . he tried to say.

Linnea's instructions hovered just at the edge of his thoughts. He needed to . . . what was it he needed? To close his eyes and drift . . . to allow the currents to carry him where they would . . .

. . . *to get up and walk . . . to use movement to anchor his mind to his body . . . to stabilize his balance centers . . .*

Dimly he felt his body struggling, his movements weak and uncoordinated. The ground disappeared from under him, and he was falling, falling . . . twisting in the void . . .

Stars whirled, dissolving, scattering into pinpoint glints of brilliance, a sea of them . . . He was drifting through that endless galaxy . . .

"Garrin." The voice was almost too low to make out, a breath against his hair. He felt the softness of a cheek against his. Arms held him . . . warmth . . .

Rahelle.

"Garrin, hold on. I've got you."

Something fell into place, like a latch clicking open, and then he was back in his body, still nauseated but steady. When he swallowed, his throat felt as if it had been scrubbed with sand. He opened his eyes to discover that they now focused normally. He knew who and where he was.

He was lying on one of the beds in the barracks, curled on his side. Rahelle sat cross-legged by his feet, watching him. She must have dragged him here.

Rahelle.

He remembered her arms around him and her voice in his ear, her presence like a fixed star in the midst of a maelstrom.

He pushed himself up on one elbow. To his relief, no waves of dizziness followed.

"What happened?" His throat was so dry, he could hardly force out the question.

"What do you mean, *what happened?* You fainted!"

Gareth shook his head, then thought better of it. "Hayat . . ." *took the amulet . . . my starstone . . .* "How long . . .?"

Her eyes went flat and grim.

She'd stayed. Or come back, he couldn't be sure.

He pushed himself to his feet. The interior of the barracks swirled in his vision, a moment of disorientation, nothing more. He swayed on his feet, then Rahelle caught him, her body solid against his as she pulled his arm across her shoulders. Outside, the base appeared to be deserted. All the horses were gone as well.

"The ridge trail!" Gareth gasped. "Hurry!"

Rahelle darted back into the barracks and emerged a moment later with one of the off-worlders' hand lamps. Gareth stared at her. He had no idea how she'd learned to use them.

"Come on!" She grabbed his sleeve and pulled him toward the ridge.

The first few steps were the hardest. By the time they reached the perimeter of the base, he no longer needed her support and was able to manage a shambling run.

They headed into the night.

Filmy shapes like wisps of vapor hung in the air, blowing away into nothingness as they approached. Rahelle took no notice of them, so Gareth decided they existed only in his own mind. It took all his concentration to keep moving, putting one foot in front of the other.

The terrain became rougher. Gareth stumbled, catching himself on his hands and knees. Rahelle, who had been a little ahead of him, whirled and raced back.

"N-no! K-k-keep going!"

She grabbed his hand and pulled him up.

After that, Gareth tried to keep his pace even. He dared not fall, dared not slow their headlong flight. If he did, Rahelle wouldn't leave him.

Ahead of them, the ridge blocked the lower horizon. The sight of it infused Gareth with a renewed burst of energy. He was breathing hard, and the muscles of his legs were beginning to ache, but his mind was clearing.

Rahelle played the light beam over the ground ahead of them. She cried out, "There!" as it illuminated the bottom of the trail.

Side by side, they clambered up the slope. The trail rose gradually at first, then more steeply. Gareth's breathing turned harsh. His ears filled with the laboring of his heart. He had no idea how much time they had or how far they had to run to be safe, how wide an area Poulos meant to destroy. He was a little surprised they'd made it this far . . . he could not tell how long he'd wandered in psychic shock . . . unless Poulos had lied and it was all an empty threat. No, there had been truth in the smuggler captain's thoughts.

This section of trail looked vaguely familiar as it curved into a series of switchbacks, following the contour of the hillside. In places, it slipped between the ridge and massive boulders, rocky shoulders that obscured the view below. If his memory was right, they'd made it at least a third of the way to the crest.

The light beam wavered as Rahelle faltered. She couldn't keep up this pace for much longer. Gareth shortened his stride for her to come even. The hand lamp limned the outlines of her features, but he could not read her expression. She must be thinking the same thing, that they needed every morsel of speed they could wring from their bodies. Even a few moments of respite might cost their lives—

Light flashed behind them, followed an instant later by a roar like a thousand simultaneous claps of thunder. Gareth threw himself between Rahelle and the blast. His weight carried both of them to the ground, narrowly missing a half-buried boulder.

Heat came boiling up from the crater. Huddled in the lee of the boulder, Gareth felt it on his back and face. The rock shielded them from the worst of it, but even so, it was as if he'd come within a hair's-breadth of the open door of a furnace. Beneath him, Rahelle whimpered.

The light faded.

Gareth realized he'd been holding his breath. His lungs ached. His heart hammered in his chest. His skin was hot and slick, and so was Rahelle's. He rolled off her, being careful to keep his body between hers and the downward trail.

She lay on her back, gulping in one breath after another. The hand lamp had rolled a little distance and come to rest at the foot of a smaller rock. By some chance, it hadn't gone out.

Gareth managed to get to his hands and knees. He crawled the few feet to the lamp and switched it off. He didn't know how long it might last or how much they would need it later. Then he eased himself back to their little shelter.

Rahelle had recovered enough breath to gasp, "We've got to—keep going—"

"The worst—" he forced out between breaths, "—is over."

No, some part of his mind prickled. *The worst is yet to come. Hayat is on the way to Shainsa, armed with blasters. The privateers will soon aim their weapons at the Thendara spaceport.* And he could do nothing about it, not even give a warning!

Was that any excuse not to try?

He knew he wasn't thinking clearly. The separation from his starstone had left him disoriented, and he was still drenched in adrenaline from the flight from the smuggler base.

Yet he had heard stories, pure imaginings he'd thought at the time, but perhaps fiction had at its core the germ of reality . . . Rare though it was, Mikhail and Marguerida were able to reach each other's minds over long distances. Grandfather Regis was said to possess the Hastur Gift, that of being a *living* matrix. That meant he didn't need a starstone to use his *laran.* The story went that he'd summoned the incarnation of Aldones, Lord of Light, with his unaided mind . . . but the legends about Regis Hastur were many.

If there was even a morsel of truth to the tale . . . Gareth was not his grandfather, or even his father. He was not even the least of the novices at Comyn Tower. But he was all there was. If he could not send a warning, it would never be sent.

"Rahelle . . ." As her name left his lips, he realized what a rare gift it was to be able to call her as she truly was, neither horse boy nor apprentice, but a woman of courage. "We're safe enough where we are. I'm going to—I may appear to be asleep or as if I've fainted again. Don't try to wake me. If I don't come out of it, you must go on by yourself. Please."

By the rustling of cloth and the faint scuffing sounds, Rahelle was pushing herself to sitting. "What are you saying? What do you mean to do?"

Gareth's first impulse was to brush off her questions, to say it would be too complicated to explain. He'd sound like a complete madman, and likely she wouldn't believe him, anyway. The intimacy of having spoken her name aloud still lingered in his mind, in his heart. He might not survive, still impaired by the loss of his starstone and physically drained as well. If this was the last time he'd ever speak to her, did he want it to be a lie?

"I'm going to try to reach my friends in Thendara. With my mind. To warn them about Hayat and about the Federation ships."

For a long moment, a moment in which his heart beat shifted to an oddly syncopated rhythm, there was no response. Then Rahelle said, "With your mind, you said? How is that possible? You're not . . . you *are*, aren't you?"

"Comyn. Yes."

"That explains how good you are with a sword. Your accent. All the times you acted as if you owned the world." She paused. "Garrin isn't your real name, is it?"

"Gareth." He could stop there and it would be the truth. But it would still be a lie. "Gareth Marius-Danvan Elhalyn y Hastur."

"*That* Gareth?"

"That Gareth." *Do you despise me now?*

After another pause, she said, "It doesn't change who you are, you know. You're not a congenital incompetent, just the result of everyone else doing things for you. So what do you need me to do while you work your Comyn sorcery?"

He smiled into the darkness. What he proposed was not sorcery but madness.

"Just what I said. Don't break my concentration. Don't put yourself at risk if I don't come back. If Adahab's kept his word, he'll be waiting at Nuriya. He'll guide you across the Sands of the Sun—"

"I won't go without you."

"Rahelle," he said, and then realized it was no use. She'd stayed in the smuggler base. She'd turned back on the trail. Zandru's seventh frozen hell, she'd refused to leave Nuriya. Nothing he said would change her mind.

Surrendering, he lowered himself into the most comfortable position he could find and closed his eyes. As he'd been taught, he slowed his breathing, shifting it into his belly. His mind, already fragilely tethered to his body, began to drift.

"I will watch over you," Rahelle murmured. "Wherever you go and as long as you wander, I will keep you safe."

Gareth could not imagine how to answer. If he opened his mouth, he would not be able to speak, only to weep.

He cast his thoughts out into the void.

Traceries of light flashed across his inner vision, only to dissolve into looping patterns of color and movement, shapes that elongated sickeningly as he watched, now motes like tiny globules of jelly, now as solid as a stone wall, now dissolving into torrents of sleet. Crystals scintillated, drifting across his eyes. He blinked, struggling to focus his thoughts.

Grandmother Linnea . . .

Of all the *leroni* he knew, of all the trained and Gifted minds, the one he stood the greatest chance of reaching was his own Keeper. He fastened on her name, on the memory of her face and the sound of her voice.

Grandmother! Help me!

Again and again, he sent out his plea. Each time, he failed . . . yet with each attempt, he came away with the certainty that someone was there, just beyond his reach.

Help me!

If he could stretch just a bit farther . . . But he had nowhere to stand. His mind was as formless and unstable as the vortex outside, clashing and shifting into stomach-churning iridescence.

Hold fast . . .

Gareth could not tell if the thought was his own or the distorted echo of someone else's . . .

Hold fast. The words were like a tiny seed, a pebble . . . a shard of crystal.

Hold.

The psychic firmament shuddered under a renewed lash of whirling currents, of colors colliding and jumbling together, shapes forming and elongating and shredding into glittering crystal dust . . .

Crystal . . . He clung to the image, clear and hard-edged, facets reflecting pale blue light, shimmers of brightness, one moment extending to the ends of the cosmos and the next, infinitesimally small.

I am that crystal . . . I hold fast . . . The world swayed and pitched and then all chaos fell away.

Who?

The question almost broke his focus, it was so unexpected. The moment stretched into an eon. He floated in a void in which only two things existed: the crystal that housed a blue-white flicker and the memory of that question.

Who calls?

He had no idea how to answer. Who was he? What was he? What was it he needed more than help?

In the dim under-caverns of his mind, men came riding over hillocks of sand, pale-haired men who held aloft strange devices. Wherever they passed, fire burst forth from their upraised hands. It blasted rock and tree, men and beasts, mountains and stars. The earth trembled under the galloping hooves of their horses, horses with bare skulls for heads and scorpion stingers for tails. They left behind a trail of blood that burst into crimson flames. The fire died, leaving blackened patches like charred glass.

Who? Where?

Around him, the blue crystal walls solidified. He felt them hold him, cradle him. The voice that spoke in his mind took on a fierce clarity.

Where?

He recognized the disciplined mental pattern of a Keeper, but not Grandmother Linnea. He did not know this woman—it was a woman, of that he was certain—but he had no doubt of the power that allowed her to hear him across so many miles.

The blackened patches shrank in size, or rather his own perspective broadened, no longer some ancient desiccated seabed, but the center of a city. He struggled to visualize the steel and glass of the Terran Headquarters, the ancient walls of Comyn Tower, the spaceport as he had last seen it.

The flames returned, wilder than before. They spread past the boundaries of the landing fields and through the surrounding Terran

Zone . . . the Trade City and up the slopes to the wealthier residential areas . . . lapping at Comyn Castle . . . stone cracked under the heat . . . walls tumbled . . . men burned like torches, their bones blowing away as soot-dark dust . . .

And above it all, huge elongated ships of gleaming metal . . . ships that belched fire . . .

A pause followed in which he sensed the Keeper absorbing what he had just communicated to her.

He felt a pressure in his mind, a shimmering of the faceted blue-tinted light. For an instant, he had the sensation of looking into a mirror, seeing not a literal image of his mind, but one that shared some essential quality. He could not have named it or even known until that moment that it was his. In this other woman's mind, he saw his own.

Then she was gone, or perhaps he was the one who left her, falling slowly but surely through a whorl of stars, until he opened his eyes and saw Rahelle smiling at him.

29

In her sitting room at Nevarsin Tower, Silvana roused from her trance, gasping. The images of fire and destruction still lingered in her mind. No mere dream could have affected her or evoked such fear. It had been a long time since she'd woken from nightmares of faceless, menacing figures. She had never dreamed of consuming fire or of riders who left rivers of blood and ashes in their wake.

Her starstone lay in the palm of her hand, warmed by her skin. She clutched it to her breast, drew her shawl more tightly around her shoulders, and forced herself to analyze the situation.

She had been working with the stone as had become her daily habit since returning from the Yellow Forest, using the matrix to amplify her natural Gift to further develop her sensitivity and control. As a Keeper, she had mastered the skills of gathering and integrating the mental energies of the people in her circle; now she forced her own mind into greater suppleness and strength. And discipline as well, to resist the lure of the heartstone.

If the chieri *can sense that space ships have landed in the Dry Towns, then perhaps I can, too.*

At first, her efforts had left her exhausted and confused. Even enhanced by the starstone, her mind did not seem capable of reaching across such vast distances. But she had persisted, partly out of stubbornness, partly out of memory of the concern in Lian's voice.

Weakness lapped at her, such as she had not known since her days as a novice. She needed to replenish the energy her body had expended. In a moment, she promised herself.

While in trance, her mind had been barricaded against every starstone except her own. Yet . . .

Yet *someone* had touched her mind. Not only touched her, but transmitted images of such desperation that she still reacted viscerally to their vividness.

Nausea nudged her, a sign of her body's depletion. She could not think clearly or act rationally in such a state. As usual, she had placed a dish of concentrated morsels within easy reach. She took a handful of dried cherries and a nut-crusted honey roll.

The identity of her communicant she set aside for the moment. It had been a man, young she thought, but not any Tower worker she knew.

What he had sent to her mind, on the other hand, could not be set aside. The pale-haired riders could be Ridenow, but she did not think so. That Domain was peaceful and well-regulated under its current Warden.

They had ridden over sand . . . sand suggested the Dry Towns.

Dry Towners, armed with weapons of such power?

How could that be possible? The Dry Towners had never possessed such things, not even during the Ages of Chaos, when the Seven Domains had been torn with *laran* warfare. As far as she knew, the *Terranan* had never traded with them—the ships Lian had spoken of, *"up there, passing . . . and setting down far across the sands."*

Stop. Breathe. Think.

If the fiery weapons seemed fantastical, then so did the horses, with their scorpion tails and bare-skull heads. So the image could not have been an actual memory, unless the sender had been insane. The message did not bear the stamp of a hallucination. She had tended enough men whose minds had been broken to feel sure of that. No, this person was distraught, but not mad.

So the images were not literal but metaphorical. Metaphors for what?

Silvana downed a second cup of watered wine. The trembling in her limbs eased and her vision steadied, but she could not think what the horse-beasts and their riders might represent. They seemed like the stuff of childhood nightmares.

She could not think what, if anything, should be done about the threat from the Dry Towns, if indeed there were one. She set aside that train of thought and turned to the images of the starships.

. . . ships aloft, raining fire upon a city . . . a city of towers, a castle in the old Comyn style . . . *Thendara, it must be Thendara* . . . a broad paved expanse beyond which rose rectangular edifices of glass and metal . . . *the spaceport?*

She had seen the Federation spaceport as a child. Regis had taken her there, during that brief time when it had been safe, when they had been a family together. She had seen ships like the ones in the vision, waiting to launch themselves into space. And she remembered sensing her father's longing to take passage on them. This memory she set aside, thinking, *We all yearn for things we cannot have. We all, in our own ways, must answer the demands of duty and honor.*

Whoever had sent those images believed the Thendara spaceport was at risk. Dirav and the others, had they sensed it, too?

As to who had sent the warning . . .

Someone who had received information that the Dry Towners had or might have obtained Compact-banned weapons.

Someone who believed fervently that the spaceport was in danger of a devastating attack.

Someone who had been able to reach her mind, unaided.

Someone with the Hastur Gift.

Silvana closed her eyes, willing her pulse to slow. Her body, disciplined by years of rigorous physiological control, responded. She wrapped the shawl around her body and shoved her feet into her felted slippers. The chamber housing the relays would be cold, particularly the stone floor.

It was time to call her mother.

—✦—

Silvana settled herself before the relay screens, making sure her spine was correctly aligned and her shawl tucked around her to retain body warmth. Except for that one message she had been called to receive in person, she had not worked the relays in many years. In the interim, the screens had been attuned for other minds. She spared a little time to recalibrate the linkages to her own preferences. What she intended was going to be difficult enough without the added irritation of even a slight amount of distortion. She needed to be able to communicate as clearly as possible.

When she had adjusted the matrix to her satisfaction, she entered the psychoactive crystal lattice. Although Comyn Tower had not been operational when she trained on the relays as a novice, she found no difficulty in locating it.

Comyn Tower . . .

She slipped into contact with the presence on the other end of the relay.

Nevarsin Tower—Silvana, is that you? It's Illona! The younger woman's joy sparkled through the psychic connection.

Silvana felt as if a constricting band had been released from around her heart. Illona Rider, who had served as her own under-Keeper, whom she loved as a daughter, had gone to Thendara as under-Keeper.

Chiya, *how wonderful to speak with you. Are you well?*

More than well! I am—Illona broke off coherent thought and projected a mental image of herself, radiant with health and happiness—*pregnant!*

Silvana's delight faltered. Could this be safe, to work as a *leronis* when carrying a child?

Illona replied with an arpeggio of silent laughter. *Linnea assures me that it is, as long as I allow her to monitor me regularly. I must have something useful to do or I would run away to join the Travelers again! It's much better to do the work I was trained for.*

For a long moment, Silvana struggled to collect her own thoughts. She had been immune from the dilemma faced by so many of the women of her caste, for she had never taken a lover since entering the Tower. Now she understood how her own mother had struggled with the choice between her work as a Keeper and her family.

How terrified she must have been when those children were being kidnapped, after everything she had sacrificed for me.

Would Illona have easier choices? Knowing the young woman's self-reliance and fierce spirit, Silvana doubted that she would be cowed into traditional roles.

Forgive my outburst, Illona said. *I had not expected to encounter you on the relays. Has something happened, that you are now breaking your seclusion?*

It is a matter between Keepers. Silvana sent a pulse of affection to temper the formality of her statement. *I would speak with the Keeper of Comyn Tower.*

Of course. The flicker of curiosity from Illona's mind vanished, replaced by practicality. *She is not working in the circle tonight. I will bring her as quickly as I can.*

Not too quickly, for I would not be the cause of your falling down the stairs!

I shall go carefully . . . but quickly!

Only a short time later, the relay came alive as Linnea established connection. Silvana felt a tremendous sense of presence, of stillness, of listening. The excitement of their previous contact was gone, mastered as only a Keeper could master such feelings. Not even a hint of anxiety leaked through the linkage.

Comyn Tower, Nevarsin sends greetings. Silvana's greeting was overly formal, so she was a little surprised by the cordiality of the response. The words were formulaic, the phrasing traditional, yet permeated with a sense of gracious welcome.

As Keeper of Comyn Tower and as a representative of the Keepers' Council, I greet you in return. Again came a moment of undemanding silence.

I have received a report—perhaps a rumor only—of a danger threatening the Domains. I cannot vouch for its credibility, only the earnestness of its source.

What danger?

Silvana related her analysis of the images, both the Dry Towns riders with their star-bright weapons, and the even more devastating attack from space.

Thank you for the warning . . . for breaking your long silence, Linnea said. *These reports are troubling indeed.*

Silvana agreed. *Neither seems likely, but if they are true, the results could be dreadful.*

I will ensure that both possibilities are investigated. If the Dry Towners have somehow obtained illegal weaponry, the entire balance of power with the Domains is at risk. The Regent has agents who send him information from at least as far as Carthon. Perhaps they can look into the matter and either verify or disprove it.

That will take time, Silvana pointed out.

Time in which we can prepare, should this rumor prove accurate. As for the starships . . . we never expected Darkover to remain isolated forever. Once the Federation conflict is over, they will return for the same reasons they sought us out in the first place. Meanwhile, the scanning and communications equipment at the old base is still operable. Jeram, whom you may remember, has been training young people in its use.

Jeram? Silvana recalled the Terran deserter as he had arrived at Nevarsin Tower, a man wounded in spirit as well as body. His friendship with Lew Alton had begun the process of healing, but when he'd left Nevarsin, she had lost track of him and knew of him only through reports. She had no idea what one person might do against devices of such appalling power, but Jeram was a man of considerable resources. He had been a soldier, trained in off-world military technology.

You believe your informant? Linnea inquired. *On what basis? How does he or she come to this knowledge?*

Silvana hesitated. Her first intention had been only to pass on the warning, trusting that Linnea, both as Keeper and as the dowager Lady Hastur, would take the necessary steps. She was still not easy in her own mind about how much personal contact she wanted with her mother. Her sojourn with the *chieri* and the new knowledge that her father had indeed tried to find her had given her a new understanding.

Silvana remembered sitting with her mother at High Windward and then in the townhouse in Thendara, making music together, their voices and minds in effortless rapport. She had always been in their hearts, as they had always been in hers. Yes, that was true, just as Lian and David and Keral and Dirav would always be with her.

Within the little pouch hanging from its cord around her neck, the heartstone radiated a pulse of gentle warmth. She sensed it even through the layers of insulating silk. But it was not time. Not yet.

Let me show you . . . Silvana opened her memory of that desperate mental sending. Across the relays, she felt as if her mother had clasped hands with her. Their minds joined so seamlessly that everything Silvana had seen and sensed appeared in perfect replica in Linnea's mind. Silvana turned her thoughts to the one who had sent the warning, the man with the Hastur Gift.

It must be Gareth. Linnea sounded distressed.

Gareth?

Your brother Dani's son. I do not understand how he was able to do this, to reach you without the aid of a relay or even his own starstone . . . but there is no one else it could be. When Regis died, we all thought the Hastur Gift died with him.

Was Gareth not tested for the Gift?

You do not know his history. Even if his parents had agreed, the Council would never have sanctioned it. I taught him privately, as much for the discipline as for the development of the laran *he would never be allowed to use.*

Gareth must have found himself in desperate circumstances to bring a deeply buried Gift to life.

He has been missing for more than a tenday now, Linnea said, and Silvana sensed a flicker of inner conflict, as if Linnea were struggling with a difficult decision, perhaps whether or not to reveal something told to her in confidence.

As a boy, Linnea went on, *he indulged in a lot of romantic daydreams about adventures. Given the chance, he might well have made his way to Carthon. I hoped he had the sense not to venture further, but Gareth is . . . impulsive. We all thought he had outgrown it, but perhaps he only learned to mask it better.* Her mental voice sounded disappointed, as if she had just learned the worst about someone she loved and had once believed in.

Silvana found herself in unexpected sympathy with Gareth. She knew nothing of him beyond what Linnea had just told her, and the enormous effort and natural talent it must have taken to communicate without a starstone across such a distance. It was not credible that a *leronis* of Linnea's skill would not have detected Gareth's intentions to seek adventure in the Dry Towns, not when he was her student. Not when she had taught him how to use his starstone—*his starstone.*

If he has a starstone, Silvana said, *why would he be driven to such desperate measures as to activate the Hastur Gift? It could not have been taken from him, or he would not have survived.*

Only if another person, other than a Keeper, handled it.

But then it must be insulated—

Very well insulated. In a locket shaped like an amulet of Nebran, the Toad God of the Dry Towns.

It was as much an admission as Silvana was likely to receive. Linnea had known that Gareth would go to the Dry Towns; she had not been able to dissuade him, so she had given him the best protection she could. Something had happened, most likely not in Carthon but in one of the other cities—Shainsa, perhaps, or Daillon—or in the barren lands beyond. The image of the riders armed with off-world weapons now seemed even more likely.

And the ships raining down their nightmare attack from the skies? How had Gareth learned of them?

What is going on in the Dry Towns?

I don't know. Only when Linnea answered, her emotions once again under impeccable control, did Silvana realize she'd mentally spoken the question in both their thoughts.

"Others . . ." Lian had said, *". . . landing far across the sands."*

Dirav had spoken of *all* of Darkover's defenses. *"Just because we have withdrawn to the planet of our origin does not mean we have forgotten what we once knew, during those times when we were equally at home in the vast reaches of space."*

Then Dirav had given her the heartstone.

30

Below, in the blackened ruins of Nuriya, a fire was burning.

Gareth braced himself on one arm against the rock face and studied it. His vision was still unreliable, going double or distorting objects at odd, unexpected intervals. Even when he blinked, the yellow-orange flame still shone in the darkness. It must be real, then, and neither memory nor imagining.

Rahelle touched his shoulder gently, so as not to startle him. She'd been unusually solicitous since his attempt to reach his grandmother with his *laran*. Even now, he wasn't entirely certain whom he had contacted, whose competent, keen mind he had touched—if it had been anyone at all and not some figment of his disordered consciousness. He did not have the strength to try again. Weakness lapped at him. In the absence of food, his body was consuming its own substance to replenish the energy he'd so recklessly expended. Rahelle must have sensed what it had cost him, what it was still costing him, but there was nothing either of them could do but to press on and hope they'd find a cache of supplies in the village.

As they neared the bottom of the trail, Gareth was better able to judge the size of the fire. It was a small one, well contained. He could not make out any figures around it, but along the perimeter of its radiance he caught the shapes of *oudrakhi*. That was a hopeful sign, and he managed to find the energy to hurry his steps.

They stumbled through the rubble, heading for the fire. Before they reached it, the man who had been hunkered down beside it rose up. Silhouetted against the blaze, he came toward them, arms outstretched.

"My friends and the delight of my eyes! I weep with gladness to see you again!"

Just at that moment, a shift in the air carried the aroma of roasting meat and the piquant spices of the Dry Towns. Gareth's senses blurred and his knees gave way. Rahelle caught him under one shoulder and, an instant later, Adahab took the other. They set him down next to the fire. Gareth couldn't understand what they were saying, what Adahab was doing, only the plate of steaming slivers of meat and the pile of tiny beans that smelled astonishingly good.

"Eat now," Adahab instructed. "Stories later."

At first, all Gareth could do was lift one morsel after another to his mouth. The food was intensely, intoxicating flavorful. Warmth, both from the cooking temperature and the seasonings, flowed down his throat and filled his belly. His hands stopped trembling. Adahab filled his plate again, and then a third time. When at last Gareth set down his empty plate, both his vision and his nerves felt steady. The loss of his starstone still hampered him; he could see and hear well enough, but his *laran* senses had gone numb.

While Gareth ate, Rahelle had sketched out their story for Adahab. The villager made a gesture of disbelief at the folly of it all, and Gareth was struck by the essential decency of the man. Honor had brought Adahab back to ruined Nuriya after seeing the surviving villagers safe in Duruhl-ya, and Adahab had intended to remain until he had scoured all the ridge in fulfillment of his promise. All Adahab wanted was to court the woman he intended to marry, to care for his parents and his flocks, and to live a good life according to his beliefs. He had no interest in invading or conquering anyone.

Such men are not my enemy. Drought and disease and the arrogance of men like Hayat, those were the enemies. If Hayat attacked the Domains, Gareth's own people would suffer, but so would men like Adahab.

Gareth felt so sleepy, so replete and yet so drained, that he could barely keep his eyes open. He swayed as he sat, but before he could say anything, Adahab guided him to an unrolled blanket. Gareth fell asleep only a moment after curling up on it.

He awoke to sun overhead, the muted grumbling of the *oudrakhi*, and a pungent, minty aroma. The morning was well advanced, but Rahelle had insisted that Gareth sleep as long as he could.

Gareth ate the food left for him and drank the stimulant tea. As he chewed, he glanced upward, wondering what was happening with the *Lamonica* and the Castor Sector ship, whether the privateers had arrived or how long before they did. He tried without success to convince himself that if both the smugglers and the rebels had departed, their pursuers would surely follow.

The little burst of strength from last night had faded. He felt half-blind, half-deaf, swaddled in layers of insulation, alone as he had not been alone since his talent woke with puberty, alone except for his own fears.

Adahab had found a couple of the village *oudrakhi* wandering nearby, so there were mounts for everyone. They finished the food and packed up the animals, giving them a last drink at the well. Rahelle smothered a laugh at Gareth's expression as the great desert beasts moved off. The *oudrakhi* were not only taller than horses, but their gait, a lumbering same-sided stride, creating an alarming swaying sensation. Gareth felt a twinge of nausea before Rahelle suggested that he keep his focus on the horizon, not the ground. After that, the movement helped to loosen his muscles.

They set off across the Sands of the Sun, retracing the their previous route. *Oudrakhi* were not as fast as horses—Gareth did not know if they could run at all—but they maintained a steady pace for hour after hour. Unlike horses, they could go for several days without drinking. The endurance of the riders, not the mounts, limited how far they could travel each day.

Once Gareth adjusted to the *oudrakhi's* rocking gait, he had time to think. From Adahab's village, Kharsalla, the way lay open to Shainsa and from there, Carthon. And from there, home.

Shainsa. Where Hayat had surely returned, triumphant and exulting in his new weapons. Hayat, who had in his possession the Nebran amulet . . .

If Rahelle guessed what he was thinking, she would point out the folly of seeking Hayat out. He could almost hear her say, *"Are you* trying *to get yourself killed?"*

He could do nothing about the starships. He could do nothing about the blasters. He had already tried to send a warning, and he still was not sure if he had reached anyone or if it had all been a hallucination born of the shock of having his starstone wrenched from him.

There was one thing he could still do. He must discredit Hayat so completely that Dayan would reject the blasters. The only way he could think to accomplish that was to challenge Hayat, to make the issue one of *kihar*, of honor. He would have to prove the rightness of his own position by being willing to die for it, to be executed for it, because even if—by some absurd stroke of luck—he survived, he could not risk Dayan taking further steps or seeking revenge. Dayan was a cunning and dangerous man, but he was not an impetuous one. If all went well, there would be an end to the Shainsa blasters. In that moment, it did not matter to Gareth that he might not be alive to see it.

He wouldn't need to persuade Rahelle of his plan, only keep it secret. Cyrillon was still in Shainsa and Rahelle would be safe with him.

Rahelle. Safe.

He felt a pang, a mixture of relief that she would have a measure of protection and of grief for the time they would never spend together, the things he would never say to her.

He could not accost Hayat on the street. The Dry Towns lordling was too well guarded. As one who had already been presented at the Great House, however, Gareth could legitimately request a hearing with Lord Dayan.

What had Adahab said? *"Swords and whips, tools of the* kifurgh," the *kifurgh* that was the ritualized duel of honor among the Dry Towners. Such a challenge, uttered before the High Lord of the city, must be answered.

Gareth was no duelist, even with weapons in which he was trained.

There was no possibility he could win. But he did not need to win. He only had to take Hayat down with him.

Adahab went no farther than Kharsalla, where he made a great show of presenting Gareth and Rahelle with their *oudrakhi.* The generosity of the gift clearly enhanced his prestige, even more than the animals themselves would have. From the little village, Rahelle had no trouble acting as guide to Shainsa.

Dusty and tired, they arrived at the outskirts of Shainsa just as pools of crimson-tinted shadows lengthened across the sand.

With an unexpected pang, Gareth realized that after today, Rahelle would never argue with him or try to rescue him. Yet he could not think of how to frame any sort of farewell without arousing her suspicions.

After spending the last of their coin on gate fees, they approached the broad, unpaved square with its common well, where Cyrillon had set up camp among the other traders. Here they dismounted.

Although daylight was fast fading, the market still abounded in buyers and sellers taking advantage of the relative coolness. Gareth peered through the gathering dusk, but he could not make out Cyrillon's tent. Using the well as a landmark, they searched the area. Traders looked up from their evening preparations, and a few called out in greeting. Rahelle answered them with a distracted gesture. With each circuit, she grew palpably more frustrated.

"I could have sworn—no, I was right. *This* is where my father was!" She indicated a spot now occupied by a group of leather traders, who seemed to take her gesture as a signal of her interest in their wares.

"Surely he would not have left Shainsa without—" At her wide-eyed glance, Gareth broke off. He handed the reins of his *oudrakhi* to Rahelle and approached the leather traders.

"Heya!" one of them exclaimed. "Move those smelly beasts elsewhere! They're bad for business!"

"A belt, fine sir?" inquired his fellow. "We offer the finest tanned leather in all of Shainsa."

"Do you know what happened to the man who used to be on this spot? A trader out of Carthon?" Gareth asked, waving away the proffered belt.

The leather trader shrugged with exaggerated indifference. "I might remember, or I might not."

The game of bargaining irritated Gareth's already frayed nerves. "I don't need a belt. I don't *want* a belt. I haven't money to buy a belt—"

"But the man who was here does," Rahelle cut in smoothly.

Gareth picked up the story. "He's got our wages, see, and we were to collect them here. There's nothing we'd like better than a new belt for each of us, once we get paid."

The trader who'd offered the belt muttered something about penniless riffraff. His comrade, the one who'd made the comment about the smelly *oudrakhi*, said, "Word is he's taken lodgings in the city. Street of the Three Goats, I think it was, or somewhere near that."

The tension lifted from Rahelle's muscles. Gareth said, "Our thanks, friend."

The trader made a sucking noise through the gap between his front teeth and squinted at the *oudrakhi*. "You can't take 'em into that district. New orders from Lord Dayan."

"Yar," said the other, the one who'd tried to sell Gareth the belt. "Want to get rid of 'em? I can't give you much, not in that condition, but the price of grain's gone up fierce. It'll cost you more than they're worth to feed 'em."

Rahelle turned to Gareth. "My father must have stabled his own animals on the outskirts."

"Go to him, then." Taking the reins of the *oudrakhi*, he said, "I'll take care of them." He almost added, *"I'll join you later,"* but the lie stuck in his throat. She was so eager to see her father again, she didn't notice. Now that the moment of parting had come upon him, there was so much he wanted to say to her, but none of it was possible. He just nodded and watched her hurry off toward the city.

"Well, what about it?" the leather trader asked.

Gareth shook his head. He wasn't much for bargaining, but he knew he'd not receive a fair price. Selling them here would solve the problem of what to do with them, but the animals were not truly his. They belonged as much to Rahelle as to him, and he dared not trust anyone in Shainsa with the money.

After a few inquiries, Gareth found a livestock yard owner who charged neither too much nor too little and whose animals looked in decent condition. He had very little to offer in payment. His boot knife would have made a generous fee, but he might need it. In the end, he settled for one of the saddles, which the yardsman accepted happily in payment. Gareth gave the name of the owner as Cyrillon Sensar, lodging in the Street of the Three Goats, and asked that word be sent to the apprentice, Rakhal, in two days. If by some chance the duel were postponed until tomorrow, it would still be over by the time Rahelle received the message.

The yard owner, perhaps considering the imbalance in the agreement, included a meal of flatbread spread with a thick, spicy paste of beans and garlic. Gareth ate lightly, just enough to feel renewed strength but not to overfill his belly.

Night had almost blanketed the city when Gareth took his leave. Flickering torchlight softened the walls of sandstone and dried mud brick. Passing along a row of inns, he slowed to watch the light streaming from their open windows and to catch the fragments of song, voices raised in laughter, and the sweet lilt of a flute. He thought of Rahelle—but no, he must not dwell on what was forever lost.

Finally he emerged into the open square bounded on one side by the great square building that was the House of Dayan. The place seemed at once familiar and utterly alien, as if glimpsed in a fever dream. The sparse crowd parted before him. He could not tell if this was some random movement that his mind wove into a sense of approaching destiny, or whether some aspect of his bearing or expression caused the people to retreat.

Guards stood to either side of the double doors. They watched Gareth approach. Both were large men, garbed in Dayan's colorful livery, and well armed.

Gareth assumed his most imperious manner. He reminded himself that the guards might think whatever they wished about him, so long as they admitted him.

"I am Garrin of Carthon, with a message for Hayat, son of Dayan of this house."

The shorter and broader of the two guards lifted one corner of his mouth in a contemptuous expression. "I do not recognize you, gutter-dust. And the Heir to Shainsa does not treat with rabble."

"The Heir of Shainsa does not take his orders from you," Gareth replied in much the same tone. "And Lord Dayan has already recognized me on my previous visit. I doubt he would be pleased to have a guest treated in such a disrespectful fashion because of my current unfortunate appearance."

The guard's mouth tightened and his gaze flickered to his comrade. Gareth imagined him weighing the relative risk of admitting a man who carried himself like royalty although he was undeniably as filthy and ragged as any beggar, or facing Dayan's wrath at a violation of hospitality toward a known guest.

"Well?" Gareth demanded. "Are you going to make me wait all night? Are you going to make *Lord Dayan* wait all night?"

The taller guard broke first, stepping back as he opened one of the double doors. "In with you, then, and upon your head be it if the Great Lord is in any way displeased." He jerked his chin toward his comrade, who visibly suppressed a sigh before leading the way inside.

The entrance hall and colonnade appeared much as Gareth remembered, bathed in the wavering light of torches. Incense-laden smoke curled from a pair of braziers, each of them of brass and so finely wrought they must be worth the price of an entire village. There were more grim-faced men in livery and fewer ordinary people than on Gareth's previous visit with Cyrillon, but that had been during the day . . . and Hayat had not yet returned with the blasters.

The guard's soft-soled boots made hardly a sound on the paving stones, yet each step reverberated through Gareth's marrow, each step bringing him closer to his destiny. He thought how foolish he had been. He should have thought it all through. He should have rested overnight instead of rushing here, still weary from his journey. He should have—

It was too late now, and what did it matter, so long as he took Hayat with him? He needed only that much strength, that much quickness, that much luck. No more.

With a start, Gareth realized that they had arrived at the presence hall. When the guard swung the door open, Gareth glimpsed the interior, bright with banks of torches. Smoke mixed with incense to create a haze through which all the riches of Lord Dayan's court seemed like a mirage.

The guard spoke a few words to another liveried man just inside the door, then gestured for Gareth to enter. Mouth suddenly dry, Gareth stepped inside. The liveried man escorted Gareth toward where Lord Dayan sat. As if in a dream, Gareth made his way through the assembly of courtiers and lesser lords in their robes and shirtcloaks of jewel-toned silks, seated on their brocaded cushions or standing well back, the servants and the armed guards moving about their duties. At some point, when Gareth and his escort had proceeded perhaps halfway to the single chair at the far end, the assembly took notice of him. Muted conversations ceased, so that he heard Hayat's distinctive voice, followed by a rumbled comment.

Hayat was seated at his father's right hand, dressed in a robe that gleamed with threads of gold. The neck opening was unfastened, so that Gareth caught the glimmer of something silver at Hayat's throat—the Nebran amulet. As Hayat spoke, he gesticulated with one hand while he brandished a blaster with the other. A pile of the off-world weapons, most likely the entire lot, sat at Dayan's feet. Dayan stared at them with the same intense gaze Gareth remembered from his first audience. As before, the Shainsa lord wore dark clothing.

Merach, standing behind Dayan's left shoulder, was the first to react to Gareth's approach. He did not draw his sword, but he shifted one hand to the hilt and positioned himself in such a way that he could easily slip it free as he stepped between his lord and any threat.

Dayan waved Gareth's escort closer, and the two exchanged murmured words.

"What message do you have for my son?" Dayan's voice, although not loud, carried well. He placed a subtle emphasis on the word *you* that conveyed his rejection of Gareth's legitimacy: *What gives rubbish like you the right to sully the air I breathe?*

Even the poorest beggar, Gareth thought hotly, *can speak the truth.*

Slowly, deliberately, Gareth shifted his gaze from Dayan to Hayat. He had no idea how Dry Towners framed a formal challenge, nor did it matter.

"You, Hayat, son of Dayan, are a thief and a liar! I name you so before these great men of Shainsa and before all the gods!"

Shock and silence answered him.

Hayat scrambled to his feet, his sword already half drawn. An ugly flush sprang to his cheeks.

"Hold!" Dayan's command cracked like of a whip. "This man has uttered grave accusations indeed, in these charges of dishonor."

"But Father, he's just a stupid villager who was laboring for the off-worlders. He has no clan or kin, no *kihar*! I should trounce him like the troublemaker he is and be done with it."

As Dayan regarded his son, the tiny muscles around his eyes tightened. "Would the Heir of Shainsa allow these charges to go unanswered?"

The air, so thick with smoke and incense, turned chill. Gareth felt a stirring of compassion for Hayat, who did not even realize how he had just disgraced himself.

"He's nobody, a piece of lying, treacherous offal!" Hayat rushed on, seemingly unaware of the darkening of his father's countenance. "He deserves no answer! Father, you can't be serious in suggesting I should . . ." His voice trailed away as a measure of comprehension sank in. No one dared to whisper the word, *coward.*

"Your Magnificence," Merach spoke into the lapse. "These are grave charges, yet any lout can bandy about insults in order to make mischief for his betters. Would it not be prudent to investigate the basis on which they are made before deciding on a proper response?"

Dayan shifted in his chair, turning his attention back to Gareth. Once Gareth would have quailed under such scrutiny, but Dayan no longer had the power to intimidate him. To gain his objective, Gareth must be as provocative as possible. He lifted his chin and glared back.

"I am listening," Dayan said.

"He is a thief because he has stolen from me," Gareth said. "He has taken an item that belongs to me, without lawful right. He is a liar—and a traitor as well—because he has told you that these blasters will give you the power to conquer your rivals and go to war with the Seven Domains!"

Dayan's face showed an instant of surprise before he settled once more into preternatural stillness. Hayat cried, "I swear I never told him!"

"Shut up, fool!" Dayan snapped.

"Even a man of no learning could guess how you would use the fire-weapons," Merach said. Dayan dipped his chin in agreement. "Until now, your enemies have had equal resources. It is common knowledge, is it not, that only the resulting stalemate has prevented Shainsa from expansion."

"You!" Dayan said to Gareth. "My son brings me the means of victory and you accuse him of treachery! I should have you stripped naked and whipped through the market for your vile lies!"

"Go ahead." Gareth put a bit of a swagger into his step as moved closer. "My discomfort will not alter the truth. You will discover soon enough how reliable the off-world blasters are. They are quite spectacular, as your son has undoubtedly informed you. They can kill at a distance, and there is no defense against their power. But *for how long*? What happens when they cease working in the middle of a battle?"

Dayan frowned.

"Did Hayat also tell you that the first lot of blasters ran out of power within a day?" Gareth went on. "A day of light use, not heavy fighting? Did he tell you that the off-world captain had played a similar trick on the headman of the nearby village? And—" lowering his voice for dramatic effect, "—did he tell you whether he has tested these blasters to ascertain whether or not they, too, are almost drained?"

By Hayat's flare of anger, Gareth knew he had not tested the blasters. He wanted to conserve their charges.

Gareth returned his attention to Dayan. "What assurance do you have, then, that they will not fail you at the most critical time, when you are in heated battle with the armies of the Domains? Once your blasters are gone, what is to stop their sorcerers from razing Shainsa to the ground . . ." Gareth reached for the *laran* that was not quite there and aimed his final words at the entire assembly ". . . all on the word of a thief?"

Red-faced, Hayat drew breath to respond, but Merach restrained him with a touch on his arm.

Dayan's voice was as quiet as Gareth's, as powerful in its delivery. "What do you claim my son has taken from you?"

"Lord Hayat stole a silver amulet in the form of Nebran the Toad God. If you would determine the truth of my words, seek for it on his person."

The guards standing closest to Hayat hesitated, the fear on their faces plain. It would mean death to lay hands upon the Heir to Shainsa, but death also to disobey Dayan's command.

"There is no need," Merach said in the grimmest tone Gareth had ever heard him use. "I myself witnessed the deed. Lord Hayat acted out of belief that this man—" indicating Gareth without naming him, "—had forfeited Nebran's favor."

"I had every right to put a halt to his sacrilege!" Hayat said.

"What led you to judge another man's soul?" Dayan asked, and not for all the gold in Shainsa would Gareth have been in Hayat's place.

"He served the off-worlders! He tried to prevent them from giving me the fire-weapons, as had been agreed!"

A long moment of silence answered him.

"This matter cannot be judged by mortal means," Dayan said heavily, "but by the ancient test of *kifurgh*. The contest will take place within the hour."

31

Within a quarter-hour, a fighting circle had been laid out in the square outside the Great House. A small army of servants set about raking the sand, placing torches, and erecting a dais for Dayan's chair, while others of higher rank carried the ceremonial gear: masks, whips, and enormous padded gloves from which protruded three sets of long, curved, razor-edged claws. Gareth had heard stories of such weapons and how the Dry Towners were said to have adopted this style of fighting from the catmen.

Hayat went aside with three of the most elaborately garbed guards. Merach gestured for the other arms-bearer to follow him. Gareth watched, puzzled, as the Dry Towns lord motioned for Gareth to hold out his left hand.

"I don't understand," Gareth muttered. "You are Lord Dayan's man, and you served Hayat. Why would you do this for me?"

"You know little of the ways of *kihar*, man of Carthon, for all that you have your share of bravery. By assigning his most trusted advisor to make certain all is correct with your weapons, my lord ensures that all the world knows of his impartiality." Merach tightened the laces around Gareth's wrists, then tested the glove to make sure it would not slip. "Let no man claim that any advantage was taken this night."

"What about swords?" Gareth asked as Merach slipped the leather mask over his head. Gareth caught only a glimpse of the painted design, the exaggerated outlines of lips, the broad feline nose. The mask had a faint, unpleasantly musty smell, but the eyeholes were wide enough to not seriously impair his vision.

"In ancient times, we did not use swords." Merach turned his body slightly so that Gareth, following the movement, saw one of the guards placing a single sword, point down, into the sand at the center of the arena. The first part of the duel would be fought with whips and claws, each striving to entangle the other, to weaken him with pain and blood loss. It would take a long time or extraordinary luck to kill a man that way. The sword was the prize and the key to victory.

Gareth flexed the fingers of his left hand to test the action of the claws. He wondered how much experience Hayat had with them. The glove felt like an alien thing grafted on to his own hand, yet it was not a dishonorable weapon like the *Terranan* blasters. Whoever used it must place himself within equal risk from his opponent.

The whip was of braided leather, except for the tip, which terminated in a handful of short thongs. It was stiff as if from disuse, with a heavy knot at the end of the handle that fit snugly into Gareth's palm. He tested the balance, keeping his wrist loose. He'd probably get only one or two chances, with no time to practice, but a quick glance told him that Hayat was no expert, either.

As Merach finished checking Gareth's gear, the sound from the crowd increased. Through the mask, it sounded like the rumble of thunder on distant peaks. It seemed that half of Shainsa had heard of the duel and gathered to watch. Then Dayan's voice cut through and the murmurs died away.

Dayan, having commanded the attention of the audience, recited a brief speech in a dialect so archaic, so filled with unfamiliar terms and hissing accents, that Gareth wondered if it were not half in the speech of the catmen.

"The rules are these," Merach said, bending close so that Gareth could understand his words, even through the mask. "You must stay within the arena. You must fight until one of you is slain or has yielded, in which case he may be killed as one without *kihar*. No one else may assist you. Do you understand?"

Gareth suppressed a shiver. There were no restrictions on the fight itself. He felt as if he had broken into a dozen pieces, one part of his thoughts trying to understand these unfamiliar weapons, another inventing a strategy of how he could possibly put an end to Hayat under these conditions, yet another part grappled with the certainty of his own death, all the while laboring under the dullness that had smothered his inner senses since Hayat had seized the Nebran amulet. . . .

"Take your place." Merach pointed to a spot along the rim of the circle, directly opposite where Hayat waited. "Bow first to Lord Dayan and then to your opponent. Lord Dayan will then signal the commencement of the duel."

How? Gareth wondered, but his mouth had gone too dry for speech.

The torches around the circumference of the arena flared, filling the center with surging red and orange light. The *Terranan* were said to believe in a fiery hell, and Gareth thought it might resemble this.

Dayan lifted both arms, and Gareth stepped into the off-worlders' hell.

Across the circle, Hayat did the same. He crouched slightly, shoulders hunched. The Nebran amulet glinted from his open shirtfront.

Gareth kept his muscles loose, his grip on the whip just firm enough for control.

Dayan brought both arms down.

With a wordless scream, Hayat leaped forward. By some trick of the light, his eyes gleamed as if they had burst into flames. Instantly, Gareth saw that Hayat meant to seize the sword right away.

Gareth rushed forward, although he could not close the distance quickly enough. Then, as if a veil had been lifted from his sight, his vision came clear. He could see every detail of the fire-lit arena, every grain of sand, every star overhead.

He slowed, setting his balance, and brought the whip around in back of himself and then over his head. The thong uncurled in a long, lazy arc. His hand passed the top of the circle. His ears caught the faint whistle as leather cut through air, moving faster now, downward, and faster yet as he stretched out his arm. The tips of the thongs shot out with a thunderous *crack!*

Hayat skidded to a halt and scrambled backward. Whirling, he faced Gareth across the embedded sword.

Without taking his eyes off Hayat, Gareth circled to the left, keeping his whip hand toward his opponent. If he went for the sword, he'd be putting himself at the same disadvantage as Hayat had. Hayat had already shown he could be startled, perhaps even precipitated into panic.

Someone in the crowd began shouting, words Gareth couldn't make out, only the general sense of them, urging the fighters to get on with it. Gareth struggled to block out the sound. This wasn't like practice with a swordmaster, where the goal was the perfection of skill, the seamless flow of will and muscle and steel. It wasn't like the ambush on the Carthon trail; then he had been taken by surprise, they all had, and he'd fought to save the lives of his comrades. This ritualized violence was another matter altogether, exultant in its cruelty.

Hayat took visible heart from the shouting. He straightened from his crouch. A swagger marked his step as he spiraled toward the center, his gaze fixed not on the sword but on Gareth.

"How long do you think you can stand against me, puny sandal wearer? Look at you, half-dead, shriveled up from the desert, your strength draining away . . ." As he spoke, Hayat's voice settled into a rhythm, half sneer, half singsong. He flicked his whip once, twice, always following the rhythm of his words.

Gareth allowed his shoulders to sag, as if he knew he had no chance and there was no way out. He shrugged, dragging the long line of his own whip to the side, where a quick flip of his forearm would be enough to snap it out.

Hayat kept swinging his whip, fast and jerky. Every four or five steps, he let out a roar and made a swiping motion with his clawed glove. The claws fell so far short, they represented no credible threat. Hayat was indulging in empty show for the approval of the onlookers.

No, Gareth corrected himself as one of Hayat's whip strikes came perilously close. Hayat was blustering as a distraction while he sidled closer.

Gareth jumped back, narrowly avoiding the tip of Hayat's whip. He could see the pattern now, but his body was reacting too slowly. The energy from the meal eaten earlier with the yard owner would not last. His muscles felt thick with fatigue. He'd have to force the fight, and soon.

He gathered his ragged strength, lunging for Hayat as he brought his own whip around. Although he was not at all certain of his control, he directed the arc at Hayat's face. Hayat swerved just as the whip cracked. A cry went up from the crowd, a mixture of outrage and scattered applause. Gareth couldn't tell if he'd actually struck the other man.

Hayat lurched backward, but he didn't drop his whip. He scuttled to the very edge of the arena. Chest heaving, he wiped his face in the crook of the elbow of his gloved hand. In the wavering torchlight, Gareth saw the blood welling from a small cut in Hayat's forehead, just above the top of the mask.

For an instant, Hayat stared at his sleeve as if he could not believe he'd been cut. Screaming, swinging his whip with frenzied abandon, he hurled himself at Gareth.

Whipcracks shocked through the air, one after another. Swirls of dust and fine-grained sand shot upward as the tip of the whip struck the ground.

Gareth sank into a fighting stance, knees bent, weight balanced on both feet. Hayat was swinging so fast and closing so rapidly, timing would be tricky. If Gareth moved too soon, Hayat might swerve or back off or redouble the attack, but there was no way of knowing which.

Instinct urged Gareth to back away, to run. It took all his focus to hold his ground, to wait—wait—until Hayat's whip came within reach.

Now!

Gareth pivoted, using his body to bring his own whip around in a horizontal path. The whip unfurled just as Hayat's whip came down. The two whips tangled, faster than the eye could follow, twining around one another like snakes. The impact almost tore Gareth's whip from his hand, but he was ready for it, his fingers tight around the handle knot.

Bracing his feet, Gareth jerked as hard as he could. Hayat, still holding on to his own whip, was pulled forward, but not close enough to come within reach of Gareth's claws.

Hayat stumbled as he lost his grip. The crowd responded with a burst of shouting. Adrenaline and dust saturated the air.

The sudden lack of resistance almost broke Gareth's balance. He recovered more quickly than Hayat did, tossing aside the entangled whips. His right hand was now free to grab the sword.

An instant later, Hayat regained his feet, blocking the way.

Gareth swiped at Hayat. The claws slashed through empty air. Hayat reeled backward, but now Gareth had the measure of his reach. He followed, striving to close the distance before Hayat recovered.

The oblique angle of Hayat's leap took him beyond the arc of Gareth's claws. With surprising speed, he jabbed his claws at Gareth, aiming for Gareth's unprotected side. Gareth whirled, blocking with his glove. The two sets of claws gave a nerve-jangling shriek as they collided and slid past one another.

Hayat grabbed Gareth's mask, bearing down with his greater weight. The mask twisted askew, partly blocking Gareth's vision.

Gareth floundered, trying to escape the sudden, crushing load on his neck. He couldn't see, and in another moment, Hayat would slam him into the ground. A muffled roaring filled his skull. The pounding of his heart and his labored breath mixed with the screaming of the onlookers.

Desperate, Gareth reached around with his free hand. Something cold lanced across his forearm. His fingers slipped over a rounded surface—*Hayat's mask?*—and then found an opening, a hole.

Suddenly Gareth lost his balance. As he fell, he hooked his fingers into the opening. Hayat came down on top of him in a sprawling jumble of arms and legs and thrashing claws. Gareth dug his heels into the sand, fighting for traction, and tried to worm out from under his opponent. His fingertips met something soft and moist. With what little traction he had, he pushed as hard as he could.

Shrieking, Hayat arched backwards.

Gareth felt the lifting of Hayat's weight. Rolling in the opposite direction, Gareth scrambled to his feet. He could see a little through one edge of the eyehole, enough to make out Hayat's position. Gareth risked trying to shift his mask and by luck managed to get it more or less back in place.

Hayat clambered to his feet, his free hand covering his eye. Gareth judged the distance to the sword. He had only a fraction of a moment, a heartbeat, nothing more, before Hayat reacted.

Overhead, the night sky exploded in light.

32

Gareth staggered under the sudden brightness, as if the heavens had burst apart. His vision, adapted to the torchlit dark, hazed into gray. Muffled, his *laran* senses caught the onslaught of minds shrilling in terror and pain. Around him, as if in counterpoint, scattered voices howled.

"Aiie!" cried one and then another of the onlookers. "Sorcery! Devil-magic!"

By far the greater portion of the crowd had fallen silent.

Blinking, Gareth straightened up. The glare overhead faded. He made out the brightest of the stars and the glimmering violet crescent of Liriel . . . then a starburst of white-gold . . . and another, and a quick series of explosions . . . two, five, each overlapping the other.

A hush fell over the audience, except for a man here and there blubbering in fear.

Poulos was right to warn us.

"You brought this on us!" came a scream from behind him. "Die, witch spawn!"

Gareth spun around just as Hayat charged, sword extended. If they'd been any closer, Gareth would have been run through before he could react. As it was, the sword ripped through his shirt, slicing open his side. He felt a line of burning cold along his ribs, but his body was already in motion, pivoting as he had been drilled by the best swordmasters in Thendara.

Gareth stepped outside the sweep of Hayat's sword and let the other man rush past him. Hayat had swung wildly, and the stroke had pulled him off-balance. Now he was committed, for the sword had too much momentum to easily reverse direction. Gareth sidled in closer. He reached for Hayat's shoulder, thinking to control the other man's sword arm.

Another explosion whitened the sky. Hayat's eyes glittered in the harsh light. His lips drew back from his teeth. He jabbed his claws at Gareth's face.

Gareth ducked. One of the claws caught in the stiff leather of his mask. Unbalanced, he toppled to one side. He twisted as he fell, trying to keep Hayat from landing on top of him.

They rolled over one another, thrashing and struggling. For a hideous moment, Gareth felt himself pinned against the sand. His side flared into agony. A wildfire ignited in his flesh. Claws caught the light from overhead, then passed out of his limited range of vision.

Gareth's lungs ached, and his breath came hoarse and heavy. A faint, distant ringing filled his ears, blotting out all other sound. Dimly, he felt his arms and legs thrusting. With each second, his movements grew weaker, his muscles less responsive. He heard a sickening *snap!* above the sounds of the struggle. The pain in his side receded, as if it were happening to someone else.

He yearned, with every fiber of mind and body, to let go. To sink into the darkness. To have it all be over. No one would expect him to keep fighting, not against such odds, not when he was already wounded, perhaps fatally. Not when he had never thought he would survive.

Always, always, he had lived his life according to the expectations of others—his Grandmother Javanne, his parents, the Comyn, Mikhail, Domenic, Danilo, Grandmother Linnea.

Everyone except himself.

He had sworn himself to this last deed. Not aloud, in words, but where it mattered even more, in his heart. And now, he would give up because it was *difficult?*

Aldones, Lord of Light, father of my fathers, help me finish this fight!

With an inarticulate cry, Gareth redoubled his struggle. Strength flowed into him, strength he had not known he owned. Hayat's body was as dense, as weighty as ever, but somehow Gareth managed to find a hold here, a leverage there. He shoved and twisted and pulled as if all of Darkover and everyone he held dear depended upon it. His lungs burned. His heart pounded as if set upon by a demented drummer. His vision went from gray to white to incandescent blue.

He was no longer seeing with his physical eyes, but with deeper senses. Above him hovered two ships, elongated teardrops of metal. He sensed the men and women onboard, their desperate fear, felt the creak of warping steel, tasted acrid smoke, shuddered with impact after blasting impact . . .

Images wavered in and out of focus, not visual pictures but impressions, all haloed in blue-white, heat and chemical reeks and taut determination, thoughts rather than words,

Captain, we're hit—

We've got to surrender, send a message—

No prisoners.

Fire! Fire! Fire!

Flames racing down corridors, oxygen spilling out into space, fueling the blaze . . . muttered prayers, a man's face lit by flashing lights—red, blue, red . . .

Blue.

And then a terrible glory burst across his mind, across the heavens, blotting out the sweep of moon and stars . . .

A single point of brightness, trailing cometary mists . . . slowly dropping, slowly disappearing in the direction of Thendara.

Sobbing brought Gareth back to himself. He was standing, although he had no memory of having gotten to his feet. By the rush of wet heat down his side, he knew he was bleeding hard. Between one blink of his eyes and the next, the blue-white aura died away. His mouth tasted of ashes.

He swayed with sudden, overwhelming weakness. Someone caught him. A voice whispered in his ear, tickling the fine hairs on his neck. He could not understand the words.

Overhead, the stars glimmered, serene in their beauty, as if nothing had happened.

The arena blurred with overlapping images, like oddly doubled sight. A short distance away, a man bent over a rounded shape. Was it he who wept? Or had Gareth only imagined that sound?

"Lord Hayat," said the man who held Gareth upright.

Gareth found his balance and took a step toward the crouching man. It was Dayan, and at his feet lay his son, stretched across the fallen sword. No, Dayan still sat in his chair, anchored there by pride and custom. It was his spirit that had rushed to his son's side, while the demands of authority held him fast.

Gently, the guard who had stood as Hayat's aide rolled him on to his back. Blood saturated Hayat's shirt. His left arm was bent at an unnatural angle. The tips of his glove were snug against his chest.

Again, Gareth caught a wail of loss, a keening too intense for words, and this time he knew he did not hear it with his ears but with his inner senses. With his unamplified *laran.*

He should not be listening, for there was something overwhelmingly private in Dayan's grief. Yet before Gareth could raise his barriers and shut out the older man's emotions, he sensed something else . . . from Hayat.

Gareth held out his gloved hand, fumbling at the laces. Merach yanked at the knots and then Gareth pulled free.

His side throbbed, but he had not lost too much blood, not yet. He had just enough strength to do what must be done.

The guard looked up, dry-eyed, hard-eyed, as Gareth knelt. Gareth placed his right hand flat on Hayat's chest beside the embedded claws. Ribs lifted, too shallowly to be seen, only felt. Gareth closed his eyes in relief.

He reached for the Nebran amulet, but his fingers were too slippery with blood to manage the chain. The guard slipped it over Hayat's head and handed it to Gareth. By sheer luck, Gareth found the clasp right away. The locket popped open and his starstone fell into the palm of his hand.

The starstone flared like a miniature blue-white sun, more brilliant than Gareth had ever seen it. Its light bleached Hayat's ashen features. The guard said nothing, but his eyes went wide. Someone behind him spat out a curse before Merach motioned to clear the arena.

Fingers curled around his matrix stone, Gareth focused his mind on the psychoactive gem. For an instant, he had the sensation of squeezing himself into the rigid confines of a prism. He had become so accustomed to the unaided use of his *laran* that he had almost forgotten how to attune his mind to the stone. A moment later, he settled into its pattern and felt the surge as it amplified the natural psychic energy of his mind.

Although his eyes were closed, the arena leapt into vivid detail, the sand, the onlookers, the guards, the city with its taverns and walled gardens, livestock yards and market squares, women weeping in their chains and men imprisoned by their pride. Closer, he felt Merach's intricate mind, the loyalty that burned like a steady flame, and Dayan whose world had just shattered . . . and Hayat, his mind gone blank and dark, his body a web of dying colors. . . .

Gareth dropped into those sluggishly pulsing strands. He had not been trained as a healer, and yet he had managed to bring not one but two men back from the edge of death. Now, as then, he must let instinct, the strength and nature of his own Gift, guide him.

He must allow it to use him, to work through him, rather than force it to obey his will.

With that thought, his awareness shifted once again. He sensed the infinitesimal sparks of living cells and the clusters of blood-starved tissues, the cool mineral of bone, the gossamer threads of nerves . . . the choked darkness of torn flesh, sliced blood vessels . . . the eerie resonances of metal, some of it very old and from some other world—

Was it true that the Dry Towners descended not from the lost colony ships but from another planet, perhaps Wolf, during the Ages of Chaos?

—the outlines of cartilage and connective tissue. Gareth had got his bearings now. The claws had slipped between the attachments of ribs to sternum. They had pierced the membrane covering the lungs and severed a number of small blood vessels. The luck of Aldones, or perhaps Nebran, had been with Hayat, for the claws had missed his heart and the big artery. However, blood was pooling between his chest wall and his lung. The next moment, the lung collapsed. Hayat's entire body shuddered. The pattern of life energy dimmed.

Fighting off the urge to act quickly, Gareth studied the area around the tips of the claws. He did not know if it would be better to leave the claws in place, hoping that they were exerting pressure to limit the bleeding, or to remove them. If he did that, he might damage the lung tissue even more and precipitate a massive hemorrhage.

Try as he might, Gareth could not get a clear appraisal of the risks of removing the claws. He knew with growing certainty, however, that although the trauma of dragging them out might well end Hayat's life, to leave them would certainly mean his death. Dayan believed his son was already gone—what was there to lose?

Only Gareth's own integrity, because he *had* wished Hayat ill, because he *had* intended to kill him, and now he must act with such clarity of purpose that he would never look back and see himself as murdering a gravely injured man.

Gareth remembered what he had been like as an adolescent, how he had demanded the throne, insisting on his right to be king. He could not blame Grandmother Javanne entirely. The truth was that he and Hayat were not all that unlike, both having weak temperaments rendered arrogant by circumstance and rank.

With one hand, he pressed the starstone against Hayat's chest wall, close to the entry point of the claws. The fingers of his other hand closed around the glove, sodden with blood. He sensed Hayat's pulse, its thready rhythm growing weaker as Hayat descended further into shock.

Bracing his body, Gareth pulled. At first, nothing happened. The claws seemed fused to Hayat's chest. Gareth eased up on the traction, trying for a smooth, slow draw. The glove resisted, then something gave way. Blood rushed into the space around the claws. The curving metal knives slipped free.

Gareth jerked back into his normal senses. He had not expected so much blood. He yanked his shirt over his head. Wadding the fabric, he pressed it over the dripping wound. At least, the blood was flowing evenly, not gushing from an artery.

Hands closed over his, taking over the pressure. He turned his head to see Merach.

"I've stanched wounds far worse than this," Merach said.

Gareth eased back on his haunches, still holding the starstone. Hayat's blood, sticky now that it was beginning to clot, made it adhere to the palm of his hand. When he closed his fingers around the crystal, it flared again. He felt as if he were standing inside one gem and holding another. Blue-white light reflected from the faceted surfaces, amplified so that he could not tell where it originated.

Gareth began shaping the light, the power that ran through the brilliance. His *laran* senses sharpened, as if he were looking through the most powerful magnifying lens imaginable. Effortlessly, he surveyed Hayat's body, the wound, the bleeding, the distorted tissue of the collapsed lung . . . and old injuries, too, not of bone and sinew but of mind. The physical damage was simple enough to repair, now that he could see it. But the warping of Hayat the boy, Hayat the youth, the thousand times he had been told *be this* and *do that* when all he had wanted was his father's love, the indulgences, the privileges he had never earned, the callous disregard for any feelings but his own—*those* could be mended as well. Or if not mended, then amended.

Changed.

Hayat, near death, was incapable of asking to be healed; the assumption in such cases was that the person wanted to live.

Every Tower worker took an oath never to enter the mind of another without permission, and then only to help. Gareth had never formally sworn, although the precept ran like a living stream through Linnea's teachings.

He could change Hayat in any way he wanted, expunge the braggart and give him modesty and a burning drive to serve his people. He could shape Hayat into a leader committed to peace with the Domains and prosperity for both their peoples. He could implant an abiding horror for Compact-forbidden weapons, indeed, for all warfare. Then it would not matter how many blasters were smuggled into the Dry Lands, for the next Lord of Shainsa would never use them.

The cause was just—the current threat eliminated, peace for the future, peace for all their children. Still, Gareth hesitated. If he used his *laran* to remake Hayat's character, who would then be the tyrant, who the victim? Did the resulting good justify such an action? Was it not Gareth's *duty* as heir to the throne, as Hastur, to save his people by any means possible?

If he did not do this thing, if Hayat recovered and invaded the Domains with his blasters, on whose head would be the blood of the slain? Hayat's, when it was his training to be ruthless? Or Gareth's, because he could have stopped Hayat and did not?

He had come to the Dry Lands to prevent the great lords from obtaining banned military technology—was this not the purpose of his journey, the reason for everything he had endured? Why then did he hesitate?

The first thought that came to him was that he could be wrong. He had been in error about so many things in his life, could he trust any decision made under circumstances like these? This notion quickly gave way to the realization that once he gave way to the seductive lure of meddling with another man's mind, no matter how justified the cause at the time, there would always be *another* good reason to do it again, another crisis, another irresistible cause. In the end, the thought that shook him to his core was that he would rather die than have this same thing done to him. His life was a pathetic thing, but it was his own. For good or ill, he had made choices, tried or not tried, acted in ways that mostly brought shame but sometimes a morsel of pride.

He, and no other.

He had made his choices, but if he took that same freedom away from Hayat, he would become far worse.

The light began to fade, as if the blue-white flame at its heart were burning itself out. He was near the limit of his strength. In his spasm of indecision, he had delayed almost too long.

Gareth gathered his waning energies and set about repairing the most critical damage to Hayat's chest. First, he sealed off torn vessels so that no more blood pooled in the pleural cavity. The strands of light carrying Hayat's vital energies brightened, but as Gareth poured forth his psychic energy, gray lapped at the edges of his senses.

Removing the blood to relieve the pressure was another matter. There was too much for Hayat's body to reabsorb it, and Gareth dared not enlarge the wound to allow it to drain. Then he remembered Linnea describing how Tower circles were able to lift small quantities of metals from deep within the planet's crust to the surface.

Envisioning the pool of blood like a bladder filled with liquid was easy. With his *laran*, he spun a membrane around the tiny lake. He had only to move it from *here* to *there* . . .

The blood resisted, dense with inertia. He shoved again, but his mental control was erratic and ragged. The bubble wobbled alarmingly, as if it were about to burst.

Exhaustion gnawed at him. He was running out of strength, running out of time. He fought the urge to tighten his mental grip on the blood bubble or to hurry the process. He realized, with some dim and distant part of his mind, that he had already gone too far. He no longer had the strength to save both himself and this other man.

Softly, softly . . .

Gareth could not tell whether the voice was real or an echo from some buried memory. All hesitation vanished; he had all the time in the world, enough to do what must be done.

He imagined enveloping the bubble in downy feathers, in layer upon layer of spidersilk. Then, instead of trying to forcibly shift it, he simply *saw* it in a different place, no longer within Hayat's chest but resting gently on his shirt, the membrane dissolving, the blood being absorbed into the cloth of his shirt . . .

"Garrin . . . Garrin, man! Wake up!"

With a sickening wave of dizziness, Gareth snapped back into his ordinary senses. He was still on his knees beside Hayat, who was moaning and moving his good arm. All Gareth could think was that he should not be alive.

Merach, who had been shaking Gareth by the shoulders, released him suddenly. Not far away, a man was shouting—Dayan, Gareth thought. He fumbled for the locket and managed to drop the starstone into it and snap it closed. Men lifted Hayat and carried him away.

With Merach's help, Gareth managed to get to his feet. Now that he was back in his physical body, every part of him ached, except for the slash in his side, which felt as if a fiery brand had buried itself in his flesh. He desperately wanted to get away from the arena, but had no idea where he might go.

"You there!"

Gareth jumped at the sound of Dayan's voice. The crowd drew apart as the Shainsa lord strode up. Gareth's vision wavered so badly, he could not make out Dayan's expression. In a moment, he would collapse, and no shouting would be able to rouse him.

Dayan's gaze burned with an icy flame. "My son was near death, beyond the aid of ordinary men. Not even the most learned of our physicians could have saved him as you just did."

Gareth shook his head. Something was rising up in him, washing away the ache in his limbs and the fire in his side.

"Who are you, truly? To whom do I owe the life of my son?"

Gareth would have fled into silence, but the thing moving in him seized him, put thoughts into his mind, and spoke with his voice.

"I am Gareth Marius-Danvan Elhalyn y Hastur, Heir to the Comyn and the Seven Domains! I have come here to prevent your people and mine from massacring one another. If what I have done for your son means anything, let it stand as a token of that goodwill. And if you would repay that debt, all I ask is that you cast aside the coward's weapons. Bury them deep in the cleansing sands, and let that be the end to it."

Storm-tide currents of night swirled around the edges of Gareth's vision. He shivered, suddenly cold. Dayan spoke, but Gareth could not understand the words.

He felt himself falling, slipping down through space, slipping endlessly . . .

Hands caught him, lowered him to a surface that was surprisingly soft. Something pressed against the wound in his side.

A figure bent over him, features cloaked in shadow. Warm breath brushed his cheek. Soft and sweet came the voice he had never expected to hear again.

"Can't you stay out of trouble for even one night?"

33

Linnea felt as unsettled as if a Hellers thunderstorm were gathering overhead. While she was working, she had been able to focus her mind, but during her private waking hours, as now, when she was attempting to knit a blanket for Illona's baby, she had less success in disciplining her thoughts. After learning of Gareth's disappearance, Domenic had sent a message to Mikhail, still in Armida, and then dispatched Danilo Syrtis to Carthon to continue his investigations there.

Try as she might, Linnea could not dispel her anxiety about what might be happening in the skies, in the Dry Towns. She thought of what Kierestelli had said about the fleeting contact with Gareth. At least, she presumed it was Gareth. The possibility of Gareth inheriting the Hastur Gift, of being a living matrix, was theoretically possible, although she had never seen any sign of it. That in itself was not final. Regis had not demonstrated the Gift until it flowered full-force under conditions of desperate need.

Stitch, stitch . . . The knitting needles, cherry wood sanded to satiny smoothness, slid over one another.

What had happened to bring Gareth to such a point? What had happened to his own starstone? She shuddered at the possibilities.

Gareth . . . the Dry Towners . . . the off-worlders . . . She would go mad if she allowed herself to brood on things over which she had no control.

She'd dropped a stitch. Rather than unravel the last four rows, she set her work down in her lap.

The sole good thing to emerge from the current situation was that Kierestelli was willing to speak with her. No, she reminded herself, she must call her daughter by her chosen name, Silvana. *Lady of the Forest.* Yes, that was apt, considering where Silvana had passed the greater portion of her life.

What did she look like? Was her hair the same shade of copper? Did she play music, as they had when she was a child? Was her laughter still as light and fluid as a mountain stream?

A tapping at the door interrupted Linnea's musings. She softened her *laran* barriers enough to sense who waited outside.

Ah. Brunina Alazar.

"Come in, *chiya*."

The young novice entered, her cheeks flushed but her movements under perfect control. "One of the Regent's aides requests your presence at the listening station in the Terran Zone." If her delivery was a trifle breathless, that was to be excused, as she had clearly run up the two flights of stairs.

Linnea set aside her knitting and reached for the hooded cloak that hung beside her door. She didn't really need its warmth, not at this season, but since taking up her post as Keeper of Comyn Tower, she had become accustomed to shielding her face when out in public.

There was no point in asking why she had been requested to come, for Brunina would have included that information if she'd been given it. The younger woman was watching her for any hint of what this unusual event indicated. No one outside the small group—Domenic and Danilo, of course, and Jeram and a few of his most trusted assistants, and herself—knew about the possibility of an attack either from the Dry Towns or the Federation.

Her escort was no cadet, such as might normally be sent to deliver a message, but one of Mikhail's senior officers. She did not know his name. He greeted her with the respect due a Keeper. He'd readied a pair of horses from the Castle stables, a serviceable cob for himself and for

Linnea the sweet-gaited gray mare that Marguerida kept for her lady guests.

At a brisk trot, they angled through the Old Town toward the Terran Zone. The market square teemed with vendors and buyers, street performers and urchins. The air smelled of roasted fowl, served on skewers with spiced onions, and everywhere there were barkers crying out their wares, music, and ripples of childish laughter. Linnea remembered how Regis loved to walk the streets. Time after time, he would be recognized by his hair and his beauty, if not his regal dress, but after each disappointment, he would return.

It began to rain, one of the sudden downpours typical of the season. Linnea pulled her hood more snugly around her face, but the guard took no apparent notice of the weather.

They crossed the cracked tarmac. Much of this area was still cordoned off, and very few of the buildings had been taken over by city dwellers. The circumstances of the Federation withdrawal, culminating in the ambush on the Old North Road, lingered like a miasma. The metal and glass might wait for a hundred years before becoming part of the living city.

A pair of guards, alert and armed, waited for them at the entrance to the headquarters building. One of them took charge of the horses.

"*Vai leronis*, will you be so kind as to follow me?" said the second guard.

She followed him through the entrance hall, at least that's what the space would have been in a Darkovan building. The interior smelled of chemicals, the air stale and flat. Her cloak dripped, but the place felt so cold to her mind, she was loath to set it aside.

Shortly, Linnea sensed the psychic energies emanating from a chamber halfway down the corridor and recognized Jeram among them. His Gift had not wakened until after the Federation departed, but the *leroni* of Nevarsin Tower had saved him and taught him basic skills.

My daughter was his Keeper. She knew him. Linnea reminded herself to be careful; neither Jeram nor anyone else outside the two of them knew of her relationship to Silvana. Silvana had not given Linnea permission to divulge her identity.

Trust must be earned.

Another pair of guards bracketed the door. They stepped aside as Linnea approached. One of them opened the door and stood back for her to enter. Beyond lay a chamber made cavernous by the absence of windows and filled with large mechanisms. Small, focused lights cast misshapen shadows on the walls. Banks of instruments hummed softly, like slumbering giants.

So much metal! Linnea thought. Like any true Darkovan, she was astonished by the casually extravagant use of what was rare and precious. She could not imagine what kind of people would simply walk off and leave such wealth, but *Terranan* did not think like ordinary folk. They had taken their armaments, anything that had a military use, and abandoned the rest.

Linnea went in. The floor was some kind of nonreflective material and gave a little under her feet. The chamber was not as devoid of human life as the first glance suggested. A group of men and women clustered around a bank of machinery. Their Darkovan clothing seemed out of place between the sterile gray walls. Besides Jeram and Domenic, Linnea recognized Hermes Aldaran, who had once represented Darkover in the Federation Senate, and Marguerida's friend Ethan MacDoevid. Ethan had never given up his enthusiasm for space travel, even when the Federation withdrew.

Linnea didn't know the young woman with the dark hair, snub nose, and wide, mobile mouth, although when Jeram introduced the girl as Cassandra Haldin, Linnea recognized the name. The story was that Cassandra's father had been a Federation technician stationed in Thendara for a few years. When he left Darkover, he'd abandoned the girl and her mother, as had so many others before him. Linnea sensed no trace of *laran* from the young woman, although clearly Cassandra had an aptitude for the off-world devices. She had the slightly distracted look of someone focused on listening. An apparatus of off-world design covered her ears. Her hands hovered over a panel of colored lights as she stared at the screen before her.

Domenic and Ethan rose and bowed as Linnea entered. Jeram, not trained since birth in Darkovan reverence for Keepers, lifted one hand in greeting. Cassandra was so absorbed in her work that for a long moment she did not notice; when she did, she scrambled up, although she did not remove the listening device.

"Please, be at your ease," Linnea said, and was pleased when the girl returned immediately to her work.

"*Su serva, vai domna,*" Domenic said with an easy, engaging grin.

Before Linnea could inquire why she had been summoned, Jeram motioned for quiet. He indicated the screen. "There they are."

Linnea peered over his shoulder, but she could make no sense of the symbols, bright against a black background, or the curved lines that slowly moved across the screen.

"I've got a clear signal," Cassandra said. Her voice was so beautiful, Linnea thought she must have trained as a singer.

Jeram touched several small colored pads on the console and began speaking in Terran Standard. Linnea knew a little of that language, enough to deduce that he was hailing a starship.

The ship of Silvana's message?

A tendril of fear coiled around the nape of her neck before she reined her emotions under control. Although she could not follow the literal meaning of the conversation, she noted the tension in Jeram's voice and the tautness in the muscles around his eyes. After a pause, a voice answered.

During the exchange, one of the guards brought up a seat for Linnea, a Temoran-style folding chair, uncushioned but shaped for comfort. She nodded her thanks and settled into it.

Mouth grim, Jeram turned away from the screen. "Here's the situation. Two days ago, the *Grissom* out of Castor Sector, in orbit around Darkover, was attacked by a privateer licensed under the Nagy Star Alliance. They managed to destroy it, but they're badly damaged and need to set down for repairs. They wouldn't say what they were doing here, but they're assuming that since Darkover never applied for full Federation membership, we're sympathetic to their goal of independence."

Domenic nodded. "They're right."

"Castor Sector has every reason to resent the Federation's military bullying, that's true enough," Hermes said. "But we don't know what's been going on or who has the upper hand. This is the first we've heard of this *Nagy Alliance*. Sandra Nagy was never our friend, even before she disbanded the Senate. That does not mean that anyone who opposes her has our best interests at heart."

"The Federation never used privateers or bounty hunters," Jeram said with a trace of heat.

"Not the Federation we knew," Hermes reminded him.

Domenic said nothing, but he looked thoughtful.

"They destroyed the privateer, so there's no reason not to allow them to land in the spaceport, is there?" Ethan pointed out. "Their first message sounded desperate. They can't leave the Cottman system, and they can't sustain themselves in orbit. Don't we have a moral obligation to help them?"

Jeram's gaze flickered to Linnea, then back to Domenic.

Hermes shook his head. "We have to consider our own position. It's imperative that we avoid even the appearance of taking sides. We don't know who else might be after the *Grissom*."

"They destroyed the privateer," Ethan repeated with a trace of stubbornness.

Domenic turned to Hermes. "What are you saying?"

"The Feds are not to be trusted," Hermes replied.

Jeram spoke up. "Hermes, as you yourself pointed out, these are not Feds. Even if they were, Ethan raises a valid point. Regardless of their political affiliation, the people on the *Grissom* need our help. Their stellar drive is damaged, and they have nowhere else to go."

"They're armed, need I remind you, with Compact-forbidden weapons." Hermes paused to let the implications sink in. "If we let them land, what is to stop them from taking whatever they want? Staying for as long as they want? Turning the spaceport here into a base of operations?"

Memory tugged at Linnea, the vivid images she'd received over the relays from Silvana . . .

. . . *ships aloft, raining fire upon a city, upon Thendara* . . . This *ship?*

Fears, she told herself, *not omens or visions of the future.*

Hermes appealed to Jeram. "You know what I'm talking about! Tell them!"

Linnea caught the quick jerk of Jeram's head, a subconscious gesture of repugnance.

Domenic was listening carefully as the arguments unfolded. *He hasn't made up his mind*, Linnea thought. *He's weighing the risks . . . and the demands of duty and humanity. But in the end, he will decide. For this he was trained, and Mikhail was right to leave him in charge.*

"If we don't allow them to land," Cassandra said in her clear, musical voice, "they may do so anyway, with prejudice against us. We cannot prevent them. I do not know these people, but I know *you*, Jeram. You would honor the laws of hospitality, would you not? Is not our best chance for a peaceful outcome to extend our friendship so that they will do so in return?"

"You don't know these factions the way I do," Hermes said.

"That much is true," Domenic broke the awkward silence that followed. He did not say so aloud, but Linnea caught the unguarded edge of his thought, *My friend Hermes, you were too long among dishonorable people in the Federation; their taint lingers in your thoughts.* "Until we meet these people face to face, we cannot judge their character. We can know only our own hearts and minds. In our dealings with the *Terranan*, we have sought to follow our own path, to create a future that honors the best of our traditions."

Cassandra's eyes brightened and Ethan nodded. Jeram sat very still, carefully avoiding even the appearance of giving advice.

"*Domna* Linnea," Domenic said, "what are your thoughts on the matter?"

"No one can know what is to come," she said. "Even the Aldaran Gift is unpredictable and shows only what *might* come to pass. We have only the present, and what we must live with if we fail to live up to our highest standards of honor."

Domenic cleared his throat. "Then we will offer this ship the use of our spaceport and any other help and materials we can. Tell them so, Jeram, but emphasize that in doing this, we are not committing ourselves to any military or political treaties. In this quarrel with the Federation—or Nagy's Alliance—Darkover must remain strictly neutral."

Jeram spoke into the apparatus. His tone sounded so tightly controlled as to be devoid of emotion. Domenic could as well have done it, for Marguerida had insisted all her children learned Terran Standard. It was a nice subtlety of negotiation to speak through a representative instead.

"The captain says they're fighting for Darkover's freedom as well as their own," Jeram said. "He reminds us that Nagy's Star Alliance does not recognize local autonomy. It's little better than a military dictatorship."

Hermes stifled an expression that clearly meant, *I told you so.*

"Tell him we insist on neutrality nevertheless," Domenic said. "Our offer of assistance is conditional upon certain terms. In exchange for the use of our spaceport, we require their agreement to observe local laws, in particular the Compact. Explain what that means and point out that the Federation, like the Empire before it, honored it."

In the end, the Castor Sector captain agreed to the terms, stipulating that if they were fired on, they would use whatever means necessary to defend themselves. Through Jeram, Domenic reiterated that if they obeyed the laws of Darkover, they would be secure.

"They've begun their descent now," Cassandra said.

"Ask him if the privateer sent a message before it was destroyed," Linnea said with sudden urgency.

Before Jeram could convey her question, however, the *Grissom* cut off communications. Jeram said this sometimes happened during landings under adverse circumstances. Linnea reached out with her *laran*, trying to sense what was happening overhead, but felt nothing. The Terran building smothered her senses. A sudden desire to stand under the open sky engulfed her.

"I must see this ship with my own eyes," she said, rising. After a moment's discussion, it was decided that Domenic would go with her to the landing area. The others needed to remain behind to coordinate preparations. Linnea didn't understand the details, but she gathered that various pieces of equipment were needed to secure the ship and transport people and goods to and from its doors. All of this had once been handled by Federation personnel, and no one was sure how much of the equipment was still functional. She was happy to escape the discussion.

In the time she'd been indoors, the rain had eased up, although the overcast still extended, unbroken, over the city. The exterior of the building gleamed wetly. The headquarters was part of the spaceport complex, but various sorts of barriers, many of them badly weathered, obscured the landing areas. One of the guards pointed out a tall building that had once housed an enclosed viewing terrace. Once, the guard told her, you could go up there, carried by an *elevator*, but after the Terrans departed, the power to that part of the complex had been shut down.

"We don't know how long the power will last, so it was thought best to save it for essential functions," he explained.

They followed the guard past a series of fences to the edge of an enormous paved area. Overlapping circles marked the surface, relics of the years when ships regularly used this field. Partly dismantled scaffolding and things that might have been loading platforms stood here and there. Dead leaves had piled around their bases.

"*Vai dom, vai leronis,* it should be safe to observe from here," said the guard.

"If it becomes imprudent to remain, we will defer to your judgment," Linnea replied.

The rain had become a fine mist, and the day smelled fresh as only a summer shower could leave it. At last came a sound like a distant waterfall. Linnea squinted up at the sky, clearer now with the thinning of the clouds, but could see nothing. The noise increased in volume, rising in pitch until it seemed the sky was screaming. She covered her ears with her hands.

"There!" Domenic cried. She could not hear him above the shrieking din, but she followed the direction in which he pointed.

His younger eyes had spotted it first, a mote of shadow and colorless flame against the brightness of the sky. She opened her mind and sensed the wrenching of air, the fury of the currents, as rockets fired to slow the descent. Winds sprang up, lifting her cloak and tugging at her hair. It was a storm like those that swept the Hellers, scouring away all softness, slicing through flesh to chill her very marrow. Only this was no natural storm, not a thing born of snow and rock and the sheer faces of the peaks. This was a storm created by men's machines, a storm from space.

The city aflame—

She glanced up again. Now the contours of the ship were visible. Its bulk loomed above them. The guard touched Linnea's arm with the hesitancy of one trained never to lay hands upon a *leronis*. He wanted her to withdraw, and she had agreed to abide by his judgment. If she, who was Keeper and Comynara, did not honor her word, what hope was there for any of them?

Drawing her cloak tighter, Linnea nodded her assent. They withdrew behind the second range of barricades, which buffered the wind and, to a certain degree, the noise. In the process, she got a long look at the ship right before it touched down. Through the churned dust and the wind, she made out a tapering cylinder scored almost its entire length with lines of jagged-edged black. The surrounding surfaces were buckled and twisted. It was as if some giant of space had raked the ship with a molten lance. Then the ship disappeared behind the barrier.

Domenic was not wearing gloves; perhaps he had left his at the communications chamber. Linnea pulled off one of hers and slipped her bare hand into his. He met her gaze as the contact of skin on skin enhanced their telepathic contact.

Domenic, I understand why you are here to witness this. In your father's absence, you speak for the Comyn Council. Someone must negotiate and make decisions about how to respond to these off-worlders, what to commit ourselves to and what to withhold. But why have you brought me *here?*

We can't go back to the days when one man had so much power that his word was law, he answered. *This is a momentous event, for good or ill. No one person should be burdened with the responsibility of decision. Isn't that what Great-Uncle Regis tried to do with the Telepath Council? Isn't that what the Darkover Council is about? You represent the Keepers Council, even as I speak for the Comyn. I need wise ears and sound reasoning, as well, and the expert knowledge of* Dom *Hermes and Jeram.*

Linnea's heart went out to Domenic. Despite his reasoned words, he sounded very young. He was only a few years older than Gareth, after all. None of his training as Heir to the Regency could have prepared him for this encounter.

She thought, but only to herself, *We are none of us truly prepared. Not Regis, for all his charisma, nor any of the other great statesmen of our age. Certainly not me. We do the best we can with what we have been given.*

Since the Ages of Chaos, the Towers have kept ourselves apart from politics, she reminded him. *I cannot advise you there.*

Domenic nodded his understanding. *I need to know if these men are telling the truth. If they will use our hospitality to seize control, to exploit Darkover.*

Domenic was Gifted, without question, but his *laran* had an unusual character. He could sense things that none other in recorded history could, but many of the ordinary aspects of telepathy and empathy, sensing another's surface emotions, were difficult for him. Even if they were not, he could not negotiate and observe at the same time. Mikhail and Marguerida would have been better suited to the task, true partners in every sense of the word, two halves of the same whole.

The world goes as it does, and not how you and I would have it, she reflected.

With a clap like stone splitting, the sounds shifted, gradually dimming in intensity. The shrill harmonics gave way to whirring.

Your pardon? Domenic asked.

An idle thought. Very well, then. I will be your truth tester as best I can. I will not enter their minds or read their thoughts without their leave, but I may well be able to detect an intent to deceive.

I cannot ask for more.

The rain held off for the rest of the day, although the wind carried the promise of more. As soon as the landing patch had cooled sufficiently, the crew of the *Grissom* swarmed over the damaged areas of their ship, aided by Ethan and a handful of Jeram's best apprentices. From the vantage point where she watched with Domenic, Jeram, and Hermes, Linnea could see them struggling to maneuver cartloads of parts and machining equipment from the headquarters complex.

Two members of the *Grissom* crew came out to watch with them, a stocky, dusky-skinned woman and a young man of the same racial type, both in rumpled, soot-smeared jumpsuits without any rank insignia. The psychic aura of battle frenzy hung about them. Neither was visibly armed, although both wore small instruments that clung to the skin of their temples, presumably communication devices. What would they think, these space-farers, about the ability to speak directly, one mind to another?

To what use would they put such a Gift?

Linnea had no doubts as to who was in command, and neither did Domenic, in light rapport. The woman gave off a subtle nimbus of authority, and yet of sadness as well, a darkness of the spirit. She hesitated, a fraction of an instant only, when the younger man called her *Captain Harris*, and Linnea knew then that there had been another Captain Harris and this one had set aside her grief to step into his place.

Captain Harris narrowed her eyes when Jeram first spoke, perhaps recognizing his accent. She did not ask where he had come from or what he was doing on Darkover but rather turned her attention to Domenic. She had a nice grasp of diplomacy, for all the roughness in her voice, to recognize that despite his youth, Domenic was the one in charge.

"We offer our deepest thanks for your assistance." The captain's gaze flickered to the cloud-laced skies. The wind was rising. Linnea sensed rather than heard her thought, *We're running out of time.*

Linnea could not follow the exact wording in Terran Standard, but Harris was giving off such strong mental images, Linnea had no difficulty understand her general meaning. From time to time, Domenic would signal a pause, and Jeram would translate for Linnea. Harris looked a trace confused at this subtle deference. Clearly, she could not place Linnea in the local hierarchy.

"If your people wish to visit the city, I will arrange for guides and translators," Domenic said. "It has not been so long since the Federation departed; many of our people still speak Terran Standard from the years of trade and cultural exchange." His gambit paid off in the sudden flare of fear from the captain's mind. Both Linnea and Domenic sensed it.

"Perhaps when all the fighting is done and the Federation is back in place, a real Federation with a representative Senate and not Nagy's Star Alliance, then we can come back," Harris said with commendable calm.

"We all hope for a peaceful future. May this be only the first of many cooperative exchanges between Darkover and the Castor Sector," Domenic replied.

Nico . . . ask if the privateer was able to send a distress call before it was destroyed, Linnea said telepathically.

As he did so, Harris pressed her lips together. Her skin was too dark to show any blanching from emotion. "I won't lie to you, not after you've been so hospitable. When the shark blew, the electromagnetic pulse scrambled our sensors. She could have gotten off a signal right before then. I can't be sure one way or the other. The sooner we're on our way, the better for everyone."

Domenic's tight rein over his emotions faltered. Linnea sent him a pulse of mental calm. *There's nothing we can do about it.*

Except to pray that if the Star Alliance ships do arrive, they'll respect our neutrality.

In that brief moment, the captain bowed, a brief inclination of her head. "I'll take my leave, then, and see if I can light a fire under some lazy asses and get us out of your hair even sooner."

"If—" Domenic began, then cut himself off. "No, you're right. I won't detain you any longer. Ask Jeram for whatever else you need."

What I need, the captain's expression said, *is time I don't have.*

Before Harris had crossed half the distance to the ship, Cassandra burst from the headquarters building. She raced across the landing area at a pace that would have done a senior cadet in the City Guards proud.

"Come, oh, hurry, come!" The girl was all but falling over herself in agitation, shouting as she ran. "We've got a new contact! They say they're the Federation!"

Almost at the same moment, Harris paused, one hand over the communications device over her ear. She turned back, her expression eloquent in its stoniness.

"Go!" Domenic cried. "We'll buy you as much time as we can!"

She saluted him before bolting for her ship, shouting out orders to her aide. The young man trotted back to where Linnea and the others stood. "I'm to go with you as liaison."

And stay behind, if it's necessary for my ship to get away, he meant.

"It's not the worst fate," Jeram said, but not unkindly.

Cassandra reached them, breathing heavily. "*Vai leronis . . . vai dom,*" she stammered, as if the honorific phrases were proof against disaster. "Please—"

They hurried back to the communications chamber. Linnea did not know what use she might be in the current situation, but she was nonetheless relieved that no one suggested she be escorted to a place of greater safety. If Silvana's vision came to pass, there would be no refuge anywhere in Thendara.

Domenic managed a composed demeanor, but through their rapport, she sensed his tension. Jeram, on the other hand, felt like a rock, immovable in his focus—no, an arrow fixed on its target, awaiting only the right moment to act.

Of course, she thought. Jeram had been a soldier; he had fought, however misguided his orders, at Old North Road, and who knew how many other encounters that no one but he and perhaps his Keeper knew?

Domenic was yet untried in battle.

And battle this will be, whether of words or of missiles.

Jeram set the apparatus so that they could all hear the incoming transmission. At first, all Linnea could make out were bursts of raucous noise. Then a voice resolved from the din. With a few more adjustments, the reception sharpened.

"This is the *Dauntless*, security enforcement chartered under the Star Alliance, hailing Cottman IV. Do you receive?" After a brief pause, the message repeated in such a uniform pronunciation and phrasing that Linnea wondered if it had been mechanically produced.

Star Alliance. And *security enforcement* didn't sound good, either.

"Where are they?" Domenic asked. "How far?" *And how long can we delay answering?*

Jeram consulted the instruments, touching a panel here and there. One of the screens shifted to a display of numbers, another to what must have been a diagram of the planetary system. "Depending on their trajectory, they could be here in two to four hours."

"What does *here* mean?"

"Firing range."

Domenic glanced at the young *Grissom* officer. "Can you finish your repairs by then?"

"We'll try."

He means no.

The message cycled again. The light in the chamber seemed to dim.

"There's no point in pretending we can't understand their hail," Hermes said. "They'll keep coming, regardless."

Domenic chewed on his lip, then told Jeram, "Say something friendly. Then ask them to hold their position while we verify their identity in our Federation records."

"They won't be there," Hermes protested.

Domenic grinned. Nodding, Jeram settled himself in the seat and began a long, formally cadenced oration. After he'd finished, there was a long pause.

The response was, "Cottman IV, we do not recognize the requirement of local permission to enter orbit," or something to that effect.

The *Grissom* officer went off in a corner, talking in a low voice through his communication device. Domenic got up and started pacing.

Jeram launched into a long argument about Darkover being a Class D Closed World, and the *Dauntless* insisted that the old regulations of the Federation were obsolete. They had license to go wherever they wanted and do whatever would earn them their fee, which was undoubtedly a bounty on capturing the Castor Sector ship.

Domenic paused as the *Grissom* officer returned to the others. "Any progress?"

The off-worlder shook his head. "The—" he used a word Linnea did not recognize "—blew up on us. It'll be another day, probably two, before we can jury-rig a patch. That's assuming it's even possible." He blinked, struggling to focus. "They know we're here. It's only a matter of time."

"Darkover is a neutral party, and we've given you sanctuary." Domenic said. "You're under our protection."

"You don't understand! They don't mean to capture us, and even if they did, they would not need your permission. This is no corvette, it's a modified aventour! She's got the firepower to blow the whole city to smithereens. No, they mean to make sure the weapons we just loaded never leave this planet."

"*You've* got weapons," Hermes said.

"There's nothing we'd like better than to blow them out of the sky!" the young officer shot back. "Even if we had a chance against an aventour, we can't fire our weapons from the ground."

"They never identified the class of their vessel," Jeram said quietly. "How do you know the capabilities of the *Dauntless*?"

"I—we—"

"You know that ship, don't you?" Jeram pressed.

The boy gulped.

"Exactly how?" asked Domenic.

"No point in hiding it, not now. The *Dauntless* has been on our tail across five systems now. We thought we'd lost her after that last firefight. There was no sign of her when we made orbit here, just the corvette, and we took care of her. I guess . . . we were wrong."

"You led that ship *here*, to *us*?" Hermes managed to suffuse each syllable with outrage.

The boy swayed on his feet. "I'm sorry," he whispered. "I'm so sorry."

"*Dom* Hermes," Linnea said gently, "these people are fighting for their lives, making the best choices they can under terrible pressure. Can you hold this child responsible for an outcome none of them foresaw? Or do you truly believe that Captain Harris had some nefarious purpose in coming here?"

The young off-worlder could not understand her *casta*, but he responded to her tone and the pulse of kindness she sent in his direction.

"Does it matter? Now we'll be the ones *fighting for our lives*, as you put it, *vai leronis*!" Hermes relented visibly. "It's not your fault, lad," he said, switching to Terran Standard.

"If your people idolize supernatural beings, now is the time to pray to them." The young officer's voice failed him. He straightened his shoulders and stood at attention before Domenic. "Request permission to return to my ship. Sir."

To be with his comrades, Linnea thought. *Maybe his family.*

It struck her that this young man might well be the son of the captain or her younger brother. She didn't think he was exaggerating. He truly believed he was about to die.

"Then you had best go," Domenic said quietly. "And may the blessings of whatever gods you worship go with you."

The young man hurried from the chamber.

"Jeram." Domenic turned to the older man.

"He's right, you know," Jeram said darkly. "A fully armed aventour could do a lot of damage. It couldn't destroy the whole planet. You'd need a dreadnaught for that. But it could level Thendara."

"There's got to be a way out of this," Domenic said. "Keep them talking—Zandru's seven frozen hells, let me do it!" He reached for one of the headsets.

"Are you sure that's wise?" Hermes said. "Negotiating directly?"

"Do you have a better idea?" Domenic snapped.

Hermes seemed to gather himself. "If diplomatic speech can be of any help, I'm the one to do it. I've had years of experience negotiating with Nagy's cronies in the Senate. Let me throw around some names. Maybe those connections still carry some clout."

At Domenic's nod, Hermes took the place beside Jeram. Linnea noted the change in his posture and vocal tone as he began to speak. He reminded her of Dyan Ardais, the old lord, not the current Warden, who had been misguided but no less passionate in his loyalty to the Comyn. Phrase after phrase rolled out, as fluent as if Hermes had rehearsed for a tenday. Linnea watched the man she knew, however slightly, transform into a stranger.

At last, Hermes paused for a reply. The voice from the *Dauntless* repeated that Darkover had no standing in the Star Alliance. Hermes spoke again, and then again, always with the same result.

"Do you think they're using a recording?" Jeram said. From his expression, he was rapidly losing hope.

A new voice blared across the speaker: "Cottman IV, we have a duly authorized warrant for the capture or destruction of the renegade vessel *Grissom*."

Domenic, his features even more grim than before, gestured for the headset. Shoulders sagging, Hermes passed it to him.

"This is *Dom* Domenic Alton-Hastur, Acting Regent of the Comyn of the Seven Domains. I remind you that Darkover is a Closed Planet and has declared itself neutral territory."

"We do not recognize—"

"And *we* do not recognize the authority of the Star Alliance or any other institution claiming to be the successor to the duly constituted Federation! We have no part in your dispute. Any specific claims you have against the *Grissom* and her crew must be filed with the *cortes*, which will adjudicate the matter according to our laws. Do you wish to do so?"

"What can they do to us?" Cassandra said, her voice on the edge of a sob.

"The kid from the *Grissom* wasn't kidding about their firepower. Look . . ." Jeram indicated one of the screens. Symbols scrolled across a diagram of a ship, an elongated tapering cylinder. "Here, here . . . and here. Those are plasma fusion missiles. The propellant reactors are almost fully charged. And there—" cluster after cluster of motes shimmered a poisonous green, "those are—"

"We don't need to know," Domenic cut him off. "How many different ways can they kill us?"

Linnea got up and, overcoming the natural aversion of a telepath for casual touch, put her arms around Cassandra. The girl was trembling so hard, her next words came out as a squeak.

"Are we going to die?"

"Hush, *chiya*. No one knows for sure."

Hermes turned to Jeram. "How long before they attack? How much time do we have?"

"Maybe an hour to optimum range."

"*Dauntless*, we are unable to comply with your request," Domenic said. "We urge you to send down a representative to discuss the situation."

"What are you doing?" Hermes said, aghast.

"Buying us more time."

A heartbeat passed, and then another, and still the Star Alliance ship did not respond. Jeram switched the transmission to his own headset

"*Dauntless*, do you receive our last message? We are unable to comply."

Again, only silence answered him. Cassandra was on the verge of tears, and Hermes had turned ashen.

Domenic looked as if he could not quite comprehend the enormity of the threat. The light in his gray eyes was all but quenched. "Repeat, unable to comply. Please acknowledge."

In the pause that followed, Linnea imagined the Star Alliance ship like an enormous predator of the sea, such as those that sometimes wrecked ships off the Temora coast, now moving with quiet, deadly intent toward its prey.

"Th-that's it, then?" Cassandra stammered. "There's nothing to do but wait?"

"And go home to our families," Hermes said in a voice gone suddenly hoarse. "An hour . . . there's not enough time to get out of the city. At least the Regent has not returned." He swallowed audibly. "Something may yet be salvaged."

Domenic roused, visibly gathering himself. "We must not give up!"

Jeram shook his head. "I can keep trying . . ."

"What's the point?" Hermes paused on his way to the door. "They won't listen, they won't talk to us! We can't negotiate our way through this one. We have no weapons, no way to defend ourselves. The Compact is all very well, but not when it's left us vulnerable to pirates who take delight in the ruin of those less powerful. They're just the kind of monsters Nagy would use to squash resistance. I should have known—I've seen enough of their kind before." He stormed out of the chamber.

"Wh-what about the *Grissom*?" Cassandra said.

"You heard," Linnea murmured. "They cannot even help themselves."

"I know it looks hopeless," Domenic said, pacing the center of the room, "but there must be *something* . . . The reason we adopted the Compact was not to control physical weapons, it was to safeguard against the powers of the mind. *Laran* has been our greatest strength and what sets us apart from other low-industry worlds. *Domna* Linnea, could Comyn Tower create a *laran* shield—or disarm the missiles? Or—" his voice shook, "or blast the *Dauntless* before it can fire?"

Linnea remembered the disaster at Caer Donn, how an outlaw circle had used the immensely powerful Sharra matrix to destroy a spaceport and the spaceship there. But that ship had been on the ground, not high in orbit.

And we do not have any matrix of the magnitude of Sharra, if indeed any such still exist.

The chances of having even the slightest effect on the machinery of the *Dauntless* were impossibly slim. Perhaps the combined telepathic powers of a circle might be able to reach the mind of its captain or crew . . . but that would take an enormous amount of psychic energy, a suicidal effort. Linnea had never heard of any group of *leroni* being able to cross such a distance.

For every deed, there is a first time.

"If it can be done, we will do it," she said aloud. Gently, she set Cassandra from her and gathered her cloak. The girl slumped into a seat beside Jeram.

He nodded, understanding how little chance they had. "I'll come with you. Illona—"

"The choice is hers," Linnea said, meaning that under ordinary circumstances, no Keeper would allow a pregnant woman to work in a circle. *But if we fail, there will be no future for either her or her child.*

When the message came that Linnea of Comyn Tower wished to speak with her on the relays, Silvana knew immediately that something was wrong. It was mostly likely news of Gareth, and how could that be good? Anything not urgent would wait until a more convenient time.

She settled herself on the bench in front of the relay screens, aware of the increase in her heart rate, the rise in adrenaline in her blood. Usually she could focus her mind in only a few breaths, but now she achieved the necessary clarity with difficulty.

The linked stones of the relay screen wavered, as if blurred by unshed tears, as she softened the focus of her eyes. Turning her vision inward, she established the connection with the psychoactive device. The crystals trembled as energy coursed through them.

Stelli . . .

Silvana shuddered, knowing that her childhood name was not deliberately used. She was sensing something deeper in the pattern of her mother's thoughts, her very emotions.

Mother?

Silvana. The mental voice was firmer now, as if Linnea were once more in control of her sendings.

Mother, what is wrong? What has happened to Gareth?

There is no time to explain it all. A starship arrived—rebels against the Alliance that has taken the place of the Federation. They'd been damaged in a fight and needed repairs. We allowed them to set down, but before they could take off again, another ship arrived—

Silvana's blood felt like glacial meltwater in her veins. Images flickered at the back of her mind—the sky fractured with light as destruction rained down on a city, *on Thendara*, from above—flame and ash and the screams of the dying.

—refused to recognize Darkover's sovereign rights or our neutrality. They mean to destroy Thendara in order to eliminate the rebel ship. Nothing any of us said made a difference. Our only chance is for the circle here to reach them. I don't have much hope, but we have to try.

Silvana rocked back on her bench, her thoughts reeling. Did Linnea understand what she was saying? Did she know that to even attempt such a thing amounted to a death sentence? No human mind could sustain the strain of communicating over so great a distance. If, by the grace of all the gods of Darkover and everywhere else, Linnea survived, it might be better if she had not.

Yes, she knew. She'd called to say good-bye.

Silvana understood, without having to ask, that they had only a few moments together. Linnea would have to prepare herself and enter the state of deep concentration from which she would gather together the *laran* of her circle, focused through their starstones. Perhaps she might use one of the higher-order matrix screens, if such were available at Comyn Tower, to amplify the unified psychic energy.

Now, when there was no time, Silvana realized how much she wanted to say.

I never stopped loving you, was all she could think to say. The words seemed so paltry, so poor, so inadequate to what she felt.

And I, you. Remember me, caria preciosa*, and live a long and happy life.*

Then Linnea's presence disappeared. The matrix stones still vibrated with Silvana's own mental energy. There was no one at the other end.

For a long moment, Silvana sat in front of the relay screen, her mind too numb and her heart too full to know what to do.

"In time of need," she murmured, echoing Dirav's words, and reached for the heartstone.

In her palm the stone glimmered with its own inner light. It seemed to wink at her, to pulsate like a living heart, but its crimson brilliance in no way reminded her of blood. Instead, her mind brought forth images of sunset on the Hellers snowpack, rubies from Ardcarran, the first blush of color in an apple, the glory of autumn . . .

And then she was *within* the heartstone, or perhaps it was inside her. Far from being alone, she felt a multitude of entities, many either too vast or too minute for human comprehension. She sensed an ineffable comfort, as if she were cradled by the natural beauty of her world and its creatures.

Gradually—or perhaps quickly, for she could not judge the passing of time in that place—she became aware of the presence of the *chieri.* She first recognized those she knew best, Keral and Dirav. And Lian, *Ah, Lian!* Then came a sense of connection with others, *chieri* she had never encountered in the flesh. The union was like and yet fundamentally different from being in a circle. No Tower circle she had ever heard of was this large or stretched over this wide an area. Physical distance did not seem to matter, as it did for ordinary *laran.*

We are with one another, as we have always been. Words formed in her mind, and she knew it was her own human thoughts that gave them form. *As we are with you now.*

*The ship—Thendara—*Silvana began, and then realized she had no need for explanations. Certainly not for explanations in words. Nor did she need to consciously draw forth Gareth's fractured images and Linnea's message. All she had to do was soften the boundaries of her own mind, to open the doors between one set of memories and another. It was in many ways a reversal of what she had trained to do as a *leronis* and then as Keeper. She had learned to compartmentalize her thoughts, to set her emotions behind an unbreachable wall so that no personal concern would affect her concentration.

Now the heartstone demanded a different discipline, one of opening communication, of seeking integration. In order to reach unity with the shared consciousness of the *chieri*, she had to first become whole within herself.

For a terrible moment, she feared she could not do it, that the combination of early grief and years of practice had left her so fragmented that it was impossible to overcome the divisions between past and present, between heart and logic.

Over the years, she had helped many to heal from injuries to both body and spirit. Was she herself truly such a broken, scarred thing as to be beyond hope?

Look . . . A thought that bore the stamp of Lian's mind brushed hers. *Look back to the time when there were no divisions. Only love.*

As if across an enormous distance, she caught the faint ripple of a harp . . . a woman's voice, singing . . . the vitality of her own body at play . . . trees dancing in the wind, trees of silver and green . . . arms holding her, a man's arms—*her father's* arms—and a sense of such joy rising up in her that she could not contain it . . .

The crimson gem resonated in response.

He never forgot me, nor did she, Silvana thought. *They were in my heart all along, even as I was in theirs.*

It seemed to her, even as the idea formed and dissolved, that this was true for the oneness of the *chieri*, bound for that moment to one another and to Darkover itself.

The heartstone brightened, a surge of psychic energy. As it heightened the natural powers of each mind in the unity, it also drew from them. The sensation was so rapturous, so intoxicating, Silvana longed to give herself utterly over to it, to soar on that tide, to merge with it—but that way lay danger. Her Keeper's training recoiled at such a surrender.

Even now, she felt the draw of the heartstone, not only its seduction but its price. It was far more than a circle, but a sphere, remarkable in its capacity to join so many minds across such distance. That unity came at an enormous cost in mental energy. The stone itself was neither benevolent nor evil, not like the great matrix of Sharra, which could never be used for good. What the heartstone allowed those who wielded it to do required enormous psychic power. The *chieri* were stronger than she, with all her training, but they were far fewer in number than those who had created the heartstone. They could use it for only a short period of time, and that was quickly passing.

With a Keeper's deft touch, Silvana shifted the focus of the unified heartstone consciousness to the skies above Thendara.

A ship appeared in the scarlet firmament, a thing of cold metal, of ceramic and glass, of intricate machinery and things that glowed with venomous fire. Below it, the city glittered with life, pinpoints of ordinary minds like grains of sand, marked here and there with flaring blue-white light . . . Comyn Castle, the Tower . . .

Silvana visualized the Terran Zone, then an open space and another ship, smaller than the one aloft, touched with the same smoldering poison but, unlike the first ship, this one's weapons were quiescent, untriggered.

Weapons, yes . . .

The *chieri* minds recognized the materials, the explosives, the apparatus to rip apart the very fabric of stone and soil, of water and air. Silvana sensed not only the nature of the devices and chemicals, but the *intent* behind their manufacture. Every morsel of her being shuddered in revulsion. This ship and its armaments went beyond what the Compact forbade, weapons that killed at a distance without placing the one who used them at equal risk. This was far more hideous, aimed as it was not at an opponent but at the very land on which he stood. The attack, when it came, would be like burning down an entire forest to destroy a single splinter.

The ship was arming itself . . . it was almost ready to strike. From the buildings below, she felt a flare of terror, a quivering along the airwaves, a voice pleading, but so faint she could not make out more than its tone of desperation.

Silvana managed to hold her focus, to not flinch or withdraw even in the slightest degree. Too much depended on maintaining the full strength of the heartstone sphere. On a wordless, intuitive level, she understood why the *chieri* were delving so deeply into the mechanisms of destruction, the many links now forming between weapon and target. In their long history, they had passed beyond retaliation as a response to aggression. But they had not forgotten.

They had long since given up the capability to blast the intruder out of Darkover's skies. They no longer needed it.

The heartstone gathered up the minds within it, or so it seemed to Silvana. Its collective sensitivity far exceeded that of any individual, and so did its power. She gave herself, her mind, her *laran*, completely over to the guidance of something greater than herself.

The process was not unlike those Silvana had herself used in manufacturing compounds for firefighting or in mining, transporting minerals in extremely small quantities from beneath the surface. She sensed the manipulation of molecular structures, breaking a chemical bond here, detaching an atom from one position and moving it to another there. One aspect was new, and that was taking the energy released from the breaking up of certain compounds and using it to melt some structures and fuse others.

At times, it felt as if the entire procedure required hours and days, so meticulous was the work. While in a circle, it was very common to lose track of the passage of time. In a Tower, a trained monitor ensured that neither physical harm nor distracting discomfort affected concentration. Even without that safeguard, Silvana had absolute confidence in the heartstone sphere. In all likelihood, the *chieri* knew her limits better than she herself did.

In the weapons mechanisms, one connection after another was replaced by a gap, and new bonds were created where they had not existed before. The vibrational pattern of the explosive and radiation-producing materials shifted. Some parts darkened as they went inert. Others became bright, white and yellow instead of denser grays and browns. The motes danced like little flames, flaring before winking out.

With care, the *chieri* bypassed the ship's communications and propulsion equipment, as well as the apparatus that kept the atmosphere breathable.

Silvana became aware of the taste of adrenaline in the air within the ship, and then a bee-storm of confusion and urgency. The ship's crew knew something was wrong. Perhaps they'd tried unsuccessfully to discharge their weapons. Someone was shouting orders; she couldn't understand the words, only wave after wave of frenzied reverberations in the emotional miasma.

The heartstone sphere wavered, fading with the diminution of the psychic energy feeding it. Here and there, one of the minds winked out, but whether in exhaustion or death, Silvana could not tell. She herself, for all the power of her *laran* and her training, could not sustain the link for much longer. She was human, her Gift finite. The *chieri* had greater natural talent, but many were aged, even for their race. The vigor of those remaining in the sphere burned like a flame, hot and brief.

Is it enough? she wondered as she felt herself drifting toward her separate body.

Her question went unanswered. She sensed the others straining to hold the unity just a little longer, to complete the last chemical reactions, to sever the remaining crucial circuits. If the weapons could still operate, or if there was a were to repair them, then all their exertions would have been for naught.

Silvana forced herself to concentrate. She fought to remain in the sphere, alert and active. Over the years, she had grown accustomed to directing her mind effortlessly, but now the exertion tore at her, as if she were being dragged across a field of razor-edged gravel. Instinct urged her to pull back, but she resisted. The connection held, but for how much longer she could not tell.

Only a little longer, a few moments... She told herself that she could accomplish anything, withstand anything, for such a short period of time.

Searching within herself, she discovered a small reserve of energy. This she poured into the sphere, heedless of the pain. She was a Keeper, and she was Comynara, although she had never claimed it. And Hastur, daughter of kings, although she had never wanted that distinction, either.

My father did not falter when he faced the wrath of Sharra, when he called upon Aldones, Lord of Light. He never paused to consider the cost. Can I do any less?

Trembling swept through her, shaking the psychic firmament. They were all near the end of their strength.

Just a little more . . .

Dimly she sensed that she could die like this, her mind too drained to return to her physical body. Would she wander the Overworld, endlessly seeking those she loved? Would Regis be waiting for her? She wanted desperately to see him again . . .

Yet she had *chosen* to pick up the heartstone, *chosen* to open her mind to its power. In a sense, it was she and not the *chieri* who had created the sphere.

She had no choice but to see it through.

Enough.

For a moment, she could not be sure if the thought was hers, formed in fear and hope, or that of another mind.

Stelli, heart friend . . .

Lian?

A pulse of tenderness answered her. *You must leave us now or suffer grave injury.*

Can the sphere still function if I break away?

We have accomplished what is necessary. Some—I do not know the word for these things—remain, but not enough to accomplish anything of significance. Already we sense changes in the ship's navigational system that indicate preparations to withdraw.

Relief blanketed her, almost smothering her. Her mind felt thick and numb, unable to form a response.

Done, she thought. *It's done. The city is safe.*

The rapport faded, slowly at first, like the light from the twilit western sky, before fragmenting into the individual minds of the *chieri.*

She felt the confines of her own mind grow solid, a familiar prison. Although she might and undoubtedly would merge into the rapport of a circle again, it would never be the same as what she had just experienced.

Under her, the bench was hard and smooth. The room had gone chill. She ought to call for someone to stir the fire to life and bring her hot food. In a moment, she would do so.

For now, however, she would honor what had been given, what had been lost, what had been won, what had been sacrificed.

What she had become, what she would never be again. What had been taken from her.

What remained forever.

Gareth paused at a side entrance to the great ballroom of Comyn Castle. A breath brought him the smells of flowers, the greenery traditional at Midsummer Festival, and pungent balsam incense.

As he'd ridden through the city, he'd been surrounded by merrymaking, a profusion of decorations and music. It was nearly noontime, and the sun hung clear and bright in a cloudless sky. Already, people were drinking and dancing in the street.

He'd risen early enough to leave baskets of fruit and flowers for his kinswomen in honor of the Blessed Cassilda. Never had there been so many, besides his mother and his sisters. Since he was not permitted inside the Tower, he'd left gifts for Grandmother Linnea and Aunt Silvana at the door. There had been one more, one made with his own hands, one about which he had not breathed a word: a cup of plaited reeds with a single perfect white rosalys from the town house garden, tied with a garland of silver ribbons.

Now here he was, dressed in his holiday best, his skin still tanned enough to make him stand out amid the pale faces of the Comyn. He had never felt more out of place or less like he belonged. All his old hopes of making a place for himself in this society, of redeeming himself, had evaporated in the truth of what he was and how much pain he had caused. His dreams of adventure taunted him like ale to a drunkard; he could not think of Special Agent Race Cargill without feeling a mixture of regret and sadness, and so he did not. No such person had ever existed.

"Gareth?" Danilo Syrtis had come up quietly to stand beside him. A tartan in the colors of Ardais, his adopted Domain, brightened his usual somber attire.

Gareth squared his shoulders. It was time and past time to go in. *Tío* Danilo stayed him with a touch.

"Do not doubt your welcome, lad. We all know what you've been through."

Gareth suppressed a response, *No, you don't know half of it.* Perhaps they did, *Tío* Danilo and Grandmother Linnea, and *Domna* Silvana—he still could not comprehend that she was his father's sister—who knew him in some ways better than he knew himself, having been inside his mind and having guided his *laran* when he'd healed Viss, having heard his desperate warning about the attack from space. His family loved him, even if they didn't understand him.

For all the reminders of love, his heart still beat with a dull, dispirited ache, as if it belonged to someone else and had been his only on loan. He hadn't seen Rahelle since their arrival in Thendara, when he'd been whisked away in one direction, and she and her father in another. It was too much to hope he'd have a chance to sneak away to the house Cyrillon had rented. Gareth had no doubt that after his foray into the Dry Towns, he would not easily escape supervision.

For now, at any rate. But that is about to change.

Gareth clamped his *laran* barriers tight. The last thing he wanted was to sense the thoughts of anyone in the hall or for them to read his.

They went in, Danilo leading. The ballroom blazed with color—the ribbons and flower-graced garlands, the spidersilk gowns of the women, and the finery of the men. The colors of the Domains created a riot of brilliance, enhanced by the tartans of the individual families. Jewels glittered at throats and around wrists; pearls gleamed from their settings in lace or golden earrings.

To Gareth's relief, there was a only little flurry when he entered. *Domna* Marguerida glanced his way, at present occupied in conversation with Hermes and Katherine Aldaran. Grandmother Linnea and *Domna* Silvana stood in the opposite corner with a group of Tower folk.

Silvana turned her head to listen to one of the other Keepers, and Gareth noticed she'd pinned his flowers in her hair. Although older than his father, she looked much younger, her hair the same flame-bright hue as a girl's, her face unlined. She held herself with that almost inhuman stillness he associated with Grandmother Linnea when she was working as a Keeper, and yet a mantle of joy seemed to surround her. He thought he'd never before seen anyone so intensely alive, so thoroughly present. Linnea inclined her head toward Silvana, and their eyes met for an instant. The intensity of that glance was almost overpowering, even from across the room.

Gareth turned away. The rest of the assembled merrymakers blurred into a sea of finery, of laughter and the sound of the musicians tuning their instruments.

Ordinarily, Gareth took as much pleasure in dancing as any Darkovan, but now he just wanted this night to be over. The sooner he made his announcement, the sooner he might be able to manage an escape. First, however, he must present himself to *Dom* Mikhail, who was acting as host of the evening.

Mikhail was, for once, not at Marguerida's side but some distance away. He was talking with Domenic, his second son, Rory, and a handful of senior City Guard officers. Gareth took his leave of Danilo and made his way toward them. He bowed in precisely the correct manner of a prince toward his regent and recited the appropriate greetings.

"We're all happy you're here to celebrate this festival with us." Mikhail responded.

Touched by sudden warmth for the man who ruled the Domains so ably and who had never taken advantage of his position, Gareth returned Mikhail's smile.

"You'll have to tell us the whole story," Domenic said without a trace of censure. "We've heard only bits and pieces from Cyrillon."

"My story's far less interesting than what's been happening here in Thendara," Gareth said. "A Federation-licensed bounty hunter threatens to attack Thendara and then withdraws peacefully? Their quarry—rebels, you say?—then has time to make repairs and escape?" He shook his head. "Whoever accomplished that is the true hero, not me."

"Modesty ill becomes an Elhalyn prince!" Rory joked.

Gareth shrugged. The real heroes were Jeram and Grandmother Linnea, who'd stopped the Star Alliance ship from bombing the city. No one seemed clear on exactly how, not that it mattered.

"We're not teasing you, lad," Mikhail said. "What you've done may not furnish material for ballads, but it is no less vital to our future. You have accomplished what no other Comyn has. You have brought us a treaty with a Dry Towns lord. Not since the founding of the Domains have we welcomed a representative of the Great House of Shainsa."

A murmur of excitement drew Gareth's attention to the primary entrance. People surged forward for a closer look, obscuring his view. He couldn't understand what they were saying, so many were speaking at once, and the musicians had begun playing notes in unison.

Someone near the door tapped a cymbal, creating a metallic cascade more suited to the Great House of Shainsa than Comyn Castle. Then, by chance, the knot of people between him and the door unraveled and he watched as Merach strode into the room, followed by two flaxen-haired men in the livery of Lord Dayan and a servant carrying a small jewel-crusted casket.

Gareth had not seen Merach since their party had arrived at the gates of Thendara. Despite Rahelle's nursing, Gareth had been feverish for much of the return journey. He remembered very little of it until they reached Cyrillon's compound in Carthon, where Rahelle had argued strenuously and unsuccessfully for him to remain behind.

Merach carried himself with studied gravity, ignoring the hundred inadvertent offenses that would, in Shainsa, have been cause for a duel to the death. His hair, loose around his shoulders, gleamed like polished gold against the inky blue silk of his shirt cloak. By the way Merach walked, Gareth saw the pride not only of the man himself but of those he represented—his lord, his city. His people.

Glancing around, Gareth could also see that to most of the assembly, Merach appeared as a savage, enamored of garish dress and boastful speech. They had no notion of the honor and dignity of this man, and they judged him by his lack of *laran.*

All this transpired in a moment, a doubled heartbeat and there, following respectfully after Merach, came Cyrillon, also finely dressed but more in the fashion of the Domains. A woman walked at his side, her head high, her flowing robes of gold-shot rose.

Gareth did not recognize Rahelle at first. He saw the fierce pride of her carriage, the gorgeousness of her dress . . . and then the chains. No, not chains. The belt and bracelets of gold filigree were worth a noble's ransom. Delicate chains swung freely from the center loop of the belt as she walked, unattached to her wrists.

I am a woman of the Dry Towns, she proclaimed. *And I am as free as any of you.*

The ballroom suddenly seemed too bright. He thought, *Freedom is a matter of how we choose our chains. Who is more honest, my love, you who carry yours openly, or I who wear them invisibly?*

As if his thought had whispered in her ear, she turned and looked him full in the face. He was not sure if she smiled.

Merach halted in the middle of the chamber. Murmurs died as Mikhail came forward and welcomed Merach as the first official ambassador from Shainsa to the Comyn. Merach in turn presented the casket as a token of Lord Dayan's goodwill and hopes for an amicable and mutually profitable relationship. The audience pressed forward for a look at its contents, but Gareth held back. He did not care about riches, not even exotic Dry Towns metal work and gemstones.

He wished there were some way to speak to Rahelle. She was standing beside her father, who was talking with *Tío* Danilo and Domenic. Gareth watched them from a distance while dancers lined up in the center of the room. Mikhail and Marguerida, as hosts of the evening, led the first dance.

Gareth placed himself in the appropriate place so that the various dignitaries could offer polite greetings. He had no importance to them except as the Heir to Elhalyn, the prince in eternal waiting. His parents tried to draw him into conversation, an attempt at joviality, but he had not the heart for pretense. When he had spoken with everyone that protocol demanded, he escaped before men like Octavien MacEwain, not to mention mothers bent on throwing their marriageable daughters in his path, could corner him.

He made his way through the crowd to Mikhail and said he had a brief announcement to make. Mikhail gave him a hard look, as if to ask whether Gareth were planning on disgracing himself again, but then said, with some kindliness, "When the musicians take their break."

Alone in the midst of the celebrations, Gareth closed his eyes. He could not decide if a weight had been lifted from his shoulders or dropped there.

A touch, light as butterfly wings, brushed the back of one wrist. He opened his eyes to see Silvana. The physical contact dissolved his *laran* barriers, bringing them into a rapport. It felt like soaring through a field of stars.

She waited until the moment of astonishment faded. "You have done well."

He shook his head. *I have made one mistake after another, endangering the lives of others as well as my own poor existence. After this night, however, my folly will no longer place anyone else at risk.*

A ripple like silvery bells accompanied her next thoughts. *Perhaps you are right, and as long as you remain here, beset by the ghosts of your own failures, you will never be able to see how we are all bound together. You are no more to blame for the smugglers or the Star Alliance ship than I am for the World Wreckers or the death of my father. But you had a part in bringing Darkover through that crisis . . . and in reuniting me with my family. With my families.* Her gaze flickered to where Linnea was dancing with Hermes Aldaran. *For this, if for nothing else, I thank you.*

Gareth did not know what to say. She had given him so much, had guided him when he felt most in need, and now it would be cruel to rebuff her gratitude. He felt a blossom of warmth in his chest, as if her heart had kissed his own. Then she was gone, moving through the crowd as gracefully as a *chieri* dancing in a forest.

The music continued for a time with a tune composed by Marguerida to traditional dance steps. When it drew to a close and the assembly had finished applauding, Mikhail made a brief speech. He blended the customary festival wishes with his personal hopes for a new and brighter future for all Darkover, Domains and Dry Towns alike. Merach unbent enough to acknowledge his own round of welcoming applause.

"Now *Dom* Gareth has something to say to us all," Mikhail concluded.

Gareth had been standing in the inner row of listeners, or, rather, the others had positioned themselves so as to not block his view. Now they withdrew even farther, so that he had no need to step forward.

"Kinsmen, nobles, Comynari," he began with the time-honored greeting. Aware that he would never open a session of the Council in this manner, he added, "and honored friends. This is a season of rejoicing and a time of change for us all. A time to set aside old quarrels—" with a glance at Merach, who returned his gaze steadily "—and to renew old ties." This time he looked meaningfully at his grandmother, standing beside her grown daughter. He thought she had never looked so happy.

"As for myself, I too must adapt to the new order. I can no longer continue as a useless parasite."

"What did he say? A parasite?"

"Blessed Evanda, he's gone off in his head again!"

A sound rippled through the room, the rustling of cloth and the murmur of voices. It fell away into expectant silence.

"I hereby abdicate my position as Heir to Elhalyn and to the throne of the Seven Domains."

Gareth paused to let his meaning sink in. His mother smothered an outcry and clasped his father's arm. His father looked as if he might protest but then thought better of it. Domenic startled visibly. Mikhail did not move, but his brows drew together. Marguerida, at her husband's side, spoke a quiet word in his ear. Not all the reactions were negative, however. Her lips curving in understanding, Silvana inclined her head in a nod.

Gareth could not bring himself to look at Rahelle. He managed to hold himself upright as the furor died down.

Mikhail stirred. "Have you thought this through, *Dom* Gareth? Once taken, such a decision cannot be reversed."

"Sir, I have. I have never been more sure of any course. Elhalyn will be in good hands with my brother Derek, although I pray it will not be for many years. As for the Comyn, Domenic will be a far better Regent than I ever would have been a king, and he deserves to know that his position will never be challenged."

The words came more easily than any speech he'd ever made. If he had had any doubts about his decision, this moment of clarity erased them.

"And so," he turned to encompass the entire room with his next words, "I take my leave of you. May the gods grant you all long life and happiness."

Then, with the best speed still within the bounds of courtesy, he headed for the nearest exit. It opened not on the corridors leading to either the interior of the Castle or toward the main gate, but onto a veranda. Fortunately, everyone had come inside to hear the speeches, so he did not need to contend immediately with well-meaning but importunate questions.

Closing the door behind him, he stepped onto the veranda. The night was cooling rapidly, but the scent of the flowers in the adjacent courtyard perfumed the air. Overhead, three of the four moons swung serenely across a sea of glorious light. He inhaled, releasing a band of tension around his ribs.

It was done. *For good or ill*, as the saying went. He could never put this chick back into its egg. He was as free as any man might be, which was to say, not very.

The door opened. He turned, ready to make his excuses before he could be snared into a conversation. A slim, feminine figure slipped through. A whiff of spicy scent reached him.

Rahelle placed herself in front of him. By her posture, she wanted to shake him. "Are you insane or just delirious? Sunsick? In a trance? Whatever induced you give up your birthright?"

So she did not suspect.

He shrugged. "My life here was a cage, without purpose or meaning. At least, in Carthon I may set up a business and be of some use to someone. Importing lenses, you know." He managed a smile.

"You are exactly as well-suited to trading as you are to—to flapping your arms and flying to Mormallor! You have strength. I have seen it! But it does not lie in the buying and selling of objects." She paused, breathing hard. "You have lied to me before. Do not lie to me now. Tell me what is going on and why you have made this choice."

Gareth shifted his gaze toward the festivities and then back to Rahelle. "If they knew of that strength—that Gift—then they would lock me up in a Tower and use it for their own purposes. Good purposes, honorable purposes, true, but I've seen enough of that life to know I do not belong there." He fought the urge to pace up and down. "A short while ago, *Dom* Mikhail told me I'd been able accomplish something no one else had—the first step toward a lasting peace, a bridge between your people and mine. He was right."

Her eyes widened but she said nothing.

"No Comyn or Dry Towns lord could have offered the hand of friendship," he said without any hint of false modesty. "Only a man that neither side took seriously, a man with no *kihar* at stake, a man with nothing to lose, only he—*I*—could get both entrenched sides to listen. I have made a start. I mean to continue, and a bumbling, inconsequential lens merchant seems as good a pretext as any."

"Surely you could work toward that goal and remain Prince of the Comyn, or whatever your title was."

"True enough." He paused, thinking that if he did not speak now, he would never have the courage. "But then—I would never be free to marry as I choose. It runs in the family. My father gave up being Heir to Hastur for that very reason."

"To marry—" Her words skittered to a halt. He could almost hear her heart beating, wild and fast.

He went to her and took her hands, her unchained hands, in his. Raising them, he brushed her knuckles with his lips. "If you will have me."

"*If I will*— You idiot!" Rahelle laced her fingers around his so tightly that he could not have pulled free even if he had wanted to.

She drew him close and kissed him. Her mouth was the softest, most intoxicating thing he had ever felt. The kiss went right down to the soles of his feet, sending fire through his belly and sweet melting rain to his heart. He wanted to dance, to weep, to fly. Somehow he got his hands free and wrapped his arms around her.

"After all," she breathed against the side of his neck, "*someone's* got to keep you out of trouble."